C000176455

"This book is a work of fiction, bu contain perhaps more truth than first intended, and therein lies the magic."

TWPB1:
ISBN: 978-0-9567700-0-4
Second Edition 2011
Published by BenGalley.com

Cover Design by Mikael Westman

Original Illustration by Claudia West

Professional Dreaming by Ben Galley

Printing by Lightning Source

about the author

Ben Galley is a young author from sunny England, and still thinks dragons are real. He currently spends his time writing strange fiction and daydreaming, and is forever grateful for the invention of the spellchecker. He wrote this book especially for you and he hopes that you enjoy it.

Find out more at:
www.bengalley.com

Say hello at:
hello@bengalley.com

The Written

By Ben Galley

My eternal thanks to Claudia, Charlie, Sarah, and the Clarks, without whose help I would have surely succumbed to a mind-numbing banality.

This book was written for my parents, because without them I wouldn't be where I am right now, nor would any of us.

part one

it begins with snow

chapter 1

"...when the sons of gods went to the daughters of man and had children by their wombs, they became the giants of old, the nefalim, "men" of renown and infamy, dangerous like wolves amongst sheep..."
From the 'Gathered Prophetics'

It was snowing outside. The white flakes fell lazily in the night breeze, dusting the rocky mountainside with an ivory blanket. Little crystals of ice, each as perfect as the next, flurried and spun and danced through the cold air. A tall spire rose from an outcrop of quiet buildings amongst the snowy crags, where one lonely yellow window glowed brightly through the blizzard. Framed by the light, a very old man stood at the windowsill with his arms crossed. He sighed with tiredness and fought back yet another yawn. He shivered and rubbed his arms as if it would help, but still he did not move away from the window. He found the cold weather outside calming after a long day of hard study. And it had been a hard day of study indeed.

Behind him, gathered around a desk and poring over a small square book, sat a group of four equally aged men. The room was cavernous and packed floor to ceiling with bursting bookshelves, each one filled with an impossible amount of paper and knowledge. Loose pages were everywhere and scrolls lay under dust and old maps, littering the floors and shelves like dried autumn leaves. One single candle, almost at the end of its wick, clung to life on the corner of the wooden desk, throwing distorted shadows against the walls.

'I don't even think it's Siren,' said the man at the window. He absently twisted a bit of his long white hair around a wrinkled finger and sipped at warm wine. The papery wattle of skin around his neck made his chin disappear.

'Of course it is, Innel, just look at the scales of the front cover!' replied one of the others. He waved his hand in a somewhat dismissive gesture. He coughed hoarsely, as if the cough had caught him by surprise, and dabbed a careful handkerchief to his lips. Spectacles made from slices of rare crystal balanced precariously on his nose and a long beard, streaked with grey, covered his chin and neck. The group of scholars mused for a few moments. 'Where was it found again?' asked another, peering at his colleagues from under wiry grey eyebrows.

The bespectacled man spoke up again. 'No one knows exactly, some village in southern Nelska,' he said, and there was a silence.

'Fifteen years later and only now do we get to study this manuscript. Who knows the incalculable value of the magick held inside this book,' said Innel, tugging his long blue robe about him. It was now too cold. He shivered as he pulled the stained glass windows shut with a bang. He turned and sighed, leaning back against the stone sill and looking to the man with the tiny glasses. 'So the question remains, how do we get the confounded thing open? Have we had a reply from Krauslung yet, Gernn?'

'No, no not as yet. They're always late...' he trailed off, distracted. He leant forward to take a closer look at the book lying on the desk. It was small for a start, no bigger than a man's hand. Several black dragon scales adorned the cover, pressed flat and trimmed to fit its square shape. Probably from an infant wyrm, thought Gernn, as he let his fingers trace the ridges and dips of the cover. A thick gold lock, simple but firm, held the small book shut, with no keyhole or opening mechanism anywhere to be seen. The ancient pages poking out from the edges were torn and dirty. The man tried once again to split a few pages apart with a long yellow fingernail, but the book was locked fast, and not even the tip of a knife blade could squeeze between them. After a rather dramatic sigh that was probably much louder than necessary he entwined his fingers and leant back in his chair, and the ornate wood creaked as he did so.

'Well nothing's changed since this afternoon. The bloody thing's still locked tighter than a vampyre's coffin. And as none of us here possess the skill to unlock it, or even know what spell could force it open, I suggest we just wait for...' But Gernn was interrupted by the sounds of heavy boots on stone.

A loud voice made them all turn. 'Having trouble, wise men of Arfell?' A tall hooded man suddenly emerged from the doorway, hands clasped behind his back and a warm smile on his face. The tall newcomer walked from the door to the desk in a few long strides and stomped the last bits of snow from his black leather boots. The scholars were a little startled but as he moved from the shadows and into the candlelight they quickly recognised a familiar face. The man threw back his hood. A chorus of respectful smiles followed.

Innel jumped up from the windowsill to greet the man with a warm handshake, the wattle of skin beneath his neck wobbling like a turkey's. 'Your Mage, what an unexpected honour! What, with the weather and all we didn't expect you or Åddren to arrive for another two days,' he said.

The tall mage kept his smile, while he removed his hooded green and gold robe and folded it neatly over an armchair with one fluid move. There was a long sword at his waist, in an ornate scabbard, and his expensive tunic was made of a fine emerald cloth trimmed with white and gold. 'Don't be ridiculous, the weather has never stopped me,' he chuckled. 'When we heard that you had uncovered a long lost book of secrets, I decided that no time should be wasted in coming to see it!' The man crossed his muscular arms and looked at each of them with dark nut-brown hazel eyes. 'Please, show me what you have found,' he said, as Innel retreated slowly to a chair.

Gernn rose, obviously eager to impress, while the others remained silent and seated, fingers entwined in their long flowing beards. 'It is most definitely Siren, sire, as we thought,' at this point he threw his colleagues a quick sideways look. 'But this book is not from the time of the war, it seems to be very different from the other texts we have recovered from the dragon-riders, perhaps older…'

'Continue,' said the mage.

Gernn took a quick breath before carrying on, and pointed to the gold on the black cover. 'It does have some sort of magick lock on the cover, with no key to unlock it. We've come across this type of thing before but this is too powerful and too old for us. So as yet we have been unable to read it,' Gernn shrugged and thoughtfully rubbed his beard once more, gazing wistfully at the little book. There was a moment of silence and the tall man let a satisfied smile creep over his wind-burnt face before turning to the others. 'Perhaps I could help with that part,' he said. His hazel eyes flicked around the circle. 'If I can get it open, can you translate it?'

'If it's legible, then we can read it. We men of Arfell have come across all of the languages that have ever been heard in Emaneska. There isn't a book we've seen that we couldn't translate,' answered a third man, with a slow and constant nodding of his head. He looked to be the oldest by many a mile, greyer than a winter's day and waiting patiently at death's doorstep. The others murmured their assent with a symphony of throat-clearing and more rubbing of chins and facial hair.

'Good.' The mage strode forward and flexed his hands. He briefly took a moment to think and then leant over the oak desk, humming and musing and making a sucking noise with his teeth. The scholars watched him think and looked between themselves with a mixture of intrigue and uncertainty.

The tall man muttered something, perhaps an incantation, as he reached towards the book with his fingers rigid and outspread. A tiny ripple of air pulsated from his hand like a wave of heat over a fire. A purple spark danced over the cover, and he whispered something, muttering again, but louder this time. 'This book is strong,' he mumbled from between pursed lips. He seemed to be straining to keep his fingers spread. The mage's hand pulsed again and he took a firmer stance this time, spreading his feet and gripping the edge of the table. More sparks fizzed over the cover and then, quite abruptly, the thick lock made a little click, and smoothly rolled open.

The scholars all leant forward with open mouths and wide eyes, eager to see what the dark book held between its dusty yellow pages. The tall mage wiped a single drop of sweat from his brow and smiled, clenching his fist a few times to get rid of the numbness. 'Read your book, gentlemen.' He smiled like a wolf approaching a trapped rabbit.

The oldest scholar wiped something from his nose and moved to carefully lift the scaly cover. With agonising slowness he turned it and then he paused, smoothing out the first page with his hands. Peering through misty eyes at the thick writing, he nodded and scanned the script. 'It's elvish, dark elf, if I'm not mistaken. I... I haven't seen a text like this for years,' he said, somewhat shakily.

'Elvish. That is an old language indeed,' commented the tall mage. It may have been the flickering candlelight, but it seemed to Innel that the mage's eyes widened ever so slightly at the news. 'The oldest, your mage,' he answered.

Beside them the old scholar shuddered as he read onwards. He coughed briefly and turned the next page. 'It reads...' he paused, tracing the script. '*The Testament of Bringing*. But that word could also mean, erm *creating*, or...'

Gernn adjusted his crystal spectacles and peered at the writing. '*Summoning*.'

The mage turned to him, looking down his nose at the scholar. 'Summoning?'

Gernn nodded eagerly, almost losing his glasses. 'Yes, as I'm sure you know sire, the dark elves were powerful creatures, capable of controlling the darkest of all magicks.'

'It's a summoning manual?' asked the man.

'Yes your Mage. Their acolytes could summon huge beasts from the darkest places of the world at the cast of a single spell.' Innel went to a bookshelf and brought back a rare slice of tapestry covered with crude pictures depicting battles with strange goblin-type animals and giant winged creatures with many horns wearing what looked to be golden crowns.

'I remember,' muttered the mage as he turned the tapestry to face him. The others looked up questioningly. 'I said I remember seeing something like this before, in other books and old paintings at the citadel.'

'Of course sire,' Innel nodded, wondering if he had seen any such paintings in Krauslung. There was something like an itch in his mind.

'Where are the keys?' The mage asked quickly, tapping the page with a finger. Keys could be found in every spell book and any book without them was useless. They were the start of any incantation, the unlocking words to begin a spell.

The oldest scholar turned a few pages carefully, where more runes were scribbled. He pointed to a few random symbols hiding at the corners of one page. 'For the spell? Erm, there, and the other, there. These are the main words, *me* and *hear*. Saying them in the other order, of course, would open the spell. I don't dare to read aloud any further; it seems we have uncovered a very special book indeed. It must be over a thousand years old...' his voice cracked and his words trailed off into silence. The scholar's hand was shaking more than usual.

'This needs careful translation, look, it seems to reference something called *thy darkness swallowed,* or... *mouths of darkness,* yes that's it, over and over again on these pages.' Gernn waved his hands as he gingerly flipped through the ancient book. His eyes were wide.

'And you are sure this book is not another fake?' The man asked, looking hungrily at the men. The wolf and the grey-haired rabbits. His arms were crossed still, but his voice was now low and dangerous, dark brown eyes roaming the pages and pictures spread over the desk.

Innel nodded. That itch was bothering him now, something he had missed, something he couldn't begin to put his finger on. 'It's real, sire, an elven summoning manual, if you asked me.'

'It's dangerous, whatever it is,' said Gernn.

The man smiled, flashing teeth. 'How interesting this all is.' He drummed his fingers on the desk absently. 'Well, it seems you have been most useful to me this evening. I am sure Åddren will be as pleased as I am to hear about this.'

The oldest scholar rose shakily from his chair and bowed his head. 'Thank you sire. We will continue to study this manual with diligence, there is much more knowledge to be gained from it, and without you, my lord, we would probably still have a locked book.' He smiled, and the other scholars managed a polite laugh. The air had become stale and thick.

The tall mage laughed heartily, startling them slightly as the noise rang out in the small room. 'Haha, and without *you*, old fools, I would have nothing!' The smile was instantly gone, replaced by thin lips and a narrowed gaze. With a sudden burst of immense speed the mage drew his sword in a silver blur and furiously slammed the blade into Innel's chest. He fell with a terrified gurgling scream. The mage swung right and brutally cut the throat of the old scholar with a single swing. Dark blood painted the books and pages scattered around the room. Sparks of electricity danced around the mage's fingers and a huge bolt of lightning flew into the others, burning them to a crisp in a matter of seconds. An acrid smoke filled the room.

His business concluded, the mage calmly sheathed his sword and took the black book from the desk. Wiping the blood from its cover, he turned on his heel, picked up his robes from the chair, and left without another sound.

Hundreds of miles away, in the west, dawn was breaking over an empty countryside. The cold morning light shone through the skeletal trees and scattered across winter snow drifts and dead leaves. The still wilderness was undulating, with rolling hills and patches of woods springing up between boulders, frozen streams, and endless snow. Apart from the drip of melting ice and the rattle of wind in the finger-like branches, not a sound could be heard.

A broken castle rose from a tall mound, crowned by concentric rings of ruined walls and dilapidated stone ramparts. A round tower squatted in disrepair at the centre of the castle still sporting an empty flagpole. The massive stones of the walls were covered in brown moss and hanging icicles, the crenellations adorned with cuts and gashes made by the war engines of old.

Soon the pale morning was disturbed by the faint noise of a heavy-breathing newcomer. A hooded figure came from the south trudging through the deep snow towards the castle, his long brown cloak billowed behind him in the icy breeze. Hot breath escaped in smoky plumes from his mouth and the sound of his labouring was loud against the dripping silence. The man stopped and pulled his clothing around him. He took a minute to catch his breath. In the half light of the early morning his grey-green eyes could pick out a low arched door set deep into the thick outer wall.

'Carn Breagh,' muttered the stranger, lowering a plain red scarf from his face. Clearing his throat he checked the woods to the left and right with a wary glance, and then trudged on through the deep snow. Beneath his cloak the man wore light steel plate armour over his shoulders, chest, and thighs, which clanked together softly as he moved. A black and brown tunic lay underneath with a thick leather belt holding onto his supplies and an old sword encased in a dark red scabbard. Something gold and scarlet and metal peeked out from beneath the sleeves of his thick cloak. The man's sturdy black boots wearily plunged into the pure white snow, making creaking noises with every step.

The stranger reached the old wall and the small stone archway and spread his hands over the thick oak door, feeling the splintered wood and the thick spikes that held the gate together. The man gave it a light push but nothing budged. It was locked tight from the inside. He shoved a shoulder against it in a futile attempt to move the ancient wood. But still nothing. He looked at the door quizzically. The planks were weathered from hundreds of years of wind and snow, yet for some reason they had not rotted away like the other wooden features of the ancient castle.

The hooded man stretched his back and neck and rolled up the sleeves of his cloak. Adorning his wrists and lower forearms were thick vambraces made of interwoven red and gold metal scales that glittered faintly in the dawn light. They clinked as he held them together. He closed his eyes briefly and then placed his palms on the door. All of a sudden a pulse rippled across the wood and there was a dull clang from the other side. The man gave it a little push and the door swung open with a creak.

He allowed himself a faint smile and pulled his cloak around him as he peered into the gloom. The man wrinkled his nose. It smelled like a thousand years of damp and there was the faint sound of dripping on stonework coming from somewhere in the darkness. Mould hid between the cracks in the walls. Without a sound the man ducked under the thick stone archway and stood in the dim corridor, listening. He made a fist. White light shivered around his fingers and suddenly the corridor was bathed in a pale moon-like glow.

Surrounded by his light the stranger began to investigate the old castle, poking around in holes and long-lost underground chambers. Cavernous halls and old rooms spread out like a warren left and right as the explorer went deeper and deeper into the castle. Everything was rotting and damp. Old curtains decayed where they had been thrown, chests and furniture had been smashed against walls and lay in dark heaps and broken postures. In old abandoned barracks benches and tables were pushed up against splintered doors. Rusty swords hid under the rubble.

For hours he searched the dank castle and found nothing except darkness and ruin. In a tiny room deep underground, the cloaked man carefully took a seat on one of the less broken chairs and rested his feet for a moment. He was beginning to get a little tired from keeping up his light spell, but he was sure there had to be something inside the old castle. Absently he picked up a small piece of rubble and toyed with it for a few moments before tossing it across the room in boredom. To his surprise the stone sailed straight through a frayed tapestry and disappeared, landing with a clang somewhere far behind it. The man clenched his fist again and a fresh wave of light penetrated the gloom. Eagerly he tore the tapestry from its rusted hangings and threw it on the dusty floor. Hidden behind it was a staircase that spiralled down into the dark shadows. Curiosity sparked in his mind he jogged down the steps, his footsteps echoing against the narrow walls.

All of a sudden the stairs came to a halt and a long hallway snaked around a corner. Sconces holding long torches poked out from recesses in the walls. The man moved to the nearest one and felt the oil-soaked wick between his finger and thumb. It was dry enough so the man clicked his fingers over the torch. Sparks flew from his fingers and sent flame curling up the wall.

Dousing his light spell he continued down the corridor lighting each torch as he went, and it was not long before he came across a huge door set deep into the stonework, held by thick hinges and a massive bolt that seemed to be fused to the metal bracing it. Eyes closed, the man ran his hand over the wood, searching for the right spell to use, but when he threw a wave of magick at it the door didn't even move an inch. Irritated, he tried again and the air hummed as he hit the wood with another spell. Nothing happened. He rubbed his stubbled chin and thought for a moment, adjusting the red scarf around his neck. All of a sudden a deep boom rang out somewhere below his feet and made the torches shiver in their sconces. The man slowly, and gently, drew his sword from its scabbard as a few specks of dust fell from the ceiling. He squinted at the torches as something caught his eye. The flames were shifting and leaning far out from the wall as if blown by a stiff breeze. He listened and watched, ready for anything. Nothing came, and all was silent again in the castle.

Bored, the stranger turned and sheathed his sword with a loud metallic ringing noise. He climbed the stairs, turning left, then right, then left again, up more stairs, retracing his steps. Abruptly he was out in the snow once more and the bright morning sun was stinging his eyes. He slammed the small door behind him and stepped out into the icy glare.

'Hmm,' mused the cloaked figure. He bent to pick up a handful of snow and rubbed it between his fingers to wipe off the dust from the castle. As he moved to pick up another handful a shadow passed over him without a sound, a flitting shape momentarily darkening the snow. The man sighed and stood up straight, throwing off his cloak and drawing his sword with a flourish. Spinning his blade in his right hand he surveyed the peaceful countryside calmly. Steel glinted in the sunlight.

'It's not even noon yet and a man has to deal with dragons,' muttered the stranger to himself as he let his eyes rove over the horizon.

A huge screeching roar came from the skies above him and the man darted sideways with a running leap, narrowly missing a massive shape that plummeted into the snow behind him with a huge crash and a shower of snow. The man got to his feet and disdainfully brushed the white powder from his armour. He looked up. Out of the white haze there was a snarl and a creature reared its ugly blue head, shaking its horns with a rattling shiver and spreading stunted turquoise wings. A ridge of sharp brown spikes ran from its head to the tip of its serpentine tail. The monster's claws dragged at the snow, razor sharp and curved like a cat's, and its eyes were like black pools of jet. The wyrm let out a deafening hornlike scream and took one step forward, hissing at the man in the snow and rattling its aquamarine scales.

It had been a while since the man had seen such a large wild dragon, and even though it was a juvenile, no more than a wild wyrm, it still towered above him. The creature stank of old meat and a musky reptilian scent. The stranger began to circle the creature, holding his sword out straight towards it.

'Leave now, or this will end badly for you,' said the man in a measured tone, still treading sideways through the deep snow. The dragon snarled, obviously lacking the capacity to understand him, and stamped its enormous feet menacingly like an impatient bull. It roared an ear-splitting roar and foul spit flew into the man's face.

The stranger grimaced and wiped the grotesque phlegm from his cheek and forehead, careful to keep his eyes on the snarling dragon. 'I will take that as a no then, shall I?' he replied, and before the words had left his mouth the beast charged with frightening speed. But the man was more than ready. Swiftly dropping to one knee he dug his blade into the snow with a rasping thud. A solid wall of magick tore through the snow like a rippling earthquake and knocked the terrifying reptile back with a low and somewhat disappointed whine. The man jumped up and swung his sword at the surprised beast. The blade cut a long path across its scaly back and blue blood splashed the snow.

Very suddenly and seemingly out of nowhere, the beast's whip-like tail lashed out and struck the stranger hard in the chest. He flew into a nearby snowdrift with a crunch of armour. A star or two swam before his eyes. The man winced and sat up, but before he had time to take a breath the hungry dragon ran at him again. It snarled and spat and it scratched and it dug, furiously lashing out at the snow and at the man with its razor-like claws. He wildly waved his sword in front of him in an effort to keep the claws at bay, but a stray talon scraped across his armour and found his soft pale skin underneath. With a pained expression he rolled sideways through the snow and somehow managed to escape the long claws. Red blood stained the dirty snow beneath him.

Getting swiftly to his feet the man smacked his two vambraces together and a blast of flame shook the cold air. The fireball hit the wyrm in the chest and sent the creature reeling backwards. It roared with pain and frantically shook its rattling spikes, in an effort to fend off the stranger, but it was already too late for the hungry beast. The stranger sprinted forward, dodging another tail swipe. A light pulsed down his forearm and his blue-stained sword burst into flame. As he ran he hurled the glowing weapon with both hands and like a bolt of fiery lightning it buried itself hilt-deep in the dragon's ribcage with a thud and a flash of scorching fire. The beast uttered a last mournful whistle and toppled over against a nearby tree with a crash and a bang and a shower of pine needles.

Breathing a little on the heavy side and wiping snow from his face the man slowed himself to a calm walk and strode forward to wrench his blade from the ribs of the smoking reptile. He put a hand to his side and winced , feeling the wet blood seeping from the long cut. Retrieving his cold cloak he sighed and began to slowly follow his footprints back in the direction he had come from.

chapter 2

"The Long Winter started gradually during the years of our long war with the Sirens. The heat was slowly taken from our days, one by one, and the sun from our sky, until our seventy-sixth year, the year of our last summer. The snow storms gathered and the ice fields grew, creeping inexorably south until they almost threatened to cover Nelska, and ever since the end of the war our weather has remained cold and bitter, and the proud mountains of Össfen stay covered by the eternal snow."
From writings found in the libraries of Arfell

The hooded stranger travelled without rest for two days, heading south through field and forest and river and hill. By the second day the man crested a muddy knoll and took a moment to catch his breath. Before him in the valley lay a small village called Leath, built on a rocky crag that overlooked a metallic-looking river and muddy fields. He narrowed his eyes at the tiny town. Its inhabitants had always been wary of strangers, and feared his kind especially. They were a superstitious lot, concerned only with their farming and their drinking. The cloaked man decided to give the village his usual wide berth and take the winding route back to the Arkabbey. He hopped over a few rocks and slid over some shale, and then headed west around the town, sticking to the wilder roads and the copses.

A few hours later the man was treading through the thick loam of the Forest of Durn, a shady wood south of Leath that was seldom entered or explored by the villagers. Rumour had it that a fierce vampyre lived somewhere amongst the dark trees, feeding off the blood of any Albion soul that would trespass in his woods. The stranger obviously didn't believe in any such rumour, and paid attention only to the surrounding forest that was still deep in the clutches of winter. The trees were alive with the breath of a light wind, whispering branches and creaking bark. A few animals scuttled around in the frozen loam. Somewhere a bird cried out. The stranger kept walking.

Soon the hooded man made it to his destination, and found a small winding trail in between a path of bushes and pine trees. Brown needles crunched under his feet as he picked his way under branches and around rocks. After a while he spotted the light of a hidden clearing ahead and he walked towards it, still careful to follow the almost indistinguishable trail through the undergrowth. All of a sudden the trees gave way, revealing a small glade and a tall brick building that had been completely concealed by the forest. This was the Arkabbey, one of many like it that had been quietly built around the lands of Albion and Emaneska. Smoke rose from the windows of the kitchen and the noise of wood chopping and other work echoed over the grounds. The tall bell tower rose high above the trees, with glass windows and balconies punctuating its thick granite walls. The bell had been silent for decades, and the man couldn't remember the last time he had heard its doleful pealing. Workers and other people were milling around the gardens and taking in the brisk air. The man nodded to a few familiar faces as he walked across the lawn towards an open doorway. The cold grass underneath his boots was slippery and looked well tended to, clipped short and tidy, if not a little brown. There were a few beehives to his left amongst the trees. They seemed lifeless and quiet. There was a calmness floating on the chill breeze.

An armoured soldier standing by the door saluted him with his spear while staring straight ahead.

The man strode inside the arch and felt the warmth of the busy building on his cold skin. He rubbed his hands and shook the mud and ice from his boots and listened to the sounds of cooking and working echoing on the stone walls. With a tired sigh the man walked on, up a few flights of stairs, down a few corridors, and around a few corners until he came to a simple oak door. He pushed it open with a bang.

A woman jumped and dropped the bundle of tunics she was carrying and put her hand to her chest in fright. 'Oh! Farden, it's you,' she flapped her hand like a fan.

'Same old.' The man threw his hood back and smiled at the girl. Elessi was his maid and somewhat of a friend to him, and had done a bit more than just picking up after him over the years. She always seemed to be wearing a cherubic smile or a concerned frown, and her deep brown eyes were always wide, as if she had just been handed the juiciest titbit of gossip. Farden would never had admitted it, but Elessi's stubbornness had kept him on track more than once in the last few years.

Blowing her curly brown hair from her round and blushing cheeks, the maid started to pick up the dropped clothes. 'You could have knocked,' she said, flustered.

'To my own room? You shouldn't be sneaking around in here.' Farden threw her a quick smile to melt her icy stare. He threw his cloak on the small bed and sat on the windowsill, watching the trees shiver outside.

'Gods know someone needs to look after you magick lot. Where've you been to this time? Oh! Is that blood on your side?' Her face instantly creased up with worry and she rushed to the window to see.

Farden glanced down at the roughly-bandaged gash that the

dragon had given him along the right side of his ribs. He waved Elessi away as she tried to see the damage. 'Don't worry about it, you know it will heal... Elessi calm down it's fine!' He shooed her away gently and covered it up with a shred of tunic.

'Well what was it this time? Another minotaur? It was a bandit wasn't it, I knew it.' Elessi stood there with her hands on her hips like a scolding mother. Farden looked at her.

'Elessi, we've known each other a long while, and you've seen me heal from worse wounds before,' he said. She just raised her eyebrows at him. He stretched and grimaced as he moved around. 'I'll be fine in a day,' he said, then closed his eyes and leant back against the stone to end the matter. 'It was a wild dragon. They hunt magick.'

'Well no matter what it was, it looks bad to me. At least let me put a poultice on it to bring out any poison,' Elessi asked. 'You're not indestructible, Farden and gods know I've told you before, jus' like his lordship in the bell tower!'

'A thousand times,' muttered Farden, listening to her earnest rustling. She moved to a nearby jug of water and brought back a wet cloth. The chambermaid dabbed the crusted blood from his ribs and Farden clenched his teeth. There was a moment of silence. 'Sometimes I think you like throwing yourself into danger all the time,' she said.

Farden didn't answer. Instead he opened his eyes and stared at the leafless trees waving at him outside. Her hands were cold and so was the water but it felt good on the burning skin, dry and dusty from the long walk south. He felt her hands stray to his back and the silence became a little too awkward. The mage spun around and deftly caught her wrist. 'How many times do I have to tell you?' asked Farden in a low voice, with more than a hint of severity. He stared into her chestnut eyes, and slowly and gently let go of her arms.

Elessi looked upset. 'I'm sorry, I just wanted to s…' she began, but Farden held up a hand. He rested his head against the wall and closed his eyes again.

'Enough,' he said, and the maid backed away. She picked up his cloak and some other clothes and turned to leave. 'Durnus is waiting for you upstairs,' she said.

Farden nodded and heard the wooden door click shut. With a sigh he held the wet cloth to his side. Elessi was a kind soul and she looked after him well, but her curiosity was dangerous. It might have seemed harsh keeping her at arm's length but it had to be done, and her feelings had to be sacrificed in the process for her safety. There were rules, and even though she was his friend, rules and the Arka came first. It was refreshing though, to be treated with respect, as opposed to the usual uncertainty and fear he received from most of the population of Albion. Farden was usually treated with a mild neglect here, as more of a dark omen than a blessing, stared at with wary melancholy eyes, at a lone foreign soldier passing through. Farden didn't really like people. People were rude, people were ignorant, oblivious to how the real world worked and moved, like ants.

He grunted and scratched at his back and bloodied side. His vambraces felt heavy and he could feel weariness slowly creeping over him, but with resolve he made for the door. Time to see Durnus.

A thin old man sat with his back to the door, watching the flames crackle and pop in the fireplace. Drapes hung thick and heavy over the windows, making the huge room dim and full of flickering shadows. Candles dotted the floors and walls, ensconced in holders and perching on tall piles of books. A massive map of Albion hung on the far wall, showing the distant shores of Nelska, and the cliff cities of Halôrn to the southeast. Farden quietly closed the door behind him, completely silent. His bare feet slowly crept across the cold stone floor towards the old man in his comfy chair.

'You're late,' said the old man in a raspy voice. The noise made Farden flinch. The travel-weary mage laughed and moved forward to an empty chair by the fire. 'For gods' sake, Durnus how do you do that?' The man laughed a whispering cackle, and grinned widely, baring sharp fangs. Farden slumped into the comfy armchair and sighed, wincing as his wound scraped against his tunic.

'You never remember that I have the hearing to rival that of a bat Farden, whereas you have the footfall of a work-horse.' Durnus chuckled again and poked at the fire with a long metal rod. 'The sun is still up then I take it?'

Farden nodded, and stared into the fire in silence. The old figure in the chair next to him was one of his oldest friends, and one of Emaneska's sharpest historical minds. Durnus's eyes were a blue so pale that they almost bordered on white, and his skin was like white paper stretched over a thin frame. His features were sharp and bony and his greying hair was swept back and slicked down, neatly curled behind his tall ears and stopping just short of his shoulders. His fangs peeked from behind pale lips when he laughed. Farden had often wondered how old he truly was.

'Good,' he said. The vampyre settled back in his chair and closed his eyes. 'Report,' he whispered.

Farden went to it with a will, recalling every detail of his journey to Carn Breagh, telling Durnus of the strange corridor inside the bowels of the castle and his fight with the wild wyrm. The vampyre merely nodded along, musing at the appropriate points, occasionally clearing his throat and stroking his sharp chin with a frail hand. After a while, Farden ran out of information and Durnus opened his eyes. 'I shall send a full account to the Arkathedral in the morning, but Carn Breagh can wait for now. Something terrible has happened in Arfell,' he said, and his face turned very grave.

Farden looked confused. 'The library?'

Durnus nodded. 'The very same. I received a hawk this morning from Krauslung, relaying some of the darkest news I have heard in a long time.' He paused for some sort of dramatic effect. Farden knew the old vampyre loved mystery and intrigue, and he waited. After a moment he continued. 'Two nights ago, someone broke into the library and murdered five of the scholars in cold blood. It was late at night, and nobody saw or heard anything. Two of the scholars were found burnt to a crisp. It seems that a valuable object, a book of some kind, is the only thing that's missing.' Durnus crossed his legs and drummed his nails on the arm of the chair.

Farden let the information sink in. 'Well what was it?' he asked.

'No one knows. A message had come to the Arkathedral only that day, saying that the scholars in question had found a book in their collection, a powerful Siren book that we had taken years ago during the war. The scholars had only just begun to work at it, but requested that the Arkmages should travel to Arfell to help with the translations.' Durnus leant forward.

'This book must have been special to request the presence of the Arkmages,' mused Farden.

'Exactly. The message came to the council, and before Åddren or Helyard had a chance to leave, the scholars were murdered and the book was stolen. And let me tell you, from what I gathered in the message the Arkathedral is in uproar. Helyard is blaming everyone under the sky, especially the Sirens, and the good Lord Vice has ordered a regiment of his guards up to the mountains to see if the assassin returns,' said Durnus, his eyes wide with excitement.

'Well what is this book about? Why is it so powerful?'

'Again nobody has a clue. The hawk sent by the library wasn't exactly full of information. You know what the old men at

Arfell are like, full of secrecy and intrigue. All the message said was that the book was in good condition, locked, and of the utmost importance. Apparently it was small, covered in black dragon scales and was protected by a powerful golden seal, with a spell that would require one of the powerful Arkmages to crack. They assumed it was Siren or perhaps even older, and that it might contain an immense amount of formidable magick. That was it.'

'Sounds dangerous,' Farden said. He got up and revived the dying fire with a few logs and a spark of flame from his hands. Durnus flicked a tongue around one of his sharp teeth in thought. 'Indeed.'

Farden knew his friend had a theory, but that he was waiting to be asked, so he relented, and smiled. 'What are you thinking?'

Durnus leant further out of his chair and made the frame squeak. 'One of the explanations I can muster is that the Sirens have a spy in the council. They were the ones who we stole it from in the first place, it seems sensible to assume they would want it back.'

'A fair idea, but we can't dismiss that it was someone other than the dragon-riders. It's been fifteen years since the war and the ceasefire has never been broken, so why would they risk breaking it to retrieve one little book?' Farden asked.

'That depends on the value hidden within its pages. But who else then friend? Skölgard has no interest in magick like we do, nor could their sorcerers even know of such a book's existence. We ourselves didn't even know of it until a couple of days ago. If this book is as powerful as we think it might be, then the Siren wizards would most definitely risk a ceasefire to get it back into their scaly hands.' Durnus's words made sense, but Farden didn't like the sound of them. Something did not feel quite right. The old vampyre spoke up again. 'The Arkmages have sent word that you are to find a man named Jergan in the south of Albion. My research indicates that he might know what this book is, and who could have stolen it.'

'Jergan. Who is he?'

'It would seem that he was once a scholar in his own right, who lived at Arfell before the war. He might have come across this book before when he lived with the dragon-riders.'

'Jergan worked with the Sirens?'

Durnus made a face. 'He is Siren. He returned to Nelska and studied in Hjaussfen before the war broke out. But apparently ten years ago he was attacked by a lycan somewhere on the ice fields and fled to Albion, living in the mountains to the north where he's been under the wolf-curse ever since. I've just heard word that a year ago he took up residence in the Dornoch hills in the south and is now living alone somewhere on the moors. It would seem the locals have lost many a sheep,' he paused. 'Even the thought of a lycan makes me sick. Ugh.' Durnus shuddered. Farden smiled, distracted. A lycan in Albion sounded dangerous. 'When do I leave?' he said, and stood up to stretch. But as much as he tried to shake himself awake, the more he could feel the tiredness creeping over him. The fatigue spell he had cast the day before to keep him moving was finally starting to wear off.

The vampyre wagged a finger at him. 'Tonight Farden, you rest, and no arguments. You have plenty of time for a good night's rest and slumber. It's not as though the Arka will fall apart overnight,' said Durnus.

'As long as nothing happens to their gold, then I think we're safe,' murmured Farden, and the vampyre laughed. 'Politics, Farden, politics and rules. That's all they care about. People like us belong out here on the fringes, where it matters. Somehow I can't see us cooped up in a hall debating the finer points of civilisation,' he said.

The mage nodded. He wandered around the vampyre's room and flicked through interesting-looking parchments and book covers. 'So you don't miss it then?' he asked. Durnus threw him a quizzical look.

'The city?'

'Being in the thick of it.'

Durnus shook his head. 'No. I thought that was one of the reasons you came here Farden, like I did, to get away from all the pressure and the gossip and the politics.'

Farden muttered something to himself as he picked up another book. 'I know,' he said aloud. Durnus looked at the sleepy mage. 'What's wrong?' he asked.

The mage shook his head wearily and he managed a smile. 'I'm fine, don't worry.' The vampyre nodded and grinned, showing a sliver of fang between his chalk lips. 'Fancy some wine?' he offered, and pointed to table in the corner of the room. An ornate green bottle filled with a dark liquid sat there, with two glasses nearby. Farden picked up the bottle and wiggled the wooden stopper until it came free, and gave the liquid a careful sniff. 'As long as it's not the blood of some poor local, then yes, I would, please,' he said, narrowing his eyes at his friend. Durnus laughed, and gestured to the chair. Farden sat.

Despite his tiredness the mage remained holed up in Durnus's room for the rest of the evening, their tongues wagging over war, peace, murder and magick, washing their words down with plenty of wine. After a while the night stretched into early morning and Farden finally left the vampyre's room. His head spun with tiredness and long conversation. He could feel himself starting down a trail of thought that he disliked very much.

The mage wandered through the dark corridors of the Arkabbey and tried to calm himself.

As Farden lay down on his cold bed thoughts began to bounce around his head like insects around a candle, second-guessing and doubts rife in his shallow dozing. Smothered by the darkness of his room he tossed and turned until finally he banged his fist on the pillow in frustration. The mage got up and stumbled across the stone floor until his foot kicked at his travelling bag, full of supplies. He rummaged around for a few seconds before finding what he was looking for. Going to the door he locked it quietly and started unwrapping a small scrunched up bit of bark-cloth. He stopped for a second to listen to the noises of the night, and then quietly put a small bit of something on his tongue. Farden went to the windowsill and stood there looking at the dark forest outside his room. He closed his eyes and chewed, and waited. After a while the mage felt the numb feeling gradually climbing his spine, and the stuff began to sour in his mouth. Farden spat, and heard the shadowy thoughts slowly quieten, felt himself slowly forgetting. Before he felt too dizzy he grabbed a nearby candlestick and wedged the bundle of bark-cloth into its hollow base. With a thud he put the candlestick back on the bedside table and let his world begin to melt. His head felt heavy and his breathing slowed as the drug started to make his head spin. Farden fell back onto his bed with a bang and slowly let sleep take him hostage, all problems forgotten.

The mage was in a desert. The thought that he might not have ever seen a desert had not yet occurred to him, but he stood in a desert nonetheless, and lifted his hands to the feel the hot rays of the strange red sun dance across his skin. He wore only his trousers and the red-gold vambraces, and his feet were bare. The cracked dusty earth quivered and shook in the heat. Pebbles floated from side to side and tried to hide from him. In the haze of the distance the horizon was darkened by huge black mountains scraping at the heavens. Farden looked up and around him, in all directions, he had never seen a sky so big, so massive, or so empty and blue.

He felt something scratching at his leg and looked down to find a skinny black cat impatiently clawing at him. The thing mewed at him, and yawned cavernously, a yawn too big for a cat that small, he thought, and he stared, and watched the thing scratch about. It fixed him with an obsidian gaze, eyes like two black scrying mirrors, and cocked its head on one side.

'What?' asked Farden, but nothing happened. Then, slowly at first, he became aware of his skin starting to tingle and shiver, and sparks of pain began to shoot up his arms, as if he had slept on them for too long. Confused, Farden looked down to see flakes of burning skin peel from his hands and wrists in great quantities, his arms and chest started to brown and blacken, and the veins and arteries under the skin melted into rivers of fire. His vambraces cracked and splintered into pieces before his eyes, and fell to the dusty earth with a dull clang that reverberated and roared and became an unbearable noise in his ears, like the mountains were dragging themselves forward, towards him, inch by inch, closing in. He lifted his hands to his face and felt the charred bone underneath, and watched shreds of flaming skin fill the air like a swarm of locusts in the sudden hot wind. Farden opened his mouth to scream but his tongue was too dry, and refused to move, and sat smouldering between his black teeth. Before his eyes were burnt away, he looked down at the cat. It stared at him with a placid, and bored look, then its tiny mouth seemed to curl into a smile. The mage heard a voice in his head speak clearly over the fire and the roaring wind.

Follow the dragons, said the voice, and then the wind swallowed him.

❦

Sunlight streamed in through the open window, piercing the sleeping mage's eyelids like a yellow spear, and sending a spark of pain jolting through his skull. Farden swore darkly and hoisted himself out of bed. Remnants of a dream swirled around him, and dissolved to nothing in the morning light. Soon there was a knock on the door and Elessi came in to the cold room holding a small wooden cup of something and a bowl of homemade porridge.

'Good morning,' she said with a bright smile, her face the opposite of Farden's mood.

'Is it?' Farden coughed and tried to look awake, fighting off the effects of the night before. He grabbed a nearby shirt and threw it on to cover his wound. Elessi put the breakfast on a table in the corner of the room and began to sort out clothes for his journey. Farden stalked over to the table and sniffed the juice. Apple. He downed it in one gulp and grabbed a spoonful of porridge. He managed one mouthful before feeling ill.

'How'd you sleep?' Asked Elessi as she cleaned part of his armour. His battered sword was on the bed. The tired mage swept the blade from his scabbard and looked at the notched edge, scarred from many a battle.

'I need a new sword,' he said absently, then turned his attention to the maid bustling around in his room. 'I slept well, thank you for asking. Durnus and I talked long into the night. Is he up yet or should I go wake him?'

'Rumour has it he went out hunting last night, but he should be in his room. It makes my skin crawl when I think of what he's been up to.' Elessi shivered momentarily.

'He can't help his nature. And it does wonders to keep the villagers out of the forest.' Farden smiled wanly at his own joke. His head pounded like a drum.

'Your armour is all cleaned, and there's a fresh cloak and tunic here for you. Fresh supplies are in your 'aversack as usual. I know how you don't like searching the kitchens for food, what with the other maids there,' she said, and made to leave. She lingered at the door for a moment.

'Thank you Elessi,' said Farden as he tried another spoon of breakfast. She look as if she were about to say something but thought better of it and closed the door.

Farden milled around in his room for a bit, struggling to shake the numbness he still felt from the drug, the nevermar, the night before, and the strange remnants of a vivid dream he could have sworn was so real. The mage rubbed his cold skin and shook his head slowly.

He could feel the hangover dimming his magick, like alcohol and the ability to walk in a straight line. Farden took a warm cloth from a bowl of warm water and dabbed it at the wound at his side. It was healing up nicely, but was still an angry red and sore. It would be healed by the next day. His fingers traced something on his back for just a second and then he turned to face a bronze mirror in the corner of his modest room and stared at his reflection.

Farden looked exhausted. His dark, almost black, hair, was in a bit of a wilder state than usual, and from behind the tangled strands that lay across his face he could see dark rings surrounding his grey-green eyes. The mage ran an exploratory hand across his face, and examined the rest of him, rubbing stubble and dust between his fingertips and blinking at his bronze alter-ego to try to make it more acceptable. He was a tall man, just over six foot and well built, perhaps a few years over thirty. Nobody but Farden was sure. His arms and body bore countless scars from blade and magick, random streaks of pinky white criss-crossing his already pale skin like the paths of a snail. There was a small tattoo on each of his wrists, a black circular symbol with a line of thin script passing through it towards his hand in a key shape. He scratched at them briefly and then put on his red and gold vambraces to cover them up. Next came a brown tunic made of rough cloth, and over that went his thick and simple armour made from steel plates. It hugged his body closely, but still allowed him to jump and move like a mountain wolf if needed, unlike the thicker, more elaborate suits of armour from Skölgard or Nelska.

Farden strapped on a thick rust-coloured belt, some more plate armour for his thighs, and heavy black ranger's boots. Lastly he donned a long black cloak with a hood and strapped his sword into its scabbard on his back, arranging the red scarf to wrap around his neck. Despite the pounding headache and dizzy stomach Farden smiled a rare smile. He was ready to go once again.

The hooded soldier slammed the door to his room and bounded downstairs, barging past a few kitchen boys carrying pitchers of milk. They stood dumbstruck as the dark character swept off down the hallway, muttering only the briefest of apologies. Farden walked into the main hall of the Arkabbey, where a small shrine sat against the north wall and his footsteps echoed loudly. Farden bowed his head and briefly knelt before the effigy of a powerful looking woman holding scales in front of her, as if asking for something. Her stern stone gaze looked out over the myriad of candles that had been lit on her plinth. She was Evernia, goddess of power to the Arka, and keeper of balance. Farden whispered a standard prayer to the goddess and put a small coin on a stone dish. The old gods didn't interfere in the lands of Emaneska like they did in the ancient days, but it was still wise to stay on good terms with the fickle creatures.

Durnus dropped to one knee next to Farden and whispered something to the stone statue. There was a moment of silence as he finished his prayer. 'I don't often see you paying homage to the old ones,' he commented in a hoarse voice.

Farden shrugged. 'It seems like a good idea to keep on their good sides,' he said. The vampyre nodded. 'That it does. How did you sleep?' he asked. Durnus himself looked tired. His eyes were even paler than usual, and the large hooded cloak he wore did nothing to hide the fatigue hiding in bags under his skin.

'Everyone always asks me that as if I were a stranger to a bed.' Farden smiled. 'Well, thank you. I take it you had a good night then?' he asked as he ran his hand across the rough granite floor.

'Gods damn those maids, they have tongues like town criers. I would cast a mute spell on every last one of them if I had the chance to do so. I take it Elessi told you about that?' Durnus cursed, bowing his head to the statue as he stood up. He turned to leave and Farden followed him towards a thin door. The thick cloth curtains shifted in a chill draught.

'She does like to talk that one,' grinned Farden. They walked down a dark corridor. The Arkabbey was still in the process of waking up. The servants were preparing breakfast for the slumbering soldiers, and a few scribes wandered the halls, rubbing sleepy eyes and yawning.

'So I have noticed. You haven't said anything to her about what happened at Arfell have you?' Durnus's pale eyes grew narrow and he furrowed his brow as he looked at his friend.

Farden shook his head 'No. I went straight to bed after I left your room last night. I barely talked to her at all this morning when she woke me with breakfast. I know the rules, and with a dangerous matter like what happened at Arfell, I wouldn't exactly go shouting it around,' he said.

'Good,' said Durnus The vampyre seemed satisfied and sniffed imperiously. He ducked under a momentary shaft of sunlight coming from a high window and folded his gloved hands behind his back. The two walked slowly and silently for a moment before the vampyre spoke up. 'You look tired Farden, anything wrong?' asked the vampyre.

A massive headache and mind-numbing dizziness, thought the mage. 'Absolutely nothing. Deep sleep and I'm still waking up,' said Farden. An easy lie.

'Now remember, get as much information out of him as you can. I'm not sure how he's fared since his exile and the wolf-curse does strange things to a man, so be wary of his answers. After all he may have a mind like that of soft cheese, and he could be completely useless, but make sure above all that you get the truth! If the Arkmages are going to base their actions on your words then they better be the right ones,' lectured Durnus. Farden's head ached. His old friend pulled a rolled up scrap of parchment from the folds in his cloak. 'Jergan was last seen somewhere near Beinnh south of the Dornoch hills. You can rest up in the town and then face him the day after. Unfortunately for you the pull of the moon is strong this month, so he'll be able to change at will.'

Farden nodded. 'Trust me, I can handle it.'

Durnus flashed him a toothy smile. 'It's not you I'm worried about, my dear mage. He's the only lead we've got to putting an end to this book debacle. That means don't kill him, Farden,' said the vampyre. Both of them knew there was a dark undertone to the order.

'I won't.' Farden stopped at an arched doorway. Durnus stayed in the shadows of the door and away from the light outside. Farden held out a strong hand. The vampyre gripped the mage's hand in an iron handshake, and smiled.

'Don't wait up for me,' said the mage, pulling his red scarf around his neck and chin.

'I never do,' chuckled Durnus. Farden turned around and jogged over the wet lawn and into the thick forest. The mage disappeared behind the trees, and Durnus returned to his room, saying more than a few charms for luck.

chapter 3

*"A dragon's claws are curved and deadly, much like the strange
daggers from the east. Beware the teeth too, a large dragon can have
up to three rows of teeth and gnash them in a fearsome manner before
eating. A dragon may have a long or short tail, but either invariably
have a forked or barbed tip, that swishes around angrily should a
traveller choose to approach! Their scales have the power to mystify,
with rippling colours that can hypnotise the unwary, and some may
even change colour to match their backgrounds..."*
'Dragons and their Features: Lessons in Identifying the Siren Beast' by
Master Wird

It was raining hard when Farden walked through the
industrious streets of Beinnh. Townfolk and strangers trotted though
the muddy streets and carts pulled by cows and donkeys splashed
through puddles, soaking the passers-by and dirtying the colours of
the market stalls lining the road. People crowded in the shadows of
the tall houses, the wooden buildings leant over the thoroughfares as
though they would topple at any moment, heavy with tall arched slate
roofs, brick chimneys, and dripping gutters.

Farden shrugged rainwater from his cloak for the hundredth
time and drove his hands deeper into the pockets, hoping to find a dry
spot somewhere. His grey eyes roved over the various wares that
were on offer in the little tents, their tables adorned with food,

clothing, weapons, and cheap trinkets. The shopkeepers shouted through the downpour with offers of bargains and special prices. Ahead, a building jutted into the road. A striped tent had been hoisted up to cover some benches and a well, where gloomy figures hunched over pots of ale, plates of bread and *farska*, a cheap beef stew sold in taverns all over dreary Albion. Farden trudged through the muddy puddles and cart ruts, dodging the brown rivers of rubbish. After three long days of urgent travel, he was starting to run out of food.

As he neared the tent the mage spied a small blacksmith's shop nestled in the back of the building. A table of shining weapons glinted in the bright firelight from the forge and a thin soot-smeared man stood holding a file to an axe. Patrons milled around the tables holding various blades and sharp objects, stocky grim men with dark aspirations and malicious inclinations. A group of them hunched over the end of the table, clad in long dark cloaks and smoking cheap tobacco from even cheaper pipes.

Farden made his way to the front of a table and ran his hands over the shining swords and knives. His eyes picked out a longsword, sheathed in a thick black leather scabbard, posing with thick crossbars and a long steel leatherbound handle with a pommel shaped like a huge black diamond. Farden unsheathed the weapon and ran a careful thumb over the thick blade and its sharp edges.

'See something you like, boy?' A bald skeleton of a man croaked in a thick Albion drawl. The dirty blacksmith tugged at the grey-white gloves covering his bony hands. They were made from salamander wool, impervious to fire and perfect for working a forge.

'How much for this, old man?' Farden asked, waving the sword at him.

The smith looked at the blade and chewed something in the back of his mouth. 'Hmm... one 'undred, silver.'

'One hundred? You've got to be joking. I'll give you sixty, fair price for this blade.' Farden shook his head and crossed his arms.

The other men had gone silent, intrigued by the sale and the foreign-looking mage.

'Eighty, or no sale.' The old man put a greasy palm out.

The mage unbuckled the old sword from his back and with a grunt tossed it to the blacksmith. 'Sixty, and you can have that old man, it's still got a few swings in it.' Farden strapped the deadly longsword to his back and fastened the thick buckle around his armoured chest. The old man grudgingly cleared his throat, shrugged, and finally nodded. Farden took his money bag from his travel pack at his side and gave the man sixty silver pieces. Farden noticed the silence at the table and turned to meet the stare of a bald thug on his left with a scar across his forehead. The man held the mage's piercing gaze a moment before turning away to grin at his mates. He walked off and his minions followed him like loyal dogs in their master's wake.

Farden finished counting out the pieces and the man began putting them into his dirty apron, proudly dropping each individual coin into a pocket with relish. As the mage turned to go a polished reflection of the hot forge caught his attention on a nearby table. A shiny little hand mirror lay propped up against a wooden post at the far corner of the stall, surrounded by cheap cutlery and ornaments. 'Hey smith! Is that mirror silver?' asked Farden.

The old man turned and looked at the glimmering object and rubbed his filthy chin with equally filthy fingers. 'Yeah I made it last week, for the posh ladies of the town y'see, give 'em somethin' to look at their pretty faces with,' the smith leered, exposing empty gums where teeth should have been. He paused to spit in a clay pot near the crackling forge. 'Ye want that too?'

'This is important old man,' Farden pointed a warning finger at the blacksmith. The mage knew his magick lore, and of the rules that bound each creature. If Jergan was a lycan, then he would fear silver. The rumours about using silver blades or arrows to kill the creatures were absolute rubbish: any blade would do as long as it was sharp enough and thrusted into the right place. But if a lycan saw their reflection in something like a silver mirror, however, then the curse would break momentarily, and they would return to their naked, shivering, human forms, dizzy and exhausted after the sudden transformation. It would give him an hour, maybe two at most.

Farden had faced a lycan only once before, on the ice fields in the far north. He had been let off easily that time: the creature had merely stalked him for a day or two at the most, only once getting close enough for a spell, but otherwise keeping its distance. Farden remembered the fear as if it were yesterday. Lycans were incredibly dangerous. Their massive claws and vicious teeth were matched only by their inhuman strength and lightning speed. And of course, it only took one bite or a single scratch.

Farden looked around to see if anyone was watching. 'This mirror has to be *pure* silver you understand? If I find out it's a fake there's going to be trouble between you and me, and more than just the mirror will be returned to you.' Farden tapped the new sword's hilt menacingly with one hand and with the other he summoned a little flame to burn on his palm. The old man took a step back warily and began to bite a dirty finger nervously. He held up an anxious hand 'Easy, easy, ain't a reason to get violent here. It's silver, have no fear mate.' The smith flashed an uneasy and disarming smile and held up both empty hands.

'How 'bout a special price of twenny five silver? Between you and me?' he offered. Farden didn't trust him at all, but he needed something shiny and silver, and he had forgotten to find one before he left. The mage nodded, and the smith rushed to fetch the mirror from amongst the other trinkets at the back of the oak table.

Farden looked about him once again. The nevermar was still numbing his magick ability and now a fresh throbbing had taken up residence in his head. Assured that nobody had seen his little demonstration Farden counted out the overpriced sum of twenty five silver coins to the fidgety little man. He put the mirror in his travel bag and let the smith scurry back to the safety of his smouldering forge.

The mage stepped back into the pouring rain and went to look for a few food supplies for the last part of his journey. After purchasing some dried meat, tough biscuits and apples, he headed down the hill towards the south gate of the muddy town.

❦

A while later Farden was wandering slowly through a quiet road near the south wall. Night was slowly approaching and lamps were being lit all over Beinnh, the twinkling lights hiding behind curtains and doorways and iron sconces. It was still raining hard and the downpour was now driven by the approaching wind, sending the thick blanket of clouds sprinting across the dim sky above him. In the distance white lightning ripped through the darkness. The flashes tore the horizon and shook the hills with rumbling cracks and deep booms.

Farden watched his own boots tread through the mud, sending little brown rivers flying through the air with every step. It was foul Albion weather as always but his cloak was warm and was keeping him nicely away from the elements. This new sword was heavier, he thought, but it felt good to have a decent sword for once. Through his musings he heard a muffled cough from behind him and turned to see a burly figure following him. Turning back, Farden looked around at the silent dripping houses and tiny alleyways. Another man, skinny and bedraggled, was leaning against a wall smoking a pipe. To the front yet another thug was coming up the road towards him. The rain pattered noisily on the puddles and the sounds of splashing strides were ominously loud. Farden clicked his neck and mentally tensed his wiry muscles, summoning the magick from the base of his skull. A wave of hangover washed over him, dimming his magick and sending throbbing waves of pain ricocheting behind his eyes. Farden would have to wait to use his bigger spells.

The thug in front suddenly brandished a knife in his right hand, the thin blade glinting from a far off glow of the town. It was the bald man from earlier at the forge, and in the half light of dusk Farden could see the rain bouncing off his shiny head and running down the scar on his brow. He grinned and waved his dagger at the smoker and the man behind Farden.

'Jus' give us yer silver and we'll be on our way,' warned the lout in a low voice. 'Let's not 'ave any trouble 'ere mate.'

'If you and your men know what's best for you then you'd be on your way now. I don't want to hurt you,' said Farden as the men surrounded him, keeping their distance and brandishing cheap weapons. He took a wider stance and stood firm.

'I don't know if yer noticed but there's three of us, an' one of you, so it ain't looking too good for yer mate. Like I said, give us the silver and the gold an' we won't 'ave to leave yer for the guards to find dead in an alleyway.' The bald man made little cutting motions in the air with his kitchen knife. He was a brute of a man. His small bald head sat atop a thick grubby neck and his cloak hung from wide hunched shoulders.

Farden sighed. He should have known better than to splash his coins around in the view of ugly men like this.

'You idiots don't get it do you? Leave me alone or you won't live to see another day.' Farden's eyes bored into the dimwitted frog-like stare of the bald thug. The man leered and spat. 'Get 'im lads! Get 'is coins!' He yelled and ran wildly at the lone mage, feet pounding through the muddy street and dagger flailing. Farden took a step forward.

The two men collided with a massive crash as Farden turned to the side and met the man's face with his elbow, stopping him dead in his tracks and knocking the knife from his hand in one swift strike. The thug's legs flew out from under him and he crashed heavily in a shower of brown water. In an instant the mage dropped to his knees and drew his sword with a loud metallic ring, waiting for his prey to come to him. The next assailant sprinted to attack and Farden swung the longsword left in a wide arc. The blade caught the thief square in the ribs and there was a sickening crunch as it smashed through the bone to hit flesh and spine. The man let out a petrifying scream and crumpled to a bloody heap next to the first, writhing and spilling vital organs into the incarnadined mud.

With a shout the last thug ran towards the powerful mage wielding a long club high above his head. 'I'll kill yer!' he yelled. Farden smacked his wrists together and threw a quick bolt of fire into the night. The sizzling bolt burst against the man's chest with a blinding flash of light that burnt the clothes from his skin. He hit the mud flat on his back with a short yelp and choked on rainwater. Farden dashed towards the charred man while he struggled to lift his head up from the clogging mud. Without missing a stride he sent his boot flying into the grimy thug's nose with a lethal kick. The man's face exploded with blood and bone and his head slammed back into the ground with a nauseating thud. He did not move again. Farden skidded to a halt and then leapt to his feet, and listened to nothing but the dripping rain.

The bald man stirred under the carcass of the other bandit. His face looked like a crimson landslide and he lifted shaking fingers to feel the damage, breathing through cracked teeth. Farden retrieved his grimy sword and wiped it on the leg of one of the downed men. Farden watched him struggle. Durnus would not have been happy with such a vicious display, he realised. But Durnus wasn't there. Farden shrugged to himself and spat on the bald thug, sheathed his sword, and left.

The mage walked alone, letting the rain drip down his face

and cool his hot angry skin. He let the fight replay in his head. A smirk curled at the corner of his mouth. Might as well start the night as he meant to go on, he thought. He reached into his pocket and pulled out the soaking piece of parchment, looked at the lines and contours of the map, at the word *Jergan*, and then shoved it back into his pocket. He doubled his pace and jogged into the night.

Eight hours later a lone figure crouched on the summit of a low hill, his long cloak billowing in the stormy wind, rain lashing his unblinking features. The man was staring avidly at a small hovel cowering in a shallow valley between two hills. It was barely surviving the weather, its rough wood and stacked stone walls were shaking violently in the howling gale. A single struggling candle peeked from a tiny window. The man's eyes flicked to the cloudy sky as a fleeting gap in the clouds revealed the white saucer of the full moon, radiating blue light down on the hills for a split second. His watchful gaze returned to the hut.

Farden had been watching this poor excuse for a house since finding it three hours before. His headache had finally gone, and he could feel the power swelling in his wrists and head now, magick running through his veins like a strong river pulsing and surging through a canyon. A faint glow came from under his cloak, but he tried to keep it under control; creatures like Jergan could sense magick, smell it, like the wyrm in the north. They hunted it, given the chance. The rain slammed into him with hurricane force and rain pelted his face and yet Farden didn't even blink, completely focused on his task.

Suddenly in the corner of his eye something seemed to move on the hillside. The mage snapped his head in its direction and stood upright just to make sure. Slowly he inched his sword from its sheath and stood ready. Nervousness crept over him and his breathing became short and quick.

For an age Farden didn't move, watching the stormy hillside getting lashed with curtains of rain. He slowly crouched down again with sword in hand and looked back at the hut. The candle had gone out.

From absolutely nowhere a massive shape bowled out of the rain and barrelled into the mage, driving the air from his lungs. He flew down the hill, barely rolling as the hairy creature fell with him and snarled savagely in his ear. His sword fell from his hand and dug into the grass. Farden let the creature slide off him and he skidded to a halt. He scrabbled to get upright and once he had he thumped the ground hard with his fist. A searing light cut through the darkness of the stormy night, revealing a hulking creature standing a dozen yards down the hillside, matted hair drenched with rain and plumes of hot breath escaping from a mouthful of fangs. It growled and snarled, words slipping through yellowed daggers of teeth.

'Leave this place,' barked the monstrosity. Its long arms were hanging low beside muscular legs, and its stretched hands and curving claws were dripping with water.

'I've come to find Jergan! I must speak with him!' Farden shouted above the gale. He slowly moved back towards his sword and the creature menacingly took a step forward in return. The thing's eyes were red pools of pure madness Farden slid a hand into his travel pack and searched for something shiny.

'Jergan is dead! He doesn't live here and never has so LEAVE!' The lycan crouched low and his thick mane stood up and flapped in the wind. Farden took another step back and a sword hilt knocked against his leg. The mage held out a hand, warding the animal off, trying to get through to the man inside him.

'I don't want to hurt you, Jergan, I just want to talk!' Farden's heart was beating double time against his breastplate.

'Arrrgh!' The lycan snarled and leapt towards the mage. Farden smacked his wrists together again and stamped his foot. A wall of fire billowed out of the ground towards the beast and ripped through the rain, but with a roar the agile creature jumped over the flames and bared his teeth in the red glow.

Farden whirled his sword and dodged to his right as Jergan flew past him. The lycan skidded on the wet grass and with a terrible clicking he unhinged his jaw even wider. The mage summoned a huge globe of fire and aimed a blow at the growling animal. The fireball smacked into the lycan's shoulder blade and sent him sprawling. Farden bravely strode forward and held his curved longsword high. Jergan jumped to his feet and roared deafeningly. He sprinted towards the mage and swung his claws in mad arcs. Farden blocked and cut straight across Jergan's left arm. It sent the lycan reeling backwards, yelping, but he managed to reach out with one deadly punch. The swipe caught Farden on the breastplate, winding him and cracking a rib. But the mage did not falter and jabbed at Jergan, finding the skin beneath matted hair at his neck. With incredible speed Farden yanked the mirror from his bag and showed it to the cowering lycan, lifting his light spell to blinding levels.

'Look at this!' the mage yelled. Jergan blinked and squinted at the silver trinket, covering his eyes with bleeding hands.

'Look!' Farden strode forward, marching his mirror before him into the face of the lycan. But the beast suddenly barked a guttural laugh and shouted above the rain.

'You should tell your maid not to buy you cheap silver mirrors mage!' he cackled, and kicked out at Farden's chest with a long hind leg. The huge foot caught him hard right below his throat and the mage tumbled backwards with a cry, but as he fell he threw three small bolts of blistering fire at Jergan and the lycan stepped back quickly swiping fire from his face. Farden rolled backwards skilfully and regained his stance, the wind blowing the smell of charred hair and flesh to his keen nose. He threw a massive fire blast at the creature and followed it up with a quick spell to drain the lycan's strength. Jergan yelped and barked as he threw a rock at Farden. The powerful mage deflected the missile with his sword and kept throwing spell after spell at Jergan. A few more firebolts and a blast of lightning threw the lycan to the ground. Farden summoned a dark well of strength and threw his arms out wildly. A ripple of magick ripped through the ground like a carpet being shaken and rocks flew in all directions. The quake spell hit the lycan in the back and the crack of several bones was audible. Farden reeled from the massive spell, cramp striking his arms like a hammer bouncing off an anvil. The mage gritted his teeth and still strode forward, watching the beast scrabble to get upright. Jergan's fur and skin were raw in patches, and blood gushed from his arm wound.

'Leave!' the lycan hissed.

Farden halted and watched the creature pick itself up. 'Let me talk to Jergan! I know he's in there somewhere,' he held his arms wide, twin balls of fire spinning in each hands as he struggled to keep up the level of spell casting, but he knew it was the only way he could make the lycan retreat.

'NO!' Jergan pounced and Farden clapped his hands together with a blast of flame. But the lycan had been too quick and the spell broke, the two of them falling back to the ground. Farden struggled for his life as razor teeth snapped an inch from his face. Claws dug deep furrows in the grass next to his head and the lycan spat and roared in his face. Farden was using all his strength to hold back the massive shoulders of the beast with his sword, backing up his efforts with an iron spell of force.

'Get....off!' Farden shouted and rolled over. His blade sliced across Jergan's hand again and skilfully reversing his grip he raked the sword across the lycan's side. The beast snarled and leapt away, but not before scraping a claw across Farden's chest, luckily only finding armour beneath. The blade swung again and caught a hind leg. Farden could not chance even getting a small scratch from one of Jergan's teeth. so he kept swinging his sword in a vain attempt to ward the animal back to a safe distance. Relentless magick was the only weapon that could keep Jergan at bay. If they had to fight until the sun came up then so be it, Farden thought grimly.

Lightning forked the sky above them and a roar of thunder followed it. Jergan howled a haunting cry, arching his head towards the heavy clouds. Farden spun away from the lycan and the two of them circled again, both breathing hard and shaking with effort. The creature was bleeding from multiple places but the wounds already seemed to be healing and scabbing over. Farden cursed the lycan's regeneration ability.

The mage ran the flat of his sword over his left gauntlet and the blade burst into flame, spitting and crackling. He threw two more spears of fire at the lycan and swung his sword at the lycan's skull. Jergan ducked and rolled, the flames licking his flanks. Sparks of electricity leapt over him as Farden hit him with another jolt. Jergan was getting tired and he knew it, the lycan's spell starting to break under the pressure of such powerful magick. Farden was starting to crack as well, keeping up such powerful spells was draining him, and badly. Remembering Durnus's words he extinguished the sword in the ground and began to concentrate on the wind around him, forcing a vortex of rain to spin around the snarling lycan. The wind howled keenly and the rain battered Jergan as Farden sent wall after wall of wind at the beast. Farden mercilessly drove a few more blasts of energy at the wolf-like creature. The wind tore back his hood and the cloak flapped while rain lashed the mage's face. His jaw was set and the effort drained his stern features of colour. The lycan stumbled back again and spluttered as rain water filled his face. Lightning ripped through the sky.

'Leave me alone!' shrieked Jergan. He scrambled backwards

to get free of the powerful onslaught. He turned tail and stumbled away from Farden's vortex spell. The lycan ran off into the night, howling as he disappeared.

Farden swayed on his feet as the wind died back to its normal level. He lowered his hands and collapsed into the soaking grass with exhaustion, still trying to keep his eyes open and fixed on the hills around him.

❦

Morning brought him iron skies and a light drizzling rain. The rolling green hills lay quiet and sodden, the grey outcrops of rock scattering the scarred grass from the night before. Farden lay in a trance, hunched up with his knees at his chin, cloak gathered around him in a tight bundle. He had forced down some meat and water earlier in an attempt to stay awake and alive. The exhausted mage wiped rain from his face for the thousandth time. His eyes were surrounded by dark rings once more, and his lips were white with the cold. Farden's sodden hair covered his face and a beard was starting to decorate his chin. In the valley before him lay the tiny wooden hut Jergan had retreated to earlier that morning. After the battle the lycan had disappeared into the storm, howling occasionally and spying on Farden from a nearby hill. When dawn finally broke over the moors Jergan had begun to transform and so he had slunk back into his hovel.

Farden stood up resiliently and drew his sword. He gripped the cold steel and bound leather with his weary frozen fingers and cleared his dry throat with a crumbly, hoarse cough. After taking a final swig of rainwater and relieving himself gratefully behind a boulder the mage determinedly strode forward down the sloping hill towards the hut.

'Jergan! Come out here and talk! Don't make me cut your

head off you cur!' barked Farden. He marched up to the door and banged loudly on the rough wooden planks. No answer.

'Jergan! Get up!' Farden kicked the door in and cast a light spell to burn through the darkness of the messy cabin. The rancid smell of wet dog and rotten meat made the mage gag. A clatter of pans came from the corner behind the door and Farden stormed into the tiny room.

'Don't! Don't kill me!' shouted Jergan. He held up his muddy hands in defence and covered his eyes. Pale skinny legs flailed in the air as the gaunt man scrabbled in the dirt. The mage's magick burnt his eyes. Jergan spluttered and coughed. 'Please, I'll do whatever you want!' he managed, and Farden let his spell die. He looked at the poor excuse for a man lying on the floor.

Jergan looked as though the years had eaten away at him. His arms were thin and bony and his brown fingernails were long and chipped, and now starting to curl with age. A scrap of cloth barely covered him, and it was soiled with mud and blood, leaving his ribs poking through papery skin. His straggly white hair hung thick over a weary face, and dull violet eyes poked from deep holes above sharp cheekbones and cracked lips. Scales adorned his chin amidst grey stubble. Proud flecks of blue striped his cheeks and ears. He was the complete opposite of the foul creature he had faced last night, the antithesis of threatening, a broken old man lying in the dust, and the mage felt a tinge of pity for him. Scaly feet and ankles kicked pans as the exhausted Siren lycan hauled himself to a sitting position, a dishevelled crossbreed of bad luck.

Farden leant against the doorpost and waggled the fierce tip of his sword at the cowering man. 'You'd better have whatever I came for, or you'll wish I had killed you last night,' he spat.

Jergan was still breathing heavily, and his bony chest heaved up and down with his panting. 'I thought you were here for sport, like the many others that have come here and tried to hunt me. How was I supposed to know who you were and what you want, I haven't spoken to anyone in months, or years...' He glowered at the mage, and then cocked his head on one side, like a dog. 'What do you want from me Arka?'

Farden sheathed his sword. 'Information that you have, old man, or had.'

Jergan shook his head, as if his fate had already been decided for him. 'What could I possibly know that's of any value to you?'

Farden scowled, and 'Well let's find out, shall we? Three days ago something was stolen from my people...' he began.

'And you think I had something to do with it?' He glared again, and Farden felt the anger boiling in his chest. The cursed old skeleton was being petulant. Farden crouched down and brought his eyes close to Jergan's. 'Listen here, old man, and listen well. After last night you're lucky I didn't set fire to your hut and be done with you. But I've been sent here for information, and I don't intend leaving without it. I suggest that you give me what I want. And if you interrupt me again, it will be the last thing you do. Tell me what I want to know and I'll leave you in peace, or end you if that is your wish.' The mage's eyes burnt with fire. The Siren looked away, and they both rose warily, Jergan taking a seat by the small stove and Farden remaining standing, arms crossed and stern. The scaly man took a few deep breaths, licked his dry cracked lips, and gestured with a wave of his papery hand. 'Please, go on.'

Farden flashed a humourless smile. 'The stolen item was a book that was taken from the Sirens during the war. It was a book of great magick, small and black with a black dragon-scale cover. My masters think you studied this book years ago when you lived in Nelska.'

The lycan looked away. 'That was a long time ago mage,' he said.

'Well I need you to remember.'

Jergan thought for a minute. His mind was full of tired headaches and ravenous hunger. 'I have tried to forget these parts of my life, and for years I've pushed them from me, or the beast has done it for me. If I can't remember having a life, then I have nothing to miss do I?' He paused again, and then narrowed his eyes with deep thought. 'A long time ago, years before the war, an expedition discovered a cave near the Tausenbar mountains, and in the depths of this cave lay a hidden fort dug out of the rocks and cliffs, and inside that we found a library filled with everything we could have dreamt of. It had been a dark elf stronghold, in the old times, now long abandoned, but it was filled with so much knowledge and countless forgotten treasures. The elves had left all their belongings in a manic retreat, leaving all their food and clothing behind in their rush. One of the tomes we found buried beneath the dust was a little black book like the one you've lost.'

'Well was it this book or not?'

'That was such a long time ago, and my mind isn't what it used to be... but it sounds the same. A small book covered with black dragon scales, and a small gold latch on the front, with a very strong spell sealing the lock.'

Farden nodded. 'That sounds like the one.'

Jergan shrugged. 'Well, there you have it.'

The mage shook his head. 'I need more than that. What was *inside* the book?'

An irritated sigh. 'We took it and the other books we found back to the halls of Nelska, and began to study them. It took years to accomplish. I happened to be one of the few men working on your book, trying to uncover the secrets of the dark elf magick.' Jergan paused for a swig of nearby water.

'You Sirens should have known better than to mess around with elven magick,' said Farden.

'We knew that, but at the time it seemed the best thing to do for our people, with power like that we would have been unstoppable,' said Jergan, grinning a little.

'Then I'm glad we started the war before you did.' Farden returned the yellow smile.

'Perhaps, but either way this book was the most fantastic example of dark elf magick we had ever seen. Once our most powerful spells had opened the book we were able to learn the summoning incantations that brought daemons, monsters, and ghosts from the other side, calling them to fight anyone who would stand in our way. We tested some of them with several prisoners from Skölgard with brutal results. The daemons would do anything we asked them, and they would fight on command until death. That is, if you were strong enough to summon one; several of our wizards died from the strain of summoning such terrible beasts.' Jergan looked wistful, remembering an age long forgotten, like a torn-out chapter of a book he had once read.

'Shame,' Farden spat.

Jergan seemed hurt, but thought better of complaining. He went on. 'The most powerful spell in the manual was for the one of the most ancient and terrifying of all dark monsters. None of us to this day knew how to raise it, and the incantation alone scared us witless. Whatever it was the Old Dragon called a stop to such free use of dark magick, and called off the whole investigation into the "evil" book. Farfallen had it banished to southern Nelska, where apparently your soldiers stole it and whisked it away back to Krauslung.' The scaly man crossed his arms.

'What was this spell about?' Farden asked as he took a seat on a small wooden box.

'We never knew, it referred to what was named...' Jergan made a guttural sound of some foreign language, and Farden shook his head. 'Something I can understand, please?'

Jergan made a face as though he were teaching a child. '*Thy mouths of darkness* or *terrible dark*, something like that. All that we managed to find out was that this thing was different from the other dark creations, a crossbreed of daemon and dragon that old Farfallen feared greatly. Luckily, none of our wizards had been strong enough to survive such a powerful incantation, and the Old Dragon put a stop to our research, so the book was sent away and we halted all other reading on dark magick. Farfallen had the practice outlawed in Nelska and none of us spoke any more of it.'

'*Research* is hardly the word I would use, but that sounds a wise thing to do, for a Siren.' The mage nodded as he searched in his travel bag for food. He tossed Jergan a red apple and munched on his. 'I will assume that was a compliment,' said the lycan, as he caught the offered fruit. 'Thank you.'

Farden shrugged. He mused as he crunched on the bruised apple, turning over words in his head. There was a moment of chewing, and then the lycan asked a question. 'I take it you are one of the Arka then? One of the Written I imagine?'

Farden set his jaw. It was an invasive question, especially from a Siren. He humoured him. 'Yes, I am.'

Jergan nodded slowly, a hint of something in his hollow eyes. 'Then I applaud you, carrying the Book is not easy task, for some,' he said, and his hungry eyes roved over the mage. 'I've heard the stories about the unlucky ones, mage, when the magick eats away at the mind.'

Farden shuffled on his little box and scowled. 'I suggest you keep your observations to yourself. Why would someone want to steal this dark manual? How much would it be worth on the magick market?'

'As I said, it has been years since I talked to barely anyone mage, as you might have guessed I usually just end up eating my guests.' Jergan's face went icy cold and his eyes glazed into a faraway look. Farden tried to find patience somewhere inside him. 'I saw as much last night. Again, why would anyone want to steal the book?'

'Power maybe? But to use the greatest spell in that book you would have to be one of the more powerful mages in Emaneska. I only know of a few, and most of them are the ones who sent you. Out of the Arka probably only the Arkmages could open the book and cast the spells within. You're probably asking the wrong person' said Jergan, but Farden didn't buy it. 'There are other powerful mages in the land these days, besides the Arkmages. A few of the wizards from your own lands could do it, and in the east Skölgard have sorcerers capable of such feats. Why would my masters steal their own book?'

'You tell me, mage. Could you do it?' Jergan asked with a nod of his head.

Farden shook his head. 'That's not the point,' he snapped, and the lycan went on.

'If someone wanted to steal it then they would have to know of its existence. Excluding the dark elves who are obviously not an option, that leaves the Sirens in Nelska or your own people. That's the truth of it.' Jergan leant back on the rickety chair. Even with the stiff breeze from outside sneaking through the open door, the air inside the hut was thick and stale. The more Farden looked at the scaly lycan, the more he pitied him. He obviously hadn't eaten anything for days; Jergan had eaten the whole apple already and had wolfed down the core and even the wooden stem. The mage shook his head, and focussed on his task.

'Then if it wasn't any of the Arka, that means the war is far from over,' concluded the mage. An ominous silence hung between them. Farden's mind ran through fields of possibilities and jumped over hedges of doubt. Had, the gods forbid, one of his own Arka committed this crime, murdered the scholars and stolen this book? Farden's mind clouded stormily with fears. He couldn't rule out the Sirens either. And there was the distinct possibility that the murderers were working completely on their own, independent of either race,

Arka or Siren. Suddenly he felt a heavy dread worrying and chilling his heart, but an equally strong sense of duty coursed through his veins, and the mage clenched his fists as he resolved to put a stop to this mess before it got out of hand. Farden had to get back to Durnus.

Jergan filled the silence. 'If the book was stolen by someone powerful enough, strong enough to summon that terrible creature, then all of Emaneska would be in danger, not just our peoples,' Jergan warned. Some colour had seemingly returned to his old skin, and he seemed more confident, eloquent. He went on. 'If you had seen the sort of caged daemons hidden in this manual like I have then you would know how important retrieving this book is. Now this is important, so listen well. It's not just being able to cast the spell that is the challenge, but this particular beast needs a powerful well of dark magick to help it cross over. The elves built deep caverns to house their magick power, much like the Book you carry.' Jergan paused to look hungrily at the mage. He continued hastily when Farden threateningly narrowed his eyes at the lycan. 'There used to be hundreds of these wells all over the lands, but when the elves left they were hunted down and destroyed. I'm sure you know of them: "lost by dark ones all forgotten..." ' he recited.

' "...Lakes of magick below paths untrodden." Yes we've all heard the stories and the riddles to find the last few elven treasure troves. But they're all gone, lost to time. Where else would someone take the book to release its power?' Farden crouched forward, elbows on knees. Against his better judgement he was beginning to trust this Siren's words.

'That's assuming that you're wrong and not all the wells have vanished?' The corner of Jergan's mouth rose ever so slightly, as if he had a won a small hand in a verbal card game against the interrogative mage. But Farden wasn't in the mood for playing games. 'Then tell me where I can find one.'

Jergan laughed as heartily as his starved frame would allow.

'Hah! No one has uncovered one for decades, so explain to me why I could know where to look.'

'You obviously know that there are some left in Emaneska, and creatures of your kind are drawn to magick. You might have found one in your time with the Sirens, or maybe as a lycan you know where one is,' he said. Farden had a dangerous look in his eye.

'All I know is that there a still a few left, maybe about two, or three, I don't know.' Jergan held up his scarred palms in honesty.

'But you don't know where?'

'We never found one. That was one of the reasons we never managed to summon the beast from the book.' Jergan flopped his arms on his lap. A silence sat in the room and Farden was deep in thought. 'So whoever has stolen this book intends to release this creature, but only by finding one of these wells.'

'And the only way of doing that would be through the dragons of Nelska. In the memories of the old dragon there may be a clue to where an old well may be,' offered Jergan.

'Then I suppose I'll be hunting dragons next.' Farden clenched his fists and rose. Jergan stood up with him.

'If you're going to go then I would ask one favour of you.' The Siren asked in a pleading voice, his violet eyes watching the mage adjust his belt and travel pack.

'What do you want? Farden replied sharply as he sheathed his sword.

'If you do come across any of the dragons, then at least tell them that I'm alive, and not dead. That's all I ask,' whined the man.

Farden nodded, and went to the door. The breeze was hard and cold, but sun was beginning to burn away the drizzle and the blue skies had started to scatter the clouds. Farden looked at the decrepit old man standing behind him. 'Thank you Jergan, for your help. I understand you didn't ask for this, for the life of a lycan, and I hope that you survive it a while longer.'

Jergan tried to smile, as if it was the kindest thing he had heard in decades. It probably was, he thought. 'Good luck…' said the lycan, and the mage sighed. 'Farden. If you must know,' he replied.

'Then good luck Farden.' And with that the mage was gone, jogging across the hills back towards Beinnh and the Arkabbey to the north. Jergan sat back down in his little chair and looked around at his little hovel. The wind howled through the crack in the door and rattled the walls. A little tear ran down the lycan's cheek.

Hours later, night had once again fallen upon the streets of Beinnh. Rowdy laughter rang out from tavern doorways and wild yells fell from the top floor windows of brothels. A light hammering rang through the alleyways, unnoticed or ignored. The old blacksmith was still hard at work, alone at his forge. The red glow of the fire illuminated his anvil and sparks flew from his hammer as it beat down on a glowing spear point. The thin old man was content, he had made a good profit on these cheap iron spears, they had earned him a fine bit of gold without too much trouble. The hammer sent another shower of sparks into the cool night air that scattered over his salamander wool gloves. The blacksmith pondered his next scam and started to whistle, tuneless and croaky. Something moved in the shadows behind the forge behind him. The hammer fell again and again like a beat to his dissonant warbling, and something drew closer behind him. Suddenly a hand grabbed the scruff of the old man's neck and shoved his forehead down hard onto the glowing spear point, making a scalding hiss as it collided with the blacksmith's skin.

'Aagh!' The old man cried out and fell to the dusty floor. He rubbed at his skin and howled.

'You lied to me,' the dark hooded figure spread out his fingers and a small lightning bolt flickered over his palm, dancing in an electric blue glow. Farden grabbed the smith by the wrist and covered his mouth roughly. The old man squirmed as electricity flew through his bones and rattled his spine.

'Stay quiet old man, otherwise you might make me do something I'll regret.' Nervously the blacksmith stifled his yelps and fell deadly silent, eyes wide and terrified. A few muffled questions came from behind his hand. 'You lied to me about the silver mirror, and I warned you what would happen.' Farden jolted the man again ruthlessly, and then he slowly uncovered his mouth.

The smith panted and bobbed his head. 'I remember yer, I remember! I'm sorry! I'll do whatever you want, er, you can 'ave yer money back I swear! Jus' please don't kill me...' sobbed the man. '...yer not goin' to kill me are yer?'

Farden narrowed his eyes and watched the pitiful man squirm. 'Lucky for you,' he snorted, 'you can keep your money old thief. But you *can* have your mirror back.' And with that Farden whipped the fake silver trinket from his side and hit the man full tilt in the jaw, cracking bones and snapping teeth from their roots. The smith crumpled to the earth in a flurry of glass and spit and went silent. The mirror skipped and skittered over the dusty floor and collided with the stone wall of the forge with a clang. Farden looked at his glowing face in a shard of glass, and took a deep, calming, breath.

Farden stood up quickly and pulled his hood down low over his face. Without a word, he walked down the nearest alleyway and melted into the shadows of the ugly town. Lightning flickered on the horizon as another storm approached over the faraway hills.

chapter 4

"Those of special circumstance, can find themselves alone, by the field the house the mountain crag, the blood begets the bone.
Friend of foes, and fair thee well, watch out for shadows black, for darkness comes to them too soon, a wing'd teeth, bared blades, and trap.
They want what is different, but as all, we want the same, thus blood becomes the birthright, and thy night becomes thy shame.
They judge us by the difference, they judge us from thy teeth. But we watch their necks, we'll string them up, and leave them there to bleed."
Vampyre poem of unknown origin

Durnus was dozing in his loft room, watching the fire crackle and spark as the wet wood popped occasionally. His sleepy mind was churning over thoughts of war and countries, kingdoms and traitors, and of the legends of old. He let himself melt and rove through his thoughts, listening to nothing but the rain hammering on the stained glass windows, and the wind howling through the dark afternoon. It would be night soon, and there was nothing better than hunting in the rain. He let his eyelids droop some more.

Behind his comfy chair, propped up in the corner of his room, was a tall archway made from black stone and metal scaffolding, tied and strapped to the wall with thick grey rope. The contraption leant out from the wall and over a wooden lectern holding a very thick brown book. The black stone flickered in the candlelight. The old vampyre turned his head to check on the thing in the corner, as if it might have moved, and then turned back to the fire to close his eyes and enjoy the warmth of the big armchair and the soft upholstery beneath his paper-like fingers. All was quiet in the Arkabbey. Then there came a banging noise from the corridor outside his room. Durnus sighed.

All of a sudden the door was thrown open with a startling bang and a dripping Farden burst into the warm room and collapsed to his knees, palms splayed on the stone tiles. He was breathing hard and trying to fight from coughing.

'Farden!' The vampyre hauled himself upright and rushed to the mage's side. From his hoarse gaspings, Durnus made out the word "water" and went to a pitcher on a bedside table. He filled a cup and returned to give it to the mage. Farden downed the whole thing in one go and tossed the vessel aside. He stood upright and groaned.

'By the gods that feels better. I've never run that far that fast before,' Farden took a moment to swear and then coughed again, seeking the refuge of the other comfy chair by the fire. The vampyre followed him and watched him slump into the armchair.

'You've been gone for almost a week, we were starting to get anxious,' he said. His friend was still struggling to get his breath back. 'Farden, hold still.' Durnus spread his thin fingers over the mage's forehead and the tired man went rigid. Farden's eyes shook while his vision burst into colour and vibrated with energy. The vampyre quickly removed his hand and the mage shook his head, blinking and wriggling his jaw experimentally. Farden squinted and twitched with the electricity of the strong spell. 'That felt, incredible… why've you never done that before?' He looked as though he were keeping watch on his nose as he tried to focus on the dancing lights in his eyes.

'Jolting the brain like that too many times can kill a man.

Even one as strong as you.' Durnus looked at his old friend. Mud, twigs, scrapes and wounds covered Farden's back and shoulders, his cloak was ripped to shreds and the sword dangled almost free in the loose strap around his back. Blood oozed from several wounds, some fresh, some old, and his face was a mess of stubble and bruises. He looked as if he had been dragged backwards through a forest and a river, thought Durnus, but at least he was still alive. Farden had regained his breath thanks to the spell and most of the colour had returned to his cheeks, but he still had deep black bars under his eyes and his dark hair was a bedraggled muddle.

'I have news.' Farden cleared his throat again and leant back in the encapsulating chair.

Durnus leapt back to his seat with surprising agility for someone who appeared so old. 'Well let's get to it! What happened?'

'Well, I found Jergan on the hills where you said he'd be, south of Beinnh,' Farden paused for another cough. 'And, for a hermit, he wasn't at all shy when it came to trying to kill me. Anyway, in short, you were right, Jergan and the Sirens found our book in the Tausenbar mountains before the war, in an old elf stronghold, and thought they'd try to use it. Jergan was one of the men who studied it, and with their wizards,' he said *wizards* with a hint of superiority in his voice, 'they tried to cast some of the spells. Apparently the book was some sort of dark elf summoning manual, for bringing creatures over from the other side.'

'They *cast* the spells in it?' The vampyre was shocked.

'That's what Jergan said, and for some reason I trust him. They went through it systematically from cover to cover, and their wizards tested the daemons and beasts on Skölgard prisoners. Jergan thinks that's why someone would steal the book, to get at the powerful beasts hidden in its pages.'

'But the Arka have fought daemons and ancient beasts before, you were there five years ago, when the minotaurs came out of the

Efjar wastes? Why should this book be any different?'

'He said this book held one spell that the dragon-riders feared so much they were never able to cast it.'

'What was it?' Durnus entwined his fingers in thought and stared at the fire.

'They never found out... but it was something that scared the Sirens and their dragons to death, apparently a terrifying beast referred to as the "*mouths of darkness*." They were foolish,' Farden shook his head, trying to remember the lycan's words.

'Foolish indeed,' the vampyre watched flames lick at the wood and stone.

Farden leant forward. 'Jergan also mentioned that if somebody powerful enough were to attempt to summon this thing, that...'

'That they would need a great source of magick... perhaps like one of the dark elf wells?' guessed Durnus.

'Exactly,' the mage smiled at his friend's intuition.

'As far as I know, the last one we found was near Arfell, north of the library and several miles underground.'

'And with barely any magick left in it, if I heard the stories right,' Farden pointed a finger at his friend. The heat from the fire curled around him like a blanket. 'And as far as *I* know, there aren't any left in Emaneska, but Jergan seems to think that there are a few we might have missed.'

'Indeed, I've spent almost my entire life trying to track them down.' He tapped his thin lips thoughtfully, deciding what to do. 'This is dire news, Farden, especially if the lycan is right about an undiscovered well. If we're assuming, that the thief stole the manual to get at the spells, then we have to suppose that they mean to release this beast on the world.' Durnus spoke his words with an ominous tone, a cold voice in a vacuous cave.

'And if Jergan was right about the size and power of this

creature, then we could all be in serious danger, and I don't just mean the Arka. Whoever stole that book wants to turn Emaneska upside down...' Farden looked at the vampyre and their eyes locked in a steely embrace.

'We need to get you to Krauslung with all speed.' Durnus quickly leapt from his chair and went to the pile of scaffolding in the corner. He flipped the dry pages of the dusty tome on the lectern and let his fingers scroll over the lines of brown ink.

'I'll need most of the night to prepare the quickdoor to the citadel. You need to rest. I can imagine that you've been through enough to get this information so I advise you just get some sleep friend,' he said, as his pale blue eyes scanned the book eagerly.

The mage took a deep breath and gathered his cloak behind him.

'What was it like?' asked Durnus abruptly. His finger had stopped on the page.

Farden looked over at the vampyre's back. 'Imagine seeing death in the eyes of a nine-foot tall wolf,' the mage paused, remembering that blur of a fight. Durnus turned to face him, a humorous look in his pale eyes. 'It strikes me as odd, my good friend, that you should ever see anything resembling death. Every time I fear the worst, you come back to us with no more than a handful of scratches. I envy you Farden, being out there face to face with creatures like Jergan?'

'Envy me?' Farden threw him a quizzical look. 'Are you sure?' Farden lifted his torn cloak over his breastplate and pointed to the deep groove made by the lycan's raking claws. 'This isn't a handful of scratches, an inch further up and I would be either dead or howling away somewhere out in the mountains.'

Durnus smiled and turned back to his book. 'Come now, I know you better than that. You crave danger,' there was a pause. 'That's why I'm always telling you to be careful.'

'Here we go,' muttered Farden, with a mock sigh. The vampyre turned around again as the mage slumped back into the chair. 'No, I'm not going to lecture you.'

'For a change.'

'Fine. All I'm saying is that we've known each other a long time,' Durnus tapped the side of his head with a pale finger. 'I know why you came here to Albion, and what you're trying to hide from, and I've seen how you deal with it. Just remember that we care about you, and that even you have your limits.' The vampyre crossed his arms and stared at the mage. His face was serious, and his words were sincere. Farden felt a little uncomfortable as he always did in these moments, and tapped his vambraces with his fingernail. 'It's not likely I'll find them just yet though.'

Durnus sighed and went over to the mage. 'Just be careful,' he said, and Farden nodded silently. The vampyre found himself smiling and put a thin grey hand on his friend's shoulder. 'And in truth I do envy you, because you're the one who gets to go out there and make a difference, fight the battles and the monsters, uncover the secrets and be the warrior. My days are long drawn out and my memories are slowly fading, Farden, I can't remember the last time I held a sword. By the gods it must be at least fifty years ago,' chuckled Durnus.

Farden seized the opportunity to change the subject. 'That's because you're a dusty historian, old friend. But have no fear, I'm sure there's still some fight in you yet.'

'Hah! That'll be the day.' The vampyre went back to his book laughing. To illustrate his point Farden picked up a nearby book and blew the dust from the cover. He cleaned it with the palm of his hand and squinted at the faded title. *Treatises on Shapeshifting*, that's a bit dangerous isn't it Durnus? Playing with the old daemon arts?'

Durnus looked at the book and shrugged. 'Just curious, and it's not just daemons that can shapeshift, my dear mage. What do you think I am? Or Jergan for that matter? Both curses have their roots in the ancients,' he said, and then wagged a didactive finger in the air. 'Did you know that the powers that bind a lycan are completely opposite to that of a vampyre? If a vampyre were to be bitten by a lycan, one of pure breed, then it could technically cancel the two out.'

'What would happen?' asked Farden, but the vampyre shrugged again. 'Who knows? Hence the book,' he sighed. 'But you need rest now. It'll be a while before I'm ready.' Farden nodded and stood up to stretch. 'And please heed my words Farden, as your friend. I know what your temper can be like.'

'I shall.' Farden walked towards the door and pulled it open. His old friend was right; there were a few people in the world that he cared about. Farden thought of one in particular, and suddenly an idea blossomed in his mind. 'Durnus, can you send me to the quickdoor at the Spire?'

The vampyre thought for a moment and then nodded without turning. 'I don't see why not. If that's what you want.'

'It'd be good to see Manesmark before I go to the city.' Farden left the old man to his books and turned to go. Durnus could have sworn he heard the mage whisper a thank you before he closed the door.

Elessi was wandering the corridors of the Arkabbey tower. After hearing a rumour that Farden was back, she had gone looking for him with angst in her heart, but now it was late and her search of his room and the cavernous dining hall had been fruitless. She was wandering up and down the spiral staircases of the abbey tower, peering in empty rooms and listening to the wooden doors of locked quarters and rooms home to sleeping soldiers. The earnest maid skipped up the steps to the training halls near the bell tower, holding her skirts above her shoes. A dull thudding tumbled down the stone hallway on her left and she paused in her stride. Yellow torchlight spilt from a door half-closed at the end of the corridor, and the rest of the hallway was bathed in lazy moonlight pouring from a thin arched window. Elessi crept forward, running her hand over the rough walls. Her work-worn fingers felt the cracks and pitted surface of the grey stone. The noise grew louder as she approached, like a sharp, deep crack of fire against wood.   \

She reached the doorway and peeked through the gap into the hall. Her pupils shrank in the bright yellow torchlight. Flashes of light and fire skipped over the wooden beams of the yawning roof, and she shuffled around to get a better look at the cause of the noise. There, standing shirtless and sweating, was Farden, throwing bolt after bolt of fire at a wooden man-shaped target. The mannequin swung wildly, suspended from the wall and shackled to the floor on short iron chains. It rocked and bucked under the powerful blasts of magick. He wore nothing except a pair of black trousers, and in the dim torchlight she could see Farden's chest heaving with deep arduous gulps of air and his shoulders were bathed in sweat. And there was something else. Elessi's eyes were now fixated on his back. Lines and lines of thin black script covered the mage's shoulders and lower back, punctuated by swirling elegant lines and spirals clambering over his collarbone and shoulder blades. Four symbols ran along his spine, runes with shapes and strange interwoven words. Elessi couldn't help notice the dark faces of telling bruises running through the black lettering, and every time the magick surged through his body the words flashed and glowed, sporadically lighting up all over his skin, glittering and dancing with a bright white light. The chambermaid was transfixed: her eyes locked in a mesmerised stare. She narrowed her eyes and tried to follow the lines of script and make sense of the foreign scribbly words.

Farden threw yet another bolt of fire at the target, whose

carved wooden face was now charred and smouldering. If a mannequin could look depressed, then this one did. The mage paused his onslaught for a moment and clenched his fists. A whirring, crackling sound hummed through the air, and Farden bared an open palm and sent tidal waves of sparks and lightning to wash over the wooden statue. With a crash the topmost chain melted and the mannequin fell to the floor with a burst of cinders. The mage cursed and went to find his shirt. Elessi flinched back from the door and ran back down the corridor with mixed feelings of relief and fear. That night she dreamt of wounded ghosts and hulking monsters, of deep caves and fire burning under her sheets. Sleep ran from her and Elessi awoke with red eyes and dripping with cold sweat.

Farden opened his eyes to find some more winter sunlight jabbing through his open window. He found he was lying on his front and swiftly pushed himself up and out of bed, stretching with a new-found readiness. He had rested well, in a deep dreamless sleep, and now he felt fit and eager to get going. Whatever the old vampyre had done had worked, and Farden resolved to ask him about it another time. He finished stretching and went to find his scattered clothes and armour. He ran a wet cloth over his grimy face and neck and began to wipe the dirt away. One of his teeth was loose, probably from the fight, and Farden tongued it in an investigative way. He pushed a finger to his jaw and muttered something, and the tooth settled back into its place. It didn't move again.

He moved to the window and felt the cold breeze of the morning on his face. The winter sun was still hovering near the horizon behind the trees, hiding behind the leafless branches of the Forest of Durn. A lonely bird sang somewhere below in the Arkabbey grounds. The smell of baking bread from the kitchens below hovered in the air. The mage carried on washing until he looked relatively acceptable to society, and then tried smoothing out the folds and creases in his clothes with his warm hand. He put on his tunic, his boots, and his armour, and strode out of his room.

When he reached the vampyre's room the door was unlocked and Farden went straight in. Magick throbbed and hummed in the air. The fire had long burnt out and only the candles now lit the dim room. In the corner the archway of black stone and steel was filled with a haze, as if a silk veil quivered constantly and violently in the centre of the tall doorway. The quickdoor seemed to be finished and already thrumming with energy.

Durnus reposed in a wooden chair near a desk, eyes closed and dozing. Farden walked quietly up to him and put a gentle hand on the old man's shoulder. The vampyre stirred and his eyelids fluttered.

'Farden...hmm, what time is it?' asked Durnus hoarsely.

'Just before noon, it'll be afternoon in Manesmark by now. It's time for me to go.'

'Right!' Durnus slapped his knees and stood up, all tiredness instantly forgotten, and headed to the lectern to check on the vibrating quickdoor. 'It's ready, it took me a while to do for some reason, the Albion magick seems to be weaker than normal. The quickdoor in Manesmark is a powerful one though, so it wasn't impossible,' the vampyre rambled away as he leafed through the pages, preparing the next spell.

'You know I don't understand this time and space magick my old friend, that's your area of expertise not mine.' Farden smiled warmly.

'It's all about patience my good mage.' Durnus squinted at the hazy surface of the quickdoor and ran his hand over the archway, careful not to stray too close to the buzzing threshold. The obsidian surface of the stone blocks felt alarmingly hot to the touch. 'Think of it as trying to open and close a window a thousand miles away, with no more than a rope and a long pole.'

'That doesn't really help.'

Durnus thought for a moment, looking at the ceiling. 'No it doesn't does it? Well, all seems like it's in order Farden, time to go through. Now remember, hold your breath before you step in, and watch your feet. It looks like it's snowing on the other side,' Durnus pointed.

Farden watched as little flecks of snow tumbled through the portal, settling in a little patch on the top step of the quickdoor. 'Great,' he said. He had hoped it might have been a little warmer in the city, but apparently he was wrong.

'See you soon, old friend.' Farden shook the vampyre's hand and stepped closer to the portal. Durnus flipped through pages of his book.

'Try to remember every single detail and be sure in your opinions before you voice them to the Arkmages. You have a meeting with them this evening in the great hall,' Durnus looked at the sword on the mage's back and sniffed. 'And Farden?'

The mage turned.

The vampyre narrowed his pale eyes. 'I can smell the blood on your sword... who else did you fight besides Jergan?'

Farden lingered for a moment on the best excuse. 'Some people just don't listen,' he said abruptly, with a shrug, eyes searching the wooden floor for an escape from the reprimand he knew was coming.

But the vampyre merely sighed. 'Don't get sloppy Farden. You are an instrument of the Arka first and foremost, a finely tuned weapon of precision and tact. There are rules and there are consequences for poor decisions, mage, bear them in mind next time you draw your sword. I watched your uncle go down this violent path a long time ago, and look where it got him. This is the last time I'll tell you.' Durnus's gaze was grave, and more disappointed than angry, and it stung the mage all the more. There was no need to bring up his uncle, he thought. 'I will,' he muttered in low voice, and stepped up to the doorway. Farden felt the icy blast of the quickdoor on his skin and ran his hands over the tingling threshold. As he lifted his foot the door suddenly grabbed him in a vice-like grip and dragged him forwards into a blinding white tunnel of light and noise. Wind tried to rip the breath from his lungs and freezing gales attacked his watering eyes as he plummeted through the doorway. And in a second, it was over.

Farden stumbled onto the wet frozen grass of the Manesmark hillside and put a hand in a patch of snow to steady himself. Behind him the quickdoor fizzled shut and the mage shook his head free from the stomach-churning dizziness. He rose shakily to find a soldier standing guard beside him. The early afternoon sunlight glinted off his steel breastplate and made the emblem of the Arka, a gold set of scales, shine and glitter. Farden nodded to the man, who dipped his helmet in response, and quickly wiped the amused smirk from his face. The mage threw him a narrowed look as he wiped himself down. 'I'd like to see you try to land more gracefully,' he said, and the soldier made an effort to stand a little straighter, clearing his throat timidly.

The dizzy mage said no more and walked forward to look out across the stunning countryside that he had known as a boy. The landscape was still as breathtaking as he remembered. The tall Össfen mountains stretched out for miles and miles in all directions, as far as the eye could see, puncturing the wintry sky with their snow-capped summits and scraping at the heavy grey clouds with their rocky teeth. Beneath the jagged peaks and down in the snow-locked valleys waterfalls played amongst rocks and fjords of ice and farmhouses. To the south he could see the deadly slopes of Lokki, the tallest mountain in Emaneska, towering over the vista. Below him on the steep hillsides villages sat wreathed in wood smoke, peeking out of the snowdrifts. Farden looked down the hill at Manesmark, the traditional home of the Arka's fighting forces, perched on the slope, a cluster of townhouses, inns, and barracks. The buildings were tall and proud, elegantly built from grey stone and pine and topped with tall arched wooden roofs of slate. Chimneys belched grey haze and the sounds of a busy afternoon in the market floated across the cold mountain air to Farden's wind-bitten ears.

Scattered memories ran like rabbits through the fields of the mage's mind as he walked across the hillside. Manesmark was the long-established home of the Written, and of the School where every mage studied, where Farden had studied as a child. He could still smell the strange, ever-present burning smell of the place, feel the rough wood of the floors, the beds, and taste the watery yellow gruel. The School of the Written had been a cruel world of bullying, spells, and of constant fear. Many of his classmates had died along the way: victims of an "accidental" knife thrust or perhaps caught by a wayward spell. Vicious competition plagued the prestigious School, and Farden was sure nothing had changed. His class of prospective Written had been whittled down to just three exhausted candidates, and Farden had barely made it into the final cut. He remembered standing before the elders, beaten and bruised, pulsating with magick on his final day, feeling the blood run down his brow and hearing his name on their stern lips. It had been torture, every moment, but it had made him a man, taught him the true face of magick, and shown him the wild nature behind Emaneska. Farden could still feel the Scribe's whalebone needle carving the words into his back.

The mage strode up the slippery hillside towards the Spire, a huge tower that perched on the summit of the Manesmark hillside and climbed hundreds of feet into the sky. Here the Written lived, trained, and slept when they had the chance. As he approached he could feel the power thrumming through the walls of the tall building, emanating from the countless parapets and walkways hanging from the Spire. Guards and soldiers swarmed around the base of the tower like ants, and Farden spotted a few Written amongst them, hooded and cloaked like he was. The magick council had been rebuilding the ranks of the Written ever since the war, and now, even after the problems in Efjar, their numbers were greater than ever before. From what he had gathered from Durnus there were now almost two hundred mages training in the Spire, and just over half of them carried the Book.

Farden reached the foot of the Spire and made for the entrance. As he walked closer to the door a deep vibration could be heard, like a large bell tolling under a hill.

' 'Fraid you can't go in sire, too many already in there,' said a short man in uniform who stood at the doorway. He pointed inside with his thumb. Farden peered through the doorway into the enormous atrium of the Spire, a cavernous hall filled with stairs and corridors running in every imaginable direction. Hanging in the middle of the atrium was a colossal dragon scale suspended in the air by great steel chains. It quivered with energy and was making a deep whining sound. Too many Written mages in the Spire at one time could send the other men mad from the pure power of raw magick. The beaten dragon scale was like a warning bell for the Spire, ringing whenever the magick grew to dangerous levels. It was annoying, but necessary.

Farden nodded in reluctant acquiescence and withdrew to a nearby rock. He watched several people rub at brief headaches and listened to the scale slowly become quiet again. The mage shrugged to himself: Krauslung could wait for a little while.

Cheska was standing in her room watching the messenger hawk flutter around her windowsill; the poor bird was trying to find a place to land somewhere amidst the frozen snow on the stone ledge, flapping and mewing and being altogether unsuccessful. As soon as it came close enough she quickly untied the wooden canister from its leg and the bird flew off, probably in search of food. She snapped the tube and took out the scrap of yellow parchment. Three hastily scribbled words was all she needed to read. Cheska held the note in her hand and concentrated hard with muttering lips. There was a brief flash of light and the paper note became ash in her hand. She winced and sucked her singed finger. The sound of the scale below her reached her ears and she immediately turned to leave her modest room. The young woman quickly checked herself in a polished bronze mirror and opened the door.

'Afternoon Cheska.' Brim smiled a toothy smile, and winked at her. It didn't suit him, and made him look like he had a twitch. Her only friend from the School stood in her doorway, hand poised to knock on her door.

'Oh, Brim, I was just leaving,' Cheska said.

'Well I'm going to the market, we can walk if you want?' He said.

She nodded, sighed inwardly, and let him walk her to the stairs.

Farden was quickly getting bored. Some sunlight had broken through the heavy clouds so he had thrown his hood back to soak up the rare warmth, feeling the mountain breeze toy with his dark hair. A few soldiers he recognised acknowledged him in passing with silent nods. The other Written were mostly courteous, but curious of Farden. The solitary mage had always been quiet around most of the others, preferring his own company, and it was no secret in the Spire that people thought him dangerous and wild. The mage's eyes scanned the throngs of people milling around, looking for someone in particular.

She must have heard the scale ring, Farden thought. Then he saw her. She never ceased to make his mouth hang slightly ajar. Cheska looked as stunning as ever. From his rock he watched her weave through the crowds with all the grace of a cat, letting her piercing blue eyes rove over the multitude of faces, obviously looking for someone. Her long blonde hair escaped from the edges of her hood and swayed hypnotically in the breeze. She always seemed to be smiling too, ever since he had first seen her wandering the halls of the Spire, nothing more than a scared little girl. Her skin was paler than most, and like her hair it betrayed her Skölgard ancestry. Her royal breeding was obvious in her gait and posture. Like him, she wore a dark cloak, with a tight-fitting black tunic that did nothing to hide the tantalising and untouchable curvature of her body.

It was common knowledge that Cheska was the daughter of Bane, the King of the powerful Skölgard empire in the northeast. And that made her a princess. For her to be even living with the Arka, not to mention practising their dangerous magick, had been a massive political step for both countries, and a tough one. She had been supervised by a veritable horde of Skölgard minders, every step of the way, through every year at the School, until one by one she had shrugged them off and immersed herself in the brutal world of magick. Farden had to admit, she was good, better than any he had seen so far, and it had made their little affair even more exciting and dangerous.

He let his eyes take in every inch of her. It had been a few months since he had seen her, and a warm, if not slightly unexpected, feeling spread itself across his chest. He spied that friend of hers Birn, or Bridd, or whatever his name was, following her like a loyal dog, hoping to be thrown a treat. Farden set his jaw with an inkling of jealousy. As her deep mountain-lake eyes caught his he got to his feet and grinned.

'Well well! Look what the gryphon dragged in!' Cheska

smiled as the two came close in a firm embrace. She stood on her tiptoes and threw her arms around Farden's neck. He dared to give her a small quick kiss on the cheek and she stepped backwards with a coy look. A rare smile crept over the mage's lips, and he held her eyes a moment longer than was necessary.

Brim coughed into his fist politely and they came out of their little trance. 'Oh, Farden, you remember Brim don't you? He was in the same class at...'

'We've met a few times before. Good to see you again,' Farden gripped the man's hand in an iron grip. Brim tried and failed to return his icy gaze, and winced at the handshake. 'You too sir. What brings you to Manesmark?' Like all the others at the School, Brim had heard the rumours about this mysterious character, and was more than a little intimidated by him.

'Official business in Krauslung. I have to be heading there soon.' Farden said dismissively, looking at Cheska as she ran a handful of her hair through her fingers. A flash of something red caught his eye. That warm feeling in his chest suddenly turned cold. 'Tell me that's not what I think it is...' he said stonily.

She laughed, shedding his concern. 'You're right,' She pulled back her cloak sleeves and revealed a red band of metal wrapped around her slender wrist. It was a *fjortla*, a bracelet that traditionally marked a trainee for being Written. Supposedly the rare red metal brought strength and perseverance to the wearer for the dangerous tattooing process, a three day process that only half of the candidates usually survived. Farden still had his old fjortla somewhere back at the Arkabbey. 'We both got chosen and we'll be Written in less than a month!' Cheska smiled and put her hand on Farden's arm.

'Both of you?' He asked.

'Both of us,' Brim bared his wrist and showed him his own bit of red metal.

Farden found himself filled with anxiety. He couldn't even

begin to care about Brim, but Cheska? That was a different matter. Here was one of the few people in the world he did care about, and now she was scheduled for a terrible, gruelling ritual that could easily kill her.

'Cheska this is serious…' began Farden, but Cheska shook her head defiantly.

'Don't even start with that vulnerable woman shit. You'll start to sound like my father,' she cursed. Farden glared at Brim for a moment and then thought better of arguing. 'Fair enough, I won't say another word.' He held up his hands and shrugged. 'Walk with me for a while?'

Cheska smiled. She turned to her friend as she left. 'I'll come and find you later Brim, I'll meet you in the market,' she said. The young man nodded, a little confused, and watched the two of them walk off through the throngs of people and soldiers. 'Great,' he muttered, and with a wistful sigh he turned and headed for Manesmark.

'Are you actually serious?' Farden asked gingerly.

'Oh, don't be a hypocrite, Farden. You said you couldn't wait to go through with it when they chose you.' Cheska ran a hand through her long blonde hair again. Her tunic perfectly complimented her slim curves, and Farden couldn't help but sneak quick sideways looks at her. 'What did you think would happen anyway? That I would spend all these years training and then just turn it down?' she huffed, and looked away.

'It's just dangerous Cheska, and you know…' Farden trailed off, thinking of Jergan. His boots kicked loudly at loose stones. They were walking down a quiet path that curved away from the main thoroughfare between Manesmark and Krauslung. Behind them the noisy bustle of the Spire could still be heard over the sound of flags flapping and birds twittering. Cheska stopped abruptly under a rocky outcrop that bent over the thin path. 'I know what?' She asked.

'You know.' Farden waved a hand dismissively but she caught it deftly and stepped closer to him, a coy look in her glacial eyes. Cheska pulled at the red scarf around his neck. 'Still wearing the present I got you?' she smiled. He pulled her closer and they kissed, their lips locked in a passionate embrace. Farden's hands snaked around her back and pulled her closer to him, until she stood on tiptoes and threw her arms around his neck and let her fingers tangle in his dark hair. He started to kiss her neck, letting her scent dizzy his head, and pulled her even closer as his hands moved down her back and legs.

'No, not here Farden.' She put a hand on his chest and leant back, and he released her reluctantly. 'If we get caught they'll throw you in the stocks. And who knows what my father would do.'

'They wouldn't dare,' he said with a sly grin. 'You're not a Written yet, why should it matter?'

'Not here,' Cheska smiled and kissed him again softly. 'I think I'll head back to the Spire,' she held a finger to her lips as he began to talk. 'I know you're worried, but I can do this Farden. I've spent the last twelve years training for this, and the gods know I've struggled with my father every step of the way. I'm not going to let another stubborn man get in my way. Just be here for me, Farden.'

She was right, and annoyingly she had a point, he thought. Farden nodded and sneaked another kiss on her cheek, making her laugh and leap away from his grasp. Her sparkling eyes flicked to the city in the distance. 'Be careful in Krauslung,' she said. Farden took her hand and looked at her with a rare and mischievous smirk. 'Me? Be careful? What are a bunch of bureaucrats and their politics going to do with me?' He laughed and winked. 'I'll see you soon.'

'I hope so,' said Cheska, and with that she turned to walk

back up the path. 'Tonight?' Farden hissed, and she looked back over her shoulder. 'I'll find you,' she said, and he allowed himself a small smile. The mage watched her until she had disappeared behind a little ridge. 'Politics…' he muttered with a shake of his head. 'Politics and rules.' He kicked a pebble for good measure and watched it sail down the mountainside before he left.

A few hours' walk from Manesmark, nestled in a deep valley between the twin peaks of Ursufel and Hardja, lay the immense citadel of Krauslung, capital city of the Arka, home of the Arkathedral and to the ruling powers of the magick council.

Farden reached the huge city just as the afternoon was starting to give way to the dark winter evening. The sky was still bright even through the clouds, but the cold darkness of night lingered on the horizon, ready to sneak through the mountains. The hooded mage strode over the frozen grass of the valley, staring up at the two steep mountains either side of him. Their sheer rocky faces were dark grey, sprinkled with a few hardy shrubs and pines, and they towered over the city walls. The immense ramparts of Krauslung filled the gap between the two peaks, using their cliffs as a solid foundation for their thick stone defences. Acres and acres of fields stretched out in front of the city. Houses and shacks that were home to hundreds of peasants squatted in the shadow of the soaring walls. A stream of travellers and city folk flowed through the massive main gate, its huge archway dominated by the gatehouse above it that almost rivalled the Spire at Manesmark in height. Stone battlements crested the walls, and from there a small army of guards watched over the arriving visitors and peered down from their reclusive arrow slits. The long and uneasy ceasefire with the Sirens had made the Arka guards wary and suspicious over the years, ever fearing the shadow of a dragon or a Siren spy. Even after fifteen years nobody was willing to forget.

Farden joined the slow moving throngs of people heading towards the city, boots crunching on the gravel on the wide road. He pulled his cloak around him to ward off the approaching cold. Merchants at the roadside called out to the passers-by hoping to make a few more sales before night finally fell. Pigs and goats were being herded in small groups by young children covered in mud. A few dark-skinned men from the south were sat around a campfire beside the road, curved swords at their side and muttering to each other in a low foreign tongue. The smell of exotic spices and meat tickled Farden's nose. A fat man riding a sorry-looking black bear meandered between the people, occasionally whacking it with a thin stick to make it move faster. The beast just grumbled and kept moving.

After a short time spent weaving through the ever-increasing crowds Farden reached the huge archway of the main gates. The thickness of the stone and the massive iron doors never ceased to amaze him, even for one as far-travelled as he, and the mage stared up at the murder holes and gigantic stone blocks suspended above his head in awe. The guards eyed him warily for a moment as he passed beneath them, and then, recognising what he was, they looked away quickly to glare at the next person. Farden pulled his hood down even further.

Ahead of him was the main city, and from his vantage point at the gate he could see the whole of Krauslung spread out ahead of him like an intricate carpet. The two great mountains either side dipped and fell, giving way to a narrow sloping valley that ended in a horseshoe-shaped harbour and the Port of Rös with its legendary shipyards. From there the bay and the cold Bern sea stretched out for many leagues before stumbling across the islands of Skap in the far distance, mere dark blotches that stretched out on the horizon like a half-drowned giant. The Össfen mountains marched on for miles to the east and west, steep walls warding off the bitter waves of the winter sea. The mage could smell the tangy salt in the air and hear the plaintive hungry cries of the gulls on the wind. He smiled.

Farden switched his attention back to the city. It had been many months since he had been here last and the mage had almost forgotten the impressive view. On his right, leaning against the precipitous walls of Hardja, stood the Arkathedral, forged from grey granite and white polished stone from the cliff cities in the west. A great hall perched on top of the huge hive-like building, crowned by two thin towers that stood either side of its domed roof. These towers held the twin bells that shared the names of the two mountains that flanked the city, Ursufel on the left, and Hardja on the right. Farden hadn't heard them ring in years, the last time he did had been at the end of the war. Like the layers of a gigantic cake, the Arkathedral spiralled downward to the city streets, its concentric curtain walls hiding libraries, halls, kitchens, barracks, training yards, and regal abodes for the two Arkmages and the council members. Here was the throbbing heart of the Arka, where the balance of magick was kept in check and the council played out their game of chess with the world.

The mage made his way deeper into the valley and down into the citadel. Night was starting to fall, and the city was buzzing. Down on the streets it was noisy; the gutters were full of water from the winter snows and gods know what else, people leant out of windows and shouted to others down in the street, while others gambled and bartered in the narrow alleyways, merchants hawked their wares, bellowing at passers-by, and women painted with gaudy colours whistled and grabbed at some of the finer-looking men. Farden loved it. Here nobody paid attention to him, he could melt into the dark alleyways and market stalls and nobody would look twice at the shady mage. Even the pickpocketing children ignored him, knowing better than to mess with a Written. In Krauslung everyone seemed to live on top or underneath everyone else. The buildings of Krauslung were piled storey upon storey, until each house or shop or tavern seemed to lean against the next, making the streets seem like the darkened arteries and capillaries of some immense living thing.

He finally made it onto one of the main avenues that ran through the city, and the crowds became thinner and slightly more civilised, and a bit more sunlight reached the streets. He looked up at the tallest buildings, at their stained-glass windows and their arched slate roofs, and a few faces peered back at him. From behind the coloured glass they sipped at thin goblets and picked daintily at tiny bits of something in their hands. In the city, the finer citizens claimed the upper levels. They had made social class a matter of mere physical height.

Farden snorted and carried on, taking it all in as he walked. He watched some of the more established merchants relax at their stalls after a long day of profit, smoking pipes and chewing on tough bread. Arka soldiers stood on every corner. Their polished silver armour shined in the last rays of early evening light. A tavern to Farden's right suddenly erupted with loud music as two bards, or *skalds*, rallied the patrons with loud tales of heroes and beasts and magick. The drunken men all sang along, and several spilt out into the streets to slam their tankards together in flurries of brown ale. The soldiers looked on distastefully.

To his left a group of fine ladies, their faces painted and their hair tied up high, ran gloved hands over jewellery and ornaments at a shop window. A few of the women had their pet geese by their side. The fat birds were decorated in the same colours as their owners' dresses and held on thin velvet leashes and they honked quietly and impatiently waddled from side to side. Farden smiled. The fashions of high society had always seemed a bit odd to him, but after all the wishes of the rich ladies had always commanded the coin purses of the rich men. He caught himself staring at one of the blonder women, one who looked a little like Cheska, but he pushed her from his mind and kept walking. A warm feeling spread across his chest.

Shop windows called out to him with bright colours and signs: *"Potions, Lotions and Notions, Magickal remedies for all! Vigtor Urtt: Purveyor of Blades and Pointy Weapons! Fine clothes for Fine women!"* This last one was accompanied by a little wooden notice that said *"No beggars allowed."*

This was how the city was, and more so in recent years than ever before. The poor lived below the rich, so close and yet so far, neither crossing the gap between the classes but willing to live in rough harmony as long as their peaceful way of life was maintained. And that was where Farden thought he fitted in. He was not rich, but nor was he poor, simply somewhere in the middle, an unknown stranger ignored on the streets. He thought himself part of the glue that held the Arka together, a servant of the ruling magick council whose job it was to maintain this balance, this way of life for these naïve people. It was suddenly odd in his mind, how thankless this task was, and yet somehow he was still so dedicated to it. If the world of magick was a game of chess, then Farden was a pawn.

Farden headed north along another wide street lined with houses. He fixed his eyes on the gates of the Arkathedral fortress ahead of him and started the long walk up the sloping street towards them.

 chapter 5

"See I think those Arkmages is sneaky, why else would they keep us all out of their pretty tower, secretive like. And you know I heard that there Helyard bloke can change the weather? Make it rain and all that? See now that scares me. If were up to me, I would have us people running things, making sure we're not up to no mischief and all. We're the ones who knows best.

"What, the war? Well that was all about gold or land or something, yeh it was definitely about gold..."

Overheard during a conversation in a Krauslung tavern

'Farden!' A loud voice rang out through the marble corridor. The mage turned to see a familiar face creasing with a big smile, and an outstretched hand coming towards him.

'Undermage, always a pleasure.' Farden grinned and shook the proffered hand warmly and vigourously.

'It's been too long Farden, too long, and you can dispense with that Undermage rubbish, you know me better than that,' The Lord Vice flashed a smile that was crammed with white teeth and clapped Farden on the shoulder.

'I can see you haven't changed, still playing the politician as usual,' said Farden. They both laughed and carried on walking down the corridor. Vice was an old friend and a powerful mentor to Farden, and he had known him almost all his life, ever since he had met him at the School. Back then Vice had been a lowly instructor, but step by step and bit by bit he had climbed through the ranks to sit beside the two Arkmages, the powerful Helyard and the wise Åddren. Rumour had it that Vice was actually doing some good for the council, and Farden was honoured to have a friend in such a high place, someone he could trust in the upper echelons of pompous Arka society.

Vice was quite a tall man, a good half a head taller than Farden and quite powerfully built, rather than lanky. He had a long ceremonial knife at his hip as a mark of his office and wore a long black and green robe that swished lightly against the marble floor as they walked. His dull blonde hair curled and spilt over a tall forehead that was just beginning to show the lines of stress and age. His dark brown eyes were warm and welcoming while his defined jaw and high cheekbones gave him a regal air, but Farden knew the huge power that Vice hid behind his usually calm exterior, and had seen those eyes flash with furious magick more than a few times. If Farden remembered correctly, Vice had been one of the best at the School, and had taught Farden many of his tricks and spells. But he wasn't a Written, and couldn't begin to compare himself to the power of the Arkmages.

As they walked, the affable Vice threw an arm around Farden's shoulders, steering him down the corridor. He spoke in a low voice while a few servants passed. His purposeful eyes flicked between the marble flagstones and the big arched windows lining the hallway. The sun was starting to set behind the mountains.

'This is a dark time for us Farden. I hope you have some good news,' he murmured.

'I have news, but whether it's good or not will be up to the Arkmages and you, Vice.'

'The tragedy at Arfell has hit us hard. It's one thing to lose valuable scholars in such a brutal murder, but to have a dangerous book taken from our safe hands is much worse.' Vice shook his head and clasped his hands behind his back.

'I agree,' said Farden. Two guards swung open a large door and snapped their heels together as the two men passed. They sported short spears and circular shields, and they wore the same green and black of the Undermage's position. The mage waited until they had passed through the door. 'Whatever's going on, and whoever's behind all of this, we can't afford to waste time.'

'More of your good news I assume,' said Vice drily. He rubbed his clean-shaven chin. 'We'd better discuss this with the council, they're waiting for you,' he pointed ahead to a wide gilded door, one that Farden had seldom walked through. Another two guards flanked the thick doorway in full ceremonial armour made of shiny gold and green metal. Their shields were like mirrors and their long spears were so tall they almost scraped the arched marble ceiling. Their golden helmets covered their entire face, and they nodded to Farden and Vice as they approached. Farden straightened his shoulders and cleared his throat loudly. He tried to remember the etiquette and protocol that Durnus had taught to him long ago, and not much came to mind.

'Let's go in.' Vice motioned to the guards and they pushed hard on the big doors. They swung open agonisingly slowly.

Farden stepped into the great hall and tried to keep his mouth from hanging open. It was like stepping into a white and gold cavern, and every time he came here it never ceased to amaze him. Marble pillars lined the room, tall white columns carved like tree trunks so that their bases spread over the floor like gnarled roots, and their tops flared out across the roof like thick ivory branches, and there they entangled themselves in the huge beams and gilded rafters that resembled the ribs of some huge fossilised animal. Light poured through windows that stretched from floor to ceiling, from one end of the hall to the other, fitted with the finest stained-glass that the artisans of Krauslung could ever hope to make. Farden watched the opalescent light play amongst the ivory branches and golden wood, and paint the white floor every colour he could imagine. He scanned the men and women and places frozen forever in the patterns of the coloured glass, their old faces emotionless and regal, staring impassively out of the windows at their successors.

The mage kept walking and followed Vice to the back of the great hall. Almost a hundred people stood around them, loitering amongst the pillars and benches clad in robes and dresses of various hues, talking in low voices and pointing at the mage. Farden ignored them.

In the centre of the great hall stood a statue of Evernia, surrounded by candles. Sitting at her white marbled feet were a set of gold scales, hanging balanced and even, the symbol of the Arka. High above her head a huge diamond-shaped window was open to the cold sky, and the cold wind whined across the opening. Through it Farden could see the sky turning a dusty pink with the dying sun. A single star dared to peek through the fading daylight and sparkle gently.

At the end of the room stood three giant chairs, two equally-sized ones in the centre and a smaller one to the right. Here sat the Arkmages Helyard and Åddren, rulers of the Arka and the heads of the magick council, powerful and wise and beyond contestation. Vice swept from Farden's side to take his place on the smaller marble chair. Guards stood in the shadows between the pillars. The hooded mage stopped several feet short of the three men on the chairs and bowed low to the ground, sweeping back his hood as he did so. There was silence in the great hall.

'Welcome Farden, to the Arkathedral. I trust your journey was swift?' Åddren spoke first. He was a short man, with kind blue eyes and a balding head sparsely decorated with copses of grey hair. Åddren was thin and ageing, but the powerful man still wore the long green and gold Arkmages robe with pride and a strict posture. He hadn't changed one bit since Farden had last seen him.

'It was, your Mage.' Farden rose slowly and nodded with his best courteous smile. To Åddren's right sat a tall man with a long sharp jaw and mahogany eyes that roved over Farden's clothes and apparel. For his age Helyard was surprisingly thick-set and muscular, echoes of a long life spent on the battlefield. He sat bolt upright and stern in his tall marble throne, spine and jaw stiff with pale skinned hands resting on the broad arms of the chair. Helyard's hair was cut short and dirty blonde in colour, with streaks of white beginning to surface through his trimmed curly locks, like worms appearing after a heavy rain. He had the habit of looking down his long nose at the people he addressed, and impatiently interrupting council members he deemed too unimportant to speak.

The austere Helyard sighed theatrically. 'Tell us of your findings then Farden. If this news is as urgent as I'm told, you'd best be out with it,' he said with a dismissive wave.

'Yes Lord Helyard.' Farden nodded once more and took a breath. He spoke slowly and with a measured tone, striving to remember every detail, like Durnus had told him. He was unusually nervous in front of these old men. 'The book that was stolen from Arfell is an old dark elf manual, a spell book for summoning daemons and beasts from the dark places. A few days ago I travelled further south into Albion to find a Siren hermit named Jergan. He had been part of the team of wizards and scholars that first discovered the book, in an ancient elf fortress in the mountains, the same team that went on to decipher and cast some of the spells. Jergan spoke of the worst and most powerful of them all, something he said they had called *"the mouth"* or *"mouths of darkness."* They tried, and failed, to summon it, and before they got any further the Old Dragon had the book banished to a secret location in southern Nelska, and never spoke of it again.'

The Arkmages thought in silence for a moment, and several of the council members murmured between each other conspiratorially, like gossiping maids, and then Åddren asked a question. 'What of this Jergan, could he be the one responsible?'

'No your Mage, Jergan has become a pathetic hermit, nothing but a slave to his curse,' he paused as the others threw quizzical looks at him. 'He was bitten years ago by a lycan on the ice fields, and since then has lived in hiding, a broken and pitiful man under the spell of the bite. He hasn't left Albion in years and is still hiding on the moors in a wooden cabin. He's innocent.'

'And you're sure about that,' asked Helyard pointedly.

'The murders at Arfell were committed by more than just your average magick-user, we know that,' said Vice. Åddren nodded.

Helyard licked his thin lips with a lizard tongue and tried on a hint of a white smile. 'I hear a rumour that you might be one of the finest Written we have, Farden, where were you when the book was stolen?' There was a burst of outrage in the hall, mingled with a few accusing shouts. Åddren banged his fist on his marble throne for quiet.

Farden was shocked, and momentarily speechless, standing there with his mouth open. He tried to think of a careful answer. Silence was slowly restored, and then it hung like lead in the hall. 'Your Mage, I agree that everyone is under scrutiny for this terrible crime, even our own Arka, but as for me,' he looked the Arkmage squarely in the eye, 'I was in the north of Albion, on a mission given to me by my superior.' Farden paused, and then something kindled a little rebellious streak in his heart. 'But perhaps, if I might be so bold in saying, that if that's the case, then even the magick council should be considered in this investigation.' A few more shouts from behind him and a low rumble of discontent came from the gathered council members. Arrogant bureaucrats, Farden thought, and made an effort to stand straighter.

Åddren held up his hands for silence. 'No one here is being accused. Farden is a loyal servant and has served us well through the years, Arkmage Helyard is merely being wary.' Vice agreed with a murmur, and Åddren changed the subject. 'I'm curious, why did they fail in summoning this creature?'

Farden took the hint. 'Jergan said that this spell would need one of the dark elven wells to bring the creature from the other side, and he also seems to think there may be one in Emaneska that we have yet to find.'

Helyard scoffed, and a ripple of laughter ran through the council. 'Did he draw you a map?' shouted a mocking voice from somewhere in the crowd. Farden stood even straighter. 'He knew something, and I believe him,' he said confidently, looking to Vice for help.

'If what Farden says is true, then I thank the gods that the Sirens didn't ever find one, while they had this book in their possession. Such a force would have made them unstoppable.' Vice mulled over his friend's words.

Åddren held up a solitary finger. 'If the murderers need a dark magick well to summon the creature, then we have no choice but to believe this lycan, and try to find this well. Only then can we catch the ones responsible.'

'Yes your Mage,' agreed Farden.

'Åddren, the wells have been lost to us for years! You cannot seriously believe that one still survives,' Helyard chuckled in mock humour. 'Believe me, I have led many expeditions to find one...'

'As have I, Arkmage,' interrupted Vice. 'I agree with Farden. We need to make sure that this creature, this *mouth of darkness*, is never released. The only way we can do that is by getting to a well before they do.' The Undermage looked Helyard squarely in the eye while he spoke, and the stern man snorted and looked away. Farden could have sworn, that for a mere moment, Vice flashed him a triumphant wink.

Åddren cocked his head to one side, as if waiting for the

answers to come to him. 'How then, can we find a lost well now when we have been searching for decades? No clues have been found at Arfell, nor at any of our other libraries. Our records do not simply go far back enough!'

The others in the hall were silent in thought. A few still sniggered amongst themselves, and Farden contemplated changing their minds with a quick firebolt, but he kept his hands clasped behind him and stayed where he was. And then it came to him, something Jergan had said. 'Some of the dragons could have memories of the dark elves,' he said. A strange silence came over the hall, a mixture of horror and deep thought.

Vice, eyes locked on Farden, spoke up again. 'We would need a tearbook,' he said.

Farden's interest was aroused. He had only seen a tearbook once during his skirmishes in Nelska years before. He remembered them as large tomes filled with lines and lines of dragon-script, hieroglyphs that held a dragon's memories like a sponge holding a lake. When a dragon's tear was dropped onto a blank page of an empty tearbook, the memories would write themselves over the pages, and the dragon could store his past in one single book to be read as a history of their lives. The older the dragon, the longer the tearbook, and some spanned millennia.

'The dragon-riders have been silent for years now, and not a single messenger from Nelska has passed our gates since we agreed on the ceasefire.' Helyard said, 'and that was fifteen years ago.'

Farden was starting to notice that these council sessions seemed to consist of a lot of shouting and of a lot of silence.

'Vice?' All eyes turned on the Undermage. Years ago, in one of the final battles of the war, Vice had bravely led a small group soldiers through a secret tunnel into the siege-locked fortress of Ragjarak, home of the Old Dragon Farfallen, ruler of the Sirens. After a long battle through the ice-tunnels, Vice had killed Farfallen and taken his tearbook as a trophy. It was one of the few great victories of the war, and the blow had been heavy on the Sirens. Songs were still being sung in the taverns of the great Undermage and his fight with the gold dragon.

'The tearbook is empty, and has been for years.' Vice shrugged, and a susurrus of disappointment echoed through the cavernous hall. Unfortunately for the late men of Arfell, tearbooks fade when they aren't in the presence of their dragon, and their pages go blank.

Farden thought for a moment, and then dared to speak up again. They were not going to like this. Not one bit.

'Your Mages,' he began, trepidation building inside him. 'What if we took the tearbook back to the Sirens, as a peace offering and a gesture of good will to…' But he didn't get any further: the hall exploded into outraged chaos. Shouts ricocheted around the hall.

'Madness!'

'To suggest such a thing is treason!'

'Get him out of here!'

Åddren held up his hands once again, but nothing happened. The noise was deafening. Helyard was incredulous. He leant far out of his chair and gaped wide-eyed at Farden as if the mage had just squatted down and laid a golden egg on the marble floor. 'How dare you! That is an outrage!' bellowed the Arkmage. His face turned a crimson shade of purple. Åddren banged his fist on his throne and waved his other hand for silence, but none came. Helyard was still shouting. 'How do we know the Sirens weren't responsible in the first place?!'

Farden looked to Vice for help, but he was busy shouting down another council member. The mage yelled over the pandemonium. 'The dragon-riders were the ones who originally banished the book your Mage, and if they see how dangerous the situation is they may help us in finding the well!'

Helyard slapped his thigh angrily and pointed at the mage with an accusing finger. 'Of course they will, and once we do they'll stab us in the back and summon the creature for themselves! You could start another war with your foolish actions!' He boomed.

'And you could start one with *your* inaction!' snapped Farden. He could feel the magick bubbling up in his chest. He wanted to slam his fist into the Arkmage's nose and teach him a lesson.

'How dare you lecture me!' barked Helyard, his face red and full of indignant veins, jaw pointing and condemning. 'Guards! Remove F…'

'ENOUGH!' Åddren roared, in a voice quite unnatural for his small figure, and everyone froze, and the echoes of angry words hung awkwardly in the hall. With a snort Helyard sat back in his throne and drummed his fingers on the marble.

'This is a place of reason and discussion, not petty squabbling and shouting, if you want that then go find it in the streets. I will not have it here. Now does anyone have any sense to offer?'

After a moment Vice raised a hand and spoke in a measured tone to the hall. 'I suggest, that Farden should go as an emissary to Nelska, and speak with the Siren elders.' Farden fixed Vice with a shocked look. Vice held his gaze and continued. 'I would rather gain their help, than try to face this threat alone. This concerns all of Emaneska now, not just the Arka.' Farden fidgeted with his hands behind his back, almost excited.

Åddren sighed. 'Then it is down to a vote. Helyard?' he looked at his counterpart, who still hadn't taken his stormy eyes off of Farden. 'Choose your side,' said Åddren.

Helyard was the picture of rage. Arms folded, he languished in his chair like a spiteful lizard, still boring into the mage's skull with his wooden eyes. 'I say that the dragon-riders are the ones to blame, and we'd be foolishly throwing everything, and I mean everything, into their claws. I say no,' the tall man shrugged, slouched shoulders scraping against the polished marble throne.

'Vice?'

'I say yes,' the Undermage said firmly, without even missing a beat. 'Farden should take back the tearbook to Nelska.'

Victorious drums started to play in Farden's head. A surreptitious smile started to creep into the corner of his cheek.

Åddren paused for a moment, and everybody seemed to hold their breath. The suspense verged on painful. He looked up from the marble floor. 'I say yes.'

And here entered the proud trumpets. The council rumbled with mixed opinions and a scatter of applause from about half of them. Farden saw some of them nodding and smiling to each other, while others shook their heads and crossed their arms. He looked back to the thrones, and to Vice and Åddren 'Thank you, Arkmages, I will not fail you,' Farden bowed his head with a quick nod and put a clenched fist to his breastplate, where his heart was.

'Vice will show you out, and find you accommodation in the Arkathedral. We will meet at the west pier of Rós at dawn. May Evernia bring you a restful sleep tonight, mage,' Åddren said warmly, and gestured to the doors at the back of the hall. Vice stood up quickly and went to put a friendly arm around Farden. They bowed again and turned to leave. They walked through the crowded council, who stared like hawks at the two men.

'Thank you,' hissed Farden, once they were out of earshot.

'Don't even mention it.'

The gold doors slammed shut behind them and their steps echoed loudly in the stone hallway, and somehow the narrow corridor was a relief after the claustrophobic hall. They talked and walked.

'I've never seen Helyard like that,' said the mage.

Vice nodded. 'Mhm, he's very, what's the word, *passionate*, about his views.'

'And in other words...?' Farden grinned, not convinced by

his friend's tactful words.

'He's a stubborn fuck,' said Vice, and he looked at Farden with a serious look. 'He should have been a tyrant or a warlord rather than an Arkmage, it would suit him better. There's no place in the council for people like him. It's time to compromise and open our doors, not to lock them even tighter.'

'It's been a while since I heard you speak your mind Vice, and I have to say, I prefer it to all that delicate democratic shit,' said Farden, still in a low voice. The corridor seemed empty. He looked over his shoulder to make sure.

Vice nodded. 'And so do I.'

'Åddren seems to know how to handle him.'

'After twenty-five years I would expect him to. He knows things are changing, and he's willing to change with them. The problem is Helyard has many a supporter in the council, and so Åddren has to be delicate, and democratic, and find a middle ground.'

'I could never do what you do, sit there and let all the politics wash over you,' said Farden.

'No you prefer it out there in the wilderness with fire and a sword, where it's up to you and nobody else,' chuckled the Undermage.

Farden patted the sword resting against his shoulder-blade. 'Politics can run a city, or define a nation, but men and magick are still what counts. You can't hammer in a nail with words.'

'No but you can start a war with them, that's why we still have to be careful with the Sirens,' said Vice, and he slowly came to halt. He looked at his friend. 'Can you handle this…Farden?'

The mage stopped in his tracks and crossed his arms. He frowned. 'Straight to the point. What happened to the democracy?'

'I have to ask Farden, this is bigger than anything you've ever undertaken. You'd be the first Arka, nevermind a Written, to set foot in Nelska in fifteen years. I only suggested it be you because, well who else is there?'

Farden tried to conceal his pride. He shrugged. 'It has to be done, and then, if I'm the one to do it then, well that's that, I go to Nelska.'

Vice slowly shook his head, hiding a smile. 'I always knew you were going to be difficult, the first day I met you. Just be careful, you're no use to the Arka dead.'

The two men continued to walk. 'Please, I get enough of that from Durnus,' said Farden.

'Ah, and how is that dusty old vampyre of yours?' It was Vice's turn to the frown.

'He's fine.' Farden tried to skip that particular subject; the Undermage had never been fond of Farden's placement in Albion, nor Durnus. 'Just get me on that ship with the tearbook, and I'll handle the rest,' he said.

'Alright, you heard Åddren, tomorrow, at the west pier. But you guard that thing with your life, and don't let it out of your sight while you're on the ship, or in Nelska for that matter.' Vice wagged a finger at Farden. 'Don't show them the Book either, as in...' he waved his hand towards his back. The mage understood.

'I know. They can't be trusted any more than anyone else.' Farden listened to the sound of their footsteps for a while. 'What happened at Arfell? I mean, what really happened?'

They turned a corner, and Vice looked around conspiratorially. He lowered his voice even further. 'Three of the old men were so charred and burnt, they didn't even recognise them. The other two were found dead on the floor, slashed wide open with a blade. In the morning the others smelled something burning and saw the blood seeping out from under the door.' He shot Farden a serious look. 'It was an assassination, pure and simple, and a good one at that.'

'Fuck,' said Farden. He couldn't think of anything else to say.

They came to a small spiral staircase leading downwards into the citadel and Vice stopped. 'I think it's best if you stay somewhere other than the Arkathedral tonight, after what has just happened. There's an inn nearby, on Freidja street, called the *Bearded Goat*, or something like that. I hear it's surprisingly nice by Krauslung standards.'

'You sound like an old widow,' sniggered Farden.

'And remember, dawn at the west pier.'

'I'm never late.'

'That's very funny.' The Undermage shook his head. 'I won't see you tomorrow, I have to make sure that Arfell is protected. I'll see that the tearbook is sent to Åddren tonight. Helyard has business to deal with in Albion later, and I wouldn't trust him with it anyway. He'd probably burn it,' he said with a scowl.

'Albion?' Farden looked at him questioningly.

'Something with one of the Dukes near Kiltyrin, or Dunyra, I forget. Official business,' he shrugged, and his robe rustled. Farden nodded, wondering what the Arkmage could possibly be doing in Albion. The mage stuck out a hand, and Vice shook it warmly with both of his. 'Thank you, again, for this opportunity. And for how you supported my argument in front of the Arkmages. I don't think they would have listened to me otherwise,' said Farden.

'I think you're doing the right thing friend, and I'm glad the Arka has somebody like you on our side.' Vice clapped the mage on the arm. 'Now be careful in Nelska, and remember what I said about words. Diplomacy is sometimes necessary.'

'I'll see you soon Vice,' Farden spun around and disappeared into the stairwell, taking the steps two at a time.

'May the gods be with you,' the Undermage shouted after him, and then he left with a sigh.

❦

Night fell quietly, and darkness slipped unnoticed into the streets and roads of the city. Torches sparkled, and the noises of the evening began to fill the cold air. Two figures walked silently through an alleyway, cloaked and hooded, near to where the main wall met the mountain rock. As they wandered further and further away from prying eyes, hands reached out to torches and they hissed and died one by one. The shadows were as thick as black velvet, and the two strangers knew it.

Farden pulled his hood back and held Cheska tightly by her hands. He could imagine her smiling at him through the darkness. 'I told you I'd find you,' she said.

'I'm glad you did,' he replied, barely finishing his words before he felt her lips catch his. Her hands curled around his back, and they leant against a nearby wall. They kissed, hungrily, and held onto each other for what seemed like an age.

Cheska finally pulled away, almost breathless. 'How long are you staying for?'

Farden hesitated. 'They're sending me away again, tomorrow,' he said with a sigh. Even in the darkness he could see her disappointed face. Her voice was small. 'When will you be back?' Farden didn't even need to answer; she felt him shrug and shake his head.

'I suppose being Arka's finest has its drawbacks,' she said, and rested her head against his shoulder. She was usually excited by his missions. Farden stroked her hair. 'I'll be back, don't worry.'

Cheska nodded. 'I don't doubt you will, you always do, but I just want to spend more than two hours with you before you disappear again,' she said, and kissed his neck. 'I know it's dangerous for us,' she said, as if answering for him. 'And now that there's the Ritual... It'll be against the law.'

'I know.' Farden scowled at the shadows. 'But I don't care, I want you.'

'So do I,' she said, but before she could go on there was a loud shout from nearby, and the orange light of a torch started to creep up the alleyway. Someone was singing.

'Why's it so daaaaark?' sang the offkey voice. Farden growled, and moved forward to stand in front of Cheska. They put their hoods up, and let the shadows cover their face. Soon enough a man appeared around the corner, holding a candle and tottering from side to side across the cobblestones. He was drunk, and being particularly loud. Farden felt anger rising in his chest. He took a step forward, and the bleary-eyed man suddenly noticed them.

'Whoaaa! Hidin' in the shadows are we?' slurred the man as he tried to keep walking up the alleyway. He gave the hooded pair a wide stumbling berth and leered at Cheska.

'Quiet yourself, fool, before I do it for you,' snarled Farden.

'Who's your pretty friend mate? She can come home with me if ye like?' he laughed again, and the mage took another step forward. Cheska put a hand on his arm and held him back. 'Don't Farden,' she whispered, and he nodded grudgingly. Durnus's words echoed in his ears.

'Keep moving,' said Farden, and the man did, hollering and hooting with every step. The light receded with the disappearing candle, and Farden moved back into the shadows and wrapped his arms around Cheska. She toyed with his hair. 'You've always been so quick to anger, Farden.'

'I don't like people,' he scowled, watching the darkness.

'But you like me.'

'You're different,' he said, giving her another kiss. 'You're not like the others. Somehow you can keep me calm. Well, up until now.'

He heard her take a sharp intake of breath. 'Gods, Farden, you have to stop worrying about this Ritual. I'm ready for this.'

'And what does your father think of all this?'

'My father and his precious advisors gave up on arguing with me a long time ago now. He knows it's what I want and grudgingly he leaves me to it. As should you. Please stop worrying.'

'Do you blame me?' he asked.

Cheska shook her head. 'No, but we can deal with this when you get back. Not now.'

'Fine,' said Farden.

'I think it's time I left,' she whispered in his ear. She kissed his cheek. 'Please be safe, wherever you're going.'

Farden held her wrist. 'I'd tell you if I could.'

'I know,' said Cheska, and then she kissed him once more, lingering on his lips. She ran a hand over his weathered face, and then left, melting into the darkness. Farden stayed a while, waiting until it was safe, and then walked off in a different direction.

An hour later Farden was sitting in the *Bearded Goat* quietly sipping his drink and minding his own business. Vice had been right, the inn was loud and full of drunken fools, but the quality of the place and beverages and the food was good, and Farden had found a quiet corner by the fireplace in the dim recesses of the room. A skald was regaling the rumbustious crowd with stories about the faerie incident. He stood on a table near the door playing his stringed *ljot*, kicking tankards of beer with his muddy feet, and belting out the words at the top of his voice. A few women in thin frilly dresses lounged about the place, grinning at any man who came close and beckoning them closer with crooked fingers, nails painted with gaudy yellows and reds. The men cheered and clanged their tankards together, singing along, swinging some of the more sober women around in drunken jigs. The mage watched them impassively. Alcohol worked in mysterious ways.

Farden looked back into the crackling flames and swirled his sweet red wine around in the wooden cup, thinking about his day, and trying not to think about Cheska. The fire was warming his cold toes even through his thick travelling boots, and the warmth and the wine were starting to make him sleepy. He crossed his legs and shuffled slightly closer to the fireplace, and pulled his hood lower, down over his brow, blocking out the loud men and women nearer to the bar. Someone coughed and spluttered nearby, and Farden glanced in the direction of the noise.

Next to him, nearer to the wall in a shadowy corner, was an old beggar smoking a long dirty pipe. Farden had seen him earlier, snoring away to himself near the warmth of the fire, but now he was awake and peering about the place with his beady rat-eyes. The grey man was ugly, unshaven, and unkempt, with greasy hair and dirty patchwork clothes made from a thousand different garments. Sprouting from his narrow chin was a straggly beard coiled in little dirty strands and plaits, with bits of dried stew clinging to it. He busied himself by chewing on the mouthpiece of his curved pipe. Gnarled fingers drummed annoyingly on the arm of the wooden chair he was curled up in. The mage looked him up and down, and then back to his wine. The smell of his acrid tobacco tickled his nose.

Farden took another sip of his wine and tried to let his concentration melt into the warm fire, but now he could feel someone looking at him. Casually he turned to face the beggar and met his gaze. His little rodent eyes narrowed and sparkled with a cheeky glint.

'What do you want?' said Farden calmly.

The beggar chuckled, making his whole body shake with the effort. His tobacco-smoke breath rattled in his throat noisily. 'Oh nothin', thought I'd look at yer, seein' as he's lookin' at me,' said the man. He waggled his pipe in Farden's general direction. 'Yew look like a strong fellow though, don't yer, all quiet and sad on yer own,' he croaked, leering at him with a mischievous smile.

'What's it to you?'

'Oh nothin' at all friend, jus' makin' conversation s'all,' the beggar shrugged and sucked on his pipe. It rattled against his dirty yellow teeth.

'Well I'd appreciate the peace and quiet if it's all the same to you,' Farden looked away, but out of the corner of his eye he saw the man lean in closer. Smoke escaped from his mouth like thick grey liquid and coiled towards the ceiling.

'Yew that mage? The one I 'eard about?' asked the man.

Farden didn't move. 'There are a lot of mages in Krauslung old man, I'm not one of them.'

'Heehee, fair enough,' he cackled hoarsely, wheezing and slapping his knee, obviously finding great humour in the answer. 'But I seen yew around mage, runnin' here, runnin' there, yer important they say, one of the older ones. I 'eard about yew an those minotaurs sev'ral years back? Said yew almost took 'em all single 'anded. Saw yer at the Arkathedral too, an' I can spot those pretty vambraces a mile away,' the tramp winked, nodding to the gold poking from under Farden's sleeve. The mage crossed his arms and eyed the man suspiciously. He blithely wondered if he had seen this old wreck before.

'Hah, yew 'ave nothin' t' fear from me, big strong lad like yerself...' he paused, taking a drag on his foul-smelling pipe. Farden wrinkled his nose. The man sucked his blackened teeth and held it towards him. 'Fancy a bit?' he asked.

Farden looked at the mouldy pipe and shook his head with a grimace. 'I don't smoke,' he said.

The old man shrugged and looked around furtively with his rat-eyes. His voice dropped to a hoarse whisper. 'How about that then, and yer look like the manner o' man who does. Maybe you prefer to chew it.' His eager eyes scanned the mage's face and there was an awkward pause.

'I said I don't smoke, and I don't chew it either.' Farden narrowed his eyes threateningly. His patience was wearing thin.

'Wasn't talkin' 'bout tabaccy now was I...?' a sparkle in his little eyes suddenly caught the mage's attention, but he shook his head.

'This conversation is over.' Farden stared at the fire.

'I don't think it is mage,' chuckled the beggar. He cocked his head to the side like a pigeon assessing bread. 'Yew never smoked it before, 'ave yer?' He leant forward slightly, confidentially. He looked around at the unfamiliar faces at the bar and sniffed. 'Yer wastin' yer time, only chewin' it. Nevermar's meant to be smoked, mage,' said the beggar, and tapped the bowl of his pipe on the arm of the chair.

Farden opened his mouth to say something, and then closed it again. He reached out towards the fire with his hands and felt the heat creep over his skin. A loud bray of laughter came from the others at the bar. He took a deep breath through his nostrils and let the smell of pipe and wood smoke fill his head. 'How much?' he asked.

The beggar waved a bony hand and shook his head, as if he had just been insulted. 'Sometimes an old man jus' likes a body to smoke with, 'stead of bein' on his own, see? Makes a change don't it, mage,' coughed the man, with a skeletal hiss and a waft of bad breath.

'Don't call me that,' Farden warned, and the man shrugged again. 'As you wish,' he said.

Farden's mind raced while he swirled the wine around like a whirlpool in his cup. Temptation billowed in low clouds over his head and he chewed the inside of his lip. Unwelcome thoughts gathered, memories and dead faces laughed at him. Cheska hovered in his mind, pale, and still. He wanted to stop thinking.

'Fine,' he said, and then stood up to gulp down the last dregs of his drink in one swift move. 'I'm in number sixteen, if you can count that high, the one with the red door.' And with that he swept up the nearby staircase and disappeared into the shadows of the corridor. After finding his room in the gloomy hallway he opened the door and lit the fireplace with a quick spell. He opened the windows to let the cold night air chill the room and reclined in a nearby chair. He impatiently played with flashing sparks on his palm.

A short while passed and then there came a bony knock on the wooden door.

'Come in,' Farden whispered gruffly.

The old beggar shuffled through the door, hunched and crooked. Farden thought the man could have been tall once, but now his long years had bent his back and added lines to his face. In the firelight his face looked like weathered oak, and he now wore a grey cloak, also made of patches, over his rags.

'Have a seat,' gestured Farden, to the chair opposite him.

'Give me a moment.' The man ignored the offered chair and squatted in front of the fire. He pulled a few items from his pockets and placed them on the brick hearth. He toyed with them with gnarled hands. Farden pointed to one, a strange pipe, curved like his other one, but coiled in the middle. It looked like a cross between a snail and a horn. 'What's that?' the mage asked.

'Gim, skiff, redraw, blagg, nevermar, you always smoke it in a pipe,' the grey character muttered. He unfolded a little bundle of cloth and started to peel something apart, placing little crumbs of red moss into the bowl of the pipe and pushing it down with his little finger. Once the bowl seemed to be full, the man sprinkled some of his cheap tobacco on the top, and tapped the thing on the edge of the fireplace. He looked at the fire, shook his head, and then cast around for flint and tinder, then he had a sudden thought and looked up at the mage. 'D'ye mind?' he said, waving the pipe in little circular motions.

Farden fixed him with a murderous look, and then grudgingly accepted the pipe. 'If I find out that you've told anyone, *anyone* about this, then I will find you, old man, and I will kill you. Understand?'

The old man shrugged and shook his head and tried to portray the image of sincerity and trust. 'Don't know no one to tell, mage, yew can trust me.' The beggar winked.

'Don't call me that,' said Farden irritably. He held the pipe in one hand, and with the other, keeping an eye on the beggar, pointed his finger at the bowl of the pipe, and with a little flame, made the stuff crackle and hiss. He sucked on the end of the pipe and felt the acrid smoke burn and scrape his throat. He coughed and spluttered.

'Tastes good don't it,' chuckled the old man. With great difficulty he got to his feet and then instantly placed himself down in the threadbare armchair.

'It's harsh,' Farden groaned. He took another painful drag and tried to relax in his chair, feeling a slight headiness tingling all throughout his skull. He offered the pipe back to the old man and he grabbed at it with grubby fingers. After a few quick puffs he passed it back to Farden with another knowing grin. They sat in silence, listening to the music from downstairs escape into the street below the window. The man watched Farden smoke the pipe with a hungry expression, but Farden didn't even notice. He held the smoke in his chest and felt the back of his eyes shiver and his temples quiver. His arms felt a hundred feet long and his fingers moved through sickly honey.

They passed the pipe back and forth, and soon enough Farden found himself melting into the chair like an icicle in the morning sunlight. His mind ran through fields of the absurd, random music scattered between his ears, and strange shapes moved about his room, searching for reality under the bed and behind the curtains. The old tramp shook and bounced, and his jittery bed shifted around in an imaginary earthquake.

At some point Farden looked up to find the pipe in front of him again. The thing glittered like an angry torch, sparking and puffing fumes into the air. Smoke filled his eyes. Lungs burnt. An intense feeling of dizziness pounded against the inside of Farden's skull. He closed his eyes to watch colours collide, and opened them to find he was suddenly alone. The old beggar was long gone. The bed evaded him for a while but then he caught it, and fell into a lake of pillows and sheets. He kicked off boots that were hot and heavy, and his tunic was made of thick soup. A pillow hijacked his head and he drifted off into a heavy, drug-laden sleep. Gods danced around his room, and daemons watched from the corners and rafters, quoting something about blood and history. Darkness took him.

The old man slipped out from the mage's room and closed the door quietly with a slight click. He threw a hood over his greasy hair and kicked at his rough leather shoes as if they annoyed him. With great care he hobbled downstairs and weaved his way between the drinkers and singers that filled the noisy inn, still worshipping the ale that foamed in their tankards. The beggar shuffled past them, muttering quiet 'scuse me's and comin' through's as he did so, and finally he made it onto the street. He paused to stretch. After a small private grin and a satisfied slap of his thigh he disappeared down the nearest alleyway, suddenly seeming taller and more nimble with every step.

Soon a loud drunk came around a corner and careered down the narrow alley towards the strange beggar. The drunken man leant into his path, shouting and singing loudly in his face. He smell of his wine-soaked breath was a little overpowering, and the beggar fended the drunk off with a light push, but in a fit of sudden anger, he cursed and violently swung his arm in a wild punch. The beggar reacted with a speed that belied his years. A short black knife darted out from under his patchwork cloak and plunged into the drunk's side with a thud. He clamped his palm over the man's mouth and threw him hard against the nearest wall, pausing only to viciously twist the knife. The man grunted in pain and shock. Stabbing him twice more in the chest, he let the dying man slump to the floor. Without a moment of hesitation or remorse he pulled his cloak about him and silently disappeared into the night once more. Left to die alone in the cold and muddy street, the drunk gradually slipped away, a bewildered look plastered onto his pale face.

chapter 6

"Dark magick is the scourge of Emaneska. Let no Written ever be involved with it, and seek to use full force against those who practise it. Those who wield it should be warned: We will chase you into the mountains, hunt you down, and bury you under the rocks. The council has spoken."

From a speech by Arkmage Åddren in the year 879, addressing the Written after the Neffra Incident

Farden was dreaming again. He stood in the shadow of a black mountain. A hot breeze lashed his bare skin and the dust stung his eyes, and he found himself wearing only his vambraces. He could feel the sand between his toes.

The mage looked behind him and saw razor-sharp crags of rock hanging over him, a bare, faceless cliff of jet and obsidian coming straight out of the sand and towering into the sky. Shadows played in the darkness. The wind whistled through the rocks, making an eerie sound like a faraway horn crying for help, or a wounded animal wailing away its last few hours. Even in the dry heat, Farden shuddered. He looked out, away from the mountain, where the sun shone and the heat waves danced. He watched the bare earth stretch on for leagues, further than even his eyes could see. The horizon shuddered and wobbled.

Farden looked up at the sky, that pure empty sky, and felt a tranquility he had never felt before suddenly wash over him. The mage felt as though he could melt into it, into the vast blueness of it, and never have to wake up again. He could forget about the council, the book, everything, and just melt away.

A black shape fluttered in his peripheral vision, and Farden turned his head. A crow, or a raven, some sort of black bird, flapped aimlessly around the rocky ledges of the black cliff, trying to stay out of reach of a skinny black cat that danced below it on its hindlegs. The bird dithered in midair, narrowly avoiding the clawing swipes of the mangy cat, and desperately tried to find a safe place between the rocks. The cat crouched and watched its prey. Farden tried to shout and scare either of the animals away, but the hot wind snatched the words from his lips, and he yelled in complete silence. The cat hunkered down and its haunches twitched and wiggled, until suddenly, choosing its perfect moment, the cat shot into the air and dragged the bird to the sand. The thing flapped and cried, but the cat was merciless. It pinned the crow-thing to the ground with one paw and sunk its yellow teeth into its neck until it moved no more. The bird's head sagged and its beak lay open and motionless. Farden tried to move, to try to chase the cat away from the corpse, but his legs and arms refused to shift. He was glued to the sand. Something flitted from rock to rock above him, and a cackle floated on the wind. Farden looked at the cat, and saw her staring back at him with those obsidian eyes. Blood dripped from her fangs, and a black feather hovered at the corner of her mouth. The sand had become a red pool. She ripped some more flesh from the birds neck, and chewed, slowly, staring at him without emotion or even a hint of remorse. She threw her head back, swallowed, and then made a howling whining sound deep in her throat. As quickly as it had began it stopped, and the cat took a slow step forward towards him.

You're between a rock and a hard place... So to speak, it said, an echoing voice in the back of his head. Farden tried to answer, but no sound came from his mouth. The cat continued to move forward. Blood decorated her chin. Things moved and flapped above him.

They've got you all in a flap, came the next cliché. The flapping became the sound of a landslide of wings. Black shapes and beady eyes hid behind the crags and watched him. Farden struggled in vain. He looked at the desert behind him, and it had become a desert of fire. The wind blew hot dusty air in his face, and whipped his naked skin. Shapes began to fill the empty sky above him and the mountain became a black whirlwind of even darker birds, wheeling and careening through the blueness and cackling hideously. The cat had come to a halt in front of him, and she threw a curious look up at the storm of wings and beaks and claws flooding his dream. They filled every space on the rock face, stood on every inch of rock and crag. A thousand of them flapped around him.

It's you they want, just as they once wanted me. A talon sliced across his back and he felt the drip of hot blood down his skin. Farden winced, and tried with all his strength to move. Another claw across his thigh and a beak tore a hole in his side. Wings buffeted his face. Claws ripped flesh from bone.

Follow the dragons said the voice.

No more than a handful of hours after he had collapsed into his bed, the first streaks of dawn started to stretch across the dim sky, and Farden awoke with a pounding headache. He fell out of bed and collided with the cold wooden floor with a groan. The mage quickly shrugged on his clothes and armour and massaged his temples in a vain attempt to get rid of the waves of pain coursing through his head. He tried to cast a small healing spell and the magick smashed against his skull like a sledgehammer. Farden cursed and flinched, feeling the pain all the way to the tips of his toes. Every movement seemed to be a strain. He blearily looked at his surroundings. The candles in his room had burnt to their bases, and the dim morning light barely illuminated his room. The smell of acrid smoke hung in the air, and the stench made the hungover mage retch. Stoically, he hauled his sword over his back, wincing, He fastened his cloak around him and slammed the door much to the dismay of his head. He stood in the hall and rubbed his head. All seemed to be quiet in the inn, but something gnawed at the back of his head, underneath the headache, something that escaped him every time he got close to identifying it. Shadows of his dream taunted him, not daring to show their true faces. He remembered rocks, birds, or a place with sand. Farden shook his head gingerly, and tried to forget the strange nightmare.

The streets of Krauslung were gloomy in the early dawn light, the shadowy clouds hung like a blanket over the mountains and the slumbering city by the sea. Men moved around the streets, cleaning the refuse from the muddy roads while shops and houses started to wake up. A few candles still peeked through the cracks in thick drapes.

'Spare a coin sir?' whined a beggar that was slumped in a wooden box by the side of the street. Farden looked at him, after a moment realised he wasn't the same beggar, then coughed, winced, and dug a little silver piece from his pocket. He flung it into the tramp's lap, and walked off. The man bit the coin and grinned a toothless smile. 'Gods be with you sire!' he called after the mage. Farden wondered why everyone kept wishing him that.

Dawn shined in the east, and the chimneys began to belch their sooty breath over the city. Smoke mingled with granite clouds. Squawking, cackling chickens scattered around Farden's legs, and a lone goose wandered through the crowds, trailing a velvet leash in the mud behind it. People were now beginning to fill the thoroughfare, laughing and talking loudly despite the early morning. A short bearded man, who seemed to still be drunk from the night before, shouted impatiently at the closed doors of a bakery while clinging to a lamp post to keep from falling over. Farden watched an attractive peasant girl leave a rich-looking house and skip down the street with a coy little smile. She was still doing up her blouse and wiping smudged makeup from her face when she disappeared around a corner. Such was the way of Krauslung society.

Signs told Farden to head right down an alleyway if he wanted to reach the west side of the port. He walked for another half an hour before he came to a short balcony that overlooked a square and the west curve of Port Rós. The mage stood against the stone railings and sniffed the salty air, feeling the fresh breeze try to work its charm on his headache. A cold mist had crept across the sea in the night, and now it lingered in thick wisps and trails at the edges of the harbour walls. The ships in their docks rolled gently on the calm blue-green swell, crowded side-by-side and tethered by thick ropes. Wooden jetties and gangways ran vein-like through the bay, boardwalk capillaries keeping the ships alive with supplies and sailors. The muffled sounds of the ships' bells and the creaking of the docks was a gentle background noise compared to the shouts and banging of people working around him. The hammers of the shipyards were loud and clamouring. Everywhere Farden looked cargo was piling up on the side of the jetties and sailors rushed around their ships and ropes like termites over spindly tree trunks.

Seagulls mewed overhead and caught the morsels thrown into the air by the crowds of people at the dockside. The inns in the city may have closed for the night, but the inns there in the port were still thriving with raucous conversation and snippets of atonal singing. Stalls had started serving fried meat and bread, boiling cheap moss tea for the sleepy sailors. The smells of farska and fish soup and the infamous sea-serpent pie, were thick in the cold air.

Farden waited in line at a stall, hood pulled low over his baggy eyes, and grabbed a quick bread roll stuffed with cheap greasy venison. He bit into it ravenously and tried to chew in a way that didn't cause sparks to fly behind his eyes. The food tasted like ash in his mouth. A swig of brackish tea just reminded him of the herby charcoal taste of the nevermar.

The mage walked further along the wooden jetty towards the west pier. He munched on the cheap snack and dodged his way through crowds of bustling dock-workers. His sword felt heavy on his shoulders and he swayed drunkenly against the elbows of the men. He stopped for a moment by the side of a wall and slowly finished his tea. A few slow deep breaths later, the wave of nausea had passed and Farden felt a little better. He looked ahead and spied a ship flying the golden scales of the Arka. He headed off in its general direction. Farden was slowly realising how much he was dreading the ship, and the turbulent, churning journey that was waiting for him. If he hated anything, it was the open sea, and all of its grey rolling vastness. He shuddered momentarily.

'Farden!' His own name surprised him and he turned to see Åddren and Helyard flanked by a dozen or so armoured soldiers. They were heading through the crowd towards him, so he made his way in their direction. He bowed formally and then stood with his hands behind his back. Helyard didn't even look at the mage, but Åddren smiled warmly at him. He had a large sack at his side, hanging by a strap around his shoulder. The soldiers looked at him impassively.

'I trust you slept well Farden?' asked the Arkmage.

'I rested well your Mage, thank you.' Farden wanted to throw up on his expensive green robe.

'Good, we need you vigilant and well prepared for this trip. I have convinced Helyard to provide you with fair weather for as far as he can manage,' said Åddren. Helyard just grunted. Farden had heard the rumours about the Arkmage's power over the local weather, and it had been known, that on occasion, summer days would be surprised with freak snow. That had been before the days of the Long Winter.

Farden looked at the powerful man, and he wondered why he hated the Sirens so much, but Åddren was talking again. 'Meanwhile, a hawk has been sent to Nelska and the citadel of Hjaussfen to warn them of an emissary from the Arka. I did not mention the true intention of your mission in the letter.' Åddren stopped. 'Here is the tearbook.' The Arkmage led the mage away from the others and put an arm around Farden's shoulders. With his other hand he lifted the travelling sack from his shoulders and handed it to the mage. There was an earnest tone in his voice. 'Keep it safe at all times. These sailors are loyal, as are the soldiers, but greed may change their minds,' he said. Farden nodded wordlessly. Åddren gestured to the others and they walked on towards the ship.

Helyard cleared his throat noisily, and spoke up in a hoarse lecturing voice. 'Make sure you read it *first*, mage, and *with* the dragon-riders. Most importantly don't let them hold information from you, and don't you dare jeopardise this ceasefire,' he growled.

'I think he means don't lose your temper and kill anyone, Farden,' said Åddren calmly. He halted in his steps. Farden tried not to let his eyes betray him. He hadn't expected that the magick council would put any truth to the gossip about his exploits.

'Arkmage, I...' Farden began, trying to quickly conjure a lie, but the kind man held up a hand. He pointed to the ship nestling up against the wooden walkway, and the mage looked. It was a low carrack, a dark mahogany brown in colour, with tall decks and pine rails. The ship lurched on a wave and brown bilge spewed from the holes on its bow. The mage looked upward at the tall decks piled on top of each other like a deck of cards. He could see the stained glass of the captain's cabin in the stern, and briefly pondered if he could bunk there, but the sight of the crow's nest made his stomach perform a somersault, and he looked down at the waves. Barnacles and green algae festooned the battered hull, and a sad looking unicorn that had seen better days was the figurehead. Farden marvelled at the lengths of rope that seemed to hold the fat ship together, wrapped around its stout rigging and sails like a spider's web on a hedge. A string of sailors hauled boxes of lemons and hard tack bread up the steep ramp, along with an equally depressed goat, which was bleating tediously. About a score of men worked on the ship, a few already halfway up the mast, others piling up cargo on the decks and making ready to sail.

Farden eyed the ominous weather hiding behind the mist, and cast a brief look at Helyard, whose glazed eyes stared at the clouds with a concentrative look. Cold winter spray splashed over the nearby harbour wall and hissed in the wind. The harsh metallic seas pounded the black granite of the port defences like legions of icy waves drumming eagerly at the gates of the harbour. The mage was thankful that the dock was so sheltered. Someone was talking to him again.

'Farden, this is Captain Heold.' Åddren welcomed a grizzly old man to their party. He looked like an ageing pirate, who sported a grey beard that was even bigger than his round belly, with a kind weathered face and eyes as hard as blue diamonds hid behind bushy white eyebrows. He looked as though he had been born at sea. He wore a rough uniform of sorts, in the green tunic of the navy, with a black cloth hat pulled down over his head. Captain Heold offered his calloused hand and Farden shook it with a smile. 'Good to meet yer Farden, the *Sarunn* is a good ship, we should be there in about five or six days, travelling 'round the coast,' he said. Farden had met his type before, a real northerner, harsh spoken, blunt, and as superstitious as they came, but a true master of the rocky seas.

'Excellent. Thank you, Captain.' The mage struggled to return the man's vice-like grip, feeling as if he were greeting a huge crab, but fortunately before anything could be broken, the captain released him and turned to shout loudly at his motley crew.

'Right, let's step to it lively lads, prepare to cast off as soon as we can!' He bowed stiffly to the Arkmages and strode rather decisively up the ramp, still shouting.

While the accompanying guard made ready to get onto the vessel, Åddren took Farden aside again. The two men walked towards the ship's gangplank and the Arkmage whispered quietly into his ear. 'Farden, I honestly wish I didn't have to ask you to carry out this mission, but if I thought that a man better suited to the task existed, I would ask him.'

'Thank you, your Mage.' Farden didn't really recall being asked, but he still wanted the opportunity.

'And you may think that Helyard and the rest of the council are against you in this, but believe me you are doing the right thing. Not only could we have a chance to stop this malicious plot in its tracks, but we could finally have a chance of peace with the dragon-riders.'

'I know how important this is for our people Arkmage, and trust me there is no measure I won't take...'

Åddren held up an interrupting hand. 'Just...be careful mage. Helyard may be rash and swift to anger, but he does have a point. We do not yet know that the Sirens weren't responsible for the murders,' he said.

'You think that and still voted yes?' Farden looked at Åddren quizzically, and he nodded with a solemn expression.

'There are certain risks that need to be taken Farden, Vice and I saw that, and that's one of the reasons the Undermage is on the council. Sending you to the Sirens could bring peace to our people, but if Helyard is right and they were behind the atrocities at Arfell then we will find out very soon. It's a gamble in trusting them Farden, and I regret that you are the tool we must use. But now we must pray to the gods, and wait for your message,' the Arkmage looked up at the tumultuous sky and thrust his arms into his robe. 'The old ones still have sway over these lands,' he smiled and turned his gaze to the hooded Farden.

With a brisk jump Farden mounted the wooden boards and steadied the tearbook at his side. 'Let's hope then, that our gods are stronger than our enemy's.'

'Hope, there will be, Written, for the gods and for you. May Njord protect you,' Åddren said, in a louder voice and few nearby sailors rumbled in agreement, though they eyed Farden like he carried the plague. The mage sighed inwardly, nodded his thanks to his superior, bowed, and then climbed the ramp up to the ship. His sleepy brain felt like it was tumbling down a well, unable to put a stop to the journey he was about to take. Nausea groped at his gut as he felt the waves swell underneath his boots. Farden had never liked the sea. He said a swift prayer to Evernia and stepped onto the deck.

The three or four Arka soldiers had found their berths in the under decks, and the mage decided to go do the same. With one last wave to the Arkmages and their entourage he ducked under a hatch and went below. As he descended some stairs into the low humid belly of the stout ship he heard the dirty goat somewhere ahead of him. He decided to head in the other direction and soon found an empty stateroom that looked through small windows out from the back of the ship, probably beneath the captain's cabin, with the warm fire and comfortable bed, a fine breakfast... He shook his head. Farden paused outside the room, looked around for anyone nearby, and then grabbing a nearby bucket he swept into his room and locked the door.

Farden quickly went to the corner and threw his guts up in the wooden pail. His head lurched with his stomach and the world burst into sparks and leaps. Farden cursed and slumped back against the bolted-down bed, wiping the mess from his chin. He knew better but had to try a spell on the off chance the nevermar had worn off. If this lasted any longer than five or six days he was in trouble, especially seeing as he felt violently sick. The most pitiful excuse for a spark of flame flashed on his fingertip for a mere second before he doubled up in pain. His head exploded and tears squeezed their way out of clenched eyelids. Slowly, he slumped sideways to the floor to regain his breath. He had never felt this powerless before, and he just lay there breathing.

After a while Farden felt the ship drift free of the dock and the waves beneath them made the ship rock back and forth. The mage fought back bile and a pounding headache while the sailors above him sent the ship leaning into the growing wind, clearing the boardwalk and out into the mouth of the port. The mage could hear their shouts and calls. He shut his eyes, and then after a brief nauseating moment Farden felt a second wind and got to his feet, suddenly determined to see the ship leave the harbour. He made sure to lock the door behind him and then tried to negotiate the slippery corridors. He prayed he would not throw up in front of the soldiers or the stout men of the ship. At least he could pass it off as seasickness instead of a life-threatening hangover from a banned drug. That would make interesting news to the magick council, Farden thought.

He made it onto the deck, already slick with spray, and headed to the tall forecastle of the *Sarunn* and stared weakly at the turbulent seas whirling around the mouth of the huge port. The mage gripped the wood of the railing and felt the rimy spray on his chin and creased forehead. A sailor stood to the right of him, and was staring at Farden with a wary look. He felt the eyes on him and turned to face the man. The sailor turned slowly and made himself busy with coiling ropes. Farden squinted at the man but he didn't turn around again.

'Sire!' The mage turned around to find Heold briskly running up the steps, coughing steam into the cold wind. He barked a few orders back down the steps to his men and yelled course directions to the crewman at the wheel. The Captain looked at the mage and shrugged. 'Busy day fer us, mage. We jus' got back int' port last night and were sent a message from the council we 'ad to take you t'

Nelska this mornin'. Ow are yer accommodations?' The man grinned, gripping the rails with hands whose skin looked like tanned leather.

'Good thank you captain, I found them, at least,' said Farden. Heold nodded. The ship rose abruptly on a wave, and Farden grabbed at the handrail. The Captain was looking at him.

'I guess I can't ask why yer off to the land of the dragons? No body's been up there fer years I 'ear,' he appeared to make blithe conversation, but his keen flint eyes roved over Farden with a powerful curiosity.

'I'm afraid it's a quiet mission,' Farden said stonily and stared out to sea. The ship was nearing the harbour walls.

'A few degrees to port Thurgen!' Heold abruptly yelled through cupped hands. 'Excuse me. New man on t' wheel today, the other one 'ad the plague, and one o' me mates too, 'ad to replace 'im as well. Sorry t' ask 'bout yer business Farden, 'just the lads are a bit worried 'avin' you aboard. Superstitious lot.'

'I'm not dangerous, captain, tell your men that. I will be keeping mostly to myself over the course of the trip, so I'd appreciate being left alone,' Farden said, trying to make his words sound kind and courteous. The captain nodded with a grunt and watched the mage go, wobbly on his feet.

'Be some good weather comin' soon, mage, you'll see!' Heold yelled. He pointed towards the breaking clouds in the distance. Farden squinted and saw the golden sunlight glinting off the waves, but he shrugged and held his hand to his stomach. As he went below decks he could imagine Helyard back on the pier, grumpily agreeing to Åddren's stern orders. The breakers crashed around the bow of the ship again and she lurched awkwardly. Spray decorated the deck and the *Sarunn* loitered on the first few big waves before the helmsman got the hand of the winter swell and set her on course again. Heold watched Farden leave, and a disconcerting cloud of doubt filled his old mind. Mages were bad omens.

☙

The first two days of the trip were uneventful, and on the third, the *Sarunn* finally rounded the west coast and made for the channel between the beaches of west Midgrir and the cliffs of stunted Albion. The weather remained fine for the first few hundred miles or so, but then, as they rounded the coastline to head towards the Jörmunn Sea, past the cliff cities of Halôrn, the clouds started to pile up and darken, bringing squalls and bitter gales to hammer down on the ship. Farden hid in his room, feeling every pitch and roll of the vessel in his uncomfortable wooden bed. Everything in his cabin was nailed to the floor, which made sword practice a little impossible, and made everything creak and groan all the more. The bucket had been filled, and emptied, several times over the first day, and now Farden had finally gotten rid of his massive headache. His magick however, had not returned in the slightest, and he could feel his tattoo lying dormant on his back like a heavy weight. The mage spent his time meditating and trying to get his power back, or absently mapping the stars when the deck was quiet enough. More than a few times Farden found himself lying awake on the cold nights, thinking about Cheska, and waking up to find nothing and no one beside him but faded dreams. The mage tried to ignore the rolling ship and instead stared at the wooden ceiling, picturing her beautiful eyes in his tired mind and thinking long and hard about things like her body, her laugh, and a hundred other things like their future. He wondered what she was doing and where she was, and whether he would be back before she started the Ritual. The ghosts of fear slowly crept back into his mind.

On the first day a small black cat found its way into his room. Farden assumed it was the ship's cat, a little good luck charm against bad weather, and let the creature wander about his room and investigate everything. She sniffed and pawed at his clothes and every corner of the small room for an hour before finally curling into a neat black ball on his pillow. Feeling a little used, the mage consented to let the thing sleep in his room all day, until it finally disappeared at dinner time. Once, when she had looked at him, Farden had felt something scratching in his mind like déjà vu. Her little brown eyes gazed at him placidly for a while before returning to lick her paws. He dismissed it, but always found himself watching her and wondering from then on.

Once on the second day, out of pure boredom and curiosity, he took the tearbook from its satchel and idly flipped through the blank pages. They seemed pure and untouched, only yellowed at the very edges, and grey dust filled the cracks in the spine and between the overlapping dragon scales that were a dull metallic yellow. No trace of any script or writing could be found in the entire book, Farden even tried holding up the thin pages to the light streaming through his tiny window to see if anything could be seen. Nothing. He gave up with a bored sigh and slipped the tearbook under his pillow.

Farden walked along the decks at dawn, accompanied by the lithe black cat, whom he had named Lazy, and tried to cast small spells in the half-light. Much to his dismay the magick still rebounded against his head every time. Still, his study of the stars at night seemed to calm his mind, and his stomach for that matter. He still hated the water. Time felt like treacle in the ship and Farden dreaded the constant wary looks from the superstitious sailors. The previous morning he had found a greying crewman praying to the old sea god Njord outside his room and trying to attach a cheap-looking charm to his door. Farden had slammed it hard and scowled at the noises of the man nervously scuttling away down the corridor. Everyone seemed to be trying to ignore him and stay out of his way. Most of the weathered crew were scared of Farden; they saw him as a powerful sorcerer leading them towards a forbidden land, and that didn't make them happy. Their passenger was unlucky and unwanted.

On the first night the Arka soldiers had made an effort to talk to the lonely mage as he sat alone at a table. Farden hadn't been in the mood to socialise and his clipped answers had slighted the men. They made their excuses and left. What rumours they might have known about Farden seemed to have already circulated around the already superstitious crew, and now everyone seemed to be trying to ignore him and stay out of his way. And to a certain extent that suited him fine. Only Lazy seemed interested in him, and the little thing was happy to curl up beside him at night, purring away quietly like a bubbling pot all night until their morning walk.

On the third day, dawn found Farden making his way up to the forecastle. For once he had left the little feline fast asleep in his room, and he wandered across the deck alone. Fingers of light crept along the eastern horizon amongst dark clouds and faraway cliffs. The patchwork sea of blue green light and shadow foamed and roiled in deep swells. The mage stood at his usual spot at the railing and wiped rimy spray from his face for the tenth time and looked at the skies. Ahead of them a huge bank of storm clouds lingered, and the shadow of rain covered the sea. Someone coughed nearby. A man stood on watch to his right, and Farden recognised him as the man he had seen staring at him on the first day. He stood stiff and back straight, holding his arms crossed behind him and a spyglass in his left hand.

'Mornin' mate,' the man coughed a rough greeting. He had a thick accent, probably from southern Albion.

'Morning,' Farden replied. He nodded towards the black clouds. 'Weather looks bad.'

The man nodded. 'Looks fairly bad, I agree. Cap'n should ride 'er well.' He was a thin wiry man, and looked strong despite his size, with heavily calloused hands. He had a square shaped face that was punctuated by a sharp nose and short black hair slicked flat to his head. The sailor wore the dark green uniform of the ship's crew. A dark mole sat on his lip. The sailor was a head shorter than the mage, twitchy and energetic in his quick movements. He looked like a hawk waiting for his prey, in Farden's mind, and he didn't like the way the man stared at him.

'Good,' said the mage.

'Take it ye don't like the water then?' A smirk painted itself on the man's face.

'I like it fine,' Farden thought of the tearbook in the sack by his side.

The sailor chuckled. 'Karga's the name,' a hand followed the name, and Farden shook it firmly. 'Farden.'

Karga nodded. 'Aye, I know.'

'You have a fine captain it seems,' Farden made idle conversation. He listened to the splash of the waves beneath the ship.

The sailor shrugged. 'I wouldn't really know. He seems a fine fellow, but I'm jus' a stand in for this voyage. Other man got sick.'

'I see.'

'Plague probably. A lot of it goin' around in the south.'

'Mm.' Farden began to feel the conversation dwindling. He nodded to the man and made for the steps. As he was walking away the sailor called to him in a gruff voice. 'Oi mate, look at this.' The mage turned and followed the direction of his pointing hand. In the clouds up ahead something was happening that Farden has never seen before.

Between a gap in the immense storm-front wisps of cloud began to form two shapes that towered above the seas. They reared out of the clouds and stood upright to face each other, looking for all the world like two brawny men carved from cloud. And then they began to move. Thunder rumbled, and Farden moved closer to the railing to stare in amazement. One lashed out at the other with a gigantic fist, and lightning crackled from its fingers. Wind whipped the waves into foam, and the deafening burst of lightning made Farden cover his ears.

'Storm giants!' yelled Karga, and the helmsman wrenched the ship's wheel away from the stormy duel. Sudden rain lashed the ship, and Farden ran down the steps so he could watch the immense creatures battle each other. The giants lunged at each other and threw punch after punch until the sky shook and the crew cowered under the sails. But as quickly as they had appeared, they went, and after a few more thunder claps the giants melted back into the clouds. The sailor at the wheel calmly resumed course, and Heold bumbled out his cabin sleepily to see what had happened. 'What in 'ell is goin' on?' he bellowed, still adjusting his wide belt.

Karga shouted from the forecastle. 'Storm giants cap'n! They're gone now though, disappeared into the storm front!' Heold squinted at the clouds and frowned. Satisfied that he had missed most of the action and wasn't needed anymore, he headed back to his bed. 'Good, wake me in an hour,' he said. By the time he had slammed the door Farden was already back in his cabin.

Despite the rocking of the ship and the bad weather, the mage fell into a deep sleep until later the next day. He awoke to find the rain still lashing his window. He groaned and tried to pull the blanket further around his head. He had almost had enough of this voyage. The tearbook nudged his hand from its hiding place under his pillow and he pulled it towards him. The big book propped up his head nicely under the thin lump of cloth, and Farden wondered what the council would think of him using the tearbook as a pillow, or even the dragons for that matter. The mage let himself doze for about an hour before rising and heading sleepily to the galley. Lazy was nowhere to be seen.

He ducked under the door frame of the ship's kitchen and looked around. The goat was nibbling something grainy in the corner of the tiny room and the cook was cleaning dishes.

'All right there sir?' asked the cook while he wiped a bowl with a dirty cloth.

Farden stretched and stifled a yawn. 'Fine, thanks, I was just wondering if there's any lunch still left over? I missed it earlier.' He moved forward and knocked his forehead on a beam.

The man smiled, and stifled a chuckle. 'Farska's in the pan, or there's some shark 'ere that the first mate caught,' He lifted a lid on an earthen bowl, and the smell of the cheap fishy stew filled Farden with ravenous hunger. He dug in with a wooden spoon that didn't look too clean and filled a bowl that had a splintered edge. The mage was too hungry to care. He had eaten worse.

'There'll be summin' new tomorrow as well...' The cook looked at Farden and gave a faint nod in the direction of the fat goat. The poor animal stopped chewing and looked at the two men. There was an awkward silence.

'Well I'll see you tomorrow then,' Farden smiled briefly and swiftly turned to go. He carried his bowl of watery stew to his room and stared at the steel waves roll out behind the ship like angry grey foothills of ice water. The mage sighed and consigned himself to another day of feeling ill and empty from the lack of magick. A strange desire for nevermar had begun to creep into his mind over the last day, a craving to taste that acrid smoke on his tongue again, to feel that familiar numbing in his arms and legs. Farden guiltily pushed the notion from his head and tried to concentrate on his meal. The shark was salty, and the meagre vegetables floating around his bowl were bereft of colour or taste, but it was food, and Farden sipped the hot liquid carefully. The drug was forbidden for a reason, he told himself, nevermar's magick-numbing power was legendary, and for over a hundred years the council had opposed it with vicious measures. When Farden had been in training at the Spire, a mage had been caught having nevermar in his room. He had swiftly disappeared, and was never even spoken of again. It had been the death penalty for that man, dangling by his entrails from the city gate as an example to all. Farden shuddered.

But it calmed him, made him think less about the dark things in his mind, the fears, the second-guessing, and even despite its effects Farden had realised that he needed it. Over the years he had been incredibly careful to keep it a secret. The idea of anyone, especially Cheska, finding out was unthinkable, but he was too meticulous, too wary, to be discovered, and so far he hadn't done any harm to anyone besides himself. All that really mattered now was that his magick returned before they got to Nelska. He focused on getting through his bland stew, and tried to quiet his thoughts.

On the ship the mage's mind felt bored and unused. He could feel himself beginning to ramble in his own head, and was slowly going stir-crazy from constantly sitting in his tiny room. With a sigh Farden consigned himself to going outside, raining or not. He finished his shark, sipped the dregs from the bowl, and threw his hood over his head. He looked at his reflection in the dirty window and thumbed the stubble sprouting from his chin; he would have to shave before they reached Nelska. He relieved himself in the bucket in the corner and left the room.

Farden emerged onto a windblown deck and almost immediately regretted his decision. Everything had been tied down, and the deck was slick with spray and salty rain. Heold was at the helm, his beard matted and glistening from the precipitation. The big man laughed at seeing the mage. 'If ye didn't like the weather before, ye ain't goin' t' like it now!' he shouted. As if the ship had heard him, the *Sarunn* dove into a low trough between two waves and yawed sluggishly. Farden's stomach rolled with the waves. He stared at the

foam on the deck swirling around his boots and tried not to think of
the shark stew. The ship was on a roiling carpet of steel-capped waves
and overhead thick black clouds crackled with light and thunder.
Daylight was slowly fading and in the gloom the sailors clung
desperately to rigging and ropes and tried to work through the rain
and the wailing wind.

'I got bored of my room!' he shouted, and shrugged at the
Captain, but Heold was too busy fighting the wheel. A stubborn wish
to confront the awful weather made Farden want to go and stand at
his railing. The mage pulled his hood around his face to ward against
the stinging rain and headed up to the bow. From there he peered into
the storm and tried to make sense of the grey world. He couldn't even
see the difference between the waves and the granite sky. A wave hit
the poor unicorn beneath his feet and the *Sarunn* buried her nose in
the surf. Only one more day to go, Farden thought, remembering
Heold's words. Farden patted is side, and then suddenly realised that
he had left the tearbook under his pillow in his room. The mage
pivoted on his heel and ran back down the wet steps to the deck. He
felt odd, and a weird glow of unrest felt its way into his already
queasy stomach. He made his way below and pushed the door to his
cabin open with a bang.

The pillow was lying on the damp floor, and Karga stood
hunched over the bed flicking lazily through the pages of the
tearbook. The sailor looked up, mildly surprised, and the two men
shared an awkward, deadly silence.

'What the fuck are you doing?' blurted Farden, shocked.

The sailor stared at the mage with a faint smirk. 'I knew you
wouldn't leave it for long,' said Karga, and looked down at the blank
pages. 'He was right, it is empty.'

'Get away from the book,' the mage stepped further into the
room. He thought of his sword leaning against the wall behind the
door. It was just out of reach, and so he took another careful step.

'Whatever you say, Farden,' the sailor smiled, held his hands in the air, and stepped backwards. 'Whatever you say.'

'What are you doing with my book?' Farden growled. With a quick motion he grabbed his sword from behind the door and pulled it out of the scabbard. He waved it at Karga.

'You have no idea what's going on, do you?' He narrowed his eyes and flashed another toothy smile. Farden noticed scars criss-crossing his palms. The ship tilted underneath them.

'Wipe that smile off your face or I'll throw you overboard!'

'I'd like to see you try.'

Farden fumed. 'I think we should see what Heold has to say about this,' the mage motioned the door with his sword. Karga didn't move a muscle. Farden burnt with furious anger. He was confused, thrown off-guard by the sailor's smug expression. There was something very wrong.

'Move! Get out!' Farden yelled, but Karga simply reached out towards him with crooked fingers and red magma burst from his fingertips, a searing pyroclastic cloud of fire. The ball of ash hit the mage in the chest and knocked him straight through the wooden wall of his cabin. Splintered wood and flame filled the corridor. Farden coughed and spat and flailed his limbs. He swung his sword blindly in the burning smog, and dragged himself around the corner. He felt his skull throbbing and rubbed burning coals from his charred breastplate. Farden's mind raced like a falcon as he peered into the smoke.

'Come out here and fight!' shouted Karga. A screaming bolt of lightning tore through the hole in the wall and it exploded in the corridor with a bang. Somewhere in the darkness between the deck the goat bleated pitifully.

'I'm right here, Karga, come and find me!' Farden could hear the crunch of sea on the deck coming towards him. He waited and slowed his breathing and concentrated on not choking, and listened intently for the right moment to pounce. Another few footsteps, and Farden spied a shape peering through the hole. With a yell he jumped into the corridor and swung his sword at his assailant's head. But Karga spun around and held his hands up to block the swing. Just before the blade carved through his fingers a pulse of energy exploded from his palms and the sword rebounded with a clang. Farden swung again and thrust deadly steel into the man's face, but still Karga blocked and the sword whined and bounced away.

'Who are you?!' barked Farden.

He dodged another swipe and laughed. 'The man who was sent to kill you!' Karga screamed as the blade notched his shoulder. He quickly grabbed the sword with his left hand and lightning scattered along the steel.

'Argh!' Farden yelped as the magick shook him but he swiftly recovered, and with a strong step forward he slammed his forehead into Karga's nose. The sailor's head snapped backwards and blood sprayed from his face. The resilient mage followed up with a fist in his stomach and then a right elbow into the man's neck. Karga choked and fell backwards against the wall. Some of the sailors had heard the noise and gathered around a nearby hatch.

'Karga!' One of the men shouted. 'What's going on?'

The dark assailant ignored them. He breathed heavily. 'You can't fight me with magick, Farden? What's wrong? I was told you would be fun! A fair match for a sorcerer of my strength,' Karga sneered, and his eyes flashed a deep red. This man had dark magick in him, thought Farden, a servant of the forbidden, but before he could react Karga clenched his fist and shouted foreign words. All of a sudden the shadows in the dim underbelly of the ship came alive and grabbed at the mage. Farden cried out as a black hand pulled at his face and hair. Shadow fingers groped at his feet. Swinging his sword left and right he dove behind a tall pile of boxes and scrambled backwards and further into the ship. A ball of hot lava exploded over his head and sparks showered his hood. A dark shadow creature snatched at him but he escaped its grasp and ran for the galley.

'Fight me!' Karga yelled over the roar of his spells.

Farden dodged under beams and pans and grabbed the sturdy wooden rail of a ladder. Another burst of fire sent cinders flying across the ship's kitchen and singed the poor goat. Farden pushed the hatch above him and luckily it came free. Rain instantly hit his face. Quickly he ran up the ladder onto the deck, and stood with his sword low. Sailors shouted out to Heold, who was still at the wheel.

'What's goin' on 'ere?!' bellowed the big Captain. The sky flashed with white-blue light and thunder boomed. Farden yelled over the howling storm. 'It's one of your crew, Karga! He's been sent to ruin this mission!' Heold scowled, and turned his attention back to the wheel.

The mage wiped spray from his face and tried desperately to catch his breath. Gods damn that old man and his nevermar, he cursed inwardly, he needed his magick back. And fast.

A fireball streaked across the deck and exploded against the mast. The wet sails thankfully didn't catch fire but the splintered wood creaked and sparked. With fearful cries the crew dove for cover and scuttled into hiding.

'You can't win Farden!' a voice shouted over the howling rain. Karga had found his way to the stairs near the forecastle.

'And you should know better than to interfere with the magick of the elves!'

His opponent poked his head above a crate and grinned lopsidedly. 'It's not in my hands, mage, I just do what my masters tell me!' He shrugged. 'I'm just here for you.'

Farden growled. 'Where's the manual?'

Another ball of magma tore over Farden's head and ploughed into the angry sea with a hiss. Karga spat and laughed. 'You'll never find it! He sidled along the opposite side of the deck like a hungry eel. Farden crouched behind a wooden skylight and watched him. This sorcerer was strong, true, Farden thought to himself, but he was just a man, and a man can be broken. All he needed was his magick.

Karga called out to him again. 'You're wasting your time! Who knows where it could be by now,' he laughed sadistically. A sailor with an axe jumped down from the forecastle stairs and strode along the deck to face up to the dark mage, waving his weapon high over his head. Karga paused for a second and the storm howled around the two men. Every eye on the ship was upon them, silent and watching.

With lightning speed Karga pounced on the sailor, knocked the axe from his grip and put a hand around his neck. White-hot ash seared the flesh from his bones, and the man managed a gargling scream before he tumbled into the green-grey waves. The crew dissolved into pandemonium. They scurried over the deck yelling and shouting and trying to get as far away from the two mages as possible. Heold shouted from the wheel, trying to rally his men, keeping one eye on the treacherous sea and the other on the dangerous mages. 'Man the mast lads! Take those sails down!'

The *Sarunn* pitched violently over trough and crest. Farden clanged his sword off the mast and tried to block a searing ball of purple lightning, but the spell knocked Farden against the back railing, inches from the edge of the ship. He moved forward and away from the sea, and took cover behind a crate. Farden put a hand to his back and winced for a moment before the pain abruptly vanished. Something stirred in his spine, a tingling across his broad shoulders that the mage knew very well indeed. Farden smiled, and crouched low, stalking his prey. It was his turn.

Karga ducked under the railings of some stairs and peered through the pouring rain. Sparks crackled around his fingers as he waited for the mage to show his head. 'Come out, coward!' he shouted. He wiped blood from his nose and spat on the deck.

'Up here,' a gruff voice barked, and Karga looked up to see a boot heading rapidly for his face. The vicious kick sent him sprawling on the deck with a flurry of bloody seawater. Farden dropped from the forecastle to the stairs and rested his sword on his shoulder. But Karga was ready. He put his hands together and a ball of magma ripped into the mage's chest with a huge bang. Farden flew back into the wooden stairs and choked on the burning smoke. The dark sorcerer was already up and striding across the deck. Farden swung his blade up, but the man blocked it again, and again, but on the third swipe the blade sliced across his chest and cut a long gash through his sailor's tunic. Karga yelled and reeled backwards. Farden was quickly on his feet.

'You want to see some magick?' He spat salty rain to the side and ripped his hood back in defiance. His eyes blazed with white fire.

Up by the wheel Heold's face drained of colour and his shout chilled everyone on board.

'WAVE!'

And with that Farden's world seemed to pause.

His arms lifted through the slowing rain, single droplets sliding over his hands like clear mercury. A lightning bolt tore the sky and froze, paused in an eternal second. The air buzzed with magick and Farden could feel the tattoos burning white with heat and fire on his back. He braced himself on the slippery deck and felt the weight of the spell push him against the wet wood with a slow squelch in his boots. The mage took a deep breath and stared into Karga's glowing eyes. There was a paralysed look of fear suspended on his face. Farden looked up as flame trickled over his wrists, watching the rogue wave arch in slow-motion over the masthead above them. For the briefest of moments time stopped and the world around him became quiet. But it was short-lived and as the deck began to shake beneath his boots the roaring started, and time caught up with itself.

With a blinding flash of searing heat a tower of fire erupted from beneath the deck and ripped through the wood as if it were mere paper. Karga flew from the splintered deck, screaming and swathed in flames, and disappeared into the sea. Farden reeled backwards as the spell billowed upwards through the mast and the sails and into the face of the wave. Fire met water in an explosion of burning debris and steam, and then the wave hit the deck.

Heold's frenzied shouts were drowned out by the noise as the wave tumbled onto the deck with the force of a falling mountain. Farden grabbed the stair rail behind him and clung on desperately while the ship rocked under the watery avalanche. The wave washed the sailors from the deck and tossed them into the sea like broken marbles and they yelled and shrieked in the icy water. The mage was almost torn away by the rogue wave, but the water quickly receded as the *Sarunn* somehow rode the crest and recovered. Farden was washed sideways across the deck towards a hatch and he grabbed at it. His head pounded, and he felt the sickening dizziness of the spell's wake. Karga was nowhere to be seen, and the mast sounded like it was about to snap, splintering into matchsticks around the base with whip-like cracking sounds and a terrible groaning.

'Farden, what have you done?' Heold was on his belly on the top deck, wallowing like a manatee in the salty water.

'It was Karga!' lied Farden. He looked around desperately. The ship was going down fast. Water was now pouring through the gaping hole in the deck and Farden stared wide-eyed and fearful at the seawater gushing into the belly of the ship. The fire spell and the wave had ripped the *Sarunn* almost in two, and now she was foundering miles and miles from shore in a turbulent sea. Several of the crew still clung to the rigging and screamed for Njord to save them. Farden didn't expect him to intervene.

The mage half-ran half-fell down the stairs and his boots splashed in the rising water. It was icy cold, and stabbed like daggers into his waist and chest. He had to get to the tearbook.

Farden ran down the stairs and corridor and dove over broken wooden planks and floating charcoal. He pushed the door open and strode through the flotsam and jetsam floating in his room. The ship was falling apart quicker than he thought.

'Where are you?' He shouted. Farden was panicking. The tearbook wasn't on his bed, but he found it hiding under the mattress in the water. He tore away his cloak and breastplate and kicked off his heavy boots so that they didn't drown him. Grabbing the sack and the rest of his supplies, he sloshed through the seawater and made his way back up to the deck. Once there he tried to get as far away from the water as possible, and made his way to the wheel. Farden shivered in the lashing rain. The *Sarunn* was now pitching on her port side and the mast was starting to crack in two. Farden found Heold still lying on his front, shouting to his men and now clinging onto the wheel to keep from being washed away. Farden wondered if he had broken his back, and then he saw his legs. A spar of broken wood had skewered one his legs, and smashed the other to a pulp. His shins were a mass of broken bone and bloody flesh.

'Get off the ship lad! She's done fer!' the captain shouted at the mage in a hoarse voice.

'What the hell happened to you?' Farden watched him grimace in pain. 'You have to get off the ship!'

'Cap'n goes down with 'is ship is what I 'eard! Ain't no way I'll try m' chances in the sea tonight!' He bellowed, face twisted in agony again.

'Gods damn it!' Farden cursed at the defeated old man. A few sailors and one of the Arka soldiers, who was furiously shedding his heavy steel armour, clambered over the flooded deck, over rigging and drowning cargo. Farden grabbed a broken hatch cover and futilely threw it into the sea, but just then he spied a huge section of a wooden box tied to the railing. He hacked at it with his sword until it came loose and then stood holding it, waiting for the sea to swallow the ship. With growing alarm Farden watched the hungry waves lick at the deck and climb further and further into the ship with every second. He narrowed his eyes, steeled his reserve, and hauled his box to the opposite railing and threw it into the sea. The wind howled around him and threatened to rip the tearbook from his side but Farden grabbed the strap and yanked it hard to tighten it. The brave mage steadied himself on there railing against the force of the storm and waited for his moment to leap. From somewhere behind him there was a deep rending crack and something struck him heavily on the back of the head. Farden fell down into the angry sea and into a dark dream.

part two

follow the dragons

 chapter 7

"It was at this time that the Scribe came to us, the secret behind a Written's strength, and a great and powerful wing of the magick council came to exist, charged to watch over the dark forces left behind by the elves. The peers of the Arka factions were now under a great duty; to see that the powers of good were exercised in the wild lands of Emaneska, and that direction and order was brought to the people. This was of course, before the greed of the rich sought to pervert the power of the two thrones, when one by one the members of the council turned their minds from justice and good, and wanted for gold and power instead."

Arkmage Olfar, writing in the year 789

Choke.

Water flooded his nose and ran down his throat like a runaway avalanche of salty black liquid.

The sea pulled at his hands and feet and clothes with ice-cold fingers. His world switched between the roar of the storm and the inky deafness of underwater. Up was down, and water replaced air.

Lightning fizzed in the darkness. Somewhere above or below him the clouds slammed together. Stars swam in his head and invisible gods played with his rag-doll body. He felt like his body was swimming away from him, and blood ran down into his eyes. The carcass of the drowned goat knocked against him, stuck somewhere in the tangling rigging.

Breathe.

Rain-soaked air fought with bile for room in his throat. He felt something under his swollen fingers and grabbed it with the last vestiges of strength in his weary body.

Hold fast.

Ropes dragged at raw cuts and lashed him to the crate that kept him afloat. His forehead found a resting place against the salty wood.

Darkness.

Farden shivered in his desert, and rubbed at his cold arms and legs. He looked down at his pale naked body, at his skin that looked wrinkly as if from too much water, at the damp patch in the cracked earth. His vambraces lay rusty and covered in drying seaweed at his dusty feet.

Breathe said something, and Farden turned his head to see a skinny black cat, soaked to the bone, sitting near to him amongst the stones. Its ragged fur steamed in the hot sun. A dead rotting bird full of maggots sat at its feet. Beady empty eyes stared at the sky. Farden looked up, and his pale blue emptiness bubbled and wavered, as if he were looking at the surface of a placid sea. He lifted a finger and ripples spread out across the vast cloudless sky. His fingers felt wet. There was a rumbling, and the sun flashed.

'I am breathing,' he said.

Not for long said the voice, and the cat licked its bedraggled paw.

A man was walking alone on a rocky beach. Pockmarked
volcanic stones mingled amongst grey shale and pale sand crunched
under his slender boots. The spear in his hand held him steady against
the slippery stones and green seaweed. From under a white hood
purple eyes scanned the grey waves rolling up the beach and a scaly
nose sniffed the salt air. The man watched the first few shafts of new
sunlight pierce the rain clouds and felt the fresh wind coming from
the west on his skin. Should be a calm day, he thought to himself, and
he breathed deep to let the smell of the salt air fill his head. The man
pulled his white cloak about him and swapped his grip on the spear so
he could warm his cold hand in his pocket. He coughed a rattling hiss,
and walked on, still scanning the beach. Then abruptly he stopped and
crouched by a rocky outcrop. Something had caught his keen eye. A
shape lay in the surf.

The man hopped nimbly over the stones and sand flew from
his boots as he ran over the beach towards the shape. Within moments
he reached it, and circled it warily, feet splashing in the shallow
water. It looked like a crate, or a door, a mass of ropes and rigging
lying useless and tangled in the sand. Using the sharp spearpoint, he
peeled away the matted weed and knotted ropes to reveal the long
dead eyes of a goat, bloated and swollen from seawater. It grinned at
him in death, and its cloudy gaze stared off into space. He grimaced at
the sight of the dead animal and poked at the rest of the sodden lump.
The Siren spied something that looked like a shoe poking out from
under a slimy section of wood, and crouched to investigate further. It
was a boot, with a foot and leg attached to it.

The man tore apart the wooden crate in a spray of green weed
and water to find a bedraggled corpse lying curled up and half-buried
in the sand. Kneeling at its side, he poked and prodded at the face of a
beaten man. He looked to be in his thirties, probably from the
southeast, with matted dark hair and red-gold vambraces on his arms.
He put his spearblade to his mouth, and a thin mist of breath appeared

on the shiny steel. The Siren slapped the man's face, feeling his chest where his heart was with his long fingers. Something stirred there, maybe a faint hint of life. The Siren brought a fist down on the man's chest, at the point where the ribs joined, and the washed-up man suddenly spluttered and coughed, retching bile and seawater. He opened his red-rimmed eyes to find a shiny spear blade waving in his face, and closed them again to find nothing but darkness.

❦

'Where'd you find him?'

'On the beach near the southwest corner. Should have been dead, the poor bastard, but somehow there's life in him,' the soldier shrugged and tried to rub warmth back into his hands. His white cloak was dripping wet and covered in sand, and there was brown seaweed tangled in clumps around his wrists.

'Arka, by the look of him,' The healer had the look of an ageing crow, and the voice of one too. He was hunched over the wooden table and murmuring thoughtfully somewhere deep in his throat. His long hair hung in wet strands over his squinting green eyes. His scales were the colour of tree moss. He rubbed his chin and examined the man spread out on the table below him.

Farden looked like death, or something very close to it. He shivered convulsively and clawed at the wooden table as if it could give off heat. Like the soldier he was also covered in sand and seaweed, and his skin was pale like parchment and as cold as ice. His cloak and tunic were ripped and torn and snagged with splinters of driftwood. The figure looked altogether wretched. A little black bundle of something lay by his side.

'What's that?' asked the healer, pointing at the thing.

The soldier carefully turned it over to reveal a dishevelled mess of black fur and whiskers. 'I think it's a cat, it was near to where

I found him.'

'Well what's it doing here?'

'The thing's still breathing, don't ask me how, but it is. It must belong to him,' the soldier pointed to Farden. 'After all the little thing's been through…' He shrugged.

The healer shook his head despairingly. 'Fine, leave it with me. I'll have him taken to my rooms and I'll see who he is, *if* he lives that is.' The healer spied something colourful under Farden's torn sleeve. He shifted his long grey hair from his eyes and peered down his beak-like nose. He looked up, a confused look plastered in his face. 'Scalussen vambraces?'

The soldier nodded. 'I know. This isn't just some washed up sailor,' he paused, 'the others might need to hear about this.'

The healer took a moment to think, and then waved his hands with a shake of his head. 'Yes yes, after I get him back to health. He can't go far like this. Here, I'll send for my guard to take him to my house, and *yes* I'll take care of that mangy animal,' The old man gestured to someone behind him, and a nervous young boy, previously silent in a corner, ran off to fetch help.

'I'll send a messenger to the Old Dragon,' the scaly soldier turned to go, but the healer held up a hand to stop him.

'I will do that, when he is ready to be interrogated. At the moment he is too weak to be questioned. This man is at death's door.'

The soldier looked as if he were going to say something but thought better of arguing, and nodded to the grey man. 'Fine with me. Good day, sir.'

'And to you.' The healer watched the soldier go, and turned back to Farden. He poked under the red and gold vambraces and peered down his beak-like nose at the hidden symbols tattooed onto the mage's wrists. The man's emerald eyes widened. His bony hands scraped at the rotting wet tunic on his back and pulled the fabric aside to reveal something that made the breath catch in his throat. But at that moment the guards knocked on the door, and Farden was taken further into the city on a cart covered by a blanket. The grey healer had the mage put in a locked room in his house and had water and food put out for him.

That night the healer quietly padded down the corridor leading to Farden's room, holding nothing but a tallow candle tightly in his hand, a hand that quivered with anticipation and a hint of excitement. His bony fingers fiddled with the key in the lock and the man took a few breaths to calm his eager heart. The lock clicked, and he shut the door behind him. The healer lifted the candle high to light the square room. Farden lay prone and unconscious on a wooden table in the middle of the floor. Slowly the grey Siren crept forward and ran his fingers across the mage's feverish brow. He put his ear to Farden's mouth and listened to the shallow ragged breaths sneaking in and out between his cracked lips. The healer sniffed. He put the candle down on the edge of the table and pulled a slim knife from under his nightgown. It took all his strength to turn Farden over and get him onto his front, but finally he did it, and began to slice through the mage's ragged tunic. Cloth parted and betrayed the black lettering hiding underneath. The old healer grinned to himself and squinted. He balanced his little glasses on the very edge of his nose and tugged at the remaining strands of tunic. Shaking hands moved the candle closer.

After what seemed like hours, the old man paused to stretch and yawn and rub his eyes. His eyelids felt like they were burning and the yellow light of the dying candle was beginning to fade. Without taking his eyes from the writing on Farden's back the old healer moved to snuff the flickering flame. With the back of his hand he knocked it to the floor where it spat and dribbled wax on the flagstones. The Siren cursed and bent to pick it up.

He froze.

There was something in the room behind him. A huge shadow

fell over him like a blanket and the old man shivered with sudden cold. He made a brief squeaking noise as his throat closed up with fear and scrabbled for the candle. Whispering voices called his name and he rubbed his eyes again to try to rid of himself of the shadows dancing around him. He wiped his face and blood from his nose smeared his fingers. He choked on acrid smoke and tasted ice, shivered as hands groped at his legs. A terrified wail broke from the Siren's throat and he bolted for the door leaving the candle to die on the floor. Breath clogged at the very back of his throat and his heart jumped in his chest with every thundering beat. He groped for the key in the darkness. Terror gripped him and all he could do was run. He fled down the dark corridor, listening to the whispers and shrieks biting at his heels. He skidded and fell into his room, slammed the door, and groped about in the darkness for his bed, his only refuge. Ghosts threw the fingers of dead men at his door. They scraped at the walls and called his name as he quivered beneath a blanket and several pillows. Dark letters swam around his eyes and sleep flew from him like crows. They danced and fluttered their terrible black wings, swarming his room with cawing and scratching, reminding him of every mistake he had ever made, every bad thing he had ever done. The old man cried and sobbed, huddled in a ball under the blanket.

In a dark room down the corridor, a tallow candle finally burnt out on the cold flagstones. A man breathed heavily in the dark. Farden was dreaming his way through a deep, healing sleep, and the life slowly started to return to his weary body.

'Why am I here?' asked Farden.

You tell me said the voice. The cat looked at him with the same deadpan look.

'I don't even know this place,' said Farden, annoyed. He looked up and tried to melt into his cerulean sky, tried to leave the aching pain in his body behind.

It's a little of you, and a little of me.

'Well, who are you then?'

I'm trying to help.

'If you wanted to help, you'd get me out of here, you'd help me up and make the pain go away, you'd get me back to Krauslung and you'd find the book and save Emaneska.' Farden sighed, feeling the weight of his sky pushing down on him. The heat was unbearable this time. 'I never asked for this.'

The cat yawned and stretched. Its skinny black tail swished back and forth through the dust. *We never do* said the deep voice in his head. *We never ask for this, nor do we ever complain, we just do what we're told. It's what people like you and I do; we fight, and we never ask for anything in return.*

'Who are you?' asked Farden. A wind whined through the desert, a cold cackling wind that whipped the sand into spirals and eddies.

I'm just like you.

'You're nothing like me,' scoffed Farden.

The voice sounded disappointed but earnest. *Keep an eye on the weather, Farden, there's more to this than first appears. You've found the dragons, now listen to them.*

'Leave me alone, I don't need your help. I don't need anybody,' said Farden, and he crossed his arms stubbornly. The whirling sand whipped his face, and in the spinning dust he discerned faces, faces of Cheska, of Durnus, of Vice, and an old face that he hadn't seen in a very long time. Grit burnt his eyes, and hot tears were stolen by the wind.

As you wish. Keep an eye on the weather.

Something rustled near him. Hay scattered and an animal snuffled. Farden kept his eyes tightly closed. His body ached in a thousand places and wrists were screaming against the iron shackles. Straw pricked his back and the wall behind his head was ice-cold. Farden could feel the heat of a fever burning his forehead, and he slowly raised a hand to his skin to see for himself. Chains encircled his wrists, and his vambraces were gone. He was surprised to feel that he still wore his cloak, ripped and torn as it was, but the sackcloth tunic he wore under it felt strange and rough. He blithely wondered where his old one was, and who had dressed him, but a ripple of sickening dizziness brought him back to the matter at hand. He clenched his jaw and slowly, ever so slowly, opened his eyes to peer around the unfamiliar chamber. There was a disgusting stench in the air.

The room was forged from grey granite walls, square and low with a matching floor, and hay was strewn about him. The only entrance was apparently a stout pine door. The source of the smell was an upturned bucket in the corner. Its foul contents lay in a puddle on the floor. A whispering came from his right, and a nervous rattling of shackles. Farden turned his head gradually, trepidation growing in his throbbing heart. A cackle echoed in the cell.

Chained to the wall about six feet from him sat a dishevelled character, a mere shell of a Siren man inside which lunacy had taken up residence. Wide green platters of rapt madness were now peering out from the place where eyes used to be, and a wide curve of yellow teeth squatted behind dangling tendrils of matted grey hair thick with filth and dung. The Siren cackled and spat, a thin tongue darted from behind his psychotic smile.

'The... mage! Awake from sleep, dark dark sleep,' he laughed, cross-eyed.

Farden backed further away from the raving mad man. It was like stepping back in time to a painful memory. He had seen this before, in his own uncle the last time he had seen him, and the sharp similarity of it made him feel sick. The man foamed at the mouth, grinning and pawing at the mage. The Book carved into a Written's back was strictly not for reading, and the raw magick in the script could warp the mind of a weaker person. There was a reason the tattoo was placed on the shoulders and back, and the Written were sworn to keep it concealed at all times, hence why Farden was so keen to keep inquisitive people such as Elessi out of harm's way.

The mad siren kept reaching out to him, rolling his eyes madly. The resemblance to his uncle was unsettling, a dark memory dug up and dumped at his feet. His broken fingernails found cracks in the granite floor and left bloody scrapes on the stone.

'Where'd you go, mage? Where'd you go? Dark dreams you had…dark daemon dreams!' He hooted, and then muttered to himself. 'Dreamdreamdream, stuck in a desert.'

'Be quiet!' Farden shouted and the man twitched and snuffled.

'Hah! I've read your mind! Felt the lines on your back, felt the writing on my fingers calling to me.' The man grinned a scaly smile so wide Farden thought he might break his face.

'Silence!'

All of a sudden there was a bang on the door, and the heavy bolts slid from their holes. Half a dozen guards burst through the wide doorway and rushed in to grab the two prisoners. A soldier hit the mad Siren around the head with a club and he fell to the floor with a cry.

'Do not move!' Another shouted inches from Farden's face, and the mage froze. Heavy keys jiggled in the locks around his wrists and he fell to the floor with a flurry of hay. Farden was roughly hauled upright and dragged from the room, with the shouts of his crazy cellmate ringing down the corridor.

'Beware the dragons, mage! They'll steal your soul!' He was silenced by a kick.

'Where are you taking me?' Farden coughed weakly. His body screamed out to him in pain.

'Shut it, Arka, He wants to speak with you,' the man said from a mouth ringed with blue scales.

'Who... ?' managed Farden.

The Siren narrowed his eyes at the beaten mage. 'No more questions!' he elbowed him hard in an already burning rib.

Farden was silent for the rest of the journey, or dragging, and drifted in and out of a feverish consciousness. He was manhandled up steps and through corridors, along bridges and across bustling thoroughfares filled with gawking Siren citizens. Pain from a hundred cuts and bruises blurred with his fever as he was hauled onto a wide bridge that arched over a massive cave carpeted by rolling fields. The dark walls rose upwards and culminated in a huge ring of rocks like a crater. Daylight surged through the opening high above Farden's head and he could see the snow drifting gently through the cold air. As the party crossed the long road he managed to glimpse looks at the farms and buildings below him. Countless people milled around below them like ants, wandering through the furrowed fields and farmhouses, down lanes and curving roads.

A good half an hour later Farden was dumped quite unceremoniously at the top of a flight of stairs. Cold wind messed with his hair and he tried to push his head up to see, but a guard yanked him backwards, and the refreshing mountain air was taken away. Farden was dragged again, this time somewhere that swung and wallowed as if he floated. There was a creaking and he felt as though he were moving upwards. The mage tried to reserve his strength for whatever was coming, so he kept his eyes shut and concentrated on staying conscious.

After a while he was hauled across what felt like a cold shiny floor and left in a foetal position. All was silent. Behind him a large door was slammed and the sound of boots ceased. Light shimmered behind Farden's eyelids, and he waited.

'Can you stand?' asked a massive booming voice.

Farden lay still and kept his eyes closed. Feeling his fingers stretch out beneath him he pushed himself up shakily. Every limb wailed in protest. He cursed under his breath and looked for the first time at his surroundings.

There had not been many times in his life that Farden had felt such awe and shock, and been speechless because of his surroundings. This was one of those times. The humbled mage felt beyond tiny as he gazed upwards at a massive domed roof that seemed to tower effortlessly hundreds of feet above him. Thin shafts of bright light poked through the tough granite rock like holes pierced in a grey blanket and a huge skylight punctured the far side of the ceiling, a massive doorway to the snowy skies outside. At least a thousand ledges were carved into the rock, all over the hall, huge sconces carved from the stone that ran up and along the walls like countless honeycombed nests. The candlelight of hundreds of lamps flickered all around him, and dragons, scores of dragons, filled the lower ledges of the gigantic hall. They squatted and perched on piles of soft hay, surrounded by little candles and pitchers of water and accompanied by their riders. Farden noticed, with a somewhat unexpected dismay, that only half the nests in the cave seemed to be occupied, dark without their candles and visitors. He wondered what this hall would have looked like before the war. The huge lizards shuffled and shifted all around him, and the sound of their breathing and their dragon-riders whispering to each other was deafening. The smell of reptile and woodsmoke was a strange mix, but welcome after the stench of his cell. A ring of guards surrounded him and watched him carefully, but the mage's eyes were now fixed on what he saw before him.

There, laying on a huge wooden bed of autumn leaves, spotlighted by a lone shaft of sunlight, was the Old Dragon, Farfallen. He shone with a warm gold light, vibrating with an ancient magick Farden did not fully understand. The mage's head swam between disbelief and bewilderment. Vice had killed the Old Dragon, years ago in the battle of Ragjarak, and yet here he was, sitting calmly on his roost with his dragon-rider beside him.

Farfallen's Siren was a tall thin willow of a woman. Her stern lightning face was like a thin blade, serious and commanding. Her jaw was set and her thin hands were neatly folded behind her back. The woman's long green dress draped over her incredibly slender body and fell to the floor like a moss-covered tree branch. Her long autumn-gold hair was tied back apart from two long strands that fell in front of each ear, long like the fangs of a sabre-cat. She seemed to have a habit of flaring her nostrils, whether through irritation or tendency, Farden could not tell. Golden scales covered her cheekbones, and they ran in stripes up her neck to meet her chin. Her yellow eyes pierced Farden's and he felt himself blinking weakly even in the low light.

The great dragon stirred loudly behind her and she turned. He stretched out one colossal gold wing briefly like a huge canvas and blinked each golden eye separately. They were like black orbs flecked with liquid gold and stardust. Farden felt like falling into them. Farfallen finished stretching and watched the quiet mage impassively. A lizard tongue graced sharp teeth and flicked over mottled lips.

'Well met and good wishes, stranger. Can you speak?' His voice rumbled again like distant thunder.

'Yes, sire,' croaked Farden.

'From where did you come, thief?' His dragon-rider, the stern woman, spat.

'Be calm, Svarta. Speak, guest, tell us,' Farfallen lifted a huge claw to silence her and then nodded for him to carry on.

Farden took a deep breath and attempted a shaky bow. 'My name is Farden, I am an Arka mage sent here to speak with the Siren council. My masters wish you all kind greetings and express their desire to bring peace between our two peoples,' he said. Farden felt dizzy under the gaze of the dragons. There was a pause.

'You are one of the Written,' said the woman, Svarta, more of a fact than a question.

The mage suddenly grew wary. His mind turned to the raving lunatic back in his cell. 'That is true,' he answered slowly.

'Then you are a danger to us all!' Svarta opened her arms palms facing upwards and she looked up at the other dragons. 'The magick this man holds in his skin is treacherous. The healer who brought this mage back from the dead was turned to madness and lost his mind to whatever spells *you* cast on him.' Her eyes bored into Farden's skull. Some of the lofty dragons murmured in agreement, others, like rusting leaves, whispered conspiratorially to their riders.

Farden was shocked at the accusation. 'I have been unconscious for days! The first time I saw that man was in my cell just a moment ago! Whatever he did he did it to himself and without my help. I'm sure you all know what I am, and what is on my back.' Farden involuntarily pulled his tattered tunic around his shoulders and stood defiantly, still shaky. 'His fate is nothing to do with me.'

'It is *everything* to do with you! A strange man washed up on our shores half-dead, taken in by a kind healer, and suddenly he is turned into a raving lunatic? We should have left you for the gulls!' Svarta shouted. Farfallen and the council watched on calmly.

'I came here on a peaceful mission! My ship was attacked on the way here, and I was forced to take my chances in the sea. Surely a hawk has arrived with news of my arrival?' Farden tried explaining, but Svarta huffed and crossed her arms. He looked into the massive gold eyes of the Old Dragon. Farfallen took a deep breath and sighed.

'No hawk, eagle, or falcon has reached us with any missive from the Arka. We have not had any dealings with your people in years,' he said, with a tinge of looking like a distant thought had just passed through his mind like a wandering beggar. 'Who attacked your ship?'

The mage sighed. This was going to be a long story. 'Sire, this discussion might be better held in private, my mission concerns all of Emaneska.' Another grumble from the other dragons.

Farfallen waited to say something, but Svarta jumped in. 'Your mission? I assume this has something to do with…. *this!*' She reached behind her and pulled out the huge tearbook, dry and safe. A gasp came from the hall like a sudden wind, as if a forgetful guard had left a door open. The dragons flapped and moved around in their nests. Some riders perched on their partner's long serpentine necks leant forward to get a better view of the book.

Farden was shocked and relieved at the same time. He was sure that the tearbook had been lost in the waves when he jumped ship. Svarta held it aloft and showed it to the entire council. Farfallen was silent, one eye now closed, the other fixed on his tearbook.

'This man was found with this in his clutches! Farfallen's memories, long stolen from us and kept by the Arka as a trophy of the battle at Ragjarak…'

'Yes and if the message had arrived from Krauslung then you would know I was bringing it as a gesture of good faith! As a peace offering from my people!'

'You're a thief!' one Siren somewhere in the hall shouted out.

'Liar!' another shout.

'Enough!' Farfallen roared. For the first time the Old Dragon reared up from his bed and sat up straight with a loud scraping and Farden found himself gazing up at him. A thick spiky tail whipped the air with a swish and his wings beat the air like hammers as he hauled his massive weight upright. The huge golden dragon sat on his hind legs like a giant cat and his spiked tail waved impatiently. Farfallen's wings folded back with a rustle. The golden scales that covered his body undulated and quivered in the torchlight that washed over his shining body. His wings stood arched behind his shoulders, and long horns ran up his spine to meet in a wide crown above his bony brows. It was the sheer size of him that impressed Farden. The Old Dragon was at least twice the size of the worm that had attacked Farden recently, and the mage's heart thudded hard in his chest. He could see a long rippling scar that ran from Farfallen's throat down across his left forearm. The dragon flexed his snake-like neck, hinging and unhinging his jaw with a noisy click. He clicked his talons together against the rock floor.

'I will talk to the mage, but not now and not here. Let him explain himself to me.'

Svarta looked like she would say something, but Farfallen shot her a glance. 'My word is final,' he uttered. She nodded. The other dragons rumbled their assent, and several leapt into the air, flapping their wings with huge whooshing sounds. Farden's dark hair scattered in the wind as the huge beasts soared upwards and through the skylight at the far end of the hall. The mage could just about see the snow flurrying in their wake.

'Farden, walk with us.' Farfallen swapped a look with Svarta. The two of them left their platform and headed towards a low doorway in the rock wall. The mage was ushered along by two nearby guards who grabbed him roughly by the arms. Farden walked forward and the men jostled him. Despite his dizziness he was beginning to feel strength seeping back into his body; the weakness and fragility seemed to fade slowly with every step he took. He wondered if it was the effect of the dragons' magick.

Farfallen's feet pounded the stone floor ahead of him and each step shook the mage's legs. Svarta shot him a glance that spoke menace and justice. Farden coughed blandly. Randomly he wondered if it was difficult to ride a dragon.

The party strolled around a wide corridor that sloped gently further and further down into the mountain. Farfallen and Svarta were silent as they walked. Occasionally they would look at each other as if reacting to a silent rebuke or question. Farden watched them closely until Svarta chuckled slightly and then fell silent once more. She still held the big tearbook under her arm. The mage tried to remember the rumours he had heard about the mind-reading skills of dragons.

Soon they approached the end of the spiralling corridor and stopped in front of a semi-circular doorway, locked tight by thick bars of ornate wood. Two siren guards stood either side of it wearing the expressions of wax dolls. Their colourful eyes were rigid and unmoving, the tips of their sharp spears barely quivering, and their lips were drawn tight with ceremonious gravity. Formal was an understatement, Farden thought to himself. Farfallen fixed him with a golden stare momentarily and then looked away.

'Leave us,' Svarta looked over her bony shoulder and nodded to the men flanking the mage. They stepped aside, bowed, and scurried back the way they had come. Farden swayed like an old willow on his tired legs.

'Come, Farden, let us talk in private,' said the Old Dragon without turning around. He waited for the two soldiers to slide open the doors. Even though the curve of the doorway was massive, the huge lizard still had to duck his head and wings as they passed under the gilded arch. The mage followed quietly. He caught one of the soldiers stealing a glance at him as he passed. Their eyes met for a second and the soldier's head snapped back to position. Farden shrugged and hobbled into the room. A fresh arctic breeze caressed his unshaven face, and he could smell the clean, pure scent of snow and mountain air coming from somewhere nearby. The tall domed roof reminded him of the hall he just left, but the long windows lit the huge space with crisp white light that hurt his eyes. Thick carpets covered the stone floor, and wide benches and platforms followed the line of the walls, there was even a resting spot for the huge bulk of the Old Dragon. Big circular doors led to other rooms and quarters to his left and right, and thick wooden bookcases lined one far wall next to another door to a long balcony. The dragon shuffled his gold feet in that direction, and Farden followed like a loyal dog. Svarta lingered by the bookshelves.

The brisk mountain air almost knocked Farden over as he stepped over the threshold onto the expansive balcony. High overhead he could see more dragons circling, coloured shapes whirling through the sky, big and small depending on the distance and of all hues and sizes. Scattered snow drifted through the overcast skies, as if the clouds were trying but couldn't quite muster the energy for a blizzard. The thick white flakes were a stark contrast to the dusty grey clouds that rolled and yawned above, a sky so cavernous Farden was sure he had seen it before. If he stood at the railing he could see the whole mountainside spread below him, but leaning over made his stomach churn so he looked straight ahead at the mountainous countryside that stretched out into the distance like a crumpled chart. He held out a hand to let cold snowflakes land on his hot skin.

The citadel of Hjaussfen seemed to be mostly contained within the extinct volcanic shell of the mountain, but the villages and towns had pooled together around it, linking roads and boundaries to form a suburban sprawl of buildings much like the cramped streets of Krauslung. Through the curtain of snow Farden could pick out clusters of houses and low round towers poking from behind volcanic crags and rugged cliffs. Farms of dark soil popped up between the rocks every so often, now barren in the winter months. Here and there he could see flat roofs and circular areas lit by wind-blown torches. He assumed they were for dragons to land on if they so wished. Strange, he thought, how easy the harmony was achieved between these massive beasts and their Siren friends. Everything he saw was built for two different kinds of citizen, no road was too narrow, or step too tall, and everywhere he looked he could see the Sirens living in complete cooperation with the dragons. If only the social boundaries of the Arka could be so blurred, he thought.

'We love the snow.' Farfallen said from behind him. The dragon had joined him at the railing. 'Keeps us cool.'

'I've never seen so many of you in one place,' confessed Farden.

'Even in the war?'

'No,' he said, 'before my time.'

'There used to be many more of us in the world, not only in Hjaussfen or Nelska, but in every corner of Emaneska,' he sighed.

Farden thought of the empty nests in the great hall and thought about asking, but Farfallen spoke up, so he stored that question for later. 'You must be surprised to see me alive, mage, after the stories you have no doubt heard of brave Lord Vice the dragon-slayer?' A smirk curled on his lip.

Farden nodded quietly, eyeing the scar on the dragon's neck.

'It was a lucky strike, and one that almost killed me. But I think it would take a lot more than just a sword to finish the job. Vice foolishly left me for dead, and I decided it was better to stay that way, at least as far as the Arka were aware, that is,' said Farfallen with a far-off look.

Farden wondered what Vice would say when he found out. He would not be best pleased. 'There's a lot to be reconciled between our people, but I'm here for something much more important,' the mage said.

The dragon dipped his massive spiky head and cleared his throat. The noise was like a landslide under a hollow mountain. 'I assume you speak of your mission?' He rumbled.

Farden turned to face him. He closed his eyes as a wave of weakness came and went. 'I was sent here with an important task, one that is best kept as quiet as possible. We're still not sure who is behind all this, and several members of the magick council believe that some of the Sirens could be responsible.'

Farfallen matched his solemn look with both giant eyes. The reptile settled down on the cold floor and his tail swished noisily from side to side. Farden shivered in the wind. 'Tell me,' he said.

Farden told the story of what had happened at Arfell, leaving out no detail whatsoever and remembering to be exact and mind his manners. Even though he kept glancing at Farfallen's claws and teeth, something in the back of his mind told him he could trust the dragon, and he could see reliability in the dragon's eyes. So he kept talking.

When it came to the subject of Jergan, Farfallen held up a single claw to interrupt the mage.

'Jergan, the lycan?'

'You knew him?' asked Farden, confused.

Farfallen squinted into the distance and tried to think. 'Yes, a long time ago, the memories are hazy, but I remember him, or at least the memory of him.'

A voice came from behind them. 'I remember when we heard he was bitten.' Svarta glided across the flagstones, her slim green dress blowing in the wind. Farden didn't turn around and carried on staring at the rocky landscape.

'He came back covered in blood and deep scratches, soaked by the snow and half-dead from the cold. The healers knew instantly what had happened and we sent him away.' Her words sounded cruel and heartless, but Farden knew there was no easy cure for a lycan's bite; exile was the only answer.

'The wolf-curse is a strong one, and there was nothing we could do for him. He was a danger to us all.' Farfallen agreed, as if reading the mage's thoughts.

'I know. He wishes you to know that he is alive and well… sort of. I fought him in the south of Albion about a week ag…' Farden paused for a moment. 'How long have I been here?'

'We've put up with you for six days,' said the stern woman. She reached the railing and put her hands slowly on the cold stone. Her yellow eyes wandered over the view.

Farden counted the days in his head, and then realised he had no idea how long he had been stranded at sea. Eleven, twelve days altogether? With no messenger hawk the council would be getting worried, and probably fearing the worst. 'I have to send word to the Arka.'

'We'll get to that after you tell us what you're doing here, and why you had Farfallen's tearbook.' Svarta snapped.

'I came here to enlist the services of the Sirens in battling this common enemy. Whoever stole the summoning manual wants to use it against all of Emaneska, and only the memories in the tearbook can tell us where they'll try to summon this creature.' Farden crossed his arms defiantly.

'Which creature?' asked the Old Dragon.

'One spell in the book spoke of a massive, apparently unimaginably terrifying monster, the one that we think they're after. If the scholars and Jergan were right, then none of us, not the Arka nor the Sirens, could match it.' Farden explained.

The grin that ran across Svarta's face was no less than sarcastic. 'The last I heard, the Sirens weren't in favour with your court.'

'If we are to stop this from happening we need to fight together. True, there were some in the council who accused you of being responsible for this chaos, but it was the ruling of the Arkmages that I was to come here and try to make peace. Unless, of course, your pride isn't damaged in doing so?' Farden returned the grin. Svarta smouldered, but Farfallen put a huge claw on her shoulder lightly.

'We have no objection to peace, Farden, Svarta is just trying to look out for the best interests of our people. But if you found a strange foreign man washed up on one of your beaches with a stolen treasure in his hands what would you assume?' the dragon asked, and the mage had to agree with him. 'Still, I am grateful for the return of my tearbook. Since it was taken things have been hazy in my mind, not so clear. When I try to remember something it's like grasping at a wet fish. Difficult,' he said, with more than a hint of wistfulness. 'Why are my memories so important to the safety of Emaneska?'

'The spell needs a well of dark elf magick, and your memories could point to one that has survived.'

'We haven't found one in years. Jergan and his team were the last to do so.' Farfallen said.

'I know, but it's the only way they can summon the creature. If we find the well we find them.' Farden clenched a fist behind his back. He felt like he was back in the magick council, but this time there was no Vice to help him. He tried to convey the urgency of the situation to Farfallen with his mind.

'And what if you're too late?' Svarta asked. The dragon-rider turned to face the wind again.

'Then we'll just have to be quick then won't we?' Farden retorted.

'He has a point.' This came from Farfallen.

'Well there's no time to lose then. We can have the men from the library come look at the tearbook. If there's a clue to a dark elf well, they can find it,' said Svarta. Farden was unsure whether she was being sarcastic or not. She scowled at him once more and then left the balcony edge. Farden watched her leave, and turned back to the Old Dragon.

'You will have to forgive her blunt remarks.' Farfallen sighed with a strange reptilian smile. His horns shook as he turned his head into the wind. 'The wind feels good today. The snow keeps us cold you see. I think that inside we're all fire and heat, so the north always keeps us cool and comfortable. And the weather is better here too.' He chatted almost conversationally, as if the two were sharing stories and drinks in a tavern. Farden found himself liking the huge dragon, and he smiled. 'Really? I thought Krauslung was bad. But this is far too cold for me.' The mage shivered even as he said it.

Farfallen laughed his deep rumbling chuckle. 'For flying, that is.'

'I suppose that's true.' He nodded and paused. 'I'm glad that you have your tearbook back. Many things happen in war that shouldn't... if you know what I mean,' Farden shook his head at his lack of eloquence.

'I agree. I know that my forces did some terrible things to yours, and vice versa. A king never wants war on his people. If he does then he is a despot, and not a king in the first place, just like the one who sits in the throne of Skölgard. What happened between the Sirens and the Arka is now long ago, and Emaneska forgets.'

Farden simply nodded, and tried not to betray any thoughts of Cheska and her father. He quickly tried to think of a question. 'What's it like? Flying, I mean.'

Farfallen cocked his spiny head to one side for a moment. 'For us it is not about what it is like to fly, but trying to imagine living without it. Think how natural picking up a sword is for one such as yourself. You take it for granted. Now think, without your hand, how much you would miss the feel of a sword in your palm.'

'I once knew an unfortunate dragon who had sadly lost one of his wings during a terrible battle long ago. I forget his name now, but he said living without wings was like seeing without colours, a wash of grey landscapes and charcoal sunsets.' Farfallen solemnly bowed his head, and Farden felt a deep sadness. 'What happened to him?' he asked.

'If memory serves I think he ended up dying from a broken heart. It doesn't happen often to a dragon, but it can. The same happens when we lose a rider we've bonded with. Dragons are born in the air and we die in the air, so without the rush of the wind beneath our wings we feel useless. Like birds, in a way.'

'The flying part sounds intriguing.' Farden squinted at the mountainside and the grey clouds and wondered where the colour was in the first place.

'Ask Svarta, or one of the other riders about it.' It was Farfallen's turn to pause, and he looked at the mage beside him. 'What is it like?'

Farden looked confused. 'What?'

'Being a Written.'

Farden was surprised that the Old Dragon would want to know about him and his kind. He tried to put the feeling into words, and realised he had never had to explain it before. Even Durnus had never asked him. 'It's difficult,' he said. 'You can feel the power burning on your back when you cast a spell, or the sensation of the magick rushing through your veins. But then at other times it's intangible. You can't grab at it or hold it, like a dim star you can only see when you look to the side of it. Sometimes you wake up at night with a dizzy feeling when it rushes through your head. But it's dangerous, and some say that it's more of a curse than a blessing, but we're sworn to strict rules to keep others safe.'

'What are they?' asked the dragon, and Farden absently clicked his knuckles as he stared at the landscape. 'Not to breed, especially with another Written. Not to let anyone read our Book...' There was an awkward moment, and the mage looked up at Farfallen. 'And for that I apologise,' he said. But the Old Dragon shook his head slowly. 'It was his own doing. I saw that, as did Svarta. She might not admit it, but there is a lot of blame to be shared between our countries. Please, go on.'

Farden shrugged. 'Whichever way you look at it we're sworn to a life of service to the Arka, one that either ends in death or madness.' The dragon kept staring at him, taking in all the mage had to say. Farden looked into his giant eyes. He suddenly found himself talking openly to the dragon, as if they were old friends. Farfallen seemed to be a golden rock of common sense, and for some reason he felt like he could tell this giant dragon anything. His lips kept moving. 'My uncle was one of the unfortunate ones. After thirty-three years fighting for the Arka, his mind started to slip and the magick started making him see things and hear noises. It kept him awake for days on end and he ended up going mad. He convinced himself that there were things in the darkness trying to kidnap him, and he told everyone that there was a daemon trying to control him. So, one day he went out into the streets of Krauslung and killed a man for no reason. Ripped him apart and painted the walls with his blood. It was chaos. Later that morning they caught him trying to scale the city walls with a rope. He was stark naked, and had bitten the tips of his fingers off and scratched words into his arms. The last time I saw him he was being hauled away to the prisons in shackles, shouting and spitting, biting at the guards who carried him.' Farden stared at the snow.

'What happened to him?' The dragon asked quietly.

'He was cast out of the city, banished from the Arka, and sent out into the wilderness with a blanket and a gold coin.' Farfallen looked confused, so Farden explained. 'It's not the first time one of the Written has lost their minds, so when a mage gets to a certain age the council starts to watch him or her closely, to see if they act strange or different. It only happens to about one in every three Written, so it's a risk we all take when we go through the Ritual. And if you are one of the unlucky ones, like my uncle was, then you're exiled. Tradition states that you're given a blanket for the cold, and a gold coin to use however you see fit. If an exile tries to get back into the city, then it's an instant death sentence. It's been like that for centuries... that's just the way it is for us. So we fight, and we fight hard and fearlessly, and hope that death comes to us quicker than the madness does,' said the mage. He closed his eyes to feel the wind on his skin.

'It seems like a heavy weight to bear, Farden.'

'Sometimes it is. Sometimes I don't even think of it at all. The way I see it, I was born to fight for the Arka, and so fight I will. It's just hard when you have people who care about you and worry what you do.' The mage flexed his fingers and looked at the dirt under his nails, finding Durnus's words coming out of his mouth. He hoped the dragon could not feel the anger under his skin, the rage that burnt there. He thought of Beinnh, and the people he had killed. There was silence for a moment.

'There is one that cares about you more than the others I take it? A female?' Farfallen squinted. Farden didn't say anything, and kept his eyes straight ahead. 'I don't mean to pry, Farden, and your secrets are safe, but I can feel it burning inside you,' said the dragon.

Farden didn't speak for a moment, and then nodded. 'Any sort of romance, however brief, is against the law for us. So we keep it secret, and hope that one day, if we both live that long, we can find a way around it.'

'A fire burns more intensely when it is covered up, mage,' said Farfallen, and the simple truth of his words made Farden think. But the Old Dragon quickly changed the subject. 'It is strange how different our two peoples are. The way you treat magick for example. To the Arka magick is something you can learn through reading a book or a spell, something you can carve into skin. But for the Sirens it's more natural, a hereditary gift rather than a skill. They all have some magick in them, but it is an innate magick that leaks from the dragons. Have you ever wondered about why Sirens have scales like us?' asked Farfallen. The mage shook his head. 'It is the dragons. Living too close to us for too long can change a person in odd ways.'

Farden nodded, abruptly realising that was why every rider had the same colour scales as their partner. 'I could feel it as soon as I walked into the hall.'

'Not everyone does, but anyone that spends a long time in the company of dragons will feel it eventually, and by the time they realise it, they've already been changed.'

Farden thought about it. 'Maybe that's why our people have been fighting so long.'

'Perhaps. I have always been curious at the way you treat magick like a secret art, a power that must be controlled and carefully guarded from others by your council, like it's a treasure to be locked away. But I suppose on a level many Siren wizards envy the ease with which you Arka can control and bend the magick to your will,' said Farfallen with a sniff.

'I don't think I've ever thought about it like that,' the mage admitted. 'Some say we caught the magick at sea, while the Arka were just a race of fishermen, others say it came from our goddess Evernia, or the Scribe, but either way, you have a point.' He stretched and yawned. Tiredness seeped into the spaces behind his eyes and even though evening was swiftly approaching, he found himself blinking and squinting in the snowy light. He wondered how it was still so bright when he couldn't even see the sun.

'Down there, to your left, is a small room that our old servant used to occupy. It's warm, and I hear the bed isn't that uncomfortable.' The dragon flashed his weird reptilian smile again, baring a few knife-like teeth. 'Rest for now, and by tonight I think it will be time for me to see it.' He held the mage's gaze a few more seconds before turning back to face the wafting waves of cold wind on his gold face. 'Oh and something else survived the shipwreck besides you. It's in your room,' the dragon said without looking at him.

Farden nodded, slightly confused, said his thanks, and headed towards the little door hiding between the rock and the edge of the big balcony. It was unlocked, and as he pushed it forward he heard a little mewing noise, and saw a black shape trotting across the floor towards him. It was Lazy, the ship's cat. Farden was speechless, but even so he crouched down and let the little cat nibble at his fingers and rub itself against him, watching her intently. The cat must be as lucky as he was, he thought, and shook his head in disbelief. She rumbled with a happy purring, and watched him remove his cloak and tunic. The mage collapsed weakly onto the small bed and into a tangled mess of deep thoughts and cold pillows. Lazy settled down somewhere near him and fell asleep instantly.

Farden thought of dragons in the sky and dragons on the ground, and then he thought of flying, wondering whether dragons slept at all, or how they would never need a flint or tinder to light a fire for their rider, and what it must feel like to snort and breathe fire as if it were just simple air, not forgetting of course how beautiful it was to watch them fly, how they made picking up a fork look harder than merely jumping into the air, and how these were the true dragons, not just simple worms of the wilderness hunting magick. It was like what Durnus had said years ago, about dragons living for hundreds and hundreds of years, that they just keep going and going and going and going like the snowfall outside that small circular window near the door, grey and drifting like dust on his pillow…

Farden had never slept a deeper sleep.

chapter 8

"Never not to understand the beast,
for takes one bite, evermore curs'd to feast.
All morality and goodness, fair well to silver moon,
For evil take thee, wolf claws and doom."
Lycan curse

A banging awoke him. A persistent, resolute knocking that stubbornly shook his recently acquired door. The blankets tugged at him to get up, and his eyes snapped open to see a boring stone ceiling. It told him to stop staring and answer the door, so he did.

Svarta stood behind it with her arms crossed. It was now night time and the low yellow light of a nearby torch cast angular shadows across her face, accenting her stern expressions of impatience. 'I have been knocking for a long time,' she said.

'I'm sorry, I was asleep. Look, by now you must know I'm not here to harm anyone, so why can't we just forget that you want to lock me up in a cell and start over?' The Siren merely stared at him and frowned. 'Do you want to come in or something?' He asked.

She snorted and turned around to walk away. 'We don't have time for your games, mage. Follow me, and be quick about it.'

Farden smirked to himself and adjusted his rumpled clothing. He smoothed his hair back into some sort of socially acceptable order and rubbed the last vestiges of sleep from his eyes. He noticed his sword and Scalussen vambraces had been returned. He decided against taking the blade but slid the pair of vambraces onto his wrists. The metal contracted slowly around his skin with slithering whispers like a coiled snake wrapping tightly around a tree. Farden smiled. A new pair of surprisingly comfy boots had been left by the door, so he put them on. His red scarf was nowhere to be seen however, and he wondered if Cheska would mind. He had been through a shipwreck, after all. Farden then turned, ruffled Lazy's ears, and slammed the door with a bang.

'Who's *we*?' he called after the tall Siren.

The mage followed Svarta back through their huge room and out into the cavernous corridor once again. They meandered through long, seemingly endless, identical hallways that curved through the mountain like the tunnels of some monstrous rabbit warren. Farden felt completely lost already in the grand palace, but he held his tongue during the walk and walked slightly behind Svarta. She was silent and brooding, occasionally throwing him a look to see if he were still there.

After a while the mage and the Siren reached a tall set of iron doors and Svarta stopped abruptly and swivelled on one heel to face him.

'If it were up to me you wouldn't even be standing here. But Farfallen thinks there is some sort of good in you, and wishes you to be here for the reading. I for one think you should be kept under lock and key and watched like a dangerous animal. *If* it were up to me, of course.' Svarta cocked her head to one side.

'Of course,' Farden nodded and mentally rolled his eyes.

'Don't be clever with me, mage,' she snapped.

'If I had wanted to hurt anyone, then believe me I would have

done it already. If Farfallen trusts me then maybe you should too.'
Farden stared defiantly into her yellow eyes. Svarta's lips curled into
a reptilian snarl and she spun back around. She pushed against the
doors and with a huge creaking scrape they swung open.

A few torches glimmered in the shadows, trying to throw
their meagre light out into the cavernous hall as best they could.
Behind them the doors closed with a long echoing thud and Farden
tried blinking his eyes to adjust to the gloom. Between the spots
dancing in front of his vision and the yellow flickering of candles, he
could discern a massive shape at the end of the room. Farfallen
crouched in the shadows, eyes closed and quiet like an elaborate
statue.

He felt Svarta close to his ear, whispering. 'Unless someone
asks you a question, you are to be silent in this room.'

Farden nodded and took his place a dozen paces in front of
the silent dragon. He looked up at the faraway stone ceiling held high
above them by the many thick stone pillars stacked around him, like
uniform grey trees. The hall was bare, with no decoration or furniture,
and only a small shrine sat against the back wall behind Farfallen, a
powerful looking statue of what looked like something half man, half
dragon. The alabaster figure sprouted arching wings from his back
and a thick spiny tail curved around stone clouds that formed his
pedestal. Small candles hid in niches or danced gleefully in small
metal holders, sparkling for their deity, Thron, the Siren weather-god.

'Bring the book!' Svarta called to the shadows, and soon a
small man shuffled from the darkness holding the tearbook, looking
for all the world like a shrivelled shrew with glasses set into his
wrinkly face. The bespectacled man put the thick tome on a low stone
table under the dragon's chin and then backed away into the darkness.
As he did so, Farfallen opened his eyes, and Svarta moved forward to
the table and grudgingly beckoned the mage to follow. Farden did so
silently and became aware of a low hum that seemed to be coming

from the dragon, like the rumble of a distant avalanche.

Svarta turned the book over so that its back cover was facing upwards, and turned to the last page slowly. Farfallen flicked one eye to look at Farden. 'Tearbooks go backwards. The start is the first memory a dragon has, the last are the most recent,' he rumbled. A single tear rolled from the golden orb and coursed its way with agonising slowness down his scaly jaw line. The single tear quivered on the very end of his chin and hung for a long second before dropping quietly onto the book.

Farden looked down at the pages and saw them quiver with energy. Nothing happened for a moment, and then slowly, as Svarta closed her eyes and lifted the page ever so slightly, a rune slowly appeared. It was swiftly followed by another, and yet another, until the page had been completely turned. The strange foreign lettering that Farden couldn't even begin to understand kept writing itself across the next page and then the next after that, filling up every inch of blank paper. The letters danced over and over themselves, every invisible quill-stroke scurrying across the page like sand through an hourglass word by spidery word. As Svarta's page-turning became quicker, so did the letters. The lines soon scrolled across the flying pages and Farden could see the dragon's eyes twitching as he tried to follow the writing at the same pace. The mage wondered if Svarta would slow down, but her practised hand movements only sped up. The sound of her hand on the pages grew to a flurry of little papery whip-cracks that echoed around the hall.

Suddenly she stopped, and the writing slammed to a halt, letters bunching up messily at the first line as their momentum carried them forward. As slowly as she had opened the book, Svarta closed the front cover and her eyes locked with her dragon. He made a deep rumble and her neck twitched involuntarily. The next moment she relaxed and nodded and then clicked her long fingers high above her head. Once again from the shadows, shuffling inch by inch, came the same old man with the crystal spectacles. With the same deliberation and overall speed he carefully picked up the tearbook, turned, and disappeared into the shadows once more.

Farden was confused. Svarta fixed him with her usual condescending stare. 'Feel privileged, mage. Never before has an outsider watched a dragon rebond with his tearbook.'

'I'm honoured.' He said this to Farfallen.

'I can feel the memories flowing through me again. I had not realised how much had been lost to me; names, places, kings and queens, all coming back to me now...bit by bit.' The Old Dragon drew a long breath in through his nose and closed his eyes.

Farden watched him as he held it for an impossible time, and then finally he exhaled a blast of red-hot breath from each nostril. The air rippled like the heat from a blacksmith's forge. 'A long time has passed since I last breathed fire, far too long a time for a dragon.' He pushed himself up and sat upright, making his scales undulate hypnotically in the candlelight. Rearing his spiny head, Farfallen took a deep breath of air and spewed forth a deafening blast of searing fire that curled around pillars and licked at the granite ceiling. Heat bathed the two standing at his side, and Farden's eyes were wide with awe. Svarta even looked happy for a change, managing to clasp her bony hands together in what he could only guess was delight. Farfallen roared again and Farden had to cover his ears to avoid the pain. Echoes danced around the chamber like winter waves on a shore, but slowly the pillars stopped humming and vibrating, and the Old Dragon returned to crouching in front of the shrine. He closed his eyes once more and was silent.

Svarta tugged at the mage's sleeve and headed slowly for the door. She whispered to him while they walked. 'Come, I'll show you where the kitchen is. I assume the Written eat?'

Farden's eyes burnt with the after-image from the bright fire and he rubbed at them to get rid of the dancing dots that swam through his vision. 'We do eat, yes, but only live children.'

'Very funny, mage,' came the reply. 'Enough of your nonsense, let's go.'

'Do you think it will be long before you realise I'm not a spy? It's just I don't think I'll be here for that long you see and…'

'Good,' she snapped and closed the tall doors with a bang. Her fists were clenched by her sides and her chin was high, pointing the way ahead like the scaly bow of a narrow ship. She led the way down another long corridor that looked like all the others. Farden had no idea how anyone could find their way around this place. 'If you think you can toy with me, then you're mistaken. Just because Farfallen has taken a liking to you doesn't mean I have to.'

'What is your problem? What else do I have to do to prove I'm not going to murder all of you in your sleep?'

The Siren queen shot him a murderous look over her shoulder. 'There's something dark inside of you, mage, and I can feel it even if the Old Dragon can't. I won't be comfortable until you're off this island.'

Farden shook his head, and wondered how far he could push her. 'Well what am I supposed to do then, while I'm staying here?'

'Stay in the confines of the palace, and no one will harm you. No Arka has set foot in the citadel in fifteen years, so wandering around the streets is out of the question. I don't want some angry, over-zealous citizen deciding to pick a fight with you. Who knows what would happen with your witchcraft.' Svarta looked the mage up and down with a flick of her head.

'Thanks for being concerned with my safety.' Farden said dryly. Guards stared at him as they passed, and the soldiers holding the doors open watched the two with quiet whispers and not-so-subtle pointing. Maybe Svarta was right: the ceasefire had always been shaky at the best of times. 'Fine, maybe you're right. What happens to the tearbook now?' asked Farden, remembering the Arkmages' words.

'Like the Old Dragon, it must rest,' said Svarta. Farden could hear the effort to stay calm in her voice.

'Well, when can we start reading it then?'

'Soon, mage, enough with this questioning.' She glared at him. Farden scowled. 'Where can I go then? Is there anywhere I can train?'

Svarta stopped in her tracks and whirled around. 'Are you joking?'

Farden set his jaw resolutely and matched her stare. 'No, I'm deadly serious. I've been unconscious for a week and I need to regain my strength.'

'You want me to agree to you practising your dangerous Arka magick in the palace of Hjaussfen?' She was incredulous.

The mage nodded 'Yes, if it's not too inconvenient.'

'By the gods,' Svarta closed her eyes tightly for a second and clenched her fists. She breathed out heavily and spat her words at him. 'Fine, leave it to me.' And with that she turned around and resumed her fast pace.

'Thank you Svarta.'

'Don't thank me, thank Farfallen, his word is law,' she snapped, and shot him a look that would have killed a lesser man. There was an awkward silence, broken only by the smart tap of their footfalls on the rock floor. Farden was slowly realising there was a lot to the Sirens that he had never been told. 'Why Farfallen, why is he king and not one of the others?'

'He's the oldest and goldest of them all. The longer a dragon lives then the golder he gets, much the same as we go greyer with age. The golder a dragon is, the greater his right to rule. The goldest out of all of them is crowned the Old Dragon, and he rules until he dies. A few of the elders in the council are close to his age.'

'How old is he?' Another boyish question.

'We have been bonded for three hundred years, but Farfallen

is close to a thousand years old,' she said.

'You don't look older than forty,' replied Farden. It wasn't supposed to sound like a compliment, but it did, and Svarta merely nodded.

'Whatever power the dark elves left behind gave our ancestors extremely long lives, hundreds of years longer than you Arka...' Svarta said snidely.

'You must be so superior to us peasants.' Farden narrowed his eyes at her and tried to add as much sarcasm to his tone as he could. 'Speaking of the Arka, I need to send a message to the magick council.'

'You can do that after you eat.' No sooner had she said that than the two of them emerged into a long room that roared with the sound of conversation and the clattering of plates. Steam rose from pots and stoves huddling together along the far wall, mingling with cauldrons and trays of food. Farden's stomach did a little turn as the smell of broth, bread, meat, and all sorts of other victuals reached his nose. The tables filling the room were crammed with soldiers and servants. Svarta stood to his right with her arms crossed, her favourite pose. She leant to one of the guards flanking the door and whispered something. He took a quick look at the mage behind her and nodded.

'If anyone should take a disliking to you then these guards will see that you are escorted back to your rooms. I'm warning you Farden, I want no magick whatsoever while you're here in the palace.'

'Fine.' Farden watched several Sirens lift their heads from their bowls and look at him. A hush slowly crept across the room until almost everyone was staring at the strange mage standing in the doorway.

'I'll be in my room if you need me.' Svarta sneered and left, leaving him standing alone in the unfriendliest room he had ever encountered.

Farden sighed and steeled himself to walk towards the food spread out at the back of the room. A hundred pairs of suspicious eyes followed him as he walked, watching their guest navigate his way through tables and chairs. Farden had never felt so unwelcome in all his life; wandering through the towns of Albion was bliss compared to this.

Still, he persevered and reached the back wall. A cook fixed him with a disgusted look and shoved a plate into his hands. It was followed by some roast fish, a dollop of watery stew, and a brown bread roll. He nodded his thanks at the silent man and turned around. Everyone was still staring at him.

'What?' Farden shouted.

It seemed to work, and many of the Sirens returned to their meals and carried on their conversations quietly. The mage sighed again and found a place to sit up against one of the walls of the long room. The people sat nearest to him cast a few wary, untrusting scowls in his direction but Farden just busied himself with his plate of food and tried not to cause any further disruption to the mess hall.

The fish was oily, but tasty, and he found himself ravenously tearing at the bread with both hands, previously unaware of how hungry he had been. He finished his whole plate in double time and after deciding against licking the plate clean of stew he leant back against the wall and tried to relax. A torch fluttered above his head and his rambling thoughts mingled with the flickering flames until he was staring blankly into space. Tiredness crept over Farden's body like a snail, and he could feel the warmth from the fire and the torch seeping into his bones. He was getting too old for this business, he thought.

The mage could still feel the unfriendly eyes watching him from the tables nearby. Conspiratorial whispers reached his ears. Gods damn that Svarta, he cursed mentally. Leaving him here alone amongst soldiers that hated him was a sure way to get him into a fight, or worse. Farden would not be baited, not this time. In his peripheral vision he saw a tall figure stand up from a bench and make his way slowly through the chairs and tables crammed with Sirens. Farden closed his eyes and tried to ignore the stares.

'You're the one they found on the beach.' A deep voice interrupted his thoughts. Farden blinked and turned his head to see a very big man in a long brown robe standing with his arms folded into his deep sleeves. The man had lost an eye some time long ago, and a long silver scar ran across over the space it used to be and carved its way down his stubbly face to his neck. His hair was curly, dark, and hung in coiled tendrils over his remaining eye and forehead. Scales decorated his temples and neck, grey and dun-coloured like the granite walls of the palace, and there was something about his scales and the look in his one eye that seemed different to the other Sirens in the hall. He looked at Farden with a solemn, vacant expression.

'The mage?' The stranger asked again.

'I guess so,' Farden put his empty plate on the floor and rubbed his cold hands together. The man towered above him. He must have been at least a head and a half taller than the mage and rippling with muscle.

'Follow me,' the man said and nodded towards the door. The tall stranger's voice was incredibly deep even for a man of his size.

'I'm fine here, thank you. I don't want any trouble.' Farden closed his eyes again and let his head rest against the wall behind him. He heard the man crouch down next to him and lean closer, and Farden could smell the cheap wine on his breath. Magick thrummed at the base of his skull.

'You've come to the wrong place if you want to be left alone, Arka. I suggest you come with me if you don't want to find yourself in a brawl with some of the more unrestrained men.'

Farden's opened one eye and looked at the nearest table of Sirens. The men there whispered and pointed at the mage, one of them holding a fork rather menacingly. The mage considered his options: follow the big stranger or stay in the room with a score of unfriendly soldiers who with utmost certainty all wanted to cave his head in.

'Lead the way,' he sighed, blithely wondering why his decisions always seemed to be made for him, like riding a wild beast over which he held no power or sway. Durnus had always said that was the way of the Written. The man stood up and headed for the door with Farden in tow, much to the displeasure of the murmuring men clustered around the table.

Farden followed the man silently, and picked bits of leftover fish from his teeth. He rubbed his chin and wondered where he could find a blade to shave with. His sword would probably be rusted, he thought. The air was cold outside the warm mess hall, a refreshing change from the stuffy and uncomfortable atmosphere. Farden contemplated going to find Svarta and confronting her but he honestly couldn't be bothered with her foul mood. He coughed to clear his throat and the big stranger turned around questioningly.

'I've heard a lot of rumours about you, Arka, people say you sent one of the healers mad,' he said.

'People seem to be saying a lot of things about me in this place.'

'We haven't seen an outsider in years. Some of the other riders are scared of you, or are instantly hateful of you because of the war. The dragons are just curious.'

'It's the magick in my blood,' Farden said as they jogged down a tall flight of steps.

'Only wild dragons hunt magick, Arka, not the old ones,' the stranger corrected him.

'Are you a rider?' The mage asked.

There was a long pause and Farden wondered if the stranger had heard him. He watched water trickle from a little rockpool on his left.

'Yes I am,' he said finally.

The mage couldn't think of any reply besides an acquiescent hum, so he just turned his attention to where they were going and his surroundings. The corridors were starting to close in and become narrower, rockier and less grand. Springs of water started to appear in little rock pools in the floor. Some hissed at the two men, and others gave off clouds of steam that filled their hallway. Their boots splashed quietly on wet steps and the air had suddenly become hot and humid.

Soon they came to an archway and the stranger pushed a low wooden door set deep into the wall. A strong gust of air made Farden's cloak billow wildly around his legs and snow scattered around his boots as he followed the man out onto a long balcony much like the one in Farfallen's quarters. The sudden cold was bitter compared to the hot steamy corridors inside the mountain. Above him the sky was dark and heavy, streaked with low ashen clouds like the kind that always seemed to hang listlessly in the sky, somehow never moving despite the powerful wind. Stars struggled to find space in amongst the grey furrowed clouds and snow billowed out of the darkness to sting their faces. A burning torch flapped and fluttered nearby, turning the flakes into a swarm of yellow flies that melted instantly as they touched the wet floor.

The stranger headed straight for the railing and stood, shoulders hunched, staring into the night sky. Farden just pulled his cloak around him and stood arms crossed by the door, watching the big man with a wary eye. The stranger pointed a monstrous hand into the air and the mage followed his pointing finger. Above the clouds, in the very darkest parts of the sky, there were streams of light dancing and running across the black canvas. Blues, dusty greens, and charcoal whites swam through the sky like a distant stream that wavered and surged through the stars.

'The Wake,' the stranger said, and Farden could barely hear

him over the sound of the wind. 'The First Dragon is out flying tonight.'

'What do you want with me?' Farden asked the big man. His keen eyes were fixated on the swirling lights above them. He spoke without looking at him. 'Have you killed dragons, mage?'

Farden mentally tensed. 'Only wild ones, on occasion,' he said, choosing his words carefully.

The man made a sucking noise with his teeth. 'That alone is reason for the men to hate you,' he paused, still looking at the sky. 'Farfallen has asked me to watch out for you. Svarta's his rider, but he knows she isn't fond of you.'

'*Fond* isn't actually the word that best describes it.' Farden walked forward slowly and leant his back against the railing, facing the door. The huge mountain slope towered over him, a jet-black silhouette against the obsidian and mica-flecked night sky. Torches shone from a thousand windows and ledges, making the huge mountain look for all the world like a solid island in the sky covered in a myriad of campfires.

'She wants you to prove her right: that you're dangerous and need to be locked away. So by sending you into the sabre-cat's den, if it were, she was hoping you'd provoke a reaction from the other men,' the stranger fixed him with his good eye.

'I am dangerous, but not to anyone here in Hjaussfen. I'm on a peaceful mission...for once,' said Farden with a humourless chuckle at the back of his throat. He turned to look at the murky darkness of the slopes spread beneath them.

'Mhm, Farfallen's told me,' the man nodded and wiped some snow out of his curly hair.

'Who are you, anyway?' Farden asked.

'My name is Eyrum, partner of Longraid.' The man bowed his head and put a hand to his chest in a formal greeting.

'Good to meet you, I'm Farden,' the mage returned the bow

and smiled at his new ally.

'Well met and good wishes, Farden. The Old Dragon speaks highly of you, which is, needless to say, strange under the circumstances of your arrival. They say you were washed ashore after a storm?'

'I was.'

'Then it's a miracle that you survived the freezing waters, the weather-god must hold you in high favour.' Eyrum said in his deep solemn tone.

A distant flash amongst the low clouds caught Farden's eye. 'Another storm?' He asked, pointing at the sky. Eyrum squinted and another flash of light flickered on the horizon. 'No, something else entirely. Wait,' said the big man. He put a finger and thumb to his wrinkled brow. After a second he nodded to a silent reply. 'Give him a moment.'

Farden was slightly confused, but as he scanned the skies he discerned a jet-black shape darting under the low clouds. 'Is that your dragon?'

Eyrum shook his head silently and wiped more cold snow from his face. Farden hoisted his hood over his wet hair and shrugged the precipitation from his shoulders.

The dark shape swooped in a low dive to glide over the foothills far below them. Farden watched avidly and with bated breath as the object dropped further and further until it seemed to be flying mere inches above the jagged black rocks of the mountain. The big man stepped back from the railing and Farden felt he should do the same. There was a moment of silence as the shape disappeared from their view, and then suddenly a gigantic gold shape tore past the balcony with incredible speed. The thunderclap from Farfallen's massive wings was deafening and the blasts of air almost pushed the two men to the ground. The dragon climbed vertically into the night sky and pirouetted on one wing tip. Just as Farden thought the dragon would tumble from the air he somersaulted and dove for the balcony, tucking his wings in tight to his flanks like a peregrine falcon. The mage backed away towards the door, but Eyrum didn't move. It looked like Farfallen would plummet headlong into the rocks, but at the very last second his wings burst open and the dragon stopped in midair spreadeagled, gently letting his whole gargantuan weight rest like a feather on the stone railing. His claws retracted and made a little scrape on the stonework. Farfallen gave his strange reptilian smile and a tiny flame escaped from one nostril.

Farden grinned and moved closer to the dragon. 'You seem happy, maybe that tearbook has done you some good.'

Farfallen laughed with a frighteningly deep rumble and scratched his spiky chin with a claw. 'Maybe it has, mage, and I have you to thank for bringing it back to me. It has been many a year since I felt this good, like a burst of power I have not tasted in too long.'

'It was the magick council that agreed to send me here with the book.' Farden said quietly and thrust his cold hands deep into his pockets.

'And I wonder who suggested that the tearbook should be returned in the first place...?'

Farden was dumbfounded. 'How did you...?'

'There are many things about dragons you have yet to learn Farden.' Eyrum said from beside him. The mage had realised that there was a lot more to the Sirens and their dragons than he had first thought. They were nowhere near as barbaric as the Arka had portrayed them in the war; they were fierce warriors, agreed, and had fought with tooth, nail, and flame in battle, but now he could see that they were older and much wiser than his own people were. He felt guilty suddenly, and dismissed that train of thought like a traitorous slave and turned his attention to a more pressing matter. 'Have you found anything in the tearbook yet?' he asked.

'My memories are long, Farden. Once the tearbook is ready,

it may take many days for our scholars to find the location of an elven well, if one even exists at all.' Farfallen said.

'We can't rule that out. What happens if you're wrong and the creature is summoned? Even if the Sirens and the Arka fought it together I still doubt we…'

Farfallen shook his head. 'So you have said Farden, but the scholars have a thousand years of my life to sift through. Needless to say it is not a quick process.'

Farden found himself frustrated and impatient, but he knew Farfallen was right. 'Gods damn it,' he cursed and clenched his fists inside his pockets.

'Come, Svarta told me you wanted to train. Maybe it'll help you blow off some steam.' Farfallen smiled again.

'Hmm, speaking of Svarta…' Farden began, but the Old Dragon interrupted by holding up a single claw.

'I am aware of what she did, and I will talk to her in good time. You must understand she is doing what she thinks is best for our people.' Farfallen said.

'I know, and luckily you had the foresight to send Eyrum here to keep me out of trouble.' The big man to his right nodded slowly.

Farfallen edged closer to the railing and began to stretch his wings out with a satisfied groan. 'Eyrum will take you to a room where you may practise your magick. I will meet you there shortly.' And with that he flapped his huge golden wings, threatening to blow the two men from the balcony, and launched himself into the dark sky. Eyrum headed towards the doorway and Farden followed him back into the steamy corridors.

'One more time, and keep it the same level.' Farden grinned, wiping sweat from his brow, and braced himself against the wall.

Farfallen took a deep breath once more and crouched low to the floor. The great dragon closed one golden eye, took a deep breath, and a stream of fire exploded from his jaws. With lightning speed Farden threw his open hands out to meet the blast and an invisible wall slammed into the fiery onslaught mere inches in front of his fingers. Ferocious flames swirled around him and licked at his boots, but his invisible bubble held strong against them. Farden clenched his teeth and pushed harder so that the fire receded a few more inches.

Farfallen stopped and drew himself up to laugh heartily. 'Impressive, mage!' Farden breathed hard, and ran a hand through his hair. He flexed his fingers and a spark flashed across his skin. It felt good to have his magick back, he smiled to himself. 'How many are there of you now?' asked the dragon.

Farden thought. 'About a hundred, I think, maybe more. Not everyone who goes through the Ritual can actually survive it, and about half the candidates die.'

'And are they all as powerful as you?' Eyrum asked. He was standing behind and to the right of Farfallen, arms behind him. His face was expressionless, and he cocked his to one side as the Sirens have a habit of doing.

'Well, some are,' the mage shrugged. Farden had always thought of himself as simply *skilled*, rather than powerful. Compared to those of the Arkmages or Vice, Farden's spells were almost unrefined. They were the masters, and Farden, even thirteen years after his ritual, was still learning. But out of the Written, he was one of the best.

Farfallen turned his head to look at the tall silent man and smiled. 'I think Eyrum here has a few tricks of his own.' The quiet Siren shook his head and mouthed a refusal, but the dragon was not to be discouraged. 'Come now, friend, show Farden that it is not just the Arka who possess magick skills.'

'Sire it has been years since I have tried,' Eyrum mumbled

and looked around him to avoid the golden stare.

'And I am sure it will come back to you,' Farfallen looked at Farden and winked again. 'It's just like riding a dragon: you never forget.'

'My knowledge of Siren wizards is limited,' said Farden.

'I suppose you never fought any in the war? Only dragons?' Eyrum's tone had become icy.

'I never fought in the war, I was still in training.' Farden avoided the subject of killing dragons under the current company.

Eyrum untied the belt on his brown robe and cast it aside. 'Well then, cast one of your fire spells at me mage and let us see what happens,' he said, and walked to the centre of the hall.

Farden looked at the serious look in the Siren's eyes. 'Are you sure?' Eyrum simply nodded. The mage relished the challenge and so he stepped back against the wall once more and slammed his wrists together with a clang. His hands were held in front of him, curled fingers formed like a cage around nothing but air. A spark ignited and suddenly a swirling sphere of fire spun between his palms and the mage slowly drew his hands apart and spread his sturdy legs. The ball grew and raged like a trapped sun and the room tingled with heat as the fire storm hung between his hands. With a swift movement the mage spun on one foot and hurled the fireball at Eyrum, who stood dead still about forty paces from him.

Just as the fire ball was about to blast the Siren into charcoal, Eyrum simply shifted, without any obvious movement at all, and simply became a blur of a man, sliding sideways across the stone floor and dodging the flames. The fireball exploded against the opposite wall with a crash and a roar, cracking the stone and making it glow under the flames.

Farden was stunned. Eyrum now stood with his hands clasped behind his back a short distance from his previous spot, a satisfied grin threatening to creep across his scarred face. Farden grinned back at him and took a wide stance again. Sparks danced along the mage's arm and a bolt of lightning tore through the air. Eyrum merely sidestepped again and suddenly ended up a dozen paces to the left in the blink of an eye, his big bulk blurring with incredible velocity.

'Speed magick.' Farden said with an impressed smile. 'One of the few schools of magick that we Written never learn.'

Eyrum nodded again and looked to Farfallen. 'It comes from the nomadic people in the east, far off in the deserts of Paraia where they learn to catch strange tall deer that can run like the wind. My dragon, Longraid, would fly there to dodge through the dunes and canyons for sport.'

'She said that the creatures there tasted better than anything else. She loved to hunt the massive desert cats and the sand worms.' Farfallen rumbled his agreement and a moment of silence followed. Farden sensed something deep and sorrowful in the room. He could only try to imagine what it must be like to lose a dragon, or a rider, and he felt a genuine sympathy for the man.

'I'm sorry, Eyrum, for your dragon,' the mage offered, feeling awkward.

The Siren looked at him with a surprised expression for a moment, and then bowed his head low in gratitude. Farfallen chuckled with a low growl. 'Did I not tell you, Eyrum, that not all the Arka were as heartless and cruel as you thought?'

chapter 9

*"When the elves left, Emaneska was left to fend for itself amidst the
darkness and chaos that remained behind. And it was at this turbulent
time that three great nations abruptly appeared amidst the Scattered
Kingdoms.*

*"The first and greatest, the warlike Skölgard, seized the lands of the
northeast. For a hundred years they carved out their vast empire,
ruling all from Gordheim, the City of Waterfalls, on the eastern
shores. The second, the small sailing nation of the Arka, finally chose
to settle in the Össfen Mountains. They used their trade routes and
seafaring abilities to become rich and powerful, meddling in the
matters and affairs of the old magicks. The third, and most mysterious
of them all, were a more ancient and proud race, born from the dark
vestiges left by the Elves. These were the dragon-riders, the Sirens, a
strange civilisation bonded to the great dragons of the north, reptilian
in their appearance and just as fierce. They built their capital in the
ice-locked fire lands of Nelska, tunnelling deep into the mountains to
carve out their cities. Their magick was of a different ilk, more
natural than that of the bold and flashy Arka.*

*"What was strange about these three great nations? Was it not their
wild differences, their abilities and cultures? No, Emaneska has never
longed for simplicity. It was however, how quickly these simple
peoples managed to rise above the Scattered Kingdoms, to become
unified and powerful, a force beyond even the most hopeful dreams of
Halôrn, or the Dukes of Albion, or even Rassmuen. These mere*

kingdoms and fiefdoms would remain subdued and quiet, servants to
the very whim and machinations of these three great nations. "
Taken from 'The Scars of Emaneska', by the critic Áwacran

Farden had gone to bed early that morning, just as the first
fingers of dawn were reaching over the mountainous horizon. In the
candlelight of Farfallen's cavernous hall they had sipped warm wine
and dark spirit under the gaze of the half-man, half-dragon weather-
god, Thron. They had talked for hours. Farfallen had regaled them
with stories of battles and great men far into the early hours and
Eyrum had become almost jovial. Farden had not been able to tear
himself away from the Old Dragon, his tales and deep tones had been
engrossing. But finally they had retired to bed, and the mage quietly
managed to dodge Svarta when she rose to go about her morning
business.

The curtains in his room had done their best to keep the
bright sunlight out, but now, as the fiery disc began to reach its zenith,
the thick cloth glowed with pale yellow light. The mage turned with a
groan and threw a pillow over his eyes while sleep began its slow
retreat. His mouth tasted like dried wine and he found himself again
ravenously hungry. A small voice inside his head thought about trying
to find some nevermar before he left for Krauslung, but he told it to
be quiet. Lazy yawned at him, twitched her whiskers, and went back
to sleep.

After a few minutes of dozing Farden hauled himself out of
the sheets and went out onto the balcony. Sunlight burst through an
almost cloudless sky and stung his eyes, and the white of the newly
fallen snow covering the wide ledge didn't help matters. He gathered
some in his hands and spread the cold ice over his face and neck to
try to wake himself up. As his eyes adjusted to the bright day, Farden
covered his brow with a cupped hand and stared up at the reptilian

shapes wheeling overhead like massive vultures, black against the bright sky. They trumpeted and bellowed and called to one another, and he thought he could hear the muffled shouts of their riders even from far below.

Farden went back into his room and found a fresh tunic laid out for him in one of the wooden cupboards, so he changed and polished his boots before leaving. Wind tugged at his cloak as he walked across the snowy balcony. Farden was curious to find out if this country ever grew warmer, but it was winter after all, he reminded himself, and shrugged resolvedly and rubbed his hands together. His gold and red vambraces knocked together with a muted clang.

Inside on a dining table he found a big bowl full of fruits, some of them strange and foreign to him, but he ate them all the same, with a few slices of bread that had been left on the side. Maybe Svarta had poisoned the food, he wondered, but he was too hungry to care, and munched on. He pulled his cloak about him and decided that if he wasn't allowed in the citadel, then he should at least wander through the palace.

Farden spent the rest of the afternoon aimlessly ambling through the long identical corridors carved into the rock of the huge mountain. The citadel of Hjaussfen seemed to be a complex warren of polished stone hollowed out from the volcanic leftovers of the mountain and her foothills. Every hallway was arched and tall enough for the biggest of dragons, and wide too. The walls ranged from glossy black marble to flecked and veined granite, and Farden let his hand run over the surface of the smooth walls. From some of the windows he found he could peer down into the craters and crags of the city and watch the hustle and bustle below. Long roads spanned the wide gaps high above the houses and streets, and towers of black stone watched over the noisy thoroughfares crammed with people, cattle, goats, and other strange beasts for sale. Farden's keen eyes picked out a few sabre-cats gnawing at their cage bars with long deadly white teeth. He could hear their roars even from high above them in the towering mountain. The bright colours of the houses and the markets stood out against the drab greys and blacks of the rock. The mage saw a few dragons wandering through the paved streets. They shone like jewels in the sunlight. Every Siren bowed out of their way and let them pass while their riders sat on top of them, just behind the base of the neck, lounging backwards against their rippling shoulders and saddle and nodding solemnly to the people passing by. Farden watched for a while longer, and then wandered on.

The mage found some more food in a smaller mess hall that was mostly empty. The few cooks that were there stared at him with the classic mixture of fear and curiosity. The mage tried to ignore their stares and took his lunch with him to eat while he was walking. Most of the other people in the citadel just ignored him, but there were a few wary glances from the soldiers at the guard posts. They let him pass nonetheless, and none of the other soldiers, scribes, slaves, or riders that saw him bothered him in any way. Svarta's new orders, obviously, he smirked to himself.

The palace seemed abuzz with activity. Farden had no idea what was going on so he just carried on eating the bread and cheese he had gleaned from the kitchens and kept walking.

The mage soon found himself in the great hall to which he had been dragged only a day before. The sound of Sirens working and talking was a roar. A few dragons perched in their nests high up on the walls, their greens, blues, and reds sparkling in the daylight that streamed through the holes in the roof. Everywhere around him tables had been brought in and assembled and covered with scrolls, maps, books, and tomes. Hundreds of busy scribes pored over them. Men and women in white tunics and robes dashed around with parchment clenched in their fists and eagerly ran from table to table. Farden had never seen such madness. A white and yellow dragon flapped into the hall through the huge window and hovered high above them near the ceiling. It spun into a slow spiralling descent and came to rest gently beside the mage, who stood eating and holding his plate in one hand. Farden watched the dragon fold its wings and bow its head. It then closed its eyes and spoke with a low gentle voice.

'Well met and good wishes, Farden, I am Brightshow, partner of Lakkin. The Old Dragon, in all his wisdom, has sent for every scribe and scholar in the city to come and search through every historical account we can find. Some of the older dragons have leant their tearbooks to be scrutinised, in the hope that we can find this dark elf well of yours,' she said. Her flanks glittered with her white and gold-yellow colouring.

The mage bowed back. 'Good to meet you Brightshow, I take it Farfallen isn't worried about keeping this matter a secret then? What if there are spies amongst these people?'

'Farfallen has seen to that my good mage, some of our dragons have spent years honing their skills at reading the hearts and minds of men. Those ones above us, you see? They watch over these men and the soldiers, making sure that they are all as loyal as they should be,' Brightshow pointed to the three dragons perched above them with a claw, and Farden shook his head with a smile.

'You dragons never cease to amaze me,' he confessed.

'We are an ancient race blessed by the gods, Farden, but it is you men who will inherit Emaneska when we are gone.' She smiled and stretched a patchy wing. 'But not yet,' added the dragon.

Farden smiled politely. 'So,' he said, as he finished off the last of his meal. 'What now?'

'For now we let the scholars do their work, and we can get you a hawk to send a message to the Arka with all speed. Unless, of course, you can read dragonscript and feel like helping?' Brightshow smiled.

'Hah, not me, I can barely read my own writing.' Farden

laughed.

'Then allow me to fetch one of the scribes to get a messenger bird ready for you,' she beckoned to a few soldiers near to them and the armoured men clattered off into the corridors to do the dragon's bidding.

Farden watched the hustle and bustle of the great hall with amazement. At the end of every desk and table piles of useless and unhelpful scrolls were slowly growing. Pages and parchments covered every surface and rustled like the sound of a forest during a gale. Every scholar was hard at work, and even some of the soldiers were trying to make sense of the spidery dragonscript lettering covering the thousands and thousands of pages. Somewhere in the forest of tables and scrolls, was Farfallen's tearbook, slowly revealing its lost knowledge, the mage hoped. A splash of colour caught his eyes.

Decorating the smooth granite walls between the dragon nests and the many archways and corridors leading from the hall were little frescoes and wall paintings that were dotted around the hall at ground level. Farden wondered how he hadn't noticed them the first time. Most were faded with age and sunlight, but some were still perfectly coloured, beautifully chiselled and painted murals depicting great battles, heroic-looking dragons, strange ancient beasts, some of which Farden had never seen before, and great landscapes of ice and snow that seemed as real as looking out of a window.

The mage left his plate on a nearby stool and made his way through the few tables between him and the nearest painting and ran his hands over its cold dusty surface. Huge grey and brown beasts moved across a frozen landscape, tusks and long trunks towering over the tiny specks of men at their huge feet. Farden had remembered seeing such creatures during a voyage to the south long ago. The men in that foreign land had called them bastions, and their feet had shaken the ground like thunder.

In the next painting sabre-cats, long wingless worms, daemons, giant manticores, and huge rats were locked in an eternal battle, frozen with faces snarling and claws reaching, while in yet another Farden saw gryphons, giants, minotaurs, and even more dragons. They were swarming across a field and battling against gangly grey men-like creatures with long black swords. As he walked the beautiful epic scenes seemed to fade and grow older, illimitable years stretched over rock. Durnus would have given anything to study these pictures. Brightshow rejoined him and stared over the mage's shoulder.

'It's been a long time since I talked with a gryphon,' said Farden.

'There are still some, in the northern wastes, or in the east I hear, but like most of the others on these walls they have long abandoned Emaneska.' A hint of wistfulness had crept into the dragon's voice.

Farden pointed at a picture of a long sea serpent with horns and ridges of spikes sprouting from its head. It was blue in colour, like the waves, and covered in barnacles. In the mural its gigantic tail was drowning a boatful of the same tall grey men, and there was a hungry look in its row of eyes. 'I saw one of these once in the Bern sea. It sank a ship in seconds and then just disappeared under the waves,' he said.

'Leviathans. Good meat if you can get at them. Now these are, or were, phoenixes, distant cousin to the dragon. They were the first of us all to learn how to breathe and live with fire, but the dark elves hunted them all down in the name of sport.' Brightshow showed him a flock of red and orange bird-like creatures. This mural seemed to be one of the older ones. The bright fiery colours of their wings had dimmed long ago but Farden could still spy flames trailing through the sky in their wake.

The mage contemplated the history of the world spread out

on the wall before him, picture by picture, one mural at a time. After one short walk along the wall Farden had travelled at least two thousand years back in time, long before the ice had started to creep across the lands and while simple man was just a nomadic and pathetic race. Unlike the Sirens, the Arka had always hid their histories in libraries and temples, away from the commoner and only for the enjoyment of scholars and the education of the upper classes. But here in front of him he could see the old days, the great days of magick and monsters, where the elves ruled and the Arka were no more than an idea in the back of somebody's mind. Brightshow was right: men would inherit the earth, but only long after the last of these ancient creatures had left or died.

Suddenly Farden was filled with a deep sadness. The world he now knew seemed like a faded painting, a consolation prize, a leftover from a greatness and power that had now faded and been lost. His fingers traced the chiselled grooves of the mural thoughtfully and tried to imagine the older days. The dragon broke his silence.

'Nothing has changed, Farden,' said Brightshow in a soft voice. He could barely hear her over the roar of activity in the hall. 'In another thousand years it will all have changed again, and another like you will be standing here looking at pictures of ancient men and lost dragons. The world moves on. It is the way of things.' Farden nodded, vaguely recalling Farfallen saying something very similar. Emaneska had been here longer than anyone could remember, and it would still be here a thousand years from now. Farden wondered idly if anyone would ever paint a picture of him on a wall, and why. Shadows clouded his mind.

'Come, let us send your message.' Brightshow put a huge paw surprisingly gently on his shoulder and nodded towards a large doorway across the hall. Farden shook himself from his trance and smiled briefly.

They walked out of the hall and up a spiralling set of lofty stairs that led into a tall pinnacle of rock high above the busy hall. Light and snow streamed into the room through long windows carved into the rock. Their ledges were wide and strewn with comfy-looking pillows. Brightshow barely fitted into the small space, so she crouched by the bigger stairwell murmuring uncomfortably. Arranged in a big circle were about a score of cages on high stilts. Birds of prey, all shapes and types, preened and screeched between themselves. They wore little leather hoods with bells on that covered their eyes and kept them calm. Feathers covered the stone floor, and so did little patches of white mess here and there. Farden wrinkled his nose at the smell.

A greying Siren with a wide-gapped grin emerged from behind a tall desk at the back of the room. He looked Farden up and down and tried a lopsided smile. Farden wondered how long he had been left alone, but smiled warmly, and bowed back. His wispy grey hair was like a wild shrub and seemed to explode in all directions. He never seemed to stop moving, not even for a second. He nodded to Brightshow. 'Well met, friends! The guards said you might be coming up to my office, so I have prepared a hawk for you,' said the greying Siren. He seemed very excitable and rushed back and forth with a hobbling gait. He beckoned Farden to follow, and he did. He shooed a few tame sparrows that were perched on a table, and the small birds jumped into the air with annoyed chirping. The old man grabbed a small piece of parchment and a long hawk-feather quill from his cluttered desk, handing it to Farden and tapping the top of the table.

'It's been a while since we sent a message to your kind, sire. Been a long time indeed.' The man's eyes constantly flicked about the room.

Brightshow nodded and looked at the hooded birds of prey in the cages. They had become quiet and shuffled nervously as they caught her reptilian scent on the breeze.

The mage voiced a question. 'Is there a quickdoor in

Hjaussfen?'

With a vigourous nod the old Siren pointed out of the window and to somewhere beyond the rocky foothills. 'Down by the south docks, there's an old one. But I hear it still works.'

'That is, if you don't want to fly.' Brightshow smirked, revealing rows of pointy teeth.

'Maybe one day.' Farden returned the smile. He spread the small bit of rough paper between finger and thumb and dipped the quill. He scratched a brief message in red ink and tiny letters. It stained his fingers as he wrote.

ARKMAGES,

SAFE AND WELL IN THE NORTH, SIRENS PEACEFUL, SEARCHING FOR THE WELL NOW, RETURNING TODAY OR TOMORROW BY QUICKDOOR WITH NEWS. BEWARE SPIES IN MIDST, SARUNN WAS DESTROYED BY A DARK SORCERER AND ALL HANDS WERE LOST. TRUST NO ONE.

FARDEN.

There was no time for ceremony or formality in the message, thought Farden. The Arkmages would understand and hopefully get the quickdoor ready for his arrival. Farden purposefully left out the bit about Farfallen still being alive, as he had decided to tell Vice in private rather than in front of the entire council. He didn't want his friend's reputation to be tarnished.

'These birds will get your message there fast, sire, have no worries. They're a lot faster than your southern hawks I can tell you that,' the grey Siren winked at him. His scales hung from his jaw line like dark brown lichen on a tree.

'Is that so?' Farden humoured the funny old man.

He nodded quickly. 'They're fed on a strict diet of rabbit meat and lightning, makes them fast you see,' The Siren grinned at his own little joke. The mage handed him the scrap of parchment and with a deft little movement the grey man coiled it up into a small tube and twisted the ends tightly. He dipped each end in a pot of green wax that bubbled above a nearby candle. Each end of the scroll was stamped with an ivory signet ring on his finger, in the shape of a feathered wing, and then he whistled piercingly to his birds. Like an arthritic hunting cat he prowled along the front of the cages and looked for one bird in particular. He stopped when he came to a very still and composed hawk that was calmly preening its feathers.

'Aha, here she is, finest and fastest of the lot.' Without any gloves or braces at all the man thrust his skinny arm into the wooden enclosure and reached for his bird. The bell on her hood jangled as she latched onto the scaly arm with her talons and flapped her wings for balance. Her plumage was a soft russet brown flecked with dark spots, with snowy white feathers on her underside that shone in the daylight.

'Come here then, come on.' He talked softly to the hawk and brought her out into the light. 'If you don't mind I have to face her away from you madam, in case she get scared,' said the man to Brightshow, and she simply smiled and nodded.

Farden looked at the proud bird of prey that was perched so gently on the old man's arm despite her razor-sharp talons. The hawk sat tall and still while the man took off her hood and then she shrugged her wings and looked around. Her deep yellow eyes blinked in the sunlight, and then she stared at the mage with an indifferent look. Two long feathers like that of a heron stood out behind her head, and when she spread her wings, the mage could see the long dark pinion feathers shaking as if she were eager to get going already.

With a slender piece of twine the old man fastened the waxy

scroll to the bird's yellow leg and wrapped it over and over in a criss-cross pattern until it was secured safely. The man made sure that the scroll was tight enough yet not causing the hawk any trouble.

The last thing he did was to whisper in the feathery place where the hawk's ears were and then fling her from his arm towards the window. The bird screeched with a thin, piercing wail and then disappeared into the grey sky.

'Thank you,' said Farden.

The jumpy man bowed. 'My pleasure sire, always nice to be of service,' then he bowed again and Farden shook his wrinkled hand.

'Please let us know if and when a reply comes from the Arka,' said Brightshow.

'I will, madam, good wishes to the two of you,' the grey man dipped his head once more and then fidgeted with his hands as if he were unsure of what to do with himself.

Brightshow and Farden went back to the hall, where Farfallen, Svarta, Eyrum, and a few other dragons had gathered in the centre of the huge mass of tables. Svarta seemed angry, but then again Farden had never seen her be any different, and Farfallen looked disappointed and pensive. As they emerged into the light of the great hall the Old Dragon beckoned them closer with a silent wave of his great claws. The mage listened to the loud conversation between his rider and one of the scholars.

'What do you mean weeks?' Svarta asked. The man opposite her was tall and clean shaven, and had obviously drawn the short piece of straw. He was clearly nervous in front of the Siren queen, and her demanding expression and posture frightened him. He blushed through purple scales and he kept smoothing his blonde hair to his forehead anxiously. 'Even the oldest of our tearbooks don't go back as far as the Old Dragon's. As far as we can…er, ascertain, your highness, none of the scrolls or parchments here have hinted at a well, therefore it must be…' he faltered.

'What?' Svarta asked quickly. Her hands were fixed to her hips.

'It must be in your dragon's memories,' the young scholar added quickly, 'and that's the problem, it is taking far longer than we expected…' he gave up again, and pulled at his fringe some more.

'And you're telling me it would take *weeks* to search Farfallen's memories?'

The man looked behind him to his cluster of colleagues, who all bobbed and nodded frantically. One held up a hand. 'It seems so, majesty. The older his memories are the more ancient the translation, and the more difficult it is to read. It is taking us a long time, and so far we haven't found anything at all.'

Svarta huffed, but Farfallen spoke up in his deep booming voice. 'If it will take weeks, then it will take weeks. These men are trying their hardest and we must give them the time to finish their task.' The blonde man relaxed visibly. 'However!' Farfallen held up a claw and flashed a look to Farden. 'Understand that we are all in great danger, and your lives depend on finding this well before it is too late. Do you hear me?' Farfallen looked around with a raised brow and every single scribe and scholar and Siren in the room shouted loudly in agreement and scrabbled to get back to work. The hubbub began again. The Old Dragon turned to leave, and the blonde man was left looking relieved and shaky. He turned back to his little gang and breathed a heavy sigh, with a few pats on his back for good measure.

Farden followed the group of dragons and people as they left the hall, and Farfallen led them down yet another wide corridor to a long room that was missing a wall and open to the sky on one side. The cold wind swirled around the bare space, and the dragons gathered in a little group at the end of the room.

'Well, what now?' Farden asked loudly as he walked towards them, arms spread questioningly.

Farfallen looked at him, and cocked his head on one side like a giant cat. 'Now, Farden, you go home. We will continue to search through my memories and find this elf well. You can have my word that we will send our fastest dragons to you when we have success.' Farfallen said.

Farden shook his head. 'But you said yourself that will take weeks,' he objected.

'Maybe so, but if I and Svarta and the others help them search,' he said with a confident air, 'then you shall have your answer within a week.' The other dragons rumbled in agreement and looked at the mage, their colourful placid eyes gazing down at the man standing before them. 'My memories are flowing slowly back to me, like a brook, but soon I can feel they will be a great torrent in my mind. We can't rush this Farden, and we need to be careful,' and as if reading Farden's thoughts once again, he added, 'and yes, mage, we are aware of the lack of time. We want this as much as you do.'

Farden looked down at the stone floor and fought a long sigh. 'Then I will return to Krauslung. The Arka will need to be ready just in case,' he said.

The Old Dragon smiled. 'Hopefully it will not come to a fight, my good mage. But if it must, then the Sirens will stand beside you.' He looked for a moment to the other dragons before continuing. 'And tell your Arkmages that they can once again call us friends. The war ended a long time ago, and I think it is once again time for us to open our gates.' Svarta shot Farfallen a shocked glance and then, catching herself, she turned to face the mage with an expression of badly hidden anxiety.

Farden smiled and crossed his arms across a chest swelling with pride. 'Thank you Farfallen.'

'Towerdawn here will take you anywhere you want to go.'

Farfallen nodded to a stocky red dragon on his right, and the muscular beast bowed his chin to the floor with a long blink. His scarlet scales rippled in the sunlight and the dark wine-coloured crest running along his spine wobbled.

Farden bowed in return but shook his head. 'Again, thank you, but Brightshow has told me there is a quickdoor at the docks that I can use to get back to Krauslung.'

Farfallen nodded. 'Of course. It is ancient, but I know it still works. I will have one of the wizards open it immediately.'

'Then I will need to go pack.' Farden smiled. Brightshow chuckled behind him.

'Svarta will have some provisions brought up to your room.' Farfallen said, and Svarta nodded tiresomely. Farden bowed and Brightshow followed him out of the door. When they had left the room and were walking back down the corridor, the dragon sighed mockingly. 'Well! It seems we've only just met and you're already leaving.'

'It is a shame!' Farden laughed and shrugged. 'But sadly I have to be getting back to the Arkmages as soon as possible.' He had decided that he would miss Nelska and its dragons.

'I've heard one of your elders has spells that control the weather?' The dragon asked.

'Helyard yes.' Farden murmured thoughtfully, surprised that Brightshow would know that about one of the Arkmages.

'He must have the blood of the daemons in him then, one of the nefalim,' the dragon whispered as though it were heresy to say those words. She sounded like one of the superstitious sailors from the *Sarunn*.

Farden found himself laughing out loud. 'Hah! Now that I would find very hard to believe. He's a powerful mage, yes, but not a daemon, just an angry old man.' Farden shook his head and laughed quietly.

'A man who controls the weather like the gods do should be careful with his anger. He sounds dangerous to me.' Brightshow, as usual with the dragons, made a lot of sense in Farden's ears. He had thought long and hard about a traitor in the midst of the magick council, and more than once the name Helyard had crossed his mind. He would talk about this with Durnus, and Vice, when he got back. He could trust them at least.

'He does, I agree,' Farden mused for a moment. 'Do you think that Farfallen and the others can find that well in a week?'

'If Farfallen gave his word, then it will happen. That dragon doesn't often disappoint.'

'Good, because we'll need all the help we can get to stop those behind all this. I'm just praying that they don't already know where a well is.'

'We would know by now if they did.' Brightshow offered wisely.

'I suppose you're right.' Farden agreed with another shrug.

'And here we are.' Brightshow said. They had come to the large door to Farfallen's rooms, and they paused.

'It was nice to meet you.' Farden said with a smile. Her huge yellow eyes had the same kind gaze the others had and he noticed himself slowly getting lost in them.

'You also,' she said with a slow blink and a slight nod. 'It's time for me to go find my rider, Lakkin, so sadly I won't be able to see you off at the docks.'

'Well, hopefully I will see you in the days to come.'

'Perhaps. Well met and good wishes Farden.' The dragon turned and the mage ducked involuntarily as her long white tail swung high over his head.

Farden went to his little room to gather up the rest of his clothes and armour and spent the next handful of hours in deep thought. The only problem was that the people of the palace seemed intent on knocking on his door and continually delivering provisions and supplies from the Old Dragon. After three hours the mage stood surrounded by parcels of bread, cheese, meats, and fruit, haversacks filled with a mealy cake thing, a small oil lamp, two fresh tunics and a new black cloak, a length of red rope, various maps, a small book entitled *Flight for Beginners,* and an ornate vial of melted snow, for his health obviously.

As soon as he dared to assume he had seen the last of the servants, another dull thudding shook the mage's door. With an exasperated sigh Farden leapt to the door and opened it to find Eyrum standing outside. The big man said nothing and the mage gestured for him to enter and get out of the wind. Eyrum had to stoop to avoid hitting his head on the door frame.

'What brings you to my humble room?' asked Farden with a smile.

'I have a parting gift for you, before you go,' he said solemnly. The mage guessed he wasn't used to this sort of sentimentality and nodded for him to go on.

He took a breath and cleared his throat. His eyes wandered around the room and over the scattered supplies strewn over the bed. 'Seems like you've had enough from Farfallen as it is. That dragon really has taken a liking to you.'

'Gods know why,' chuckled Farden as he gathered and stacked clothes and packets and parcels to stuff into his travel bag. The supply belt around his waist was already full to bursting.

'Even so, I thought you would appreciate this.' Eyrum held out a big fist and slowly opened his fingers to reveal a small glittering object curled up on his palm. The Siren lifted the shiny pendant up by its thin metal chain and offered it to the mage. Farden took it gently and stared at the object. It looked like a thin sliver of a dragon scale, sandy orange in colour and sparkling as though it were encrusted with gold dust and hard miniature jewels. There was a warmth to it, a leftover glow that Farden could feel only if he held the scale tightly in both hands. As he was turning it over in his fingers Eyrum explained.

'When a dragon dies, their scales soak up and hold on to their luck. So if you wear this around your neck it might bring you good fortune in the weeks to come,' the man said quietly. He had hardly moved since first entering the room, he just stood still with his big hands now back in his cloak pockets.

Farden was shocked, and honoured, and confused all at the same time. He instantly handed it back to the big Siren. 'I can't take this Eyrum, it's your dragon…' But Eyrum pushed the mage's hand back, and closed his fingers around the pendant for him.

'I have a feeling you need it more than I do.' He shook his head.

Farden didn't know what to say and just stared at the pendant. A gift was a gift after all. 'Thank you Eyrum.' Farden looked fruitlessly around his room to find something to offer the monstrous man in return. 'I have nothing to give you…'

'No need, mage, it has been good enough to meet you, and to see your impressive display of magick last night. I hope that we have both learnt something while you were in Hjaussfen,' Eyrum said.

Farden smiled. 'I think that a lot of my opinions have changed since being here, and not only about dragons. If only the rest of the Arka would see it through my eyes, see that there's something deeper and more ancient about you scaly lot.'

Eyrum managed a small grin. 'Indeed! Then I think it is a good thing that you were washed up on our shores.'

'Maybe.' Farden mused, noticing that fate had once again manoeuvred his life without his control or blessing. Eyrum moved towards the door. 'I will see you at the docks Farden. The quickdoor should be ready within the next few hours.' He opened the door and let a cold breeze in.

'Thank you again, Eyrum, for the gift,' the mage looped the chain over his neck and slipped the stiff scale under his tunic. The big man said no more and quietly shut the door behind him with a click.

An hour passed, and Farden managed to squeeze the rest of the stuff into the haversack and decided to eat whatever he couldn't fit in. Lazy stretched and yawned by his side, and then got up to sniff around his packages. She looked at him with a strange look, as if she wasn't fond of change, and then sat on the corner of her bed to lick herself. Farden was munching on an apple and a slice of some dark dried meat, which seemed a bit too fish-flavoured for its colour, when yet another visitor knocked on his door.

Still chewing he opened it to find Svarta standing with her arms crossed, her face displaying a familiar annoyed expression. Farden waited to finish his mouthful of apple and looked at her. 'I'm sorry, were you waiting for long?' he said finally.

'Are you ready to go?' she asked.

'Almost, come in.' He walked back inside the room and she followed. Svarta looked around the room and the mess of packing. She eyed the cat with a curious look, and then back at the mage. She pointed a long finger at him.

'Where did you get those vambraces of yours?' she asked. Her voice was quiet and controlled, as if she were forcing herself to be civil with the mage.

Farden looked at the red and gold metal covering his wrists and forearms and wondered whether to lie or not. 'I won them years before the war, when I was hunting in the far north with some of the other Written.'

Svarta crossed her arms. 'Gambling?'

'Sort of. There was an argument that I couldn't win a fight against the champion warrior of some village. These vambraces were his wager, and the skin from my back was mine.' Farden said with a far-off look in his eyes. He could still remember that fight like it had been yesterday, every blow, every scuffle and shout of the crowd, the smell of fear, all of it painted as vividly on his memory as the murals in the dragon hall. A story for another day.

'I take it you won,' she said dryly.

'Clearly.' Farden said no more about it, and busied himself with the heavy sack of supplies and his bulging belt. Tucking the last of the meat back into his pockets Farden swung his sword over his back and strapped it tightly to his chest.

Svarta stood with her arms still firmly crossed. Her two blonde strands of hair framed her frustrated face quite perfectly. Her lips were drawn thin and she held her weight on one foot, tapping the other in some test of patience. Her long dress was shimmering blue that day, crystallised like a frozen waterfall, and the thick leather jacket on her shoulders was dusted with fresh snow. Her face was white from the cold, but the deep yellow smudge of golden scales running over her cheekbones and neck were bright and shining. Farden gave her a questioning look, and then she finally let her restraint snap. 'Look, if you think for a moment that I'm going to let the rest of the Arka traipse all over Nelska again, you've got another thing coming!'

Farden laughed out loud. 'You can't let it go, can you? This was Farfallen's decision…'

'That doesn't matter,' Svarta snapped. She clenched a fist and her blue dress shifted with a rustle. She allowed herself a small sigh. 'It may have been before your time, mage, but my people still haven't forgotten the war, even if the Old Dragon has. It will be a while before we can open our gates wide enough for the Arka.'

'I couldn't care less about that. All I'm concerned about is finding that well before the others do. Farfallen has given me his word,' said the mage.

The Siren queen slowly shook her head. 'And that unfortunately stands for both of us, for his word is mine also.' Her face hardened as if he had challenged her honour. 'You have proven your good intentions to the Old Dragon, and if he trusts you... then maybe one day I will too.' The last remark stung her as she said it, but Farden knew she was trying her best.

He pulled at the straps of his haversack and Svarta moved to the door. Farden ruffled Lazy's sable ears, and looked into the cat's brown eyes. 'Look after my cat, if you can,' he said, and the queen sighed. 'Fine.'

The mage checked he had left nothing behind and moved to join her at the door. He briefly entertained a little excited feeling at the thought of seeing Cheska again, and perhaps, if he was very lucky, getting some well-deserved time alone with her. But the cold snow that suddenly whipped his face stole away his thoughts and he pulled the hood of his new cloak over his eyes. 'Well, you can relax now that I'm going back home,' he said over the noise of the wind, and he could hear Svarta grumbling behind him.

'Unlikely, I have a tearbook to scour through,' she snorted, and slammed the door behind them.

Down at the west docks the weather was no more gracious, and the rimy sea spray stung the faces of the dragons and Sirens on the solitary pier. The sea was grey and as hard as flint, white crests swiping at the frenzied snowflakes falling from iron clouds. The earlier sunlight had gone, and had been replaced by another front of bad weather from the west. Farden wondered if Krauslung was any fairer this day, and involuntarily shuddered from the cold. The Dragons seemed to be loving the foul weather, pointing their snouts into the face of the wind and letting the snow lash their scales. The fires in their hearts must be keeping them warm, Farden thought.

The mage stood beside Farfallen, and in front of them the pier stretched out into the waves, and two thin spurs of black rock formed the gateway of the quickdoor. It thrummed with the energy and sea-spray fizzed into steam on its hazy surface. A wizard, his long red cloak wrapped tightly around him, was calling words from a spell book that looked much like the one that Durnus used. The scribe at his side was no more than a boy, and he shivered through wet clothes while trying to turn the soaking pages for his master.

'Is it ready yet?' one of the dragons called from behind them. Farfallen repeated the question to the old wizard, whose face was almost completely covered with blue scales, and the man shook his head and carried on shouting over the wind and thundering waves. Every time a grey wall of water struck the rocks under the pier a wall of spray soaked the crowd, and Farden was growing more and more eager to dive through the quickdoor with each passing minute. He turned his head to look up at the black mountain towering above them. The docks were in the shadow of the mountain's steeper slope, and the wet granite cliffs soared high into the air and leant over them like the prow of some great black ship. Farden could imagine them toppling at any moment.

'What did Eyrum give you?' Farfallen's deep voice broke through his reverie.

'A dragon scale.' Farden plucked the tiny pendant from under his cloak and showed it to the gold dragon. Farfallen hummed with a low rumble.

'That is quite a gift for a rider to give,' he said. 'That is a scale from his dragon, Longraid.'

Farden nodded without saying anything, and just stared at its ochre surface. He thumbed it and thought about trying to give it back to Eyrum. He looked like he was about to take it off when Farfallen shook his head. 'He wanted you to have it, and it is highly inappropriate in the Siren culture to return a gift, Farden. Just keep hold of it for now.' He winked, and as he did so the Siren wizard shouted and threw his hands in the air.

'It's ready!'

'Good! Now mage, are you ready?' The Old Dragon shouted to all could hear. Farden looked around him as the others gathered to watch. Svarta stood still and silent as always, arms crossed yet again, but for once her face held no anger or venom. Eyrum stood at the back of the group, hood high up over his head so that half his face was hidden. Farden nodded to the big man and Eyrum raised a hand silently. He turned back to Farfallen.

'I'm ready.' Farden walked over the slick stones with the dragon and stood in front of the quickdoor. The electricity throbbed with a low rhythmic beat and he could feel the pull of the vortex on his cloak and boots already. He looked behind him. I expect to see you flying over the Össfen mountains in less than a week,' he grinned at the Old Dragon.

'You just concentrate on getting the Arka ready, we'll do our bit.' Farfallen exposed every one of his teeth in a wide smile and the mage tensed his body, ready for the journey.

'Gods speed you Farden!' The dragons called to him as he stepped over the threshold, and then everything melted into one white blur in front of his eyes. The breath burnt in his lungs and his ribs were squashed and pressed as he flew through a tunnel of white ice. He fought to keep his eyes open. His legs felt like they would be ripped from his body any second, and wind roared past his ears like a hurricane. Farden gritted his teeth and struggled to keep his body upright for the landing.

chapter 10

"Remember also the manner in which a dragon may read your soul, and speak silently to its rider. Remark at the startling resemblance a rider displays to his dragon! The scale colours are almost always the same hue, and he or she may share the same temperament, or physical features. They boldly sit astride these enormous savage beasts, as if they were no bigger than a simple cow, riding into the cold sky with them like birds. The Sirens are truly odd!"

'Inside Nelska: A Warning Guide' by Master Wird

The sky was clear for once over Krauslung. A few thin wisps of cloud were streaked idly over the crystal blue like the accidental brush strokes of an indolent artist, white smudges over the sinking sun. There was a crisp coldness to the air, the type just after snow, and the people in the streets rummaged deep into their coats and cloaks for warmth. Clouds of breath rose from the crowded citizens gathered around the market stalls and tavern doorways. A distant bell tolled in the harbour of Rós, breaking the stillness of the frozen city.

Vice watched the crowds milling around from far above. The towering fortress walls of the Arkathedral were sheer, and he could lean out over the window ledge to watch his people rush around bundled up in coats, hats, and thick scarves wrapped tightly around their heads. They looked like mere ants from so high up, Vice thought. A man's voice broke through his little trance.

'Undermage, the quickdoor is opening.' A soldier called to him, and he spun round to face his small group of guards.

'Stand back and give him some room. Get that blanket ready, man.' He waved his hands about and the men hurried to obey him. The soldier holding the thick woollen blanket over one arm stood to the side of the quickdoor and unfolded it.

Vice stood with the other men half a dozen paces back from the quickdoor and watched intently. The small room suddenly grew hot and sparked with electricity as the tall archway began to hum and shake. A thin haze started to spread across the doorway, rolling and undulating like a thin veil of energy. Several little flashes of light flew across the door and a low rumble came from somewhere deep inside it.

Without any warning, there was a pulse of light and a gust of air that pushed all the men a step backwards. Farden came flying out of the quickdoor backwards and fell heavily towards the floor. The mage threw out a hand to stop himself but he was too late and he crumpled into a heap at the foot of the archway. Farden shivered convulsively and pulled his legs from the portal just as it began to close. He had seen enough men cut in half by closing quickdoors in his time, and didn't fancy being one of them. The soldier to his left threw a blanket over him and Vice strode forward to help him up.

'Give him some help here,' he ordered, and the men helped the mage to his feet. 'Glad to have you back, old friend,' laughed the Undermage. He grabbed Farden's hand and shook it warmly with both of his. 'No doubt you have a story to tell me?'

'Just get me some warm wine, your Mage, and I'll tell you any story you want.' Farden managed to stand on both feet, but his teeth chattered over his gasping words.

'Hah! You heard the man, get him some wine, and some *mörd* too!' Vice called to his men and two soldiers ran out of the room.

'Come on, let's get you to my rooms,' the Undermage put an

arm around the mage and hauled him forward.

❦

'Drink your wine, Farden, don't just stare at the fire.' Vice smiled and leant back into a deep armchair with a chuckle. He threw another log into the fireplace and it landed in the flames with a burst of sparks. Steaming wood cracked and spat at them.

Farden shook his head and blinked. The mage was perched on the edges of his own luxurious chair, leaning forward to be closer to the roaring fire. He grinned and sipped the steamy concoction from the silver cup in his hands. It was warm and sweet, mulled wine mixed with the infamous moonshine known as mörd or *piss* as it was more commonly known. It was a soldier's drink, devastatingly strong and as clear as ice water. He had heard many of the older veterans arguing long into the night about its magick healing powers, and Farden was beginning to agree with the bunch of gap-toothed brawlers. It was like drinking fire, but the steaming liquid warmed his throat and burnt in his belly like the wood crackling in front of him, and he was starting to feel better again. Farden squinted his eyes and looked around him.

Vice's private rooms were huge, decorated in the finest styles and crammed with couches, tables, bookcases, desks, and chairs that filled almost every available space. The difference between the Undermage's rooms and Durnus's was startling, but they were just as warm, and Farden was just as happy to be there. They hadn't changed much since his last visit, but he still found himself looking around. Trophies and paintings of his victories covered the walls and jostled for space between the long windows that stretched across the far wall. The sun was just about to disappear over the faraway sea, and the clouds were beginning to gather once again as the weather from Nelska travelled southwards. Farden turned his head to watch the red orb sinking into the sea behind the distant islands.

'I knew this weather wouldn't last,' he said.

'It's been bitterly cold since you went away. Helyard's been in a foul mood, so maybe that's why,' Vice shrugged.

'What's wrong with him now?' Farden sighed. He remembered suspicions about Helyard, but he decided to hear what Durnus had to say first before telling Vice.

'Your disappearance, my good mage! The whole council has been in uproar over the apparent loss of the tearbook. It was only when your hawk arrived that Åddren finally managed to bring peace to the council, and I was sent to get the quickdoor ready for your arrival.' Vice leant back even further into the massive chair and smiled at Farden. He entwined his fingers and hummed thoughtfully.

'Well it wasn't all fun and games for me either, but I can assure the tearbook is safely back in the hands in the dragons, and they have promised me that within the week we will have our answers.'

' "Safely back in the hands of the dragons…" is that you talking Farden? I thought you said they couldn't be trusted?' Vice spluttered.

'Well, I wasn't treated kindly at first; the Siren queen, Svarta, wanted to lock me up and throw away the key.'

'But what about the message we sent to them warning them of your arrival?'

'It never got there. I think it had to do something with the sorcerer on the boat.' Farden rubbed his chin and stared into the flames again. The cup was warm in his hands.

'Right, I'm completely lost. Start from the beginning.' Vice scrunched up his eyes as if the confusion hurt him and rubbed his eyes slowly.

'Sorry.' Farden laughed and launched straight in, shuffling in his chair to face the Undermage. 'A few days before the end of the journey I caught one of the sailors in my room trying to steal the tearbook. I thought he was just a thief, but he was a sorcerer, and a good one at that, and it turns out he had been sent by the same people who had stolen the summoning manual. I managed to fend him off but a wave hit the ship and she went down.' Farden was glad Vice wasn't as good as detecting lies as the dragons were. He sipped his mörd wine.

'So how did you get to Nelska without a ship?' asked Vice.

Farden shook his head and thought, something he had spent many hours thinking in Hjaussfen. By all rights he should have been dead. 'By some sort of absolute miracle I was washed up on the beach near the palace and a guard found me. And let's just say that there were some complications after that…'

'Tell me.' Vice said and leant forward out his chair to listen more carefully.

Farden rolled his eyes. He had hoped to skip this particular matter entirely. 'One of the Siren healers read my Book while I was unconscious, so they locked the poor lunatic in a cell with me. When I finally came to half a week later they dragged me in front of the dragons and interrogated me. They weren't the least bit happy after that debacle.'

'It was his fault, not yours, if you were unconscious. It was people like him that started the war in the first place.' Vice scowled.

'Either way, the queen, Svarta, was overruled and they let me stay in the palace, free to wander around and train,' said Farden.

'You can't be serious,' he scoffed, sceptical.

Farden nodded. 'I swear to the gods. I told them the Arka finally wanted peace and after seeing the tearbook they were convinced I wasn't there to cause any trouble. I was as surprised as you were. There's a lot more to the dragons than we've come to assume, Vice.'

The Undermage scowled again, and quaffed his drink. He put

the glass down on a nearby table with a sharp tap. 'That's another matter for another day. What will happen to the tearbook now?' he asked.

'It will stay with them for the time being, and within a week we will have the location of the well. They have every scribe in the city working through every old scroll and historical account they can get their claws on, and now that Svarta and the other dragons are working beside them I have no doubt. If there's a dark elf well left in Emaneska, then they'll find it' Farden matched Vice's intent gaze and nodded slowly as if to reiterate his point. 'There must be so much knowledge in Farfallen's memories, so many lost things, places, people,' the wine stole the mage's words, and he sipped some more.

Vice nodded slowly. 'That's why Helyard never wanted it to leave Krauslung, even though it was blank, the stupid fool,' he paused, then slapped his hand on his thigh. 'If you can trust the Sirens, then so shall I. I just hope you know what you're doing Farden, and so does the council.' Vice shrugged his shoulders and leant back into his deep chair once again.

'I have their word,' said Farden.

'Fine, but if the dragons are too late, then we must be ready to fight this creature face to face. I don't care how many men it takes, we can't let this thing survive. Åddren and Helyard share my sentiments, and I'm sure the Sirens feel the same way about the matter.'

'They do, and that's why I came back,' Farden assured him quickly.

'Good, then by tomorrow night the whole army will be ready to march. I will leave it up to you to gather the Written, old friend. You will have all the hawks you need at your disposal, and I will send word to the Spire that you are to lead the others.'

'The other Written, Vice…' Farden began, but Vice held up a silencing hand and stopped him with his mouth open.

'No, Farden, I don't want to hear another word; it's about time you had your own command, and I can't think of another better suited for it. It's time to put all these rumours and gossips behind you and stop playing the hermit.' The mage looked like he was about to protest again but Vice cast him a look that said "my word is final," so Farden sighed resignedly and swilled the last of his wine around the bottom of the cup.

'For now, you will rest, Farden. I will have a room set up for you.' Vice rubbed his hands together and stood up.

He gulped down the last of the warm drink and an idea unfurled in his head. The mage grinned. 'Thank you, friend, but there is a comfy bed in a comfy inn that has my name on it.'

'Hah, you like the old *Bearded Goat* then? It's one of the oldest taverns in the city,' he said, and pushed himself up from the chair. Vice strode across the room and left Farden to gather his things. The supplies given to him by the Sirens still threatened to burst out of his haversack, but at least he would not have to pay for dinner tonight, he thought. Farden watched the tall Undermage shuffle some scrolls on a desk and hum to himself. In a lot of ways Vice was very similar to Durnus, both of them knew him too well and cared a little too much. He was starting to realise how much he needed such friends. Farden chuckled to himself; the wine always made him think too much. Vice waved a hand at him dismissively.

'Be gone with you then, you hooligan, be here bright and early tomorrow. I'll inform the Arkmages later tonight and tomorrow we will speak to the council.' Vice said and joined the mage at the door. They shook hands warmly and the Undermage looked his friend in the eye. 'It is good to have you back with us. I was worried.'

'It's starting to seem like you'll never get rid of me.' Farden winked and turned to leave.

'I bloody hope not,' laughed Vice. He watched the door close behind the mage, then he stretched with a yawn and went to find where the rest of the mörd had gotten to.

❦

An hour later and true to form, the blue glassy skies above Krauslung were becoming crowded with billowing grey clouds rolling and piling on top of each other, blotting out the first stars of the evening. The city was starting to sparkle and glow with candles and torches and the cobbled streets were as cold as the early twilight. Farden wandered on through the streets towards his favourite inn. A spot of rain landed on the back of his hand and he licked it, tasting the cold water on his burning tongue. The wine had warmed his belly. He tilted his face to the turbulent sky to feel the soft cold rain on his sweaty skin. Thankfully, there was no wind to chase the raindrops, and Farden found himself in good spirits. Even though he missed the dragons, it was good to be back in his city again, no longer under the untrusting eyes of Siren soldiers and just another hooded stranger in the street. He felt good, and strangely calm, whole even. However brief, his stay in Nelska had done something to him, and the mage allowed himself a small smile.

Farden quickened his pace, and strode briskly through the rain and the darkness. The gloomy puddles in the street rippled with orange light under the flickering street lamps. A few passers-by coughed and shuffled on the wet flagstones but they paid him no attention and the hooded mage continued on through the night.

❦

The *Bearded Goat* was lively that evening, Farden could hear the noise echoing through the dark alleyways from at least half a mile away. At first he had thought a fight had broken out, as there were several city guards leaning on their spears in the road, but then the mage realised it was actually singing he had heard, not fighting. The guards kept leaning and laughed at the drunkards of the inn. Farden kept his hood down and passed them silently. The rain splashed in the puddles and soaked the city to the bone.

A man had collapsed in the gutter outside the inn, and he was still clutching his ale and singing random lines with little bursts of energy and volume. One of the guards tried to move him on with the butt of his spear but the drunk refused to be uprooted from the wet cobbles, and argued loudly how sober he truly was. He would probably still be there in the morning. Farden chuckled to himself, and looked through the windows at the commotion inside.

Had Farden wanted a meal and a drink in the bar he probably would have cared a lot more, but seeing as all he wanted was to get to his room, he greeted the chaos with a bemused grin. Not one, but two bards had arrived that night, and both were belting out old songs and *eddas* to the bustling crowd gathered at the bar. The mage managed to make it through the door and slowly squeezed past the drunken men, heading towards the stairs. He threw a sympathetic look to the inn-keeper as he passed the bar. The man looked stressed, and furiously doled out tankards of ale and wine in every directions. Silver and copper coins clinked together in his bursting pockets. At the end of the bar the two skalds danced on a tabletop, getting faster and faster and louder and louder with every passing second, each trying to outdo the other with longer and louder tales of war and heroism. The noisy drunk men sang the bits they knew, and shouted the bits they didn't, and drowned out the ljots with the banging of bottles and tankards on wooden tables. The whole inn was a deafening cacophony of noise, music, and laughter. Farden watched the mayhem with wonder and slowly shook his head.

To his right a man was trying to cook a half-eaten sausage on the roaring heat of the fireplace, while another skinny fellow was hidden under a table throwing up in a hat. The gentleman whose hat it was laughed and pointed, and then rambunctiously demanded he get another beer to compensate for the vomiting. The skinny man kept at it. A few soldiers were leaning against each other and the stairs, long off-duty but still in armour. They stank of cheap wine and sang their own songs over the chaos. They cheered as Farden nudged them aside with his elbows and told him to join them. The hooded mage ignored their offers and skipped up the steps to the second floor. They would be in for a surprise in the morning, he thought, when Vice assembled the army.

Once his door was shut and most of the noise had been drowned out Farden threw off his wet cloak, dropped his pack, and dropped into a nearby chair with a tired sigh. The music was like a muffled droning under his floorboards, and it permeated the walls and windows. Rain dripped and splashed onto his windowsill from the lofty gutters above. Farden stared at the wet night outside his room, thinking of the dragons and the last few days. It was a blur, and he wasn't sure what had really happened. He rifled through his bag and looked at the things the Sirens had given him. Most of it was still dry. He held the vial of ice water in his hand. It was still freezing cold. The little book on flying looked interesting, even if it was in a strange dialect. The illustrations were detailed and depicted diagrams of how to hold onto a dragon, and how a dragon moves in the skies. He tossed it on the bed for later.

After a while Farden suddenly realised that he was cold and that he needed to dry his clothes, so he shuffled into a sitting position and tossed a bolt of fire at the cold hearth. The dry wood there burst into flames with a snap and a crackle and began to burn. He went to pull the window shut and clenched his cold fists to warm them. The mage stretched out his hands to feel the warmth of the sputtering logs and then threw his cloak over the chair to dry. Farden perched on the edge of the bed, near the fireplace, and wondered what the hour was. His head still swam with the warm wine, and he could feel himself growing tired. The bed and its blankets behind him looked inviting, and he contemplated melting into it. With a grunt he allowed himself to lean back and sprawl out across the mattress with his boots still on the floor.

Farden let his mind rove and wander through the dizzy sleepiness of the alcohol. Nights like this were usually spent worrying and thinking too much, and the last night he had spent at the inn he had met the grubby old man with the pipe. But Nelska had calmed his thoughts, and the idea of nevermar seemed distant and useless. Just what the dragons had done to him he had no idea, but it had worked, and he was grateful. Farden played with the dragonscale amulet around his neck, and wondered what it would feel like to lose a dragon, or a loved one. He thought of her face, and her skin, and her mountain-lake eyes. Farden sighed. He would lie there for a moment, then unpack his things, and then head to the Spire to see the girl that had been stuck in his mind ever since he had left the city. The mage smiled to himself, and stretched. He would get up in a moment, he told himself, and closed his eyes.

Suddenly there was a quiet knock at the door, and with a great amount of effort Farden shook his head, blinked, and sat up. He looked around, blearily, and then the knock came again, louder and more impatient. The mage hauled himself from the bed and went to the door. Farden lifted the latch very slowly and peered around the edge of the door.

In the dark hallway stood a very cold and very wet Cheska, her hair bedraggled and dripping, coat gripped tightly around her. She was just on the edge of shivering, but when he opened the door her eyes sparkled and she managed a polite smile.

'Hello,' she said.

Farden's heart lurched. 'Cheska! Come in, you look like you're freezing,' he said, and ushered her in. He took a moment to look up and down the corridor to see if anyone was watching and then locked the door tightly behind him.

'Expecting someone?' she asked quietly. Cheska pulled her thin leather coat around her shoulders. Farden turned and looked at her, and realised how much he had missed her. Her voice sounded like little bells in his ears.

Farden smiled and shook his head. 'Definitely not you anyway' he said. He grabbed a blanket from his bed and wrapped it around her shivering frame. They perched on the edge of his bed in silence. The mage's eyes roved over her, and when she looked up at him he stared deep into her blue eyes. She stared back at him, waiting. 'I was going to come see you at the Spire tonight,' he said, with a smile, and Cheska made a face. She looked around, at the crackling fire and the book and the rumpled bedsheets. 'I've been waiting for hours, Farden, ever since I heard you were back.'

The mage inwardly chided himself. 'Vice and I had things to go over, there was wine. It's going to be a difficult day for us tomorrow,' he said, and reached to play with a strand of her hair. Cheska batted his hand away and started combing her wet tresses through her own pale fingers. She fixed him with a sour look. 'My Ritual starts tomorrow,' she said, waving her fjortla in front of him. Farden hesitated, searching for something appropriate to say, but all he could think of was to put his arm around her. She didn't push him away, and they let the noise of the fire and the rain fill the awkward silence. For a moment she did nothing, and then she leant her head on his shoulder. They both knew what the other was thinking, but neither wanted to voice it aloud. It had been a long time since the night in the alleyway.

'I thought you were dead,' she said finally, barely a whisper. She fiddled with the edge of the blanket. He rubbed her shoulder with his hand, and tried to put as much humour into his brief chuckle as he could. 'You know me better than that,' he said, but the awkwardness didn't die as he'd hoped. She just stared at him, and her serious face made him look away. He stared into the bright flames and sighed. 'I'm sorry,' he said, and searched for something else to say. He had always been the emotionless one, and now he struggled to put his feelings into words. She just nodded and looked away. Another moment of silence. 'I haven't stopped thinking about you,' Farden told her. 'About you and, tomorrow. I just hope you know what you're doing Cheska.'

'Farden,' she said, and turned his head with a gentle finger to look at her. Her blonde hair hung over her crystal-blue eyes but Farden did not miss the determination burning behind them. 'You know I do,' she said, and it was all he needed to hear. Since that day outside the Spire, he had tried his hardest to ignore the possibility that he might lose her to the Ritual, and up until then he had succeeded. It was another shadow in his mind that he didn't need, and now it threatened to cloud his new-found calm.

'I hope so,' he hugged her tight, sighed, and then ruffled her hair again. They said no more, and buried the matter under hope.

Her serious face warped into a tiny smile. 'See, you do care about me.' Farden narrowed his eyes. 'Hmm, don't flatter yourself,' he muttered, and Cheska slapped his arm. She stood up and went to the window to stare at the rain. 'So how was Nelska?' she asked.

Farden scowled and shook his head. 'I didn't think the news would reach the Spire that quickly,' he mumbled, and Cheska shrugged under her blanket. 'Nelska was…' he tried to search for the right word. 'Difficult,' he said.

'What happened?' she asked and Farden sighed. He had no idea where to start and how to explain it, so he started at the beginning. The mage told her about the sorcerer on the ship, the cold of the northern waters, and how he had been unconscious for almost a week, flitting in and out of sleep and dark dreams. He neglected to mention them in detail, and he didn't mention the crazy man in the cold cell, because they could be left out, but then he proceeded to go over everything he could remember about the Sirens and their dragons. He told her about Svarta, but not Farfallen, and tried to loosely explain why it was so important that they find a dark elf well. Farden trusted her, but some things could be left until this was all over. She was silent and engrossed, as if trying to imagine every fine detail. When he had finished she nodded slowly, as if her mind were trying to order and catalogue the flood of information, and came to sit next to him on the bed again. She took a big breath. 'So we're at peace with the Sirens now, and they're helping us find a magick well?'

Farden shrugged. 'If all goes to plan. And now Vice has ordered me to get all the Written ready to fight by tomorrow evening,' he said.

'You?' Cheska looked taken aback, but then put a reassuring hand on his. 'Not that I think that's a bad thing, but out of the Written everyone knows you're the outsider. And after... well,' she trailed off. 'What happened with your uncle?'

Farden had to admit she was right. He nodded and scratched an imaginary itch on the back of his hand. 'I know that, and Vice knows that, but for some reason he thinks it's a good idea.'

'Maybe it is.' Cheska offered. He shook his head. 'I don't think so, it's been years since I lived at the Spire. Half of them probably don't even know who I am, apart from the rumours.'

'Then they will soon enough. If the Undermage thinks you're capable, then so should you.'

'Perhaps.' Farden left it there, and listened to the rain on the glass. 'All that matters is stopping the people behind all of this. I can't let them get away with it.'

'You always make it your fight, don't you?' Her voice sounded distant. He nodded. Cheska looked at him with a strange expression. 'It's always got to be your fight and yours alone, ever since I've known you. Why do you put so much weight on your shoulders all the time?' she asked. Her hands were resting calmly on his leg and Farden couldn't help but stare at her.

'Because someone has to,' he said quietly.

Cheska shook her head. 'Then why you?'

Farden sighed. 'Why any of us? We're the Written, we do these things because we're the only ones who can. I've never failed a mission yet and I'm not about to start.'

'But it doesn't always have to be you, Farden, what are you trying to prove?'

'Yes it does, and I have everything to prove.' Farden shook his head stubbornly.

She sighed, exasperated. 'There's a whole tower in Manesmark filled with people like us, like you, Farden. You don't have to prove yourself anymore, don't you understand that? It's why you don't want to be in charge of the other Written, because you still think you can do this on your own. The lone wolf, Farden saves the day again, is that what you want?' Her questions were like arrows. He knew she cared, just like all the others. Farden looked deep into her eyes and clasped her smooth hands between his. 'I know what I'm doing, and right now I can't take another lecture about how I need to be careful, I get enough of those from the rest of them,' he said.

'It's because of your uncle, isn't it? she ventured, knowing how touchy a subject it was. 'That's what you're trying to fight,' Farden's face was no less flinty. 'No,' he said. 'I'm nothing like him.'

'I didn't say that,' said Cheska, and left the matter to die away with the silence. She managed a tired frown and looked away. 'One day we're going to give up trying to convince you, and one day it'll be too late,' she said, with a slow shaking of her head, and a little shiver shook her slender body.

'You're cold,' said Farden, quickly changing the subject. He got up from the bed to add to more wood to the fire. The mage picked up two logs from a little box by the window and held them in each hand. Flames trickled along his fingers and the dry logs began to spit and hiss. As the crackling bark started to burn by itself Farden dropped them gently into the fire with a little shower of sparks.

Cheska rolled her eyes. 'That was unnecessary.' She was now sitting cross-legged on the bed with the blanket gathered around her like a shroud.

Farden tidied his things and smirked at her slyly, glad to have escaped the earlier conversation. 'But it's why I'm so good; I'm always practising.'

Cheska made a laughing noise. 'I could give you a run for your coin.'

'There's a reason we've never duelled, Cheska. I'm scared I'd hurt you.' Farden leant against the fireplace and crossed his arms with a triumphant grin.

'Afraid to lose?' Came the snippy reply.

'Hah! We'll see in three days,' Farden winked and she looked for a pillow to throw at him. Joking about it didn't make it any better, and he tried to force his mind away from shadow. 'What did you choose anyway?' He asked.

'Illusion and spark.' Cheska smiled.

'Interesting. What about your friend, Burg, Brine?' Farden smirked.

'Brimm? Shadow and vortex.'

'Interesting *and* original then,' he said mockingly.

'Oh be nice.' She held out a hand for him to join her. He sat on the edge of the bed facing her. They kept hold of each other's hands. 'Brimm actually looks up to you, Farden,' said Cheska.

The mage shrugged. 'I can't imagine that, he's so protective of you.'

'He's probably just jealous of you. You should teach him some things,' she suggested.

'I don't even know how to begin to teach someone, that's for the masters at the Spire, leave it to them.' Farden snorted.

Cheska shuffled closer. 'You could take any one of them.'

'Probably,' the mage nodded reflectively. He lost his train of thought when she started to lean into his warm neck. Her voice sounded small from below his chin.

'What did you choose?' she asked quietly.

'You already know, fire and light,' he said.

There was a pause, and then she put a hand on his warm chest to feel his heartbeat. 'What about the other two?'

Farden shook his head, irritated. People were too eager to gossip about things that didn't concern them. 'Who told you about that?' he muttered.

'We all know the stories about Farden,' Cheska said. 'What are the others?' The mage sighed and looked up at the ceiling. Tonight had been for forgetting, not dredging up the past, and his calm was being put to the test.

Every Written's Book contained certain runes that gave power to certain schools of magick, like water or fire, gifting a mage with enhanced abilities in those particular skills. Back in the earlier days, when Farden had still been in training, the Scribe could write as many as four runes into a tattoo. But, in light of a few certain incidents, the council had ruled that using more runes was dangerous for a candidate, and more likely to dissolve their minds like wet sand. They were unfortunately right; the more magick that was forced upon a mage, the less they could hold onto reality as the years went on. Farden had been the last to receive four runes, and it had been a highly guarded secret, until now. Rumour had it that Farden's uncle had five runes in his Book.

'Spark and quake,' said Farden quietly.

Cheska tutted. 'There's no tact to you, is there? As subtle as a house.'

Farden wagged a finger mockingly. 'A Written isn't meant to

be delicate and quiet, Cheska, you can't win a fight with shadow magick.'

'Who says you have to fight?' she said, but Farden chuckled, and said no more. She left the subject alone. Farden looked down at her, and she up at him. They held each other's gaze for a while, and there was no sound but the dripping on the windowsill and the muffled singing from downstairs. Cheska looked down at her nails and searched for some way to say it.

'I'm scared, Farden…' she began, but Farden put a hand to her cheek and before she could go any further he kissed her. Their lips met and she let his hands wander across the soft skin of her neck and up into her hair. She threw her arms around his shoulders in a warm embrace and Farden felt her heart beat hard against his own. She was warm, intoxicating. The mage felt her hands exploring inside his tunic while they kissed, fingers running over his chest and blindly tracing ridges of old scars. Cheska pulled him backwards onto the bed and pulled the blanket around them. With a flourish of blonde hair Farden pulled her shirt over her head and began to take off the rest of her clothes. They quickly landed in a heap on the floor and were swiftly followed by Farden's tunic. Cheska bit and nibbled the mage's shoulders. Her nails dragged softly over the tattoo on his back and with one hand he entwined his fingers in hers and held her down on the bed. He ran his hands over her breasts and half-naked body. Farden let his tongue rove over her skin, and she moaned and sighed as he did so. Her beautiful skin shone pale in the dying firelight, and her eyes were sparkling with the reflections of the flames. Farden had never known her to look so beautiful. They stared at each other for a moment, and then they kissed again. He explored the curves and niches of her body and felt Cheska's hands do the same. Her slender fingers floated across his skin and moved slowly further down his stomach to his waist. Farden shifted to be closer and they pressed themselves against each other rhythmically, feeling the warmth of the other's skin and the fast heartbeats as they removed the last of their clothes and felt nothing but each other's skin. His was rough, weathered, hers was impossibly smooth. Cheska pulled him close as he moved his hands between her long slender legs. Her breathing was loud in his ear, and she smelled incredible, feminine, and the scent filled him with animal lust. She was the mountains, the sky, the crystal lake, everything, and her sharp nails raking across his back only made him want her more. The shadows burnt away from the corners of his mind and he forgot everything except her, and she was a bright island like a candle in his darkness.

His fingers moved up and down, gently at first, and then faster, sliding in and out of her until at long last she finally couldn't take any more. Cheska wrapped her legs around him and took him in her hands, drawing him ever closer, pulling, until they were one and the same. Farden held her hands above her head, pressing her into the covers and letting himself melt into every part of her, forgetting everything else in the world except her, letting the shadows finally burn away until only they existed together in the darkness.

Soon they were both tangled in the sheets and panting breathlessly as they moved and writhed back and forth. Once, she screamed his name, when she was on top of him, hands in her hair and head thrown back. The noise from downstairs drowned out the sounds of their own commotion, and by the time they finally collapsed into a deep sleep, the fire had long burnt out, exhausted and sated.

❦

Farden's dream was made of darkness. He could feel the heat of the day failing all around him, feel the hot wind dying on the horizon as it chased after the receding sun. But it was dark, impenetrable, like black hands had covered his eyes and stolen away every scrap of light. He was standing, he could feel the ground under his bare feet. He moved his toes and felt sand crunch between them. Hot sand. Farden looked to where he felt was up, and blinked.

Ever so slowly, as if the stars were forming for the first time, pinpricks of light began to puncture the blackness above him like knives through fabric. He could hear their rumbling from his place on the ground as they burnt and throbbed and shook themselves into being. Farden couldn't tear his eyes away. One by one the stars appeared, and the mage lifted a finger to count them and to trace their familiar shapes in the sky. A ribbon of light began to sparkle above him, like a milky river across the vastness, and with it he could hear the voices of countless people, yelling and moaning and crying, whimpering, plotting, convoluted whispers of ten thousand times ten thousand. The shapes moved, and the sounds of battle clashed against the shadows. The old gods galloped across the skies as they shouted and twirled. Yet more stars grew, and then suddenly, as quickly as it had started, the sky froze, the chaos halted, and earth and sky fell from the havoc. Farden heard something shuffle nearby, and he spun around. Nothing there but the thick darkness. Impenetrable. The something circled him, scratched, sniffed, yowled at the night sky. The stars cast no light, illuminated nothing. The little thing kept circling the mage, and Farden followed it with his ears and waved his unseen hands around him.

There's more to this than first appears said an all too familiar voice.

'What do you want from me?' mumbled Farden.

Whoever they are, they're not who you think. That's how they got me came the reply in his head.

'What is this place?' asked the mage. The voice paused, as did the scratching. *It's where you want to be Farden, not I. And something here feels wrong, different, ruined.*

'Show yourself!' shouted Farden, whirling around. From the

corner of his eye he saw a shape move in the sky, the shape of a man holding a bow, with a sword at his hip. Wild dogs followed in his wake. With a mighty heave he leapt across the sky, and swept a third of the stars with him, and then pulled the string of his bow to his cheek. Farden felt paralysed, cornered. He looked for somewhere to run but saw only darkness and the hunter. He loosed his arrow, and his stars began to fall. Gold, silver, purple, and blinding white they fell, ripping the sky like torn skin, bruising the mountains with fire. The noise was deafening.

This was how it all started, mage, when the stars fell, the giants of old.

'This doesn't make any sense. Why do you keep bringing me here? If you want to tell me something then just tell me and stop all this nonsense!' Farden yelled. He tried to run but he could feel his feet melting into the hot sand around him.

Be careful, Farden. Something stirs in Emaneska tonight.

'Who are you? Show me your face!'

I'm just like you, which is all the more reason to be careful.

'I told you, I'm nothing like you! Leave me alone!'

Not this time. It's only just beginning. Just promise me you'll stay alive.

The stars buried themselves in the ground around him, and in the flashes and explosions of light Farden could see a man, with a cat, and a thing with wings. 'SHOW ME!' bellowed the mage as a flaming rock struck his hand. He felt his skin sizzling in the place his arm used to be.

Keep an eye on the weather Farden.

chapter 11

"The rumours of a fierce, ravenous vampyre in our forest are completely ridiculous! Why would such a beast settle in our quiet countryside, and hunt such kind people? These goings-on are just plain and simple accidents, nasty trips and falls, or perhaps a rogue wild dog!

"Pardon me? No, I don't know anything about the bite-marks. Now if you'll excuse me..."

The Duke of Leath speaking to the townspeople after alleged "vampyre sightings" some years ago

The wind was bitingly cold, tearing at the black cloak of the figure standing in the darkness on the shore like the teeth of a thousand rats, invisible and hungry. It was a moonless night, and the clouds were spinning and twirling across the seething sky, trying to find calm after the storm earlier that day. The jagged rocks of the beach were slippery and wreathed in tangled seaweed that had been ripped apart by the waves and left to lie like dead soldiers on the shoreline. The sea crashed nosily on the rocks behind the man, and he could just about catch the shouts of the people in the small wooden boat furiously paddling against the surging waves. They were loud fools, and they would wake up the whole mountain if they weren't careful. The huge face of the fortress of Hjaussfen towered above him. The black granite cliffs were almost invisible against the dark sky, but a few yellow torches glittered from a handful of windows, betraying the citadel. To the quiet man standing alone on the beach, the weather was perfect. He smirked, a wolf's smile.

The wind howled, and the figure trudged forward, thick travelling boots crunching the grit and scraping on the wet slate. Knives dangled at his belt.

❦

In the darker shadows of the cliff face a Siren stood guard, spear held firmly and low by his side. He cleared his throat and coughed, blinking and peering into the darkness. Standing near to the mountain afforded a little shelter, but the cold still crept inside his cloak and stole his warmth. His red eyes watched the clouds racing overhead, trying to find a star in the dark sky.

Suddenly a slim hand slipped over his mouth and pulled him backwards. A sharp pain pierced his back, and a thin silver blade slid out from his chest. The soldier looked with amazement at the knife protruding from his leather tunic. There was a crunching sound as the blade was pulled out, a scrape of bone and armour. Blood gathered and bubbled in his throat. The pain started to spread, but darkness was quickly gathering at the corners of his scarlet eyes and by the time he hit the ground he was dead.

The figure wiped his long knife on the body of the Siren and sheathed it slowly. He bent to grab the man's legs and hauled the body into the shadows.

❦

On top of the cliffs, at the top of a winding staircase, was a little door cut into the rock. A lone soldier stood in the doorway, shivering in the cold and stamping his feet to try to keep warm.

Someone had taken his cloak from his cupboard, and he had only his leather armour to keep him warm. The butt of his spear tapped on the ground as he shivered. He thought about going inside and stealing a blanket from one of the other guards, but the sergeant probably wouldn't have taken too kindly to that, so he decided against it. A stone shifted somewhere on the little path to his right, just at the top of the stairs, and it made a little clattering noise as it fell. The Siren blinked against the cold and tried to focus his watering eyes on the stairs. He couldn't hear anything except the wind, so he huddled deeper against the door frame and tried to feel the warmth of the barracks inside. He could almost imagine the warmth of the beds inside. He closed his eyes and shivered.

Another noise reached his keen ears over the howling of the wind, the sound of boots on stone. The guard peered around the corner of the little door to see a tall stranger, hooded and cloaked, carrying a spear low at his side. The guard shuffled forward, hands still deep in his small pockets, and opened his mouth to hail the stranger.

Like a shadowy blur the man dropped the spear and darted forward, and the Siren panicked. While he struggled to get his hands free of his pockets, the stranger's hands shimmered with blue light. A yell caught in his throat as a bolt of lightning slammed into his chest and threw him backwards with a crack of thunder. The door splintered into a thousand pieces under him and the air was driven from his lungs. The man felt his ribs pierce his lungs as he collided with the wall at the back of the dark room. The shouts and cries of the others seemed distant and muffled from the floor.

The figure filled the doorway and a flash of light flew from his fingers, blinding the three scaly men falling out of their beds and scrabbling for their weapons. Yells filled the little room.

A flaming knife pierced the darkness and flew across the room, dispatching a bewildered Siren crawling across the floor. A gurgling cry and a crash of furniture rang out. The hooded stranger held his hands open facing upwards and sparks began to gather and spin above his hands. The ball grew and crackled, spitting light and fire as it spun inches from his crooked fingers. With a grunt the man tensed and hurled the huge bolt into the darkness, where it exploded with a massive crash against the back of another guard. The man was catapulted sideways and his forehead collided with the other soldier's face as he tried to free a sword from its scabbard. There was a sickening crunch and the two men slumped to the floor limply.

The smell of burning flesh and smouldering wood choked the room with a thick smoke, and all was silent apart from the hoarse breathing of the wounded men. The dark stranger went to each one, plunging a knife into the defenceless soldiers to make sure they sounded no alarm. He sheathed his blade and left the room quickly, scurrying out of another low door into a gloomy corridor.

Deep in the mountain a flickering torch fizzled out, pinched between quiet fingers. The spreading shadows hid the cloaked figure as he stepped lightly on the flagstones, creeping further and higher into the palace.

Around a corner, another guard stood quietly and attentively at his post. The man pressed a palm flat against the wall, and the stones shivered and rippled outward with a low rumble. Just as the guard turned his head at the noise, the first wave reached him and the wall burst apart behind him with a detonation of bricks and stone. The man was knocked flat, and while he tried to rise the figure dashed forward and ended his life with a vicious slash across the throat. Dark blood pooled on the white floor, but the stranger was already gone, running headlong down the hallway.

Soon a bell rang somewhere deep in the mountain, and the

corridors came alive with soldiers like swarming ants. They crowded the lower levels, but the stairs slowed them and the murderer was far ahead, high up at the top of the palace.

The man stood in front of a tall set of iron doors and looked up at the high arch of the door frame. He strode forward and pushed on the metal, making the door creak in protest. Slowly it swung open and the man slipped into the cavernous hall without a sound. He dodged furtively from pillar to pillar and made his way to the statue of the winged god at the end of the hall, and the little stone table sitting near it. The tearbook and a flock of papers sat on it, barely illuminated by the flickering candles around the shrine.

The hooded figure dashed to the table and seized the tearbook. He slipped it into a satchel under his cloak and stuffed the parchment beside it, making sure he got all of it. The sound of bells and horns shook the fortress around him. It was time to leave.

The man reached inside his tunic and brought forth a golden object that glittered brightly with the light from the candles. He gripped it in both hands and headed for the door. The bright corridor was full of the sounds of armour and clanging weapons, and just as he emerged from the dark hall a group of soldiers came around a corner and spotted him. The man wasted no time by lingering and broke into a fast run. The men shouted and bellowed and gave chase but the man had already reached the end of the corridor and had disappeared. Other soldiers joined them, spurred by the shouts and the yells, and soon the entire palace was racing after the hooded intruder, following the trail of dead bodies left on staircases and in doorways and slumped against walls. The Sirens wanted blood, and the stranger knew that, so he darted between rooms and corridors, leading the pursuers a merry chase towards the outside of the mountain. The palace was a warren, and he was slowly losing them.

No sooner had he thought this did he turn a corner to find a swarm of armoured soldiers, teeth bared, scales flushed, and blocking the corridor with their tall shields. The man skidded to a halt and stared at the hungry Sirens. They growled and tensed, waving their spears and blades at the intruder threateningly. The corridor was the only way out of this section on the palace, but the man had one more card to play. He looked at the gold disk in his hand, and lifted it closer to his face, lips mumbling the incantation etched into the shiny surface. Footsteps clattered behind him and a soldier rushed at him brandishing a short sword. The man ducked and spun, flinging out the hand that held the disk and catching the Siren in the face with the hard metal edge. The soldier let out a cry and threw his hands up to his nose while his feet flew out from under him. The others charged to their friend's aid, yelling war cries and screaming for revenge.

The corridor roared with noise, but the stranger held firm, holding the disk straight out in front of him and muttering the last few words of his spell. And at the very last moment, mere seconds before the spears and swords cut him into pieces, the stranger swung the disk in a wide circle and completely disappeared, slipping into the bouncing, shaking air and vanishing completely. The air in the hallway wobbled like a plucked string and then slowly came to a stop. The Sirens skidded to a halt and stumbled over each other amidst shouts of surprise and rage. They looked about them, bewildered, for any sign of the mage. But he was gone.

Back on the beach, the wind howled and the rain lashed the stones and shale. The crew in the boat had done well to bring the boat into shore again, and they crouched by the pale hull of their wooden vessel, and waited. They did not have to wait for long.

Further up the beach a pile of pebbles started to shake and jitter, rocking back and forth as the air began to hum. Suddenly there was a loud sound, like the cracking whip or a tree snapping in half, and the air split in two, leaving a hooded man standing in the darkness. He looked down at the gold disk in his hand, now caked in blood, and turned it over. Shouts rang out from the cliffs behind him, and he heard the sound of arrows against the wind. A few barbed shafts slammed into the gritty sand next to him, and he started to walk briskly back to where the waves crashed on the shore. The men in the boat were a short distance away, but the archers were slowly getting used to the range. He wiped rain and spray from his face and threw a quick look behind him. There were soldiers running along the beach from the west, and the black shapes of dragons were circling the darkened summit of Hjaussfen. Their eyes could pierce the darkness like an owl hunting a mouse, so the stranger doubled his pace, and fled towards the sea.

The men beside the boat had already pushed it into the water, and were now plying their oars against the turbulent seas. The stranger was getting closer by the moment, and he hopped from rock to slippery rock to dodge the buzzing arrows. His hands were numb from the cold, and the wind constantly buffeted him and tore at his cloak.

As he reached the shoreline he looked back at the Sirens dashing after him across the rain-lashed beach. A rancourous smirk crept across his lip, and he looked again at the bloodied disk in his hand. With a chuckle he flung it towards them and it clanged against the slippery stones. Lightning flashed above him and caught the face of the gold, and he leapt into the boat with a huge lunge. Oars and paddles instantly dug deeper into the dark water, and the vessel lurched across the roiling waves with the wind gnashing in its wake. The hooded man stood upright in the bow of the ship, peering back at the shore and holding onto his hood. A member of the crew pawed at his heel, and shouted a question over the howling wind.

'What?' snarled the man.

'Where d'ye want us t' go your Mage?!' the man asked again.

'Around the coast, and to the north. And be quick about it too if you don't want to be speared by the Sirens!' shouted the man, and the sailor nodded, blinking as a wave splashed against the side of the boat. He made to turn around, but his master grabbed his shirt sleeve before he got away. The hooded mage reached inside his cloak for the satchel.

'Put this somewhere safe,' he said, and with a flick of his wrist he tossed it at him The sailor caught it awkwardly, narrowly avoided dropping it into the iron sea, and clutched it to his chest while he cast around for a dry spot between the rowing men and the supplies.

An arrow thudded into the hull of the boat, and the crew immediately started to row faster with urgent hissing shouts. Perhaps it was the current and the winds that pushed them, or maybe it was something to do with the mage at the front of the boat, but either way they sped across the choppy seas and into the stormy night. Snatches of words, fuelled by rage, could be heard on the wind, yells, and banging. Bells and horns shook the mountain of Hjaussfen behind them, distorted and muffled by the weather. The men rowed on, and watched the dark skies with wary eyes.

part three

you only come alive in

the dark...

The Written

chapter 12

"As a whole, the people of Albion are without a doubt utterly dimwitted, displaying an idiocy only just surpassed by the foolish pomposity of their so called "Dukes." The citizens of this drab land seem to spend their time standing on street corners scratching themselves, or gambling, and gawping at the rest of the world flying past without them. In all my years I've never met a more dull set of people. But then again it's probably why I enjoy hunting them so much, they're as slow as their cows..."

From the diary of Durnus Glassren

Farden awoke when the bright sunlight climbed over the rooftops and pierced the darkness of his room. The rain had stopped in the night, and now an early morning mist filled the streets and fogged the dirty windows.

The mage, however, hadn't noticed any of this yet, and he closed his eyes tighter against the offending sunshine. The fading tendrils of the dream hovered behind his eyelids. They confused him, annoyed him, ruined his sleep. They were dreams without meaning and the mage tried to dismiss their strange words as nonsense, but he couldn't help but wondering why the voice sounded so familiar, why he felt as though he should pay attention. Farden shuddered as the hazy memories of the darkness and the sand and the falling fire came back to him. He would keep an eye on the weather, he decided, whatever that meant. Rolling over he reached out for the beautiful girl in his bed but found only empty space next to him. Farden shrugged. He had expected her to disappear during the night, careful to keep their secret a little longer.

Farden had often pondered what would happen if they were discovered, what the magick council would do, what would happen to them, and more importantly, what her father would do. Cheska was a princess and very soon she would be a Written, and that would make her by all reasons and definitions, forbidden. A wave of anxiety washed over him, but after a moment it was gone, replaced by a glimmer of hope and the feeling that his life was finally starting to make sense. He felt the small dragon scale amulet tapping against the skin of his neck, and thumbed its rough surface contemplatively. From now on, he said quietly to himself, things would get better, and then for once he let his mind go quiet.

Farden smiled to himself and put his hands behind his head, still refusing to open his eyes and admit it was daytime. He let the events of last night wander through his head. With a smile the mage stretched and his hand knocked against something small and metallic on the pillow beside him. Farden grabbed at the object and held it in front of him, blinking his sleepy eyes into focus. It was Cheska's fjortla, left for him to keep until she had passed through the gruelling Ritual. He gripped the bracelet so hard that it hurt his hand, and then forced himself to sit up. He said a small prayer to the gods to keep her safe and then got up to gather his scattered clothes.

❦

The bar area was filled with snoring or unconscious men, most of whom were sleeping under chairs and on tabletops, some covered in vomit, others lying flat on the stone floor, swollen bellies rising and falling laboriously with deep drunken breaths. The two skalds had fallen asleep leaning on each other, voices and fingers raw from performing. The innkeeper had disappeared. He was probably nursing his own throbbing head somewhere upstairs, Farden thought. He had to step over a huge man in a guard's uniform that lay blocking the doorway. His beard was still wet with ale and his chest rumbled like a storm cloud. Farden could smell the beer on his breath as he passed.

The streets were buzzing, and everyone seemed to be rushing around. It was still early morning and yet the roads were packed with noisy, bustling crowds. The mage pushed his way into the street and joined the throng of teeming citizens. Carts pulled by donkeys crowded the thoroughfares, and their drivers yelled angrily for people to move and give way. The whole city was in uproar.

Farden hoisted his hood over his head and weaved through the crowds, pushing people aside with his strong arms. Everywhere he looked he could see guards frantically running back and forth, spurred on by the shouts from their captains and sergeants. Vice and the magick council had been busy this morning, Farden thought. He dug out a piece of dark dried meat from his belt, the same fishy stuff he had eaten in Nelska, and nibbled as he walked.

Even though he was only a short distance from the Arkathedral it took him the best part of an hour to reach the tall gates of the fortress, and even there people clogged the roads and gathered at the foot of the walls. Farden squeezed through a crowd of citizens that were angrily yelling at the phalanx of soldiers standing at the gates. The armoured men repeatedly shook their heads at the people and their captain was pushing them back with a short wooden stave. Farden elbowed his way forward.

'What's going on here?' demanded Farden, once he was close enough to the officer.

'Get back from the gates!' The soldier shouted at him.

Farden yanked his hood back and held up one of his wrists to the man. The captain looked at the mage and then at the symbol on his skin and bowed instantly. 'My apologies sire, these citizens are demanding refuge in the Arkathedral, but we're under orders from the Undermage not to let anyone in besides soldiers or mages.'

'Why?' Farden looked at the man with a quizzical expression.

The man shrugged. 'They didn't say, but orders is orders and I do what I'm told. You're better off asking them inside, sir,' he nodded towards the tall gates.

'This city is a madhouse,' Farden muttered, and the soldier laughed without any humour. 'If you think this is bad, then you're not going to like it in there.' Farden nodded grimly and the man bowed. He called to his men to let the mage through and their ranks parted. Behind him he could hear the captain poking and shoving the people away with his stave. 'Back! Get back I say!'

Farden walked under the massive gateway and instantly realised the soldier had been absolutely right; the whole Arkathedral was alive and buzzing like a hornet's nest. The mage groaned. It was as if war had broken out while he had been asleep, and now the grand marble atrium was stuffed and crammed with all sorts of people. Servants scurried this way and that through clusters of workers, their arms full of supplies and boxes or pulling little carts behind them. Soldiers ran back and forth lugging armour and bundles of weapons, yelling "move!" and "mind out!" and pushing others to the floor. Guards stood at every doorway and entrance. Everybody was shouting and rushing around. Only a small few stayed relatively still amongst the disorder, and they gathered in the corners of the marble hall, hooded and conspiratorial in their little groups. Several of them noticed Farden as he stood alone in the gateway watching the chaos. One man in particular, a very thin willowy man with white-blonde hair, broke away from the group and waded through the masses towards him. The man proffered a hand, and Farden shook it warmly and smiled. The symbols on their wrists flashed momentarily as they touched skin.

'Modren, at least there's one sane person amongst this mess,' said Farden.

The man nodded. 'Good to see you again,' he said quietly. Farden could barely hear him over the roar and clatter of voices. The thin man seemed to sway gently, like a sapling in the breeze, and his eyes were a deep green that watched everything with the intensity of a hunting cat. He wore a long red coat, and there was a sword on either side of his belt. His whitish hair was short and waxed back, and a black ring hung from his left ear. 'Whatever's going on here, it's all gone to shit, I'll tell you that. Thialf and the others are over there. Freidd is coming soon. Word came to the Spire that we were needed here as soon as possible.' Modren suddenly paused and gave him a strange look. 'The order sounded like it was from you,' he said.

Farden inwardly sighed, and tried to seem confident. He matched Modren's look. 'The Undermage has put me in charge of the Written for now. We have something very dangerous to deal with.'

Modren shrugged, nodded, and then grinned, showing off a set of perfect white teeth. 'Sounds like my kind of fight,' he said with relish. 'And if you're in charge, well, so be it, couldn't think of somebody more suited to the job. Better one of us than some bureaucrat.'

Farden nodded, 'Let's hope the others feel the same.'

'Doesn't matter if they don't, Undermage's word is law.'

'What's this I see? Emaneska's most dangerous hermit is out and about for once!' laughed a gruff voice from behind them. They both turned to see a stocky mage with a shaven head and tribal tattoos covering half of his face. He was smiling lopsidedly at Farden. 'It's been a long time,' said the man. Farden nodded silently and smiled back.

Modren held out a palm to the muscular newcomer. 'Good to see you Ridda,' he said. Ridda chuckled. He still hadn't taken his eyes off of Farden. 'So what brings you out of your cave then?'

'The usual,' said the mage, 'something needs killing.'

Ridda made a humming sound, and then laughed, clapping Farden on the arm. 'Don't they always.' He rubbed his hands together and watched a servant fly past with a pile of books in his hands. 'What's all this about then, any ideas?'

Farden looked around at the bustling hall with a slow shaking of his head, marvelling at the sheer volume of people. 'I've never seen the Arkathedral this busy. How many of us are yet to arrive?' he asked. Ridda scratched his chin. 'At least a score or so are off in the east dealing with the wyverns, but there's at least sixty here and a few more in Manesmark,' he said. The man's voice was incredibly deep for a person of his stature. The brawny mage barely came up to Farden's shoulder, but he was as wide as he was tall, with a constantly narrowed gaze and mischievous smile, and rippling with muscle.

'Good,' said Farden. 'That will hopefully be enough. I need everyone here before nightfall, ready to march and ready to fight.'

Ridda looked at Modren, and then back at Farden, wearing a similar quizzical expression. 'You in charge now?' he asked.

Farden hesitated for a moment, and then cleared his throat with a hint of authority. He nodded. 'It looks that way, according to the Undermage,' he said, and then added his most assertive smile. Ridda looked confused, and then his face broke into a wide grin. 'Out of his cave and already he's causing trouble. Fine with me, better you than an old greyhair who's never cast a spell in his life,' he chuckled.

Modren nodded and clapped his hands together loudly. 'That's what I said. We'd best get to it then!'

Farden tried to hide his sigh of relief, and leant in close to the others so they could hear him over the noise. 'Get Neffra and a few others to the hawk-houses and send word to every Written that isn't within a day's march of the city, then tell the others to get their weapons and everything they need ready by tonight. We'll meet in the great hall by sunset.'

'I'll go and send the hawks,' said Ridda decisively. Without another word he slapped Farden on the shoulder and strode off into the crowds. Modren turned to Farden with a mock sigh. 'Let's go and see what all this madness is about,' he said.

'Agreed.' The two men spun smartly on their heels and strode purposefully towards the main stairs. They jostled with soldiers and servants for space, and dodged around workers and equipment that was gathering, for some reason, on the steps. They walked in silence for the most part, occasionally glaring at someone who might have barged into them. Their looks sent more than just a few people scuttling away and muttering apologies. Nobody wanted to get on the bad side of a Written.

The two mages walked side by side up the endless stairs and through the maze of corridors that would finally lead them to the great hall and hopefully to the root of all this commotion. Farden was eager to find Vice.

Once Modren broke the silence, and leant close to whisper to Farden. 'Rumour has it you were up in Nelska recently.' It was a question hid within a statement, but Farden simply nodded. The blonde mage watched his friend from the corner of his eye with a knowing smile. 'I take it I shall find out later then?'

'You never did have much patience,' the mage smirked.

'Never,' said Modren. 'In all honesty though, Farden, I haven't seen this sort of mayhem since the year those faeries escaped and got lost in the city. This has something to do with the murders at Arfell doesn't it?'

Farden warily looked about them, and waited until a group of people had passed. 'It does, but it's something much more serious than just a few dead scholars.'

Modren fell silent and ran a hand through his bright hair. 'It's never that simple is it?'

It took the mages a good half hour to reach the marbled hallways at the very top of the Arkathedral. There was a massive throng of people gathered outside the gilded doors of the great hall, but a line of soldiers in gold and green armour barred the way with their tall shields. Modren began to make his way through the yelling crowd. 'Move aside there, let us through!' he barked, and mercilessly pushed people aside. One haughty scribe in particular prodded him as he passed, referring a little too loudly to the blonde mage as a bumbling oaf. Modren rounded on him and fixed him with a stare that could have frozen the sun. 'If I were you, scribe, I'd keep your mouth shut and your fingers to yourself, otherwise you might lose one of them.' Modren punctuated his threat by clicking his fingers. Sparks flashed over his nails. The scribe and his party fell deadly silent and tried to back away further into the massed crowd. Modren huffed and pulled his long coat around him to avoid it getting trampled.

'Good work,' chuckled Farden.

Modren nodded. 'I thought so too... Let us through, gods damn it!'

Farden reached the armoured soldiers and found the man in charge. He looked the mage up and down with a wrinkle of his nose and an imperious sniff. 'State your business,' he shouted over the noise.

Farden glared at him. 'We're here on direct orders from the Undermage, I need to speak with him immediately!'

The soldier shook his head and pointed to somewhere beneath his feet, as if the answers lay on the floor. 'He ain't in here sir, and I'll doubt you'll find him with the Arkmages. Try his rooms one level down!'

'What are all these people here for?' Modren called to the

soldier.

'Everyone and their brother wants to see the Arkmages today, but we can't let 'em in until the council meeting has finished,' he shrugged and his polished armour clanked noisily.

'What the hell is going on?' Farden asked as he looked around at the chaotic crowd.

'Haven't you 'eard?' The soldier looked confused, a serious expression hovering over his face. The two mages shook their heads as one.

'The dragons are comin' to Krauslung!' the man said, wide-eyed.

Farden's eyes went wide, and he turned to Modren, who looked completely baffled. 'Did he say...?' he began but Farden cut him off.

'Yes he did, now come on, we have to find Vice!' They started to barge their way back through the crowd and out into the relative space of the white marble hallway. They quickly broke into a run and Farden led them left and down a wide curving staircase. He narrowly avoided knocking down a frightened-looking man carrying a big bundle of arrows, but the mages dodged around him and seconds later they both skidded to a halt outside the tall oak doors of Vice's rooms.

Farden banged loudly on the door and waited, breathing lightly. Modren was adjusting and tidying his clothes and smoothing his ruffled blonde hair. Farden crossed his arms and drummed his fingers with impatience.

There was a clanking noise and the door was opened by a thin servant with a kind face. He looked them up and down slowly. 'How may I help you, mages?'

'We need to find the Undermage, right away,' Farden said hurriedly.

'He is with the council, sire, in the great hall.' The servant shook his head slowly as if it were in danger of falling off. Farden snorted with frustration.

'My lord is due to return soon, if you would like to wait?' The servant opened the door a little wider and gestured for them to enter the huge room. As he did so a big spider crept from behind the door frame and sidled around the wall. Farden watched the black spindly beast slip into the hallway and disappear under another door. The man seemed not to have noticed the insect, and he looked back and forth between the two mages.

Farden shook his head. 'No, thank you, when you see the Undermage, tell him Farden is looking for him.'

'Of course, sir.' The thin man bowed and quietly closed the heavy door with no more than a little click. Modren walked to a nearby window and looked down at the crowds in the streets. The noise from the people bellowing and shouting could be heard on the chilling breeze. The sky was crystal clear once again, and the clouds had been banished behind the pale blue of the mountain sky. 'This is madness,' he said quietly, and leant forward to watch the guards at the gate below.

Farden put a hand against the marble wall and stared at the floor. He chewed at the inside of his lip. If the dragons were coming to Krauslung then it meant that they had found the dark elf well, but if that was so, then why was the city so full of fear and panic? Something was niggling at the back of his brain, but he couldn't grasp it. Just as things were starting to go right for a change too, he thought.

A booming voice suddenly echoed around the corridor. 'Farden!' The mages spun around to see Vice standing further down the hallway, arms spread questioningly and one foot on the bottom step of the staircase. He was wearing the long formal robe of his position: black cloth trimmed with green. A long curved sword was slung at his side, hanging from a golden belt. 'Where have you been?' he bellowed. He wore a stern expression.

The two mages jogged to meet him and bowed quickly. Farden pointed behind him at Vice's door. 'Trying to find you, sire,' he said. Modren nodded furiously behind him. The tall Undermage snorted and stormed up the stairs with loud heavy steps. 'You did a fine job of that, didn't you?Follow me,' he said. The mages leapt after him.

Farden moved to his side. 'The guard at the great hall said the Sirens were coming here...?'

'And you heard right,' Vice seemed furious. There was a bubbling anger simmering underneath his pale skin. He took the steps two at a time and his fists were clenched white by his sides. Farden hadn't seen him like this in a long time. 'Those bloody Sirens are up in arms about something, and they won't tell us what until they get here, which is any minute now. They've threatened war, Farden.' Vice threw him a serious look. The mage's eyes went wide. He lowered his voice and moved closer to the Undermage, struggling to keep up with Vice's long strides. 'War? So this has nothing to do with the well or the tearbook?'

'All I know is they're on their way, and whatever it is, that Siren queen of yours is not at all happy. Somehow the news of their arrival got out early this morning and everyone started to panic.'

'Gods' sake,' Farden shook his head. They emerged into the long white corridor outside the great hall.

'The Arkmages are furious,' said Vice. 'As am I, Farden, with you.' Vice abruptly stopped dead in the middle of the hallway and fixed him with an icy stare.

'With me?' the mage spluttered. Modren stayed quiet and tried not to get involved, staring at the marble decor.

Vice narrowed his gaze. 'Why didn't you tell me about the Old Dragon?'

Farden mentally reeled. In all the confusion he had forgotten about the matter completely, and was completely at a loss for an answer. 'I thought it would be best to tell you in private…' Farden groped for an explanation.

'Well, it would have been, Farden, but imagine my surprise when I was told by the Arkmages this morning that the old fiend is still alive. Helyard accused me of being in league with them!' Vice was fuming and his hazel eyes were aflame.

Farden held up his hands. 'He knows that's not true; I can explain it all.'

'And so you will, right now!' Vice spun around so fast that his long robe billowed out like a sail. Farden was left standing shocked. Modren put a thin hand on his friends shoulder and sighed.

'Better you than me, mate,' he said.

Farden was about to launch into a sarcastic retort but then Vice flashed a frosty glare to see if they were following. 'Fuck's sake,' he muttered, and quickly ran to catch up. He chided and cursed himself mentally for his laxness.

When they reached the great hall the Undermage pushed his way into the crowd as if he were tackling a troll. One of the guards spotted him and immediately began laying about with the butt of his spear. 'Let the Undermage through! Move out of the way!'

Farden and Modren followed in Vice's wake and elbowed their way through the noisy ranks of people until they were standing up against the gilded doors. Holding their shields with both hands, the soldiers braced themselves against the crowd and held them back while behind them the doors were opened just enough to let the three men through. The door slammed behind them, and they were away from the noisy masses, but they paled in comparison to the uproar of the great hall.

All around them council members argued and bellowed at the top of their voices, throwing their opinions back and forth while the Arkmages sat in their tall white thrones and talked agitatedly between themselves. Colourful patterns from the stained glass windows played on the walls and floors, painting faces all sorts of hues as they yelled at each other. It was absolute chaos. With loud sighs the three men walked into the middle of the room and stood beside the tall gold statue of the goddess Evernia, her feet still surrounded by a score of candles despite the bright daylight. As soon as Åddren noticed them he held his hands in the air authoritatively. His normally kind eyes pierced the room like blue icicles. Nothing happened, and the roar continued unabated.

'SILENCE!' Åddren's voice was like thunder. Loud words and arguments froze on the lips of the people, and an awkward stillness fell on the hall. The men and women of the council quietly shuffled to their places in between the tall tree-like pillars.

Helyard scowled about the room. 'I hope to the gods you bear some sort of explanation for this chaos, Farden. Your meddling ways have caused us enough trouble already, and now you've brought those despicable dragon-riders down upon us.' The tall Arkmage looked down his nose at the mage with his usual supercilious air.

Farden walked forward across the marble floor to stand closer to the thrones. The council whispered like autumn leaves around him. 'Your Mages, I have no idea why the Sirens are on their way to Krauslung, or why they are threatening war.' The whispering increased, 'When I left Nelska, they assured me that our two people were at peace.'

'So we heard from Lord Vice this morning, when he gave us your report…' Åddren started, but the stern Helyard leant forward in his seat and held up a bony finger.

'Which we might add, left out the important fact that Farfallen is still alive. I'm assuming that neither you nor the Undermage can explain this?' he said.

Farden looked to Vice, and then back to Åddren and Helyard. He nodded slowly. 'The Undermage is no traitor, your Mage, and it is no fault of his that Farfallen still lives. I admit that I was reticent, but

I thought it best that I tell the Undermage in private, and haven't yet had the chance to do so.' Farden eyed Helyard defiantly as he spoke, but the Arkmage snorted and looked away. Åddren opened his mouth to speak but he was interrupted by the wailing cry of distant horns ringing out along the walls of Krauslung. The magick council murmured nervously.

The dragons had arrived.

Every eye turned inexorably to the huge diamond-shaped skylight in the roof and Farden slowly retreated to stand with Vice and Modren, who had now moved further back towards the doors, necks bent backwards and scanning the blue skies. A nervous hush filled the hall. Soldiers slowly took their places in the recesses of the hall.

The pale blue sky hung above them, crisp and empty, and nothing disturbed them. The cold breeze was the only sound. But soon, from the ramparts and the tall towers of the fortress beneath them, came the long warning moans of the horns. The twin bells of Hardja and Ursufel tolled warily. A few shouts rang out, and then a huge shadow scattered over the stained glass windows. A faraway roar echoed through the valley.

Farden took a deep breath and stood with his arms by his side. He glanced at Vice and the Undermage nodded slowly at him with a look that seemed to say "well done." To his right, Modren clicked his fingers one by one, and stared at the skies. Farden tried to relax. He turned back to watch the roof as the deep sound of heavy wingbeats rocked the air, as if the clouds were tumbling down the mountains.

An audible gasp came from the crowded hall as a scarlet dragon suddenly dropped through the skylight. The great red beast momentarily folded its wings so as to fit through the gap and then blew a whining snort that deafened the nearest bystanders. It dropped to the floor in front of the statue of Evernia with a heavy thud, extinguishing more than a few of her candles with a final flap of its crimson wings. It looked like the dragon Farden had met briefly in Hjaussfen, Towerdawn. It solemnly bowed its head to the Arkmages and then stepped aside a few with ponderous steps that shook the floor. Its rider was a short woman with copper-coloured hair that cascaded over her dark metal armour like a rusty waterfall. She looked around the room with slow measured turns of her head and tawny eyes.

The next dragon to drop through the huge skylight was Brightshow. Her pale white and yellow-gold colouring glittered in the sunlight and as she bowed her head her horns shook and rattled. Her rider, Lakkin, if Farden remembered correctly, sat tall and straight in his saddle at the base of her neck. He wore black and silver armour and a very long sword was strapped between his shoulders. His black hair had been slicked back by the wind, and his keen eyes roved over the gathered council members.

Farden watched the Arka soldiers slowly manoeuvring around the hall. The tension hovered in the hall like a taut bowstring. They waited for the last dragon to arrive.

The hall was abruptly shaken by a massive roar from the skies above them, and then Farfallen descended through the skylight with a blinding flash of golden scales. He dropped to the floor with an enormous bang and then reared up to his full height as he tucked his huge wings behind him. Svarta sat tall and straight on Farfallen's long neck, with no saddle beneath her and a small bundle of cloth in her hands. She jumped from her dragon's back and stood imperiously by his side. She wore a grey leather tunic with leather and mail trousers that clung to her long legs. A black knife hung from her side. The blonde's strands of hair that hung beside her flinty face flicked from side to side while she looked around the room with quick cat-like movements. Svarta cast a glance behind her and scowled at Farden.

Farfallen took a deep breath and flared his nostrils. He looked at the Arkmages, who were now standing up in front of their tall thrones. 'Well met and good wishes, your Mages. It has been a long time since we last met, and I regret that it is under such dark circumstances that we greet each other again,' he said.

Åddren bowed low and cleared his throat. 'It seems to be the destiny of our peoples, to always be at war, Old Dragon,' he said. Farfallen nodded.

At the back of the hall, Vice folded his hands behind his back and took a few steps forward. 'Your message did not mention the purpose of your visit,' he said. He watched Farfallen suspiciously, and Farden could see his eyes flicking to the scar on the gold dragon's chest.

Svarta completely ignored the Undermage behind her. Her harsh tone bounced off the walls like pieces of shattered ice. 'We are here for an explanation, Arkmages, as to why you have attempted to betray us.'

'Betray you...?' Åddren started, but the Siren queen cut him off.

'Don't play games, Arkmage. Last night Farfallen's tearbook was stolen from us along with the translations we had been working on, and to help you Arka, I might add! A score of our Sirens were slain and the murderer disappeared into the night along with the tearbook. And now we have come here to demand retribution!' Her face was pale and lips pursed tight with restrained fury. Whispers again filled the hall. Svarta looked around her and glowered.

Åddren held a hand up and spoke in a calm voice. 'Your accusation makes no sense. Why would we send you the tearbook only to steal it back again? And why are the Arka being so readily held to blame for these crimes?'

Svarta sneered. 'You should know, Åddren, it was one of the Arkmages that committed this crime,' she said. The hall erupted with angry shouts from the Arka and Farden could see the soldiers tensing warily. Towerdawn snarled and rattled his spikes, and Brightshow bared her fangs.

Vice stormed forward. 'This is an outrage!' he bellowed, and the crowd yelled with him. The Undermage stared straight at the golden dragon and Svarta as they turned to face him. Farfallen growled deep in his throat and Farden could see flame in his eyes. Vice showed no fear. 'How dare you accuse the Arkmages of such a lie! What proof do you have, if any, of this ridiculous accusation?' he shouted. His face was flushed and his knuckles white.

But Svarta laughed contemptuously and waved the small bundle in her hands. 'You want proof, Vice? Arkmages?' Here is your proof!' She held the cloth package at one end and shook it. A blood-stained gold disk tumbled out of the fabric and fell to the floor with a metallic clang. It bounced and rattled noisily on the marble floor as it slowly spun to a rest just in front of the two thrones. As it fell silent, so did the great hall, and when the disk had stopped, everyone stared at the dried blood, and the lettering, and turned pale.

Vice was visibly shocked, and his face dropped. Svarta tossed the bloody cloth to the floor and crossed her arms with a smug expression. Modren looked to Farden, but he was watching Helyard's face closely. The Arkmage sat perched on the edge of his throne, gripping the arms with white knuckles. His face struggled to remain calm and composed. Farden could see the sweat starting to gather at the roots of his dirty blonde hair. Watching the tall man's face, his suspicions about the Arkmage were suddenly thrown into sharp and painful reality. With the apparent truth looming in front of him the mage felt a sudden sickening feeling of betrayal, as if the ice had just given way under the hall, and the Arka were falling with it. He looked at the disk.

It was a Weight, an enchanted symbol of office carried by all Arkmages since anyone could bear to remember. There were two of them; one for Åddren and one for Helyard, and together they balanced the scales sitting at Evernia's golden feet. Farden cast a quick look at scales hanging awkwardly and askew, cornered and surrounded by the remaining candles.

The Weights were essentially quickdoors, smaller and more elegant than their unwieldy cousins. Hiding under the dried blood and lettering were powerful spells that allowed its bearer to travel to anywhere they wished in mere seconds. The Weights were dangerous for a mage who wasn't strong enough to use one, and Farden had heard many stories about users getting the spell wrong and appearing on a mountain top or, in his opinion worse, half in half out of a wall, crushed and dead. Only the Arkmages could use them, and only fools tried.

Uncertainty scurried amidst the awkward silence, and there was a terrible feeling of dread in the hall. More than a few of the council members exchanged fearful looks. Svarta looked about her victoriously, challenging anyone with her scowling eyes. Farfallen was silent and brooding, waiting for someone to say something. The other two dragons were silent, but Brightshow wore a concerned look, and Farden watched her shuffle her clawed feet from side to side.

Vice looked to his superiors, and he was the first to speak. 'Your Mages?' he said. The Undermage's voice sounded strangely loud after the awkward silence, and everyone watched the two men on their tall thrones. With a terrible slowness Åddren lifted a hand and reached inside his gold and green robe. Every single eye was upon him, and he looked whiter, paler, and his sparse hair made him look suddenly very old and frail. Carefully he pulled forth a gold disk from under his robe, a disk that was identical to the one lying on the floor. He lifted it high for all to see. Åddren then turned to his friend and fixed him with a stare that could have spoken a thousand different words. Svarta sniggered and looked to the two riders flanking her and Farfallen, waiting.

'Helyard?' He said with a cracking voice, 'I think an

explanation is needed...'

The Arkmage's jaw was set, eyes stuck on the Weight on the floor. 'This is ridiculous,' he croaked, and licked his lips.

Svarta cocked her head. 'Excuse me?'

Helyard's mahogany eyes flashed with anger and Farden could have sworn he heard him growl at the Siren queen. 'I said that this is ridiculous! Gods damn it, can't you hear how absurd this accusation is, Åddren? I was here in Krauslung for the entire evening, ask anyone! This is nonsense!' His eyes were narrowed, and his expression was that of a venomous snake caught between a spade and the heel of a boot.

'I wouldn't call the death of a dozen Siren guards and the theft of the tearbook nonsense, Arkmage,' Farfallen warned. The tension was slowly being drawn tighter and tighter. Farden looked up at the skylight and noticed the clouds gathering in the sky above the great hall, marring the crystal clear morning. Several other dragons were wheeling high above, colourful specks on a greying backdrop.

Helyard thumped his fist against the marble throne. 'I am innocent of this crime! How dare you try to blame *me*, an Arkmage! I can't believe these lies are actually being listened to!' He was furious, scrabbling weakly at explanations and constantly looking to Åddren for help. Farden could see the guilt in his eyes now, and the mood in the hall had turned from uncertain fear to righteous indignant anger. Council members whispered and pointed, nodding and shaking their heads, all thinking the same. Farden felt the anger inside him welling up, and he contemplated dragging Helyard from the hall himself. 'I am not a traitor!' shouted the Arkmage.

'THEN EXPLAIN THIS!' yelled Svarta. With a snarl she kicked the Weight against the foot of his throne.

'Lies! It was stolen and...' Words caught in his throat. He blinked wide-eyed, and his mouth hung open. The clouds were darkening, and the other dragons were soaring on the approaching gale.

Svarta spread her arms wide and cast an accusing look around the hall. 'Stolen! From one of the Arkmages? Even if it had been taken from you, who else can use it, Helyard? Who?' Several of the council members shook their heads at her as if they were actually being blamed. 'I didn't think as much,' she said. Farfallen cleared his throat loudly, and gave Svarta a warning look. She retreated to her dragon's side simmering with righteous anger.

Helyard continued to splutter and shake with rage. He looked to Åddren again, but the Arkmage was now slumped in the throne with his head resting in one hand. His own Weight lay in his open palm. Vice walked calmly forward and stood beside the Arkmage to whisper confidentially to him. Farden wondered how much privacy they could muster under the watchful eyes of the dragons and the rest of the hall. Ears were pricked. Vice seemed to ask a question. Åddren shook his head once or twice, and then nodded with a look of sad resignation at the Undermage, his blue eyes looking as if they could shatter like glass at any moment. Vice bowed his head and stepped back, folding his hands in front of him calmly even though he shook with anger and disappointment. Farden watched his friend carefully, and like everyone else in the great hall he waited, and boiled with tethered, indignant fury. He shared a look with Modren. The mage was wide-eyed and unsure.

Åddren's voice sounded like a snapped twig in a silent forest. 'Guards…' he paused, and there was a moment of abject horror pasted on Helyard's pale face. The clouds above were now heavy and ominous. The verdict was in. '…remove the Arkmage from the hall,' managed Åddren in a quiet breath. Vice sighed and snapped his fingers at the armoured men standing behind the pillars. There were no shouts of protest, no whispers from the magick council this time. Everyone in the hall just watched, and glared.

'This is impossible!' Helyard shouted, his voice now high-pitched and his eyes burning. The soldiers approached him gingerly and tried to slowly uproot him from his throne. Fearful of touching him, they started to lead him across the hall. Farden half-expected the tall mage to try to fight his way out, but he just carried on shouting and protesting at the top of his voice. Once he tried to move past the guards and get away but the armoured men formed a ring around him and used their shields to move him along. Condemning shouts of "traitor!" and "snake!" came from the council. Helyard's fists pounded the air, and his eyes were wide with rage. He pointed at Svarta and spat at her venomously. 'This isn't over, Siren! I'm warning you! Åddren!' Helyard's voice echoed around the hall until he disappeared behind the gold doors with a bang.

Vice turned to Svarta and Farfallen. 'Are you happy now?' he said.

'Not in the slightest,' the Siren shook her head.

'You've got what you came for, Helyard has been exposed and will be punished accordingly,' said Vice, walking swiftly to take up his own seat near Åddren.

But Svarta wagged a finger at him. 'Not so fast, Undermage, we came here for an answers.'

Åddren exploded with sudden anger. 'And what answers would they be!?' he shouted. His face was pale and his hands were shaking with fury or grief, Farden couldn't tell, and he slammed his palm down on the marble arm of his throne with a loud slap. 'You've brought this magick council to its knees and had one of the Arkmages imprisoned for treason, what more could you possibly want! Do you want me as well? The cloak off my back? My throne? Here!' Åddren tore wildly at his gold and green robe, ripping it from his shoulders and throwing it over his head. He threw it on the marble floor next to the bloody disk and stood with his arms wide, half-naked and eyes wide. Svarta was silent for once.

'I just watched a man thrown into prison for murder and

betrayal, a man whom I have known for years, a man I trusted implicitly! And yet, under my very nose, he has plotted and he has schemed against his own people! When have you known such betrayal, Svarta? Tell me how you think that would feel!' Åddren's eyes glowed with fire as he waited for an answer, but the Siren queen said nothing and just stared at him. Farden had never seen the Arkmage like that before, and neither had the council.

Farfallen took a deep breath. 'I think we have argued enough for one day.' His deep voice appeared to calm Åddren, and he slumped wearily back into his seat. The gold dragon continued. 'But the question still remains whether Helyard was working alone, or if we should still ready ourselves for the summoning of this creature?'

Vice stood. 'I agree. Farden was attacked by a dark sorcerer while on his way to Nelska, so we must assume that there are others involved.'

Brightshow piped up. 'But without the tearbook we have nothing, not even the translations.'

The whole council sighed, and felt the first icy tendrils of failure creeping over them. Farden racked his brains, and tried to quell the anger inside him. Cheska's words from the night before echoed in his head.

Vice clicked his fingers suddenly. 'Albion,' he said, and looked around.

Åddren seemed confused. Farfallen narrowed his eyes at the Undermage. 'Albion?'

'Helyard has been travelling there at night for the past few weeks. I thought nothing of it until now.'

Farden remembered something, and spoke up. 'He went to Albion the night before I left for Nelska. The sorcerer on the ship also had an Albion accent.' The pieces began to click together.

'He said he had business with one of the Dukes,' said Åddren. Vice nodded. 'He went to Kiltyrin two nights ago, and Fidlarig before that. This has to be what we're looking for.' Åddren put a hand under his chin and quietly muttered and agreement. The council members talked amongst themselves and wagged their chins and fingers. Everybody seemed to agree.

'We can have dragons searching for the well in a few hours,' Svarta said decisively, and Farden confidently walked forward. He resisted the urge to knock the Siren queen with his shoulder, and stood in front of the thrones. He looked to Vice. 'The Written can quickdoor to the port of Dunyra, Undermage. I can have all of us there before sunset, ready to fight,' he said.

Svarta looked disgusted at the thought of an army of Written, but Vice smiled. 'We will need all the help we can get,' said Åddren. Behind them the Old Dragon settled down to sit on the floor, and rumbled thoughtfully. 'Now that Helyard's been exposed, his friends are likely to spring their trap early,' he warned.

'That's assuming they've already found a dark elf well,' Svarta said.

Åddren raised a hand and spoke in a calm measured tone. 'We cannot afford to take that chance. Who knows what Helyard has been up to all these years, what powerful friends he might have,' he let out a brief sigh. 'Vice, you will take the army to the port of Dunyra by ship or by quickdoor, find that well and destroy it. I will not allow these traitors to summon this creature, it must be killed at all costs!' The council murmured, and a few yells could be heard.

'I agree,' Farfallen growled. 'I will send my fastest dragons to Albion within the hour, and if you are willing, the rest of us will remain here to guard Krauslung for the time being. Our army will be ready to leave Nelska by the morning.'

'Please, accept my hospitality,' Åddren bowed his head with a friendly, and slightly weary, gesture. Farfallen flashed his reptilian smile and Svarta cleared her throat with some sort of icy, indifferent "thank you."

The Arkmage rapped his knuckles on the side of his throne. 'The council is now dismissed, the dragons and their riders may stay, as can you Farden.' Åddren pointed to the mage. The council slowly drifted out of the door and out into the now hushed corridor. Servants and citizens peered over the heads of guards like eager chicks in a nest, trying to see into the great hall. Modren made to leave, but Farden beckoned him forward, and he joined him in front of the thrones.

Soon the hall was empty, and the doors were locked shut from the outside. Vice sighed loudly, still eyeing the scar on Farfallen's chest. 'Farden and I will go and ready our forces. There is much to do.' His eyes flicked to the mage, and Farden nodded quickly.

Åddren spoke. 'I will talk with Farfallen for a while. I want that Weight hidden in your chambers, Vice, keep it safe and out of sight.'

The Undermage stood up and went to the blood-encrusted Weight on the floor. With the cloth he picked it up and gripped it tightly. 'I'll meet you outside, Farden,' said Vice before he left the hall.

After he left, Åddren beckoned to the mage. 'Come here, mage,' he said. Farden strode forward and bowed in front of the throne. The Arkmage leant forward and held out his own Weight. It caught the light and glistening like the sun. Åddren spoke slowly. He sounded tired. 'It seems you have proven your worth once more, Farden, and I am glad to have you back in one piece. Because you have been so loyal to the Arka in the face of such betrayal, I now want you to hold onto this, so that I may be exempt from any blame. After tonight I will stay in my chamber, and the council will be suspended until I say different.' Åddren looked to Svarta and narrowed his eyes ever so slightly. 'Vice has done well to chose you to lead the Written. I know you will not disappoint.'

Farden suddenly felt honoured, and for the first time he felt like he had escaped the shadow of his uncle's legacy, that his dedication had been noticed, that he was no longer a pawn, but a player. Farden bowed once more and thanked the Arkmage. He took the Weight, marvelling at its lightness, and slipped it inside his cloak. As he turned he looked to Farfallen, who blinked slowly and hinted at a smile, and then left with Modren trailing behind. Svarta watched him go suspiciously.

As he reached the doors, Farden stopped and turned, an idea in his head. 'If I might ask a favour of the Sirens, your Mage, I would like it if Brightshow flew me to the Arkabbey in the Forest of Durn, in Albion, if she and her rider are willing?' he asked. Modren looked aghast at the notion of dragons and flying in the same sentence.

'And what is the purpose of this diversion?' Åddren inquired.

'My superior at the Arkabbey, the vampyre Durnus,' at this Svarta looked even more disgusted, 'is one of the finest historians and scholars the Arka have. He has spent decades studying dark magick and Albion, and I think he would be invaluable in helping to find the elven well,' said Farden.

Åddren thought for a moment and then nodded. 'It makes sense, and I see no problem with it. Be quick though, Farden, we have no time to waste.' Åddren waved for him to go, and managed to give the mage a weak smile. The mage could see that the day's events had hit him hard.

'I'll meet you in front of the main gates outside your city, Farden, as soon as night falls.' Brightshow said, and her rider gave the mage a formal smile. Farden smiled at the dragon, bowed again, and left with Modren once again in tow.

Vice was waiting outside the door. The people had been ushered downstairs and swiftly out of the citadel at the behest of the Undermage's sharp tongue. His soldiers now stood at every door and corner in the fortress, green and black armour clanking loudly as they patrolled around in pairs.

'There you are,' Vice scowled at them. The door banged shut and he whispered to Farden. 'What did the Arkmage say?'

'He said you did well to choose me as leader of the Written, and he thanked me for all I did in Nelska,' said Farden. They walked as they whispered, meandering through the corridors and down into the fortress below. Modren remained a few steps behind, feeling altogether overwhelmed and left out.

Vice mused, rubbing his chin with a thoughtful hum. He smoothed his hair as he spoke. 'Helyard all along,' he said.

Farden shook his head and clenched his fists. 'He's been against our every move since the start of this whole debacle. I should have realised earlier when he tried to pin it on me.'

'None of us could have ever predicted that the traitor would be an Arkmage. Even in my wildest dreams.'

'I always knew there was something strange about him. He always was the more powerful of the two. I half expected him to try to fight his way out of there,' said Farden.

Vice agreed. 'Well he's locked away now, and I'd like to see him try to break his way out. The prison walls are bound with spells for a reason. Even air couldn't escape those cells,' he said. Farden and Modren nodded. The prisons were legendary, and every criminal's nightmare. Vice looked at the two mages. 'Are the Written going to be ready in time? As much as I distrust that golden lizard, Farfallen is right: whoever Helyard was working with could potentially release the creature at any time.'

Farden lifted his chin proudly. 'I'll assemble them now and get them through the quickdoor to Dunyra as soon as possible. We'll be at Fidlarig by nightfall.'

'Good. You're in charge now,' he paused. 'So don't let me down,' Vice threw him a sideways look and disguised the warning with a smile. Farden retorted with his own arrogant smirk. 'Never been a problem before,' he said. They jogged down a flight of steps two at a time, boots clattering on the stone. The noise from below was getting louder. 'I almost forgot, I'm collecting Durnus from the Arkabbey before I go to Dunyra.'

Vice looked confused, a little annoyed. 'Why?'

'That old vampyre has sat in his study for the last two hundred years studying the dark elf wells and their history. If we want to get to this well as quickly as possible then he's our best bet.'

'Fine, bring him,' said the Undermage reluctantly. 'I'm staying in Krauslung. Someone needs to be here to stop it falling apart. Åddren is shaken, and I don't think he'll be thinking clearly, so I want to be here in case anything goes wrong. And those dragons need watching too,' said Vice, and leant closer to whisper in Farden's ear. 'I see what you mean about that Siren bitch,' he hissed. Farden nodded and said no more.

The three of them descended into the depths of the Arkathedral fortress, their steps gradually getting faster and faster with each flight of stairs and every corridor they came across, as if success depended on their haste, and in no time at all they reached where the crowds were at their busiest. Vice paused on the steps. The noise was deafening, echoing and bouncing off the marble walls and floors, and he had to shout to be heard. 'I will join you in a few days. Don't let me down Farden! Remember, you're in charge now.'

'If there're any problems I'll be back here instantly, so keep the quickdoors open!' Farden shook Vice's hand, and Modren bowed low. The Undermage gripped the Farden's shoulder tightly and then turned to go back the way they had come. 'May the gods be with you!' he called over his shoulder.

Once he had left, Farden sighed and shrugged at Modren. His blonde friend shook his head and breathed an exasperated and somewhat tired sigh. 'You've got a lot of explaining to do.'

Farden rolled his eyes 'Tonight, when I get back from the

Arkabbey, then I'll tell you everything,' he said. 'This day has been fucked up.'

'This whole situation is fucked up! Morale's going to be terrible when word gets out about Helyard,' Modren cursed.

'I know, but we've got more dangerous things to think about now, and places to be, so get a move on. I'm going to get my things and get ready, and then we'll meet back here at sunset, like I said.'

'Fine,' said Modren, and the two mages strode purposefully down the corridor and into the atrium. It was buzzing, as it had been all day, and once again they had to push and barge and shout and squeeze to get through the mass of people. Farden waved to Modren and fought his way outside and back onto the streets. Within half an hour he was back at the *Bearded Goat* and quenching his thirst with fresh cold rainwater. The drunks had been turfed out and gotten rid of, and the inn was being slowly cleaned by a set of very tired staff indeed. The innkeeper barely said a word to the mage. He had deep purple bags under his eyes and his hair resembled a dishevelled haystack. Farden paid the man for his room and his drink, and then went upstairs to gather his things. It was just past midday, and there were at least four or five hours until sunset. He slumped onto the bed and quickly fell into a deep sleep.

When he awoke it was no more than an hour later, and he felt refreshed and eager. The sun was beginning its slow fall to the western slopes, and the city outside his window was still crowded and turbulent. He was glad he had kept the window shut. Farden stretched, and then yawned, and then got of of bed. Most of his clothes were already packed, seeing as he hadn't quite unpacked yet, but his sword was blunt and his boots were looking a little too worn. He checked his supplies, of which he had plenty thanks to the Sirens. The little vial of ice water sparkled blue in the sunlight. The maps they had given him didn't make much sense, but they could come in useful, so he packed them as well. The book followed, as did

Cheska's fjortla, and then he was ready to go. Farden grabbed his cloak from the chair and flung it around him. Something solid knocked against his shoulder, and he made a confused face. The mage rummaged around in the pockets until he found the culprit: the Weight. He brought it out into the light and ran his coarse fingers over the gold, feeling the ridges and dents of the script. The words were strange, foreign, like the old spellbooks he had seen on Durnus's shelf. Farden handled the disk as if it would explode in any moment, as if it would whisk him away to some unknown place just by holding it. He carefully put it back in his pocket, and made sure it was safe. With that, he was done, and he hoisted his pack and his sword onto his shoulders. Once again, the mage was ready to go.

Farden left the *Bearded Goat* jogging and headed towards the nearest market. People were beginning to barricade doors and windows with planks and boxes. Someone had left an old cart in the middle of the road, and a man had clambered on top of it, yelling at the top of his voice that war was coming. There was a bottle in his hand, and he swayed back and forth as the cart rocked. Soldiers stood on every street corner and patrols meandered through the crowds. They seemed restrained, edgy, and Farden didn't blame them. He looked up at the sky. The clouds were still gathering, as they had been since that morning. No doubt Helyard was up to something, sitting shackled in his cell. Shadows scuttled over the city as clouds passed over the sun, and the light of the clear day began to fade. As he strode briskly through the streets, Farden kept an eye on the weather.

The mage found the market, and crammed as it was with people, he managed to make his way to the blacksmith's forge. Weapons were piling up on the tables, and a backlogged queue of soldiers stood tapping their feet and fingers. Their expressions were of impatient boredom, and they were all silent, waiting for their turn. Farden approached the line of men. He could feel their eyes on him. As he moved to join the back of the queue, they moved, one by one, out of his way, and gestured for him to move forward. Farden nodded and smiled as each man silently shuffled aside. Word spread fast in the city.

A skinny young boy took his sword and unsheathed it, testing its edge. He couldn't have been more than ten years old, but he swung it around him once or twice, nodded, and then gave it to the man at the grindstone. He looked at it, thumbed the blade, and then spun his wheel. A shower of sparks flew from the steel and it hissed and whined as the metal moved against the rough grey edges of the stone. Farden waited, running his hands over the armour and shields on display, and thought to himself.

After a moment, the blade was finished, and the boy handed it back to the mage. Farden could see the boys eyes widen hungrily at the sight of the red and gold metal around his wrists. Farden smiled and tapped them with a finger. 'Not for all the coin in the world, boy,' he said, and walked off, nodding his thanks to the line of soldiers as he left.

Replacing his boots took a while, as it seemed difficult for the people at the stalls to find any pairs that fit him. After an hour or so he found a pair of black travelling boots which matched his black cloak, and they hugged his feet comfortably. Once they had been "blessed" by the owner of the stall, a very strange and twitchy young man, Farden left, and headed back towards the Arkathedral. He gathered a few more supplies on his way out, but just as he was about to escape the clutches of the busy market, he saw a tiny little stall, no more than a banner and a tall box, hiding under the porch of an old building on the corner of the street. A tall woman, almost taller than him, stood behind the stall and watched the passing commotion with a calm and expressionless face. He didn't have time to spare, but there was something about her wares that caught his eye. Spread out on the top of the dusty box was a white cloth, and dotting the cloth were stones and gems of all different kinds. Farden walked a little closer and looked at them.

Some had smooth surfaces, and some were rough and spiky. One glittered in the fading light and shined with every colour imaginable. Another looked like a lump of gold while the rest were collections of deep molten purples and greens, metallic mottled oranges and veiny crimson reds. Farden couldn't help but examine each of them, while the tall serene woman watched him calmly. 'Would you like help, sire?' she asked, and Farden looked up at her. She was pale, very pale, and had long jet-black hair that reached her hips. Her limbs and fingers were thin, like her face, as if her whole body had been stretched and drawn out. The woman's eyes were like a lizard's, and almost seemed to move independently of each other, dark, serene, and inexpressive like two murky rockpools of glassy water. Farden pointed to the small cabochon quartz that was nearest to him. It slowly changed colour, back and forth between green and red.

'What is this?' he asked, and she leant forward as if she had just noticed the stones for the first time. 'The bloodstone heals feuds, and protects against injustice,' her voice was small and without accent, and strangely monotone. 'Many women come to me for it, to bring back lost lovers.' She pointed to a grey stone that shimmered like steel. 'This too, they buy,' she said, and then cocked her head to one side like a bird looking at a worm. 'Are you here for a woman?'

Farden quickly shook his head. 'No, well yes, but just a present for my, er, sister. She's gone away for three days, and I wanted to get her something for when she returns,' said the mage, with a brief smile. 'Which she will,' he added.

The woman grinned back at him, but it was a tight expression that bore no emotion. 'Well then, Written, this would be a fine and useful present for her.' Her long fingers moved over the cloth slowly, and then finally rested on a brass-coloured rock. It looked like a lump of tarnished gold, full of angular faces and sparkling edges. 'These fall from the stars in the east, usually in the morning hours. Some call them the stones of fire, others daemonstones. But they show the truth of things hidden, give hope, and make an excellent present for a, a loved one.'

'My sister,' said Farden.

The woman nodded and smiled again. 'Of course.' The mage rubbed his chin. 'How much?' he asked. 'Only two silver for my trouble,' said the skinny woman. He had never really bought a present for anyone before, but it seemed nice enough, and Farden reached for his coins. He placed two silver bits on the cloth and the woman snatched them away before wrapping the small rock in a sheet of waxy brown paper. Her hands moved rapidly over the package to the sound of crackling paper, and soon enough Farden's present was wrapped, and waiting in the thin woman's hands. He smiled again, uneasily, and reached for it. From the way the corner or her mouth curled, and the way she stared at him, he half expected her to pull back and ask for something more, but she didn't move a muscle. The mage stuffed the paper package inside his cloak and made to leave. The woman looked to the grey skies with her glassy eyes and muttered to herself. 'Rain's on its way, it seems,' she said.

Farden looked up at the clouds gathering overhead, their dark bases heavy with precipitation. The Arkmage was hard at work indeed, and it was time to meet the rest of the Written. He nodded to the strange woman and left her stall, feeling her strange gaze upon his back. The gem knocked against his chest with every step he took, and every time it bumped him he thought of Cheska. Farden would keep it for her, while she was in the Spire, and after, once she was rested and healed, he would give it to her as a present. He could almost see her face lighting up in his mind. He took a deep breath, and seeing as she had kept him safe so far, he threw a quick prayer to the goddess and made his way towards the Arkathedral, just as the first heavy rain drops began to fall, and as darkness gathered in the corners of the wintry skies.

❦

Almost an hour later he reached the Arkathedral gates. Heavy raindrops splashed on the walls, soaking everything to the bone, making buildings creak and swell, a city drowned in the downpour. With the outbreak of rain the streets had quickly emptied. The angry crowds had dispersed and the people had gone home for the evening to shut their doors and pull their curtains. There was no shouting to be heard, no revelling, the news of the Arkmage's incarceration had spread fast and the blow had been heavy. Farden looked around and listened to his boots splash in the bubbling puddles. Krauslung seemed strangely subdued and quiet that evening.

Modren was waiting for him in the rain, hood up and grinning like a fool. He watched Farden striding across the cobblestones towards him and raised a hand. He walked towards him and shook himself loudly with a shiver.

'Getting cold out here,' said Modren.

'You are standing in the rain,' replied Farden. The mages walked forward to where the torches hanging from the Arkathedral walls sputtered. The gates were barely ajar, and there was a loud clamouring from behind them, a roar that rose above the noise of the raindrops. Bright light poured onto the street and the guards at the gates looked unsettled and wary. Modren leant towards Farden and whispered behind a cupped hand as they reached them. 'You wait until we get inside, mate, I haven't seen something like this in a long time.' Farden threw him a quizzical look, and then realised what he was talking about. His heart began to beat. Without any ado whatsoever the guards pushed the heavy doors open and the bright torchlight momentarily blinded the two mages. The roaring noise slowly ground to a halt, and as Farden blinked the spots from his eyes, more than a hundred faces turned to look at him. His stomach suddenly bubbled with momentary fear, or maybe stage-fright, Farden couldn't tell.

Modren had been right. The main atrium was crammed with Written. Farden wasn't sure he'd seen so many of them in his lifetime, and his heart filled with pride. They were armed, equipped, eager, and ready to fight, eyes blazing with the anticipation of battle. Farden looked over the multitude of different faces, picking out a few he had fought with many times, others he had never seen before. Fresh-faced confident youngsters stood beside grim hardened men, both standing battle-scarred and more than a little proud. Every Written wore that smile, the one the Farden had flashed countless times, that self-assured mettle that burnt across their faces and their backs. Farden tried to stand as tall as he could. He tried to look authoritative. He tried to act like he belonged to this crowd. He tried to forget that they all knew about his uncle. Any eyes that held his gaze too long he tried to drill into them, command their respect. He tried to do a hundred things, and he wanted to be everything everyone was expecting. *If the Undermage thinks you're capable, then so should you.* Cheska's words echoed in his mind.

Farden spoke clearly and with a commanding tone. 'Listen up!' he barked. Farden could hear his name being whispered around the marble hall. He ignored them. 'I'm sure you all know me, and for those who don't then I expect you soon will. No doubt you've heard about Helyard, and the traitors who killed the scholars at Arfell. Word has always travelled fast in these parts.' A few people chuckled, others nodded. There was more whispering.

'I'm not going to waste our precious time talking, so here's the problem. The ones who killed the old scholars stole a book, a powerful summoning manual from the times of the dark elves. Using this book, they want to release an ancient monster that will tear Emaneska in pieces, and now that Helyard has been thrown in jail the council have no doubt that the rest of these traitors will accelerate their plan. The only chance we have is to find a dark elf well before they do, and that's why we're going to Albion tonight, to the port of Dunyra.' Farden took a breath and looked at the calm faces of the crowd, simply waiting, staring at him, and not even the slightest bit worried. The mage didn't hesitate to continue. 'We all know that we're the best at what we do because we've spent our lives proving it. And, once again, the safety of the Arka rests on our shoulders, and we're going to put a stop to all this nonsense, the only way the Written know how. I'm not ordering you to go, I'm saying let's go do our job, so let's do it fucking well as always!'

A hundred fists punched the air to his words and the roar that echoed in the marble hall was frighteningly loud. Farden turned to Modren standing by his side with a grin. He puffed out his skinny chest and looked around at the shouting Written with a similar expression. Farden laughed out loud. Shouts filled the hall and the mages began to form long noisy lines, facing the stairs. There were a few more yells and calls, and once they were finished, they started to stamp their feet with the most impatient eagerness, warming themselves up and getting the magick ready with a great roaring throbbing sound. Farden turned to Modren and shouted in his ear. 'Get them to Dunyra, and meet up with the dragons there, if they've arrived. Make sure you don't waste an time! You're in charge while I'm gone!'

'You're going to get that vampyre of yours?'

'Durnus yes! I should be back by morning, but just make sure that if it comes to the worst, don't hesitate, understand?' he shouted. Modren nodded fervently. With a grunt Farden tightened the straps on his pack and clapped his friend on the arm. Without another word he turned and left. Modren watched him disappear behind the edge of the door, leaving the zealous stamping Written to themselves. He stood on the wet cobbled street and took a massive breath and then let it out slowly through his nose. He hadn't realised how hot he'd been, but as the cold raindrops splashed on his skin he shivered, and listened to his heart slowing down. The rain knocked against the gutters and rushed into the drains, making a noisy din as it collided with the world. Dusk was quickly approaching, sneaking along the horizon like a hungry cat. Farden waited for a moment and then he was gone again, off into the evening and towards the city gates.

It took him just under an hour, and when he got there it was dark and the downpour had only gotten worse. A couple guards had taken shelter under the thick arches. They saluted the mage as he approached and quickly hurried to part the thick iron gates. Once through Farden stood in the shadow of the wall and blew hot breath into his wet hands to try to warm them. A rumble of thunder rocked the gloomy sky and lightning split the darkness. The mage spotted Brightshow standing further up the path. She was shiny with rain and blinking water from her great eyes. She smiled toothily. 'Well met once again Farden!' she called to him over the roaring downpour.

The mage smiled to himself and went to meet the dragon. 'And good wishes no doubt!' he said as he reached her. 'Thank you again for agreeing to take me to Albion.'

'It is my pleasure! Lakkin has left his saddle on so it'll be easier to hold on in this weather. I wouldn't really recommend barescale on your first time riding a dragon.' Farden had to agree. She flicked her white and gold head to the leather seat strapped behind her at the base of her neck. Farden clenched his fists in a last effort to coax some heat into them. He looked up the hillside towards Manesmark where the lights of the Spire shone brightly. The mage took a deep breath. 'You scared?' laughed Brightshow, breaking into his thoughts.

Farden smiled. 'Hah, a little,' he confessed with a shrug.

Brightshow winked. 'I don't blame you, our riders train for years. But it's much more fun than a quickdoor I hear.'

'I'm sure it is,' he paused for a moment. Rain dripped over

the edge of his hood in tiny waterfalls. 'Shall we go?' he said.

Brightshow nodded. 'As you wish. Climb up then, before this storm gets any worse!' She bent her shoulder to the ground, and extended the edge of her wing to make a little ramp up to the saddle. After a moment of uncertainty, Farden climbed up her wet scales and tried to balance so he could slip his foot into a little leather loop that hung from a thick strap. He teetered for second but then regained his footing and quickly swung the other leg over the side so he was sitting astride the dragon. Once he had pulled the leather belts securely over his thighs and feet Brightshow stood up and spread her wings like a massive umbrella over his head. Farden made sure his supplies were all in place and not likely to fly away, and then yanked the strap that held the sword to his back.

'Are you ready?' she shouted to him.

Farden blew rain water from his face and smiled grimly. She turned her head to look at him. 'I think so!' he called, and she flashed a mouth full of teeth.

'Then let's go!' she cried. The pale dragon crouched for a mere second, just enough for Farden to suddenly regret his decision, before she exploded upwards into the sky with one giant leap, rain and wind pressing his body flat against her rough scales until that first huge flap of her enormous wings was finished. And then came another. The air howled around him as her white wings beat the air with huge deep whooshing sounds like trees falling. The mage bounced up and down in the saddle with each lurching stroke. The tight straps protested but they seemed to hold. Brightshow shifted her body and pointed her head to the sky and Farden found himself strangling the leather horn at the front of the saddle for dear life. It felt like he was in a quickdoor. The noise of the wind was deafening. He swallowed nervously as he caught a glance of his city spread out below him like an intricate model that was quickly getting smaller and smaller with every flap of the dragon's mighty wings. Somehow in the back of Farden's mind it was exhilarating to see the ground fall out from him, if not a little terrifying. His teeth chattered with excitement and the knuckles gripping the saddle were so cold and white they looked as though they were someone else's.

Farden crouched low to match her streamlined shape and started to feel the dragon's body moving through the wind, noticing the twitches and swerves of her tail keeping them steady in the face of the weather. The Össfen mountains now looked like scattered rubble beneath them, and Farden pulled his cloak around his head to shield his eyes from the stinging, biting wind.

chapter 13

"No one would ever suggest that the Written are out of control, but they seem to work best when we leave them to their own devices, and we know that. They act in pairs or they act alone and as long as the job gets done, then the council turn a blind eye to the method, but thank the gods that we ruled against the fourth and third rune. Some of the older Written are almost as skilled as I am…"

From pages found in Arkmage Helyard's rooms

Jarrick had been on watch for the last twelve hours, and he was starting to fall asleep at his post. He shook his head and sniffed, and tried to keep his drowsy eyelids from closing completely. Ganlir should be here soon, he thought to himself, but Ganlir was probably fast asleep. The guard shrugged in his heavy gold armour. Jarrick eyed the corridor to his right, a dark hallway untouched by the light of the flaming torches near the door. Further down that corridor and to the right was another door made thick with steel and strong oak, and behind that slept the traitorous Helyard, locked away in a windowless room with nothing more than straw and a scrap of sackcloth to keep him warm.

The Arkmage had been brought in almost a dozen hours ago, when Jarrick had just started his long watch. The old mage, once a proud ruler of the Arka, had been reduced to a snarling angry old man, spitting curses and threats like a common thief on the way to the stocks. Helyard had pounded on his cell door and hollered for hours until he finally gave up when night fell, and now all was silent.

Jarrick watched the shadows of the corridor for a moment and sniffed again. At least he was warm and not out on patrol in the pouring rain, he thought. Happy that nothing was amiss, the sleepy soldier turned back to his staring spot on the wall opposite, counting the bricks and patches of lichen. His eyes closed briefly, but he shook himself awake again and changed his grip on his spear. He felt the rough wood in his palm and tried to stay vigilant... where was that Ganlir fellow anyway? he pondered with a yawn.

A minute later and Jarrick was leaning gently on the cold wall, his armour grating softly against the stone as his chest rose and fell. A low snore came from his open mouth, and his eyelids fluttered in the throes of a brief dream. He did not notice the door on his left slowly creeping open, and was completely unaware of the dark shadowy figure sidling into the room, cloaked and dangerous. With slow movements the intruder pushed the door shut and reached for a set of keys on a hook. They jingled lightly in his hand. Above him was a torch hanging from a bracket in the wall. With his free he hand touched the flames and the fire seemed to flow into his skin, plunging the room into total darkness. The man listened to the shadows, but all that could be heard was the quiet snorting of Jarrick's snores.

The figure crept on and into the hallway. He found his way to a thick oak and steel door, to the right, that had been barred and bolted from the outside with intricate brass cogs and latches. The keys jingled again as he felt their jagged edges to find the right ones. With a scraping he inserted the strange shapes of metal and slid them into their holes. With a click and a brief whine something within the door came loose. The figure reached for the handle but felt something still holding it tight. An invisible face frowned in the darkness. The man's fingers rippled over the face of the door, feeling the cracks and contours of it, searching. He pressed his palm flat on the wood near the keyhole. There was a dull thud, and a pulse that rippled across the oak. The figure paused warily and then pushed the door gently forward. With a creak and a moan it shifted an inch or two, and then with a bit more persuasion, swung open into a room that smelled like sweat and frustration. The bitter scent of rank urine made the figure wrinkle his nose, but he stepped over the threshold and closed the door behind him, and locked it with a spell of his own.

Somewhere there was a quiet snuffling and a rustle of hay. A burst of flame pierced the gloom and send the shadows running. The fire burnt and crackled in the intruder's open palm and he held it high to peer around the room. Orange light scattered around him, illuminating piles of straw and a rickety cot in the corner made from a few spars of driftwood and sackcloth. Curled into a ball on the uncomfortable bed was Helyard, groaning and scrunching up his eyes. The Arkmage was covered in dust from head to toe, and his robes were stained and wet.

'What do you want from me now?' he said in a gruff voice.

The figure took a step forward. Thick travelling boots scuffed the stone as he bent close to the Arkmage's face. 'I have come to set you free, your Mage,' he whispered.

Helyard peered into the gloom but the darkness of the figure's cloak obscured and covered the man's face completely. 'Who are you?' asked the Arkmage quietly. The tall stranger stepped back and gestured towards the locked door.

'A friend,' came the reply. Helyard sat up with a tired groan and tried to steady his legs underneath him. The old man ran a hand through his dirty blonde hair. Mahogany eyes looked sadly at the hooded figure standing tall between him and the door. 'Those seem hard to come by these days,' he said, and stood up with a very tired sigh. The Arkmage waved an impatient hand. 'Well whatever it is you want from me, let's go,' he said. But the stranger just stood there. Helyard coughed quietly and crossed his arms and waited.

Underneath his hood, the man smirked and grinned wickedly. Suddenly he grunted and jabbed the air with hands held like blades. The air hummed and split and knocked the Arkmage against the stone wall behind him. His skull cracked on the stone and he tried blinked pain from his eyes. Helyard's mind spun, but he quickly threw up his hands as a lightning bolt flew towards him. The spell exploded against an invisible wall about a foot in front of the old mage. Sparks flashed and crackled angrily against his magick shield, but he stood firm and his eyes blazed defiantly. Helyard stamped his foot on the stone floor with a thud and a wall of air expanded outwards from him. It rippled through the floor like a grey wave crashing on a beach, crushing the cot into splinters against the wall. The stranger was thrown backwards against the metal door but he quickly recovered his footing. He made a claw-like shape with his bony fingers and suddenly his whole arm started to shake and convulse. The hooded man cursed and choked on the words of the spell as if they scraped at his throat like sharp sticks.

Across the room Helyard suddenly went stiff and his eyes bulged in their sockets. His legs began to dangle beneath him and his arms thrashed wildly, tearing at an unseen hand that grabbed his throat in a vice-like grip. The Arkmage gargled and croaked as the life was slowly crushed from his neck. Vertebrae audibly crunched and ground together. The stranger slowly dropped his clawed hand and Helyard was lowered inch by agonising inch, feet and arms still frantically fumbling on the floor, while his breath came in ragged gasps.

Abruptly he was released, and the Arkmage collapsed in a heap on the cold stone. He seemed paralysed, unmoving and unconscious in his fallen position. With a contemptuous snort the hooded man strode to where his victim lay on the floor and drew a long wicked knife from beneath his cloak. In three quick steps he reached him, and crouched over him. Helyard's eyes were frozen shut and screwed up in agony, so the man leant close to his face, poising the knife high above his prey and ready to strike like a cobra. But the Arkmage was waiting for him. With speed that belied his old frame, Helyard grabbed the intruder's arms and gave a guttural cry. Green light exploded from around his fingertips and the stranger flew into the air with a yell. He smacked into the ceiling under a shower of broken stone and dust that instantly choked the room. With a rending crash the man fell back to the floor and the breath escaped his lungs in a loud wheeze. Chips of stone flew in all directions and clogged the air like fog.

'Thought you could get rid of me quietly, did you?' shouted the Arkmage. 'Thought you could come in and murder the old mage in his sleep, hmm? Who are you? Answer me!' He wiped stone dust from his eyes and grabbed at the man on the floor, kicking him roughly before he could move. The old mage pulled at his cloak and seizing his opportunity he tugged his hood back and cast a light spell to reveal his assailant's face.

The knife was nothing but a long silver flash in the dusty air as it buried itself deep inside the Arkmage's chest. Blood appeared uninvited at the corner of Helyard's mouth and he blinked and gasped with a somewhat confused expression. The stranger fixed him with a burning stare, watching every emotion that crossed his opponent's face, every twitch and movement he made in his last few moments.

'You?' Helyard croaked, squinting his eyes.

'Since the beginning,' whispered the stranger in a low voice. He slowly released his grip on the knife and the Arkmage fell to his knees. He leant back on his heels and kept his eyes on the man's face. Blood was running down his chest and across his lap, but he couldn't move or wrench his eyes away, all he could do was watch a smile curl at the corner of Vice's lips, an arrogant smirk that slowly lifted his cheek to meet the victoriously evil look in his eyes.

'Since the...' Helyard gasped weakly. He rocked back and

forth on his knees and swayed like a plume of pale smoke in the breeze.

'The beginning. Yes. I have been planning this since before you were Arkmage, Helyard, since before the war,' said Vice, the once-kind gaze of his brown eyes now hard like volcanic glass and just as sharp.

Helyard took a sharp breath. 'Wh...why?'

'Why what?' Vice chuckled. He watching the old mage's life gradually slipping away and pooling on the stone floor. 'Why you?' he pointed a finger. 'You were just a diversion, Helyard, a simple parlour trick of sleight of hand to keep all eyes on you while I went about my business. You were just too easy to imitate old man, ridiculous for someone of my skills, and stealing the precious Weight from your rooms was nothing but child's play. The scholars and the Sirens had no idea,' he snorted sardonically.

Helyard swallowed blood and tried to glare at him. 'You'll never win, Vice, that creature will be thwarted by our army...'

'Our army will be several hundred miles south of where they need to be, you fool. You forget that with you gone, I alone command our men, and once I'm finished with them the Arka and their new Siren friends will be nothing more than a forgotten song on the lips of the new Emaneska,' Vice sneered and crouched opposite the dying Arkmage. 'There's not a single person who can stop me now, old man, and by the time they find you in here I'll have disappeared and my plan will be unstoppable.'

Helyard shook his head and tried to raise a hand but his eyes were slowly inexorably closing. 'You've betrayed your people...' he wheezed, half-laughing, half-coughing. Bright blood spattered his chin. 'The so-called Undermage is nothing more than traitorous scum after all. I always... knew you were a snake. Just look at you.' Helyard leered, a grin filled with bloodstained teeth. 'May the gods curse you Vice...' he chuckled.

Vice's eyes blazed with murderous fire. He grabbed the Arkmage's head with both hands and brought his face close to the old man's ear. The hilt of the knife was pressing against his own chest and he could feel Helyard writhe in his grasp as he pressed harder against him. 'The sad thing is, old friend...' he paused, leaning harder and harder still on the knife. 'They're not my people!' Vice viciously wrenched the old man sideways and threw him to the floor. A loud snap came from his neck and Helyard did not speak nor move again. He simply stared into nothing, and became still.

Vice stood up and watched the lifeless body at his feet for a moment with his head on one side. 'Let the gods curse all they want,' he muttered.

Outside, over the city, drop by drop, the rain came to a halt.

Jarrick had slept through the banging and the muffled sounds of commotion from down the hall, and he snored gently while a dust-covered figure slipped past him and silently opened the door. Vice left without a sound, and the soldier slumbered on, dreaming of nothing in particular.

chapter 14

*"...There are many faces of Evernia, many facets to her magick, and
in her kindness the goddess provided the world a multitude of powers,
schools of fire, light, and wind. It is these legacies of the goddess that
we Arka strive to protect. But after the daemons were brought from
the other side, they perverted her gifts and tainted them, soiling her
magick for the elves' use. Their despicable children, the giants of old,
the half-breeds, did no better. They were the ones who forced the gods
to leave, not us. And now we pray and wait for their return, we wait
for the day that the old ones walk our shores again and rid the world
of its evil leftovers for good."*

From the 'Matters of Magick' by Arkmage Legrar

Seven hundred miles away a white and gold dragon crashed
to the leafy floor of a dark forest clearing, sending stones and earth
flying in all directions and crushing a small sapling. Her wings
slumped to the ground with tiredness and the mage on her back
rubbed his head where it had collided with the dragon's scaly neck.

'Sorry about the landing Farden, my legs have cramped up
after that flight,' she apologised with a weary smile.

Farden rubbed the graze on his forehead and frowned. 'That's
fine,' he said and managed a smile. Trying to see if there was a blood
on his fingers in the dark wasn't really working, so he clenched his
other fist and a light spell tore through the clearing. Their distorted

shadows mingled and danced with the gloom under the low trees.

Brightshow's huge yellow eyes shrank in the light and she looked around them. 'How are you feeling?' she asked.

'Well, my hands are permanently fixed to the saddle, and my face feels like it's frozen solid, but apart from that I'm good!' Farden smiled wryly. His face felt like ice and so did his fingertips.

'It's a shame Lakkin didn't have any spare riding clothes, it would have helped,' said Brightshow with a shrug.

'Mm,' Farden mumbled. He busied himself with the tangled leather straps around his thighs. He hopped down from the saddle but he got his foot trapped in the leather stirrup and fell to the leafy ground awkwardly. He freed himself and brushed the twigs and leaves from his black leather cloak. He jiggled the sword strapped across his shoulder, checked it was still safe and sound, and then massaged his legs to try to get the feeling back in them. Brightshow hid a polite laugh, and then took stock of their surroundings while she caught her breath.

The Forest of Durn swayed gently in the calm breezes. Leafless brown trees whispered and shook at the edges of the clearing, their thick skeleton branches knocking together gently, tangling with bushes and bowing over winding goatpaths and little trails through the foliage. The sounds of the trees in the soft wind were like the gnawing and creaking of some great animal as it rustled and scratched against the murmuring firs. Farden's light spell filled the clearing with clean white light and it fell in speckled patterns and narrow shafts amongst the woods, holding back the shadows. An almost indiscernible path disappeared into the dense black undergrowth to their left, to the west.

The dragon sniffed the air and looked up. The cold sky above them was empty of clouds. Tiny stars sparkled above them, distant and lonely, and tried to piercing the night with their weak lights. A sliver of white moon lingered on the treetops, dangling quietly and unassuming. The air felt icy in her nostrils. Brightshow dug at the mouldy loam beneath her with razor claws, searching for nothing in particular except something to fill the silence. Farden adjusting his tunic again and sighed loudly. 'Right, I'm ready,' he said, patting his belt. 'I'll see you at Kiltyrin later tonight, hopefully before sunrise.'

Brightshow turned to face him. 'Hopefully your vampyre will be able to help us.'

Farden chuckled and shook his head. 'Durnus knows more about Albion than the Dukes do, have no fear.'

'Well then,' she said, rattling her scales and stretching her wings out once more. 'I'd better be going. Good luck Farden, and be as quick as you can.'

'We'll be fine,' he replied, and they said no more. He watched the dragon circle the clearing before she took off, and then with a toothy smile and a blast of air she was away again, flapping through the darkness and leaving the mage standing alone in the clearing. Farden listened to the sound of her wings fading into the distance as he disappeared into the thick forest.

A short while later, Farden emerged from the scraping branches and twigs and stepped onto the neat lawn in front of the Arkabbey. The silvery light from the moon and the pale stars had turned everything a different shade of grey, a bleached monochrome version of the night. The wind rustled across the lawn and through the trees and a small pillar of smoke rose from a chimney at a slanted angle. The Arkabbey slept on peacefully, so far untouched by the day's problems, slumbering and ignorant of the danger that waited in the south. The dark woods rustled softly behind him and Farden walked silently across the grass towards the abbey. There was no guard at the door and it was unlocked, so the mage went straight in and headed for the bell tower.

When he reached Durnus's room there was light creeping out from under his door, so Farden knocked loudly on the oak and waited. There was a little pause, and then some rustling and a bang. 'Just a minute,' came a muffled cry.

After a few more noises the door was unlatched and it swung open. Firelight spilt out into the dark corridor and framed the vampyre in an orange silhouette. The mage blinked in the bright light.

'Farden!' cried Durnus. His face creased into a wide smile and the vampyre moved forward to embrace his old friend. 'By the gods, you are alive!'

The mage clapped him on the back and grinned. 'Apparently so,' he replied.

'Come in, come in!' Durnus beckoned for Farden to enter and he followed the vampyre into the warm room. Candles flickered lazily in their holders and a weird smell hung in the room, maybe of flesh or uncooked meat. Durnus was wearing a long robe of blue and green that touched the floor. It rustled against the stone as he moved the chairs around the fire. He rubbed his hands together and turned to the mage. 'You must excuse me, Farden, you caught me in the middle of my evening meal,' he said quietly.

'Anyone I know?'

'As always, no, but you can rest assured that bothersome Duke in Leath will be most confused as to where his butler has disappeared to,' chuckled Durnus. With a great sigh he lowered himself into his comfortable armchair and a faint smile hovered on his pale lips. The vampyre seemed tired. Farden nodded and followed suit, taking his own chair in front of the crackling fire. The subject of Durnus's dinner had always made him slightly uncomfortable. But there were other things on his mind. 'There is much to discuss, old friend,' Farden started, 'and we don't have much time at all.

'In your own words, apparently so. I just received word from a hawk that Helyard has just been thrown into prison for treason. Tell me this is some sort of sick joke.' The vampyre's face was grave.

'Sadly it's not. Helyard went to Nelska last night and murdered a dozen Siren guards and stole Farfallen's tearbook…'

'Wait, I thought that Vice had…'

'There's so much to tell you, Durnus, but we don't have time to talk,' urged Farden.

But Durnus waved his hand. 'Report.'

Farden sighed. 'I went to Nelska on a peace treaty, and to enlist the help of the dragons. The Arkmages sent the tearbook with me as a gift in the hope that they could find the whereabouts of a dark elf well in Farfallen's memories. I know what you're thinking, but somehow Farfallen survived and now he's somewhere in Krauslung,' he said. Durnus looked shocked and appalled, but Farden continued. 'Last night Helyard went to Nelska to steal the tearbook and in the process he killed half the palace guard. The Sirens threatened war but Åddren and Vice managed to calm them down and forge a treaty. Unfortunately for Helyard he dropped his Weight in Nelska, and now he's locked up.'

'And how is Åddren dealing with all of this?'

'He's a broken man. He trusted Helyard implicitly for years so I think he's taking his betrayal harder than any of us. And now that Helyard's traitorous nature is public news, the city is at breaking point. You can feel it just walking down the streets. Like an awkward silence,' Farden explained.

Durnus rubbed his forehead with both hands and took a long breath. 'With Helyard gone, Åddren will stand alone, and he'll be hard pressed to keep some of the more radical and dangerous members of the council in check, even with your friend Vice there to help. There are some I am sure that will not be too keen on this peace with the Sirens, some who want to see nine more years of war,' Durnus wagged a cautionary finger.

'You said it yourself, Vice is there too, and I trust him to stand up for Åddren. Luckily he has control of the army and right now they're gathering at Dunyra, ready to face this creature.' Farden paused. 'If it should come to that.'

Durnus looked confused. 'I don't understand.'

The mage slapped a hand on his knee. 'This is what I've been trying to tell you! Helyard has been travelling back and forth between Krauslung and Albion and we think that this is where his friends plan to release the beast. Vice and the dragons think there may be a dark elf well here, somewhere we've never thought to look before now.'

Farden could see the intrigue sparkling in the vampyre's eyes. 'Where?' he asked.

'Between Kiltyrin and Fidlarig.'

It was Durnus's turn to slap his knee. 'I knew it! I've always suspected Albion of hiding a well and here it is, right under the Dukes' noses!' He quickly got up and rushed over to a desk in the corner, stepping over something as he did so. He rifled through various maps before jabbing his finger at one of them. 'There, a ruin on the side of a hill. That could be your best shot.'

Farden got up from his chair and made for the door. 'Well bring that with you then, we don't have much time.'

Durnus looked up suddenly, and there was an uncertainty on his face Farden hadn't seen before. 'Me?' he asked. 'What are you saying?'

'I'm saying we need your help old friend,' replied Farden, but the vampyre just began to shuffle the papers and parchment and shake his head. 'I haven't left this Arkabbey in years, I have a responsibility... I, oh what would I know anyway, I'm just an old bookworm!'

'Durnus!'

'No Farden, you can do this without me.'

'You've said how much you envy my position, this is your

chance to get out there and make a difference,' urged Farden, but the vampyre stayed quiet and stared at the maps on his desk.

The mage kept talking. He knew his old friend better than that. 'Lost by dark ones all forgotten, lakes of magick below paths untrodden. You taught me that. None of us know the dark wells like you do, and that's why we need your help.'

There was a moment of silence as Durnus thought quietly to himself. When he finally looked to Farden, and the mage could have sworn he saw a twinkle in those pale blue eyes. 'It has been many years since I left the comfort of this abbey, but if the fate of Emaneska is in the balance then I suppose I must acquiesce,' he smiled.

'It was an order from Åddren,' added Farden.

Durnus shrugged and began to roll up his map. 'Well, in that case.'

'Good man,' said the mage, and he grinned.

'There are still a few hours before sunrise, I will prepare the quickdoor for us. Did you say Dunyra?' Durnus walked to the corner of the room where the quickdoor sat dormant.

'Yes, near the port. It's where the other Written are meeting. By the time we get there they should already be searching the hills,' Farden said.

'Good, then let us waste not a minute more! Give me an hour, and I shall be ready to leave.' Farden nodded and left him to it. The mage shut the door quietly behind him and wandered through the dark corridors. He had no time to catch up on sleep, so he decided to make his way into the kitchens and satisfy his growling stomach.

The kitchens and dining hall were dark and silent; everyone seemed to be asleep apart from the mage and the vampyre. Farden crept around the kitchen in the orange light of the stove and gathered some bread. He reached into his pack and took out some of the supplies that the Sirens had given him. Farden found a pot of cold soup and dipped his bread in it, following it with some of the dragon-riders' chewy travelling biscuits and a weird brown fruit that tasted something like a sour apple. He made a face but finished it and searched through his pack for some more of the biscuits. Farden walked as he chewed and headed towards his room for a quick lie down.

His room seemed cold and bare compared to the cosy atmosphere of the *Bearded Goat* but it felt good to be back in familiar surroundings again. He dropped his supplies to the floor with a thud and stretched his arms. The mage walked to the window and stared at the monochrome forest and listened to an owl hoot somewhere in the trees. Farden chewed his biscuit and listened to the night sounds. The room was dark so he reached for the candlestick that sat on the bedside table. As he tried to click his fingers he knocked it clumsily and it fell to the floor with a dull clunk. Farden muttered to himself and cast a brief light spell. As he bent down to pick the candlestick up, a small bark-cloth bundle caught his eye, and he froze. Lying on the floor was the bundle of nevermar from all those weeks ago, and the hazy memory of hiding it inside the hollow candlestick suddenly came back to him. Farden made sure the door was closed and crouched down, listening for any footsteps in the corridor. He put aside his biscuit and grabbed the bundle. The nevermar smelled old, dry, and it felt as though there was only a little bit left. Farden clenched his fist around it and let his mind wander. He ground his teeth together and felt temptation prodding him with a stick as it always did. Something knocked against his collar bone, the amulet around his neck, and Farden scratched at it. He could almost taste the stuff on his tongue. He closed his eyes and gnawed at his lip. *Let it go* said a voice. The voice from his dreams. Farden sighed, and shook his head.

With a grunt the mage stood up and left his room. He ran quickly and quietly down the stairs until he reached the ground floor and then he made for the door, still gripping the bundle tightly in his hand. Farden emerged into the shadowy gardens and strode across the damp lawn without a sound. He reached the edge of the forest and ducked under a branch, wary of any sounds behind him, and then crept into the trees.

Farden walked for a minute until he was a safe distance away from the Arkabbey, careful to mind snapping twigs or anything noisy. Deep in the woods the night was thick and impenetrable. The only sounds were the whispering boughs shaking their leafless branches and the screeching of the distant owl. Farden leant up against a tree trunk. The mage lifted the little bundle to his nose and smelled the earthy, sickly-sweet scent of the nevermar. He peeled back the cloth and pinched the dry moss between his fingers. Saliva filled his mouth in anticipation, and he twirled the nevermar between his fingers and rolled it into a tiny ball. He felt the fire spell stirring in his hand.

'What are you doing?' said a voice from behind him. Farden jumped, dropping the bark-cloth and the nevermar, and in a blur his hand was on his sword handle. A light spell pierced the gloom. He whirled around to find Elessi holding her hands over her eyes. 'Farden it's me!' she cried.

'Elessi? What are you doing out here?' Farden released his sword and blew a brief sigh of relief.

'I could ask *you* the same question,' came her reply. She fiddled with her hands nervously in front of her. She was in a nightgown and sandals and her curly brown hair covered her shoulders. Her eyes were wide and hollow. She looked upset or scared, Farden couldn't tell.

'Well it's none of your business,' he said, suddenly irritated.

'You've been gone for weeks, I was starting to worry about

you…' began the maid, but Farden shook his head.

'You always worry about me Elessi, I'm fine,' hissed Farden. He looked down and surreptitiously tried to spot the bundle of the nevermar amongst the leaves.

'How can I help it Farden, when I see you sneaking into the forest in the middle of the night? I haven't seen you in days!' Her voice was full of emotion, but Farden wasn't listening.

'Where is it?' he mumbled to himself.

'What's wrong with you?' She sounded like she was about to cry. Elessi followed his gaze and spotted something by her sandal. Before he could stop her she bent to pick it up and held the little cloth package in her hand. She peered inside. The sickly-sweet smell was unmistakable, even for her. Tears instantly sprang to her eyes and Elessi looked up at Farden with a quivering lip.

'Tell me this isn't yours, Farden, please,' she said, shaking her head as if she couldn't or wouldn't believe what she had just found. The mage ground his teeth together in annoyance. He rubbed his forehead with his thumb and forefinger. 'I was getting rid of it Elessi. Just give it to me,' he muttered quietly. He held out a hand.

'No,' said Elessi. She fought back tears and clasped the nevermar to her chest. He wasn't sure if he had ever seen her cry before.

'Elessi, give it to me,' repeated Farden.

'No I won't, not until you explain what's going on here. You know this is against the rules… how could you do this to yourself?' she said, sobbing pitifully. Her face scrunched up in distress and her hollow eyes glistened with huge tears.

Farden clenched his fists by his side. 'I don't have to explain myself to you,' he growled, and his words sounded foreign even to him. Her expression said everything and screamed disappointment.

Elessi sniffed loudly and shook her head. 'Then I think Durnus would want an explanation!' she cried. The maid stumbled backwards and turned to run into the forest but Farden grabbed her arm before she could get any further. 'Wait a minute!' he hissed. The mage pulled her close and put both of his arms around her to make sure she couldn't get away.

'Let go of me!' she shouted. The maid thrashed against his chest futilely with her fists like a child, sobbing and straining to get away, but Farden held tight. 'Listen! Elessi, stop struggling!' He winced as a blow caught his chin. After a moment of struggling she gave up and simply buried her head in his tunic. He whispered in her ear as she sobbed and cried against his clothes. 'I won't hurt you Elessi but you need to listen to me! Durnus must not know about this, understand? I can't let him find out,' he said. His words flooded his heart with guilt.

'Is that all you care about? What about me?' she gasped, punctuating her words by thudding her fist against his chest. 'They will hang you for this.'

Her words were like darts and Farden's heart sank in his chest. The mage sighed heavily and rested his chin on her head. Farden looked around at the dark forest, trying to find an explanation in the shadows or in the night that surrounded the two of them. He was speechless, without excuses. He sighed. 'I kept it secret didn't I? I can deal with it,' he said in a quiet tone.

'Alone, and without help,' she sobbed, and sniffed. 'And you, of all people,' she muttered. Her words echoed ominously in his head, and somewhere deep within him it terrified Farden, even if he hadn't quite realised it yet. It was because of who he was that he started in the first place. But Elessi was right. He had always hidden it. The mage lifted his head and met her teary eyes. He had never seen her so sad. 'I came out here to burn it, I swear to you. I'm finished with it.' Farden paused, '…please,' he added.

Elessi blinked and thought for a moment, a moment that felt like forever to the mage. 'Fine, but you go back on your word and

that vampyre will be the first to hear about it, I swear to the gods.'
Her voice was hard like granite, and Farden believed her. The maid
awkwardly thumbed away a tear with sudden embarrassment and
slapped him one more time on the chest for good measure. Slowly
and gently he let go of her and then took a few steps back. Elessi
cleared her throat and in the light of his spell and the moon he
watched her blinking the last of the tears away. Her eyes were still
wide and fearful, but she tried a wan smile and Farden held out his
hand for the nevermar. At first she shook her head resolutely, but he
took a slow step forward and met her gaze with an honest look, trying
to convey as much trust as possible.

'Please,' he said, in no more than a whisper. Elessi sighed and
held out the bark-cloth in front of her with pursed lips and wary eyes.
Farden took the little bundle and closed his palm around it. There was
a burst of orange light from behind his fingers and smoke curled
around his hands like grey liquid. As the sickly smell of the drug
reached Farden's nose a pang of regret suddenly shivered across his
chest, but he shook his head and threw the burning mess into the
bushes.

'I suppose that's the first step then,' Elessi said quietly. She
clasped her hands in front of her.

'Thank you,' he said.

She shook her head at him. 'I've watched you for years and I
never suspected a thing. You've come too far to ruin it now, and I...
Well, we care too much about you.' The maid sniffed. 'I care too
much.'

Farden nodded and stretched. A stray cloud had momentarily
covered the moon. 'You always have,' he said, and she gazed at him
through the darkness with wide eyes. 'I can't help it,' she said. 'I
lo...'

But something moved in the shadows, and Farden swiftly
covered her mouth with a hand. A twig snapped under invisible boots

and the metallic whisper of swords sliding from scabbards floated on the breeze to Farden's keen ears. A twang of a bowstring rang out from somewhere behind them and with the speed of a pouncing wolf Farden threw out his spare hand. A burst of white light burnt an arrow to cinders in mid air. Elessi screamed. Farden grabbed her roughly and pushed her forward through the undergrowth, back towards the Arkabbey. She was making enough noise to wake an army. Farden kept pushing.

'Move Elessi! Go!' he yelled at her as he turned to face the attackers. The forest suddenly came alive with shouts and cries. Dark men with hidden faces swarmed through the trees towards them, waving blackened swords and curved knives. Farden crouched to the loam and put a fist to the cold ground. He shuddered as the spell ran through him. It jolted his arms but he held his stance and concentrated. Just as three men burst from the bushes mere paces from him, a black wall of rock and earth sprang from the ground, arched and rippling like a wave crashing on a shore, and collided with them in an explosion of dirt. Their cries were cut short by the thick soil filling their open mouths and roots and armour cracked noisily under the blow. They scrabbled and spluttered to their feet but the mage was already gone. He sprinted back through the forest, grabbed Elessi by the hand and led her a twisting path between trees and bushes.

'Where's the abbey?!' she wailed as branches whipped her face and scratched her arms. Farden kept going, weaving through the darkness and ignoring the angry threatening cries from behind them. 'Just keep moving!' he hissed urgently.

All of a sudden they stumbled onto the short grass of the abbey lawns and Farden was pushing her in the direction of the kitchen door. For a moment Elessi hesitated, but he waved his arms frantically for her to flee. 'Go to Durnus, he'll get you out of here!' he shouted.

Elessi's eyes were wide and flicked nervously between the forest and the mage. 'But…' she began, clinging to her nightdress.

'GO!' Farden yelled. She said no more and scurried off into the darkness towards the tall abbey with her sandals slapping against her feet. Farden turned to face the invisible foes, planting his feet wide and feeling his hands shake with magick. Their stealthy approach ruined, the attackers shouted and bellowed and crashed noisily through the forest towards him. Their shouts and cries had woken the abbey from its peaceful slumbers and a handful of guards tumbled out of the main door, still struggling with their armour and wiping tiredness from their eyes. The moon and stars bathed the abbey grounds in a pale glow and they could see dark shapes surrounding the abbey grounds. The trees shook with movement and the sound of men and metal clattering through the undergrowth grew louder by the second. The Arkabbey bell began to toll.

'Stay together!' Farden shouted to the confused and bewildered soldiers. They rushed to his side and readied their weapons, forming a little line halfway across the lawn. Arrows exploded from the trees and thudded into the grass inches from their feet but they held firm, their courage bolstered by the powerful mage standing with them pulsating with magick. Farden stretched out his hands by his side and a sudden wind flattened the grass around the group. Dead leaves scurried around their feet and cloaks clapped and fluttered, crackling like whips.

'Hold on!' Farden bellowed to the others and slowly he began to move his hands forward, inch by blustery inch. The wind howled wolfishly around them. Two men emerged from the trees and rushed forward but suddenly they seemed to collide with an invisible wall of air. Farden pushed his hands forward, shaking, and the men were plucked from the lawn and thrown backwards into the forest. Two more ran ran out of the undergrowth yelling but the wind ripped the swords and shields from their hands and they tumbled into a bush.

Farden slowly wound the spell down, but as he did so a sudden flash of light in the corner of his eye caught his attention. 'Watch out!' A shout rang out in the darkness just as a streak of fire tore through the darkness towards them. Farden spun and threw himself flat to the ground as the fireball exploded against the chest of a soldier standing behind him. Flames consumed his face and neck and he crumpled to the ground with a gurgling choke. The poor man frantically rubbed at his scorched chest as the others ran to quench the bright fire. Farden leapt to his feet and threw two of his own fireballs back in the same direction. Another arrow sprang from the forest and a soldier caught it on his shield.

Farden found himself barking orders at the men. 'You two, take that man back to the kitchens and keep him there. You, guard the main door, and wake up the others. The rest of you, follow me!' They sprang to do his bidding with alacrity, some stayed, others dashed off into the night and dragged the man with them. Farden's eyes roved over the bushes and trees, watching for movement or any glint of metal. Aside from the pealing bells it had become very quiet in the grounds. There were no shouts, no yells. They jogged towards the north side of the Arkabbey. The others at his back breathed noisily and their armour rattled but they seemed ready enough. They kept moving.

As they reached the corner of the north wall a shout rang out in the darkness and a blast of lightning struck the lawn in a shower of dirt and charred grass. They ran for the cover of the wall and crouched in the flowerbeds. Farden slammed his vambraces together and a ball of fire began to grow and spin above his palms, getting bigger and hotter with every second. The soldiers shuffled backwards and eyed the mage warily. Farden, deep in concentration, muttered one word at them. 'Ready?' he asked. To a man, they all nodded eagerly, and Farden stood up.

Another fork of lightning flashed across the lawn as the mage emerged from behind the wall with the spinning fireball balanced in his hands. A dozen yards from him two hooded sorcerers crouched between a fallen tree and a stone bench. They yelled and pointed at him and waved their swords, but it made no difference. Farden lifted the ball of searing fire above his head and it pierced the night like a miniature sun. It took all of his strength to throw the fireball but it flew through the air in a deadly white streak and exploded against the tree trunk. With a deafening boom and a searing blast of heat the trunk shattered into a thousand pieces, sending deadly shards of wood flying through the air like vicious hornets.

Farden quickly held up his arms and a bubble of air pulsed from his hands with a dullish thud. A dozen flaming daggers of wood struck the invisible wall and ricocheted to the ground and sizzled. Farden blinked and squinted the white spots from his eyes and looked at the mess he had caused. A massive smoke cloud rose like a mushroom above the crater where the tree had been, and the stone bench lay on its side with a nice new crack through its middle. To his back he could hear the soldiers gaping at the flaming scene.

A coughing came from behind a section of the tree and Farden dashed forward to investigate. He found a hooded and masked stranger lying behind the broken bench. The man's chest was punctuated by three thick chunks of wood buried deep in his ribcage, and every breath seemed to be a battle. Blood was pooling in the scorched grass and rotten splinters under his back. Farden crouched down next to him.

'Who sent you?' growled Farden.

The man attempted to laugh but just coughed instead. 'You think you scare me Farden? A hermit like you? You're a lost cause.'

With a quick flick of his hand Farden tore away the mask covering the man's face, but as he did so his stomach flipped.

Ridda grinned at him through a mask of blood and slowly whispered his last few halting words. 'Think you....can run, Farden?

Run…from the likes of him?'

'Tell me who you work for, traitor or I swear to the gods I will make you die in agony,' Farden's eyes were like flint and blue sparks hummed and spat threateningly in his palm. 'Is it Helyard? Speak! How did he get his orders to you?'

All Ridda gave was a wheezing chuckle and blood trickled down his chin He shook his head and mockingly wagged a weak finger. 'Helyard…' he paused to gulp and breathe, '…is only the beginning.'

Farden fumed. He felt a huge nauseating dread clutch his heart with the icy fingers of a corpse. The mage shook him to keep him from slipping away too soon. 'Who do you work for?' Farden's hand hovered over Ridda's leg, and a spark connected with his cloak. He flinched with a yelp and then winced as the wooden splinters twisted inside him.

'You're a…' he began, but his eyes slowly started to close. Farden jogged him with another spark.

'… dead man,' he croaked. Ridda's eyelids closed permanently.

Farden clenched his fists and roared with frustration. He got to his feet and kicked the body of the dead mage to the ground, swearing and gritting his teeth. Behind him the soldiers looked at one another and swapped nervous glances.

Just then the other masked mage emerged from behind the splintered tree and tried to limp away, but Farden's anger quickly found him. In a flash his hand flew to his sword handle and he wrenched it from its scabbard. The blade flew spinning through the air and caught the stranger between the shoulders. He fell to the floor with a crunch and didn't move again. The Arka soldiers moved to make sure the man was dead and waited until Farden joined them. When he reached the body he tore the sword and the bloody cloak from the man's back and ripped it until he could see the man's bare shoulders. His dirty skin was unmarked and clear, but Farden was still not satisfied. The soldiers muttered amongst themselves and Farden simmered with anger. All of a sudden there was a smash of glass and a limp body landed in a small bush at the foot of the wall with a horrible crunch. They all looked up to find Durnus standing at a broken window frame gazing down at them. His face was smeared with dark blood and his fangs were bared, eyes wild with the fire of battle. He shouted to the mage.

'Farden! They're inside!' he yelled, but the mage was already up and running towards the main door. The soldiers could barely keep up with him. He slid to a halt in front of the tall oak doors and darted into the darkness of the abbey. The moment he was inside a man ran at him from the shadows bearing a long knife. Farden dropped to his knees and light pulsed from his open hand. The hooded attacker stumbled and yelled, blinded by the sharp white blast. Farden punched him hard in the midriff and the man crumpled winded to the floor. The mage's knee collided with the man's forehead and he sank to the floor. Farden took the man's knife and ran on.

He leapt up the nearest stairs, taking them two at a time. He heard the clanging of swords above and below him but he kept running, heading for the vampyre's room at the top of the abbey tower. The bells were still ringing.

A young maid ran ran screaming from a doorway followed by a sinister looking man in a hood. He grabbed and snatched at her arm but she managed to escape him and cowered by the wooden banister.

Farden sped forward and plunged his blade into the man's chest, letting the attacker slump to the ground at his feet with a groan. The girl stared in horror at the dead man. She ran off whimpering into the shadows before Farden could stop her.

The mage ran on, and the shouting and sounds of fighting grew louder with every step he took. The Arkabbey was now overrun by dark invaders and servants and soldiers alike were being cut down in the darkness of the corridors. Farden ducked a spinning arrow and ran on. A hooded man appeared in a doorway and poised to strike at the mage with a snarl. Three broken ribs and a shattered skull later the stranger lay on the floor, immobile and gasping through crushed lungs, choking on the dust from Farden's boots. Shouts and curses echoed off the stone walls behind him and a long wail came from somewhere below. Farden's head spun.

Up in the far reaches of the abbey tower Durnus pressed himself against the door as the men outside charged for the tenth time. Elessi whimpered and shook her hands frantically while she paced back and forth by the fire. Her nightgown was shredded and torn, covered in dirt and more than a few specks of blood. The vampyre snarled and shoved the door again to keep it closed. He could hear blades hacking at the wood from the other side.

'What are we going to do?' Elessi moaned. She pulled agitatedly at her curly hair.

'Calm down woman. Farden will be here soon, and then we can leave!' Durnus licked his lips nervously and cast a glance at the humming quickdoor in the corner. The fire crackled quietly in its hearth. The tolling of the bells above made the room vibrate.

There was a splintering thud and a spear head wiggled its way through a gap in the wood. Durnus seized the blade and yanked it with a forceful twist. The spear haft split and there was a cry from the other side as someone tried in vain to retrieve his weapon.

The vampyre snarled through the door with a sibilant hiss. 'Leave this place before I kill you all!'

Laughter came from the corridor outside. 'We just want to talk, old man, let us in!'

'I am no man!' Durnus cursed and spat blood through the gap

in the door. His lips and face were covered in dried crimson and the look in his pale eyes was as frosty as the ice fields. He licked his deadly fangs and felt the sharp nails at his fingertips with a thumb. The door pounded and shook but Durnus steeled himself to wait for his friend. This was the fight he had waited decades for, and he wasn't about to let anyone down.

Durnus slammed his fist on the door frame and hissed with pure animal rage, baring his sharp teeth. Elessi hid behind the armchair with fright and closed her eyes tightly.

'Let us in old man!' came the taunts from outside.

'So be it,' he hissed. With a burst of inhuman strength the old vampyre suddenly ripped the door from its hinges and dove into the group of men with a vicious snarl. A knife raked his arm and fists collided with his body but Durnus felt strength and speed he hadn't known in years flowing through his dusty veins. He dodged and moved like a shadow, claws striking and ripping through cloth and flesh. He was a blur of animal rage, whirling in circles and sinking his fangs into anything that moved.

The men slowly started to back off and tried to surround the vampyre. Durnus breathed in hissing gasps like a cornered swan. He bled from a dozen scratches and cuts, painted in blood that wasn't all his own. His keen eyes could pierce the darkness better than his enemies, and he waited for them to pounce.

'Durnus!' A shout echoed down the narrow corridor just as a fireball ripped through the group and burst against the wall. Chaos erupted in the hallway. Durnus jumped on the nearest hooded figure and sank his fangs deep into the soft place under his chin. 'Get him off me!' cried the man, convulsing and stumbling under the old vampyre's weight.

Farden was suddenly amongst them, striking left and right with his knife, hacking ruthlessly at arms and legs. Men fell awkwardly crying out in pain all around. One man landed a blow on

Farden's shoulder, but he darted sideways and stabbed backwards, catching the man in the groin. His face crunched up in pain as Farden quickly grabbed his throat and sent a river of lightning through his bones. The man shook like a rag doll and then went limp and lifeless when the spell stopped his heart.

'Farden!' Durnus called out from behind him. He was pinned to the floor and was trying to stop a dagger from being pressed any closer to his throat. The man on top of him snarled as he pushed his entire weight in the handle, locked in slow battle with the old vampyre. Durnus's eyes were wide. The blackened steel tip began to tickle the papery skin of his neck.

Farden leapt forward and kicked the attacker squarely in the ribs with the thick toe of his right boot. The crack of bone was an audible snap and the man instantly collapsed by the vampyre's side in a ball. Farden kicked the dagger aside and slammed him up against the nearest wall. He tore away the face cloth, but it wasn't a face he recognised. Furious anger bubbled up inside him, building and building in his chest like one the volcanic springs at Hjaussfen. Farden shook with rage and a deep growl burnt the back of his throat. Fists clenched white, the rumbling became a guttural roar of fury and he struck the man hard in the jaw with a sickening thud. He slumped to the cold floor unconscious and silent. There were none left in the corridor to kill. The bells had fallen silent.

'Agh!' The mage pulled at his hair in exasperation.

'Farden, let's get out of here while we still can! Come on!' The vampyre tugged at the mage's cloak as he ran limping back through the broken door frame to his room. Durnus hobbled into the centre of the room and paused.

'Elessi? Elessi!' he shouted. The damn maid was nowhere to be seen.

'Can we go now?' said a voice, and a shaking hand emerged from behind one of the huge armchairs.

'Yes, now get up and come here!' The vampyre snapped impatiently. He rushed to the pedestal standing in front of the quickdoor and flipped through the pages, murmuring the incantations and spells.

'Farden?' Elessi warily crept from behind the chair and looked around for the mage. Standing outside in the corridor in the dark Farden was silently fuming and staring at the unconscious stranger on floor. His mind racked every possibility, went over every piece of information, and still nothing seemed to offer an explanation. He felt useless in the face of such deep treachery, confused and bewildered. Farden flinched as a hand alighted softly on his shoulder. It was Elessi, her eyes wide and fearful.

'Durnus is making his door thing work, it's time to leave,' she said softly.

Farden nodded and looked at the fallen bodies around them. Some were still groaning with pain. He wanted to dig a blade into every single one of them, just to teach them a lesson.

A raspy shout came from the vampyre's room. 'Farden I swear to the gods I will carry you through this door myself if you don't hurry up! It's almost ready!' With a grunt the mage hopped over the splintered mess of door and helped Elessi do the same. The air in the room crackled with the quickdoor's energy and there was a low familiar humming. Durnus whispered words to his pages as he flipped each one. Farden led the maid forward and stood her next to the vampyre. 'Keep your arms and legs tucked in, close your eyes, and try not to think too much,' he said, speaking in what he assumed to be a calming voice. Elessi was shaking already and she began to bite her nails with agitation.

'And hold your breath too,' Durnus slammed the heavy book shut with a forced grin. 'You'll be absolutely fine dear, do not worry. Now come, you first.'

'But…' She raised a finger to protest but Durnus ushered her forward to the steps. The wavering translucent surface hissed at her and she flinched. The cold wind from the other side was already starting to blow through the room. It ruffled the curtains and pulled at the fire.

'No buts Elessi, we need to go now,' said Farden.

'Does it hurt?' she asked and the vampyre sighed loudly with impatience. Shouts echoed along the corridor outside.

'Not as much as I will if you don't move that ample backside of yours and get through that door!' Durnus shouted and she darted forward with fright, half-stepping half-tripping through the fizzing surface. Her scream trailed off like a distant echo.

'Was that a bit much?' the vampyre looked to Farden.

'Maybe. You'll find out on the other side,' the mage shrugged and winked. He looked behind him as he heard the sound of a blade on stone.

Durnus put a hand on his friend's shoulder. 'Thank you Farden, for coming for us. I don't think I would have…' he began.

'Nonsense old friend, you finally got the chance you were looking for,' Farden smiled. 'This is a conversation for later Durnus, go, before it closes!' The vampyre moved forward and waited on the steps of the quickdoor, watching his bold friend. The mage kicked an armchair aside and stood in front of the broken doorway with fire starting to wander over his fingers.

'You have time!' cried Durnus. 'Farden! There's no shame in running to fight another day!'

'They can follow us! Go! Before it's too late and we're both stuck here!' Farden met Durnus's gaze, and the look in his pale eyes was grave. They both understood the situation and Farden knew what had to be done. The vampyre nodded and jumped into the quickdoor. Just as he disappeared the arches shook and with a gurgling whine the portal vanished. Farden gritted his teeth and smiled from the corner of his mouth. He relished a good fight.

The first man through the door received a face full of flame and ran around the room screaming. The mage ducked an ambitious sword swing from the next and a punch to the stomach winded the man. Farden's skull smashing into his nose made him drop his weapon. Before the men could recover he had already disappeared down the corridor.

The mage careened around corners and flew down stairs, jumping entire flights in windmilling leaps. Screams and shouts now came from every corner of the abbey and bodies were piling up in the corridors and doorways. Righteous anger pounded in Farden's chest as he ran to where the sounds of battle were loudest.

'Jus' tell us where 'e is an' we won't af to 'urt you, will we my pretty?' The thug's leering grin made the young maid shiver even more. Half a dozen other servants sat kneeling around the statue of Evernia in the main hall, cowering and frightened. A score of men stood around them holding blades and eying the shadows, bedecked in scruffy armour and raggedy clothes. The flickering candlelight threw grotesque shadows across their faces.

'Where is 'e?' asked the man again. The servant girl shook her head and her lip quivered as he ran dirty fingers along her chin. The thug was hideous, bald with a scar on his brow and a recently broken nose. His hand moved down across her breasts and down to grip her thigh, but a hooded figure whacked him hard on the shoulder.

'Control yourself. There'll be time for that later,' he said and the ugly man retreated to stand with the others.

Moving slowly between the scared prisoners the stranger looked at each one of them in turn, choosing his victim. He grabbed a young soldier with a black eye and a nasty cut along his forehead. He lifted him up by the throat and a strange green light started to move across his gloved hands. 'Where is Farden?' he whispered from behind his mask.

The boy panicked and tried to wriggle out of the man's strong grasp. 'I... I told you I don't know, he comes and goes, we never see him!' he choked.

With a snarl he threw him back on the floor and pointed his finger at the others. 'If I don't start hearing the answers I want to hear, people are going to start dying all over again, understand?' Renewed crying and sobbing broke out amongst the terrified captives.

The ugly man spoke up again. 'One of yer must 'ave seen the bastard! Eh?' When nobody answered he shook his head. 'By the tits of Evernia this is useless,' he cursed.

The hooded man sighed. 'Be patient. He'll come to us.'

'You'd better 'ope so, mage, my men are gettin' restless...' His voice trailed off as the other man turned on him.

'Is that a threat? Because if it is then I can always leave you and your men to explain to my employer why you came back without Farden's head in a bag.' He let the words sink in for a moment. The other men muttered and whispered in the candlelight 'No? I thought not. Now get the fuck out of my way and do what you're paid to do.' He barged him aside and walked off towards the main door, leaving the thug to clear his throat and try to to save face in front of his men.

The hooded figure strode through the shadows towards the doors, cursing the Albion reprobates he had been forced to work with. Give him a handful of mages and this Farden would have been trussed up and stuffed like a boar by now, if only he...

But a sword suddenly weaved its way between the man's ribs with a crunch. He looked down in amazement at the black steel poking from his chest. He could hear the blood pooling in his lungs, and as the blade twisted and moved the shadows leapt up to greet him. The hooded man was dead before he hit the floor. Farden hauled the body further into the shadows and pulled the cloak up to see the man's back. In the dim candlelight the mage could see the black script etched into the pale skin, weaving across his shoulders between bloodstained runes and symbols. Two runes meant new blood. Farden didn't recognise the man, but he was Written, Arka born and bred, and that made the mage's blood boil.

He gritted his teeth and strode boldly into the middle of the hall where a single shaft of moonlight pierced the shadows. 'Hey!' he yelled and all eyes were suddenly upon him. Farden grinned and shouted at the top of his voice. 'If you want me, then come and get me!'

The ugly man went purple with rage and waved his sword in wide circles. 'After 'im!' he shouted and with a snarl he broke into an ungainly run with the rest of his crew behind him baying like a pack of wild animals. With lightning swiftness Farden spun on his heel and dashed off in the opposite direction, leading the hooded attackers away from the prisoners and out into the cold night.

part four

and it ends with fire

chapter 15

*"Beware the monster behind the door, watch out for the spiders all
over the floor.
Be brave like your father, proud warrior and all,
Something is gnawing at bones in the hall.
Maybe you'll run, or maybe you'll fight,
Or maybe you'll sleep soundly all through the night.
Never you mind, now close your eyes,
Pray you sleep well, not be food for the flies."*
Skölgard nursery rhyme

Someone was screaming in the locked room at the top of the
Spire. The cries of pain were chilling, accompanied by the howling
wind that pawed at the windows and battlements of the tower. Two
soldiers holding spears stood guard at the top of a tall set of stairs.
Their gold and white ceremonial armour glittered in the light of the
flickering torches and they stared straight ahead silent and still,
seemingly oblivious to the sounds coming from the door behind them.

Behind that door was a small chamber and another door, and
through that was a small circular room, windowless and plain, with
nothing but two wooden stools and a bench for decoration. The walls
had been painted pure white like a new canvas waiting for an artist.
Scores of candles in glass jars were spread over the floor, making the
room and the walls dazzlingly bright, perfect for keeping a candidate

conscious through a Ritual. Dotted all around the room in little piles were tiny bottles of thick black ink sealed with cloth and wooden stoppers.

In the centre of the room were the two stools, and on one stool sat a wizened man white with age and with a beard so long it was wrapped around his belt. His head was bald and freckled while his shoulders were hunched like the wings of a wet crow. On his pointy nose balanced a set of intricate lenses made of stacked slices of crystal. They made his dark beady eyes look ridiculously massive. The old Scribe was fixated on his work, watching his wrinkled skeleton hands wave to and fro, pricking the pale skin in front of him with a long and delicate sliver of whale-bone. The ancient-looking Scribe hummed in a deep drone as he worked, singing forgotten tunes and songs of magick to help the ink settle around the needle's point.

Opposite him, on the other little stool, sat Cheska. Tears rolled down her face and dripped onto a floor that was already soaking wet from two days worth of crying. She was hunched over and shaking, and her knuckles had turned an unnatural whitish purple colour from gripping her knees so hard. Her arms and legs shook uncontrollably, as if she had just been pulled from a frozen lake.

Cheska had that sort of look in her eyes, when somebody isn't listening, when they're lost in their own private thoughts as though their mind had wandered off for a moment. She stared vacantly at a spot on the floor and tried to cling onto the place where the pain could be kept at bay. Cheska willed herself to feel the cold breeze of the shore near her fathers palace, the smell of the pines by the lake, the sound of the waterfalls roaring past her window, but the needle kept dragging her swiftly back to the white room. Her back stung in a thousand places and after two straight days of sitting in the same position the needle felt like a burning knife point. Sweat streamed into her eyes but she blinked it away, allowing herself one merciful look at the hourglass at the end of the room slowly dripping sand through its tiny waist. Couldn't be long now, she prayed, to whichever god was listening. Her face scrunched up with another shrill cry.

ॐ

Outside the Scribe's room, in the first chamber, Brimm sat on a low wooden bench between two servants. They wore robes bearing the rare symbol of the tattooing art of the Written, the scales of the Arka weighing a feather quill. The two men seemed almost as old as the Scribe himself with long flowing beards and calm eyes, silent and still. Shadows from the torches danced across their still and wrinkled faces.

The servants were the only people ever allowed near the Scribe at any time. They were his eyes, his ears, and his mouth in the outside world, and they were often charged with passing messages to the Arkmages in measures of absolute secrecy. No one knew where the Scribe or his servants had come from, or even how old they truly were. There were some who whispered that the Scribe was a daemon from the old times, or perhaps a man of Servaea who had escaped before it sank into the sea. But whatever he was the withered old man was an ancient mystery shrouded in deep secrecy, and the hidden treasure of the Arka.

Brimm was trembling. He wished he could put his hands to his ears and block the sounds of his friend crying and screaming. He chewed anxiously at his lip while fear squeezed his stomach. The young mage smoothed his white and gold ceremonial tunic for the hundredth time that day and ran his dry tongue along the back of his teeth. 'May I have some water, before I go in...?' he asked, looking to the old men on either side of him. They didn't move a muscle and continued to stare at the opposite wall. Brimm sighed, and tasted blood coming from his lip.

❧

Outside the door, back on the stairs, the two soldiers exchanged concerned glances as they heard loud footsteps coming up the stairs below them. They shuffled forward and peered down the steep flight of curving steps and waited to see who came round the corner. One of them lowered his spear just to be ready. The Ritual was not to be interrupted for any reason.

Soon a tall man in a long black and green robe appeared on the tall steps and strode purposefully up the stairs towards the soldiers. At his hip was a long knife in an ornate golden scabbard. As he noticed the two men ahead of him he smiled amiably and held up a hand. 'Evening gentlemen!' he said. His dark brown eyes were warm and welcoming.

'Lord Vice, an unexpected honour!' said one soldier. He saluted with his spear and the other quickly followed suit. 'Your Mage, the first candidate should be almost finished,' added the second soldier, not wishing to be to left out.

'Good, good,' replied the Undermage. Vice made it to the top of the stairs and smiled. He folded his arms behind his back and paused. The soldier asked a question. 'To, er what do we owe the pleasure sire…?'

The words had barely left his lips when the Undermage grabbed the knife from his belt buried it hilt-deep in the man's neck. The soldier sank to the floor with a loud crash and choked on steel. Vice finished him off with a bolt of fire that shattered his armour like molten glass.

'Murder!' The other soldier shouted, aghast and shocked. He made to run but in a blur Vice kicked out behind him and caught him squarely in the breastplate. The soldier staggered backwards and tried to bring his spear level to fend off the murderous mage. A firebolt ricocheted from his shield and Vice spat, cursing the magick in the gold metal. He dodged and ducked the jabbing spearpoint like a cat. The look in the soldier's eyes was of pure panic and confusion. Vice grinned and winked at his prey and the man visibly swallowed. The Undermage took a step forward and lightning exploded from his fingers. The blinding flash struck the man in the hip and with a despairing cry he was catapulted into the wall behind him. Vice was quickly after him, hands still buzzing with sparks.

The soldier hauled himself up but he soon found hot iron hands circling his neck. Vice slammed the poor man back against the wall and the crunching sound of bricks and bone cracking was nauseating. Vice shocked him again and the man went limp in his grip.

Behind the door Brimm nervously wrung his hands, desperately wondering what the loud bangs and crashes had been. The two old men swapped concerned glances, and the young mage felt like burying his head in his hands. All was silent now, no shouts, even Cheska's screams had died. Brimm's fingers twitched nervously.

Inside the white room Cheska lifted shaking hands to her face and wiped away the tears for the final time. Her back was on fire, and the smell of fear and sweat made her gag. The pain was starting to recede from the edges of her eyes, and the pounding in her head seemed to soften slightly.

The Scribe had finally stopped humming and he turned his head to watch the door behind him. His needle was on his lap, wiped clean and unmoving now, the first time it had rested in three days.

Sniffing like a rat, he wrinkled his freckled nose and squinted through his thick glasses.

Behind him the young mage was blinking dizziness from her eyes. The bright room stung her vision. Cheska tried to stretch her back and sit upright but the sensation of her skin moving and contracting felt as though she were lying in a pit of burning coals, so she stayed put and tried to stop her heart from racing.

Brimm cried out as the door suddenly burst into a thousand fragments. He fell to the floor and frantically waved his arms to keep the wooden shards from his eyes. The other two old men rose sombrely as if they hadn't even noticed the door exploding. As one they moved aside their white robes and drew long swords from hidden scabbards. Their blades were etched with unknown words and old symbols. They stood tall, silent and ready, with their swords held in front of their faces. Brimm cowered at their feet and tried to remember his spells.

There was a short moment of uneasy silence before a man in full ceremonial armour flew through the smoking door frame and crashed to the stone floor. Brimm frantically tried to cast a shadow spell but his hands were shaking too much. The incantation bounced around his head uselessly.

A tall figure appeared through the haze in the doorway and without a sound the two old servants walked forward to meet him. As they raised their sword above their heads the figure began to laugh contemptuously. Fire danced in the stranger's hands, a deep red and orange flame that crackled and popped angrily.

The two men never had a chance. The flames jumped from the man's hands and consumed the old servants with a flash of fire and black smoke. They crumpled to the floor like burnt paper and lay there smouldering, their swords forgotten in their hands. The room was quickly filling with thick smoke and smothering the candles. Brimm crouched down to try to keep from choking.

It was suddenly deathly silent, but slowly, like out of some sort of hazy nightmare, a tall figure emerged from the smoke with vicious eyes and an evil grin. With abject horror Brimm recognised the black Undermage's robe. Vice strode calmly towards him, a long knife held low at his side. Brimm slowly backed up against the wall and tried to invoke any spell he could think of that would save him.

'Any profound words in your last moments mage?' The Undermage sneered wickedly.

Brimm couldn't even speak, he just gaped and stuttered. The cold steel pressed against his throat and he stared into Vice's evil eyes with utter disbelief.

Cheska tried not to vomit for the third time and focused on not letting the room spin round again. The throbbing in her head had now turned into nauseating pain, and it felt like her stomach was trying to punch its way out. And now she could smell smoke. Through bleary eyes she could see the blurred Scribe packing away his tools. He sounded agitated, and Cheska dazedly wondered if there was a fire.

Suddenly there was a bang from somewhere. It sounded like it was outside. Cheska swallowed bile and fell to her knees. Her back burnt with excruciating pain and the sound of her stool hitting the floor sent shockwaves across her skull.

The Scribe dashed to her aid and quickly pulled her aside. He pushed her nearer to the bench at the side of the round room. Glass jars scattered under her shaking limbs and candles hissed but the Scribe urged her on, making her crawl as far under the bench as she could go. The look in his beady eyes was urgent and serious. Cheska's head swam. Wearily she put her forehead to the cold stone floor and watched the Scribe from the corner of her eye. He was rushing around the room blowing out the candles. The room slowly plunged into darkness, candle by candle, and Cheska wondered what was going on.

At that moment there was a huge crash and the Scribe spun around to see the door fly inward under a shower of sparks. A man strode through the splintered doorway and stood in the dim candlelight with his arms crossed defiantly, ignoring the orange flames that licked at his boots and black robe.

There was a moment of silence before the man took a few steps forward and spoke. His tone was cold and formal, and there was an odd familiarity to it, thought Cheska.

'I take it all is in order?' he asked quietly.

The wizened old Scribe sighed and clicked his neck to one side, then he removed his spectacles and polished them slowly with the sleeve of his tunic in small circular motions. 'Hmm, just as you required,' he paused and then sighed with a soft wheezing sound. 'I never thought it would be you,' he said. His voice was like the rasp of files on glass, hoarse as though he had spent an age in silence. The dark newcomer nodded slowly. Their eyes were now locked in a strange embrace and both seemed to be waiting for the other to move. The etiquette before the first strike.

But it never came. Cheska waited and blinked, shivering in her hiding place. She tried to make out the face of the tall man but it was now too dark in the room, and too hot. She squirmed and tried to calm her writhing stomach. It was too quiet.

'Which one of us have you come for then Vice?' asked the Scribe suddenly.

Cheska could have sworn she heard the name of the Undermage.

'Which do you think?'

The old Scribe slowly turned his head to look at the figure cowering under the bench. 'After your last experiment, I would say her, but the look in your eyes speaks differently,' he said, cocking his head on one side like an inquisitive bird. Vice lifted his knife and casually examined the blood-smeared blade. 'It's a shame that you have worn out your usefulness…' he offered with a shrug.

The Scribe shook his head, and anger flashed briefly behind his black eyes. 'The sons of Orion will get what is coming to them in the end.'

'I beg to differ,' began Vice, but the Scribe turned his back and snorted.

'It matters not, the decision it seems, is already made,' he said. The Scribe seemed to let go of a heavy weight, and his shoulders sagged a little. Cheska held her breath. Fire licked at the walls.

The Undermage lowered his knife again and slowly moved forward, closer to the old Scribe. 'I take no pleasure in doing this,' he whispered.

'You can't fool me mage, I have spent a thousand years listening to you lie,' he said with closed eyes.

Vice sneered and grabbed the back of the Scribe's neck. 'That you have,' he replied, in a voice as cold as ice. There was a quick metallic crunch and the wizened old man slumped to the floor at Vice's feet. Cheska tried to melt into the shadows of her hiding place, but she already knew what was coming. When she opened her eyes again the figure was already standing over her. He looked down and smiled at her wickedly, and he brandished a dripping knife in his hands.

chapter 16

"The mage Farden is to be commended for his outstanding efforts in the battle of Efjar. Without the aid of this brave soldier our men would surely still be deep in the marshes fighting the minotaur clans. It has been a long time since I have seen such a skilled mage in our proud ranks, not since the days of his unfortunate uncle. Let us hope he does not follow the same path as Tyrfing."
Letter to Arkmage Åddren from Lord Vice in the year 884

Nothing lived on the Dunwold moors. Nothing. If one were to find themselves standing on the rolling hills and downs of Albion's eastern coast they would find nothing but rocks and wet grass with no living thing to accompany them. Dunwold was bare, cold, and agonisingly empty, stretching on for miles and miles around as far as the human eye could see. Here and there a few stunted trees stood amongst the rocky crags and boulders, clinging to whatever life their geriatric roots could find between the grey stone and pale lichen.

After running for two days straight he had finally collapsed between two boulders in the shadow of a low hill. His heat spells had worn off and now the cold was slowly seeping into his bones. Farden had slept fitfully. The dreams hadn't returned and no voices had spoken to him, and the mage wondered if they had left him for good. He threw a cursory look at the grey skies. Nothing. Farden shifted and winced with pain. He could feel the barbed tip of the arrow in his side working its way deeper into his flesh. Blood covered the wet grass beneath him and caked his hands and clothes. The exhausted mage put a tentative hand to his ribs, not daring to even touch the broken arrow shaft. Pushing with his elbow and grunting he managed to prop himself up to peer over the edge of the boulder at the grim countryside.

Dawn was slowly creeping across the edges of the moors. The cold wind toyed with the frost-choked grass, flipping it this way and that like a cat with a dead mouse. Farden's tired eyes roved over his surroundings and watched for movement. His followers were nowhere to be seen. After halving their numbers the day before he had outran the men at some point during the night, and now it was daylight once again. The mage had intended to circle back on himself but after losing his sword, his way, and his temper in the southern marshes he had lost all hope of making it back to the Arkabbey. Farden hadn't seen or heard anything of the men since nightfall; their parting gift was still stuck in his ribs.

His heart was heavy and his head pounded and since he had left his supplies at the Arkabbey he was now also ravenously hungry. With shaking fingers he tried to peel some of the moss and lichen from the boulder and chew it. The taste was like bitter grass but he hoped the foul stuff would stop his stomach from complaining. Farden kept his eyes on the horizon while he nibbled. His instincts told him he hadn't seen the last of Ridda's cronies, and the only way to get back to the Arka was going back the way he had come, or... he quickly pushed that thought away but his hand strayed to the circular object hidden safely inside his cloak. It was Helyard's Weight.

Farden had contemplated using it that morning, shortly before he had collapsed in a heap between his two rocks. But for anyone except an Arkmage, using the Weight was almost as good as suicide. He had heard the stories. Without the necessary power or skill a user could easily end up crushed inside a mountain or at the bottom of the

Bern Sea and Farden wasn't willing to take that chance just yet.

The mage forced himself to his feet with more willpower than he knew he had. He swayed and the world did a little spin, but he swallowed and blinked the nausea away. Farden's hands were shaking and he could feel the blood seeping down his leg. He longed for the comfort of the *Bearded Goat*. The warmth of a fire, hot wine in a cup, a sip of mörd with Vice in his opulent chambers. The brisk wind tussled with his hair and made him squint.

Next to him a little pool of water had been trapped in the rock, so he bent down to look at his haggard reflection. Red eyes and thick stubble greeted him like those of a stranger. Maybe it was the clouds hanging overhead or maybe it was the rock under the almost-freezing water, Farden's skin looked pale and grey and wan like a ghost's. His face and neck were covered in scratches from the claws of trees and branches, now red and blistered, and his dark hair hung in thick dirty locks over his hollow green eyes. Farden decided he looked like hell. He looked down at the thick arrowshaft sticking out of his ribs. He had snapped off the feathered end of the arrow last night but it still protruded a good few inches from his skin. The wyrm wound from all those weeks ago was now a silvery scar across his right side. He touched the arrow gingerly and a spark of pain made him twitch. Farden tried to get his thoughts in order. Without a healer the arrow would work its way into his lungs or stomach sooner or later, and no amount of magick could save him from that.

'Fuck this,' he cursed, and put the thick collar of his black cloak between his teeth. With a deep and heavy breath his fingers wrapped tightly around the blood-caked arrowshaft and yanked. Hard.

Light exploded behind his eyes. He choked on the utter pain and fell heavily to the wet grass. But the arrow was out and lying beside him. Blood flowed freely from the horrible wound like a swollen red river. The mage groaned and clamped a hand to his ribs. He summoned the last of his energy for a healing spell and then darkness swallowed him once again.

When next he woke, the sun was just passing its zenith and peeking out from between the thick clouds that covered Dunwold and its moors. Farden's breath suddenly caught in his throat and he coughed violently. He quickly realised his painful error as his ribs screamed in fresh agony.

It took an hour to summon the energy and strength to even sit up. The arrow wound looked as ugly as sin, and even though Farden had escaped the arrow moving any deeper he had seen wounds like his catch the rot and fester in a day. He sighed and scanned the moors with tired eyes. Even armed with his spells he was still heavily wounded and an easy target for his pursuers, if the bastards were still around, he thought grimly. A little instinctive voice told him they were. Farden nibbled at some more lichen with another heavy sigh.

In the mage's mind it was like all sense of control had flown quickly out of the window and disappeared beyond the gloomy horizon once again. Whatever semblance of order and purpose he had felt on leaving Krauslung had now crumbled. Helyard was a puppet, he thought. There was no doubt. But now, whoever they were, they were after him. Ridda had been a loyal and respectable mage, so what had made him turn so readily? Whatever it was he knew there was a great evil behind all of this, and Farden could feel he was getting close to an answer. He just hoped that Durnus and Elessi were safe at Kiltyrin. Farden's heart clenched as he remembered the last time he had seen Cheska, touching the edges of sleep, her face covered by her golden hair, glowing in the dying embers of the fireplace. Farden had ran his rough hands over her skin and marvelled at the soft skin underneath his fingertips, had thought how much he didn't deserve her. He remembered the three little words he had whispered to her that night while she slept. She would be finishing the Ritual by now, he thought, or she....

He left that thought to trail off and hide like a coward. A sudden determination flushed through his veins. Whatever it took, he had to get back to Krauslung and find Cheska, and, even if it killed him, he would see an end to this betrayal once and for all.

Farden glanced down and looked at his reflection, still covered in a myriad of scratches and bruises. The image shattered like broken glass as he dashed the water away and hauled himself up with a defiant grunt. The stubborn mage took a few deep breaths and stretched his muscles with new-found resolve. Durnus might have been right, though, it seemed that only he could get into these ridiculous situations. Such is the life of a Written, he smirked, and broke into a limping jog.

An hour later Farden was leaning against a mossy boulder in a narrow gully and trying to catch his breath. The wind moaned and cried through the rocky culvert and blew Farden's sweat-soaked hair into his eyes like tiny whips. He was breathing steadier now, but the wound on his side felt like a cat was gnawing at his ribs. His lungs burnt like hot tar.

The mage froze as the wind moaned again, blowing in the direction he was heading. A faint call hung on the stiff breeze, and fell. Another, louder this time. Like a shout.

Farden turned and started to run again. There was no time to waste. He knew that as soon as he was out of the gully he would be in open view and, with the wind, in range of their deadly bows. But then again, he grimly surmised, he didn't really have a mountain of options. His tired feet pounded the frozen earth below him. Better to be caught running then hiding.

Soon he reached the end of the gully and was abruptly in plain sight again, hobbling and skipping his way across the moor like a wounded stag. He heard the angry shouts on the wind and sneaked a brief look behind him. Six men were charging towards him over the hills and waving various sharp objects in the air. They were still about half a mile behind him, but Farden's keen eyes could see they were catching up, covered in mud and furious. Spending the night in the marshes looking for an invisible mage would probably make you feel that way, he decided. Farden tried to speed up but his ribs cried out painfully.

Inch by agonising inch the six men slowly closed the gap between them and their prey. Their orders long forgotten, this was now a personal feud with the bastard mage. The ugly man from the Arkabbey ran with the wind snapping at his heels. His six cronies slavered and grunted at his side like rabid hunting dogs. His eyes were wide and red, starved of sleep, and now he was hungry for Farden's blood. A rasping shout ripped from his throat, 'Come on lads! 'E's got nowhere t' hide now! I want 'is head on a stick!' Cries went up from the rest of them and they redoubled their efforts, feet pounding across the frozen moors.

Farden could hear their baying and yelling. Rocks and shrubs flew past him. Nothing offered anything that even resembled a hiding place. Ahead the moors stretched out for miles and miles, barren and painfully open. He could feel his lungs sticking to the inside of his ribs. They were starting to seize up and slow him down. Specks of colour gathered at the corners of his eyes, and Farden could feel fatigue trying to drown him.

A heavy object banged against his side and made him wince. The Weight, he suddenly realised, Helyard's Weight. Farden skidded to a halt and turned to face his pursuers. He grabbed the gold disk from his cloak pocket and looked at the symbols and lettering on its surface. The mage thumbed the raised lettering and tried to think straight, eying the shapes of running men that were slowly getting bigger and bigger. The Weight was warm, and felt hot in his sweaty palm. Farden's heart pounded and his mind raced over options. He had to get back to Cheska, and warn Åddren or Farfallen. And Durnus, and Elessi, he had to protect them too. But this thing in his hand was dangerous and he would be no use to the others if he was dead.

Farden gritted his teeth and clenched his fingers around the gold Weight. He couldn't hear a single thought amongst the fear shouting and bellowing inside his head. He tried to remember everything Vice had ever told him about the Weights, everything that Durnus had ever tried to teach him about quickdoors, how they were like liquid, you just have to pour in the right direction. The Weight was burning his hand. The old vampyre said it was about connection, drawing a picture, where you could be at one second is where you can also be in another place. Hot tears sprung to Farden's eyes and he pushed the Weight in front of him. The gold thing shook and buckled, sending waves rippling through the air, cracks splitting the icy air of Dunwold as though it were a broken mirror. An arrow whistled past his ear like a falcon. The mage planted his tired feet into the ground and tried to bend all his being in to seeing one place. No thoughts no distractions. The Weight glowed and fractured the air, searing his hand and splitting the sky.

Everything stopped.

An arrow poised motionless in the air in front of him, dangling and hovering, slowly moving forward like a dagger through treacle.

The sound of their feet pounding on the grass and armour clanking rolled on forever, repeating and looping like a dull drone. A shout caught on the wind.

The mage watched it all for a split second, frozen like the ice fields, a painting that seems all too familiar and real. All of sudden there was a deafening crack and the air split in two, dragging Farden into the darkness and into oblivion.

The mage vanished into the shivering air and the arrow dug into the cold grass with a useless thud. In pure shock, the bald thug came to a grinding halt, breathless and stunned while the others kept running and looking around frantically with wide eyes. His mouth hung open with sort of a confused yet pained look, as if a ghost had just punched him in the stomach. It took a few moments for him to sink to all fours. Slowly, very slowly, his face began to turn a shade of purple, and he shook with frustration. The surrounding men quietly backed away.

With a guttural scream he slammed his knife into the grass. 'Aaaaagh! Curse you Farden! Curse yer t' all the gods!'

Hundreds of miles to the east the air cracked like a whip and split in two like a jagged gap in a window pane. There was a rushing, whooshing sound and then the shape of a bedraggled man appeared out of nothing. The figure flew through the air and crashed into a nearby wall with a terrible crunching sound.

Farden gasped for breath and tried to ignore the pain that had set his body on fire. What genius had put a wall here, he asked himself, nursing bruised ribs and a sizeable lump on his head. His arm throbbed with a numbing pain and he panted as he tried to lift himself to all fours. Farden scrabbled around at the base of the wall. It was getting difficult to breathe through the pain and the fatigue. He slumped to the warm grass and rolled onto his back. He opened his eyes and stared at the horizon. A nauseating dread suddenly gripped his heart when he couldn't make sense of the upside-down mountains, but he quickly managed to steady his eyes and he found himself looking at the familiar countryside of Manesmark. Farden breathed the biggest sigh of relief of his life. He rolled over and lay spreadeagled. Blearily he watched the flakes of ash land on his cheek and open hand. He watched the flickering orange and yellow glow paint the ground a strange set of colours and wondered where Cheska was.

Ash.

Farden abruptly realised something was amiss and pushed himself to his shaky feet. He collapsed and fell once but the second time he found his balance and made it to his knees. A roaring and snapping sound became loud in his ears and he rocked back on his heels to look up at the orange sky.

Flames leapt from beam to beam, licking at the stonework and battlements of the Spire. They tore at the night sky with orange and red fingers, bursting through walls and stone like paper, a huge column of fire erupting from what was left of the blackened tower. With an enormous crash a section of beams fell inwards and sent a cloud of sparks and ash belching into the sky.

Farden rolled onto his side and dragged himself away from the blistering heat. He covered his face with his hands and crawled as far as he could before running out of breath. Above him dragons circled the tower, hauling blocks of ice and huge barrels of water into the sky and dropping them onto the burning wreckage. The clouds behind them were black and ominous and thick with smoke. It rained ash.

The mage stood aghast. Hot tears stung his eyes. The shouts of countless men could be heard from all around as survivors and bystanders were hauled out of the way. Farden could see water and ice mages standing in a long line near where the main atrium used to be, where the fire seemed to be fiercest and howled like an army of daemons. The mages were painted black with smoke yet they battled on stubbornly and threw spell after spell at the inferno. Somewhere under the blackened skeleton of the once-great Spire, amidst the flames, the dragon-scale bell clanged and shook mournfully like a death rattle. The mage stood silent and disbelieving, and he watched in horror as another floor crashed inwards and collapsed. A young soldier ran past him with a leather bucket of water and Farden grabbed him roughly before he could get away. The boy, barely old enough to be in the army by the look of him, froze as the bloodied and bruised stranger seized him by the neck. He looked into the man's red-rimmed eyes.

'What happened here?' bellowed Farden.

The boy looked confused and stuttered nervously. 'Er, the... fire, sir?' he managed.

Farden shook him again. 'Tell me what happened gods damn it!'

'No one knows sir! It started last night... at the top of the Spire!' Words escaped him and he stared fearfully at the man's ripped clothes and wild face.

Farden's heart froze with icy fear. 'Was there anyone inside? Quickly boy!'

'E... Everyone sir! All those who didn't go to Albion with the others!'

The mage slowly let the young soldier go and sank to his knees once again. The boy looked confused and hesitated for a moment before running off towards the fire with his water, leaving Farden alone and silent on the hillside. Farden watched the blaze and let the orange and yellow flames burn into his eyes and the prickly heat wash over him, as if it would cure him of the pain that suddenly ached inside his chest. Cheska would have been in the very top room. Where Farden had been all those years ago for his Ritual. Where every Written went.

The mage felt tears run down his cheek. He put his head to the scorched grass and began to sob uncontrollably. Images of her trapped in a burning room and surrounded by fire sprang unbidden into his head. They taunted him cruelly with sick reality. Farden could see her beautiful blonde hair, scorched and charred like her face, could hear her smoke-choked screams. He felt a lump in his chest.

To his left he saw a small group of people that had been pulled from the fire. Their skin and clothes were black from smoke but healers were amongst them, going to and fro tending burns and handing out pitchers of ice water to stop the coughing. A desperate urgency grabbed him and lifted him from the ground. Farden broke into a limping run and hauled himself towards the pitiful group. He went from person to person and peered into their faces, trying to find a hint of cascading blonde hair. There was nobody, not a single one that even resembled her in the slightest. He circled the entire tower until he went back on himself. There was still no sign of Cheska. Defeated, the mage slumped to the grass. The roar of the fire seemed to die in his ears as sadness gripped him with cold hands.

High above him the dragons swooped and dove in and out of the plumes of smoke. Farden watched the flames dance over their iridescent scales, making the huge beasts sparkle and shine with oranges, reds, and bright, bright yellows. He saw Farfallen dive to drop an immense block of ice onto the towering pyre. The mage watched it crash through the blackened beams as it sent beams, bricks, and planks spinning. The Old Dragon shone like liquid gold in the light. Farden looked on as a mage nearer to the Spire was suddenly engulfed and swallowed by the flames. A handful of others dashed to the man's aid, beating him with wet and steaming cloths. Another mage showered them all with a waterfall spell and kept the raging inferno at bay while they dragged his smoking body from the fire.

Even though he was surrounded by people Farden felt useless

and isolated, like an island in a boiling sea. Grief and rage tore at his heart mercilessly. His only reason to keep going had been cruelly taken away, scorched to nothing, and left as ash in his hands. Farden shook with breathless sobs and put his face in the grass.

❧

It was a grey morning when Farden awoke. It was freezing, and he felt like his limbs had been fused together at the joints, unable to move and painfully numb. The mage could feel the wet, and dewy ash covering his skin, so he moved a cold hand to wipe his face.

'I didn't think you would wake up for a few more hours,' said a deep female voice from somewhere near him. Farden jumped slightly, but he opened his bloodshot eyes to find Brightshow staring down at him with a very concerned look. She was sat like a cat with her wings folded back neatly and her thick tail wrapped around her clawed feet. The spines running down her neck and back were now limp and leant to the side like the branches of a willow.

'At least I did wake up…' he muttered darkly, and the dragon pretended not to hear. She looked away and up at the sky. Farden pushed himself up from the dirty grass and sat straight, feeling his spine and back crack in all sorts of places. The wound between his ribs momentarily flared with pain. 'How long have you watched me?' he asked.

'Since we found you last night,' replied Brightshow. She did not look at him.

The Spire was now a smouldering skeleton of its former glory. Barely a single floor high, the tower walls had fallen in and the wood had burnt away to nothing, leaving the dead husk of a once-proud building. Cracked and blackened stones littered the hillside, and the bigger bits of burnt wood and charcoal were slowly being piled up by tired workers. Somewhere under the rubble the fires were still burning, and the tell tale wisps of smoke still rose into the overcast sky. The mage watched the people mill around. Some absently picked up burnt artefacts as if they would bring back those who had perished in the fire. Others scattered mountain flowers. Everyone looked the same: covered in soot and burns, tears running in rivers down ashen skin.

A dragon had died in the flames, perhaps caught in the collapsing tower, or suffocated by the thick smoke, Farden didn't know. The green beast lay still and silent amongst a pile of rubble, where he noticed that a few people had laid flowers and wreaths for the Sirens. A rider lay prostrate on the ground next to him, a single hand pressed against the faded emerald scales of his cold dragon.

Farden looked to Brightshow, who eyes were wide and huge, gold flecked orbs of sadness and solemnity. 'Did you know... anyone? In the tower I mean?' she asked.

The mage didn't have any more tears to shed. 'The only person I cared for,' he replied hoarsely. Brightshow looked at the people gathered around the smoking ruin, 'They could still be...'

'She's gone, I've looked.' The reply was stony and cold, so she let the matter drop. Farden cast a look at the dead dragon lying amongst the stones. 'I'm sorry...' was all he managed to say.

'We're all angry Farden, and some of us lost more than others,' she said, and the mage looked at the lonely rider kneeling by his dragon's side. Farden nodded, and tried to understand, but all he could see in his mind was Cheska. His love trapped in a burning room at the top of a tall tower. Sorrow got caught in his throat for a moment, but he stubbornly swallowed the pain and got to his feet with resilience he didn't know he had. Something gold caught his eye and he turned to see Farfallen and a smaller black dragon striding across the grass towards them. The Old Dragon wore a sombre look.

'Grave times are upon us mage, and it is with a heavy heart that I greet you.' He bowed his golden head for a moment, eyes closed, and then he sighed. 'I sense a deep sadness in you Farden. I wish I could help,' he said. The mage said nothing in reply and looked down at the ash-covered grass. Farfallen looked to Brightshow and she shook her head. If a dragon could shrug, then Farfallen did. He lifted a claw to point to the lithe dragon at his side. 'This is Havenhigh, one of our youngest,' he said.

The mage nodded to the lizard and turned to Farfallen. 'What happened here?'

'She will tell you, if you can stand to listen. There is an ill will behind the cause of the fire.'

Alarm bells rang in Farden's head again, and he looked to Havenhigh. The black dragon had scales like mottled silk, sleek and dangerous. Her back was dotted with many curved spines and two long black barbels hung from her chin like a carp. Her forked tail swished back and forth restlessly. As she spoke Farden could see rows of teeth lining the inside of her narrow jaw.

'This morning I saw two bodies piled near the other side of the Spire. They were scorched and burnt with something more than just fire, the holes in their breastplates told me as much. I spoke to one of your men, a soldier, and he said they had been pulled from the tower, but by who he didn't say,' Havenhigh said. Her voice was sibilant, and her words rattled strangely.

Brightshow looked confused. 'What does this mean?' she asked.

'It means...' the Old Dragon started. But Farden was already speaking.

'It means that somebody started this fire,' the mage said, eyes downcast and searching the grass. His cold words were like rocks dropped from a tall cliff. 'Are you sure about what you saw?' he asked, fixing the black dragon with an intent stare.

Havenhigh nodded eagerly and her spines wobbled. 'The bodies of the two men should still be there, your townspeople haven't cleared anything away yet.'

The mage was already leaving. He marched across the wet grass towards the other side of the Spire. Storm clouds of dark thoughts and blame gathered in his mind as he walked. He could hear the dragons following close at his heels. They were as silent as he was and just as purposeful. Brightshow and Farfallen swapped glances.

Within minutes they came upon the first pile of bodies, heaped shoulder-high and in grotesque positions at the base of what used to be the Spire. Their pace, even Farden's, slowed a little as they saw the piles. The mage looked at the collection of figures. Some were charred beyond recognition, others seemed wax-like, with their eyes open and faces painted black and grey. Even his battle-hardened stomach twitched a bit; the smell was sickening when it mingled with the acidic charcoal taste that lingered in the air.

'Havenhigh! Where are they?' he called to her.

The lithe dragon scanned the repulsive scene with her grey eyes and pursed her lips in annoyance. She took a few moments to move around the piles, looking for a glint of armour. Something gold and white caught her keen eyes and she shouted to the others.

'Here!' she hissed.

Farden was first to reach her. Part of him hoped the fire had just been some terrible accident, but the other part, the darker part, boiled with frustration. This was no accident, it was the next notch on the mysterious blade behind all of this. Farden just wanted to find the invisible hand that wielded it. He stood by the dragon's side, looking at the two bodies on the ground. They barely resembled men at all, but Farden only saw the jagged holes in their armour. Kneeling, he ran a finger across the scarred and molten surface of the breastplates and looked at how the gold was puckered and cracked. He stood up and sighed.

'This one on the left was hit by a fire bolt. The other there, see how the hole is less charred and smaller? That's spark magick,'

Farden said quietly.

'Then this was murder, and the fire was no accident,' Farfallen voiced what all the others were thinking. The great dragon sighed. 'We must take this to Åddren immediately.'

Farden looked at the dead guards lying in the wet grass. Their wide eyes were frozen in their last seconds. He thought only of Cheska. 'I think I know someone that could tell us what happened here, if we asked him right,' he growled. *Keep an eye on the weather* he thought. He would do more than just keep an eye on it. The mage let a moody flame burn in his palm for a moment before extinguishing it in a clenched fist with a hiss. Farden looked Farfallen in the eye. 'You go see the Arkmage, I'm going to pay someone little visit.'

And without a further word the mage was off, hobbling down the hill in a limping run, heading towards the dark clouds that were gathering over the city. The dragons watched him leave and Farfallen sighed quietly to himself.

The mood in Krauslung was sombre and down-trodden. Every door was closed every window latched. The taverns and drinking-holes of the city were unusually quiet, and as Farden lurched past them he watched the men in the candle-lit windows, looking at their yellow melancholy faces sipping at cold ale. Farden trudged on. Soon he began to feel the first signs of a rain storm splash on his shoulders and he heard the heavy thwack of several drops landing on his dirty hood. The rain was just the thing to brighten the mood of the city, thought the mage. He snorted. Half of Krauslung was covered by the cloud of smoke and ash that still rose from the nearby hilltop. The city mourned for its deep loss. The mood was taut like a bowstring.

Farden zig-zagged through desolate streets and alleyways

with his fists clenched in his pockets and hood pulled low over his fiery eyes. A flash of colours, gold, white, red, and black, suddenly appeared overhead between two rooftops and the mage managed to catch a glimpse of four dragons heading for the great hall. His rib still burnt with pain, but he forced himself through it, feeling that vengeance was close at hand. He thought only of Cheska.

The guards at the citadel gates were silent and wary of Farden. With angry eyes they looked at the mage as if he were someone to blame, but they did not challenge him, and so Farden limped on past.

Stairs made his wound protest and scream with fresh agony, and the long hallways seemed endless. As he made his way deeper and deeper into the fortress the white marble and gold trimmings of the Arkathedral disappeared and were gradually replaced by drab granite and gloom. Windows were replaced with stone walls and thick iron doors dotted the corridors. Guards stood quietly on every corner but they didn't bother Farden. They just stared at him blankly as he hurried past, deeper into the mountain. Like Hjaussfen, the prisons were like a warren, a labyrinth of cells and hallways designed to slow the escape of anyone who would dare. But Farden wasn't escaping. He knew exactly where he was going.

Soon he came to another thick iron door. At some point in the past someone had painted it a dull blood red, but the colour had long-since flaked away and left the metal brown and rust-coloured. Farden kicked at the door and it swung open, startling a young guard standing on the other side.

'State your business!' he demanded and the mage found a shaky spearpoint waving in his face. Farden held up both of his hands. 'I'm here to see the Arkmage,' he said.

The young man shook his head resolutely. 'Nobody's to go in there, Lord Vice's orders, under pain of death!'

Farden's patience was growing dangerously thin. 'I don't

have ti…'

'I'm sorry sir, but you'll have to leave!' The spearpoint got closer as the man took a careful step forward.

Farden he grabbed the spear shaft and swiftly broke it in two. He pushed the shocked guard backwards until his armour collided with the wall and then he sent him sprawling on the floor with a deft kick. Dazed the young guard cowered on the floor fearfully.

Farden grabbed him by the collar of his breastplate. 'I said I don't have time for this! Now where's Helyard?' he bellowed, every word making the man jump a little more. The guard pointed a shaky hand to the dark corridor leading off from the little room. 'Down th… there sir!'

'Good man,' muttered Farden. He lifted up a clenched fist and a light spell burnt the shadows away and half-blinded the young guard. Anger bubbled inside of him, and even though he had no idea quite what he was about to do somehow he was starting to sense that vengeance and answers were close at hand. Farden tried to calm his breathing. The magick ran like boiling water though his veins. He thought only of Cheska.

Farden found the cell door and gritted his teeth, spreading his palm over the cold steel and oak and letting his fingers creep over the metal. The symbols on his wrist burnt white like fire under his vambraces. The mage had no time for subtlety. He could feel the magick pulse through his forearm but he held firm and pushed with all his strength at the door, making the iron buckle and writhe under his hand. The door rippled and shook again with a terrible wrenching sound. Farden clenched his jaw even harder and pushed with every ounce of his strength. Sweat dripped from his forehead.

Suddenly there was a crunch and a metallic squeal and splinters exploded from under the metal brackets. Farden didn't even blink. With another shove the door buckled and flew open in a cloud of white dust. The mage didn't waste a second. He burst through the haze and stormed into the room, fists clenched and fire trailing around his wrists. His heart pounded and his eyes eagerly roved around the room.

Then the smell hit him, that sickly rotting smell that nobody could ever forget once they had experienced it. Farden saw the body on the floor surrounded by a dark sticky pool of blood and his heart fell in his chest like a cold rock in the colder sea. The mage walked forward slowly and knelt by the corpse's side. It was Helyard. The old man's head was twisted at a ridiculous angle and his body lay in an awkward position. A long knife was buried hilt-deep in his chest. The Arkmage's face was ashen and grey, his eyes were misted over and glazed in death and a horrified expression was frozen on his face. He looked shocked, pained, and Farden stared into his glazed eyes. He wondered what he had seen or what he had been thinking, who he had faced. The mage gingerly lifted Helyard's chin and moved his head slightly, trying to restore some sense of decorum to the old man's posture and with a gentle hand he closed his eyes for the final time. A renewed sense of loss washed over Farden like a bucket of ice water. He sighed and looked around at the room, looking at the pockmarks in the walls and the splintered remains of what looked like a cot. The floor was cracked and blistered, like the armour of the unfortunate guards at the Spire. Without a sound Farden stood up and walked out, leaving Helyard in peace. He thought only of Cheska.

chapter 17

"I am not becoming someone different, I am simply getting to know the person I already am..."
Old saying, origin unknown

For once the *Bearded Goat* was quiet and still. A few people were scattered around the bar, not bothering anyone except themselves, sipping ale and drowning their thoughts as though there were not going to be a tomorrow. Even the sound of the inn's creaky sign swinging in the breeze outside was louder than the muffled sound of conversation. The fire crackled quietly by the mage's side. Someone coughed.

Farden swilled the warm wine around his mouth. After leaving Helyard's cell he had gone straight to find Vice but the Undermage was nowhere to be found, his rooms had been empty and his servants clueless. He had gone to tell the Arkmage and the council but Åddren had merely slumped deeper into his throne and gone silent, staring blankly into space without any words of wisdom or comfort to offer the mage. Nothing. Farden had been furious.

And, to make matters worse, talk of his daughter's death had reached Bane the King of Skölgard and he had sent a dozen hawks with news of his imminent arrival to Krauslung. The King wanted an explanation as to why his only daughter and heir to the throne had died whilst in the care of the Arka. Bane had demanded retribution for

Cheska and had threatened war on the magick council. They now only had mere days before Bane and his army arrived.

The mage couldn't help but think that somehow it all rested on his shoulders. He should have been in Albion with the army but he needed time to think. Farden took a thoughtful bite of a lonely piece of bread that sat on his plate. A mixture of anger and grief momentarily flushed through him and he shuddered. Farden tore at the bread with his teeth and sent a shower of crumbs across the table. He narrowed his eyes and tried to think, tried to figure out this mess once and for all.

That evening the city was filled with lights. As night fell the stars battled with the thick cloud for a place in the darkening skies. Torches crept into the streets and candles appeared in windows. One by one people left their houses carrying candles in glass jars, or tall blazing torches, or little whale oil lamps for the children. The countless lights made their way south towards the sea, wandering through the winding streets of the city like fireflies. They mingled and they gathered, their bearers silent and sombre, and all together they quietly proceeded down towards the shore. An Arkmage had died.

Slowly the lights assembled by the sea and lined the rocky beaches. As the people gathered they did so in complete silence and let other sounds fill the wordlessness. Innumerable shoes crunched on the sand and shingle. A myriad of candles, lamps, and torches sparked and hissed in the cold night breeze. The water lapped gently at the shore and rocked the ships in the port, making their bells shake and toll quietly with low clanging moans.

After an hour the entire city had gathered at the water's edge and every single one of them was deathly quiet. The People stood in their thousands anywhere they could find the space to do so. They crowded on the dark shoreline and filled the empty jetties and walkways. Peasants and shopkeepers rubbed shoulders with aristocrats and fine ladies stood with battle-scarred soldiers. Sailors stood at the railings of their ships. Even in their thousands nobody made even the faintest sound. The silence, broken only by the gentle swish of the waves and the quiet tolling of the bells, ached.

Åddren stood alone on a rock near the front of the crowds and looked out over the calm waves that rippled across the bay of Rós and out towards the Bern sea. The dark waters seemed glasslike, mottled like obsidian, and every now and again the frothy tip of a wave caught the bright torchlight and shone orange. He let a slow sad sigh escape from his pursed lips. The night breeze made him shiver.

At that moment a lone horn rang out from somewhere in the port and nine small boats emerged from the mouth of the harbour walls. Another horn cried then, a long high-pitched wail that floated across the cold air. Everyone just watched and waited.

The boats bobbed leisurely on the waves and thudded against each other with dull knocking sounds. Another smaller boat, a skiff, made its way out to them. There was a man leaning far out from the bow holding a long pole with rags wrapped around the end of it. Slowly, and with a great deal of reverence and ceremony, the man lit the pole with flint and tinder and touched each boat with the crackling flames. One by one the boats, their sad cargoes liberally doused with a special oil, burst into flame. The man in the skiff pushed the vessels out to sea and let the waves do the rest.

The thousands gathered on the beaches and ships bowed their heads and slowly, saying their wishes and prayers to their gods, snuffed out their torches and candles. The beaches were gradually plunged into darkness until the only lights were those of the nine burning boats drifting towards the dark horizon and the islands of Skap.

Far away on the Manesmark hillside a hooded figure sat watching the ceremony with his arms resting on knees and as silent as the surrounding grass. Farden's keen eyes had long since adjusted to the darkness, and now he stared raptly at the tiny twinkling lights in the distance. He let the breeze tug at his hood, breathing slowly and listening to his mind wander through dark thoughts.

Farden absentmindedly twiddled with something between his fingers. It was Cheska's fjortla. He had toyed with it for hours but the red metal was still cold to the touch. The fact that she could have died during the Ritual and not in the fire was no comfort. He looked at it a hundred different ways but the outcome was always the same: Cheska was gone.

The night was cold but the mage was already numb and felt as lost as ever. More than once he had contemplated throwing himself onto the rocks below the hill but he knew the fall wouldn't have taken his problems away. Farden shook his head and his morbid thoughts were interrupted once again by that annoying sense of duty that seemed to incessantly poke at him. Maybe it was responsibility or maybe it was a craving for revenge, he didn't know, but something was definitely trying to keep him going and stoking the angry fires deep in his heart. But at the same time an overwhelming desire to give up and wallow in grief tugged at him from the opposite direction, and he was caught in the middle of both feelings, undecided and confused. The conviction with which he had fought everything up to this point was slowly dimming and getting lost amidst the stress and the pain. Farden was tired. As the very last of the lights disappeared on the horizon in the darkness of the bay he got to his feet with a grunt and strode off into the darkness.

The walk back into the city only took a few hours, and as Farden walked past the huge city gates it started to snow. The flakes were few and lazy at first, gently drifting down from the black sky, but Farden could feel that a blizzard was fast approaching. As he descended into the streets of Krauslung he looked up at the dark clouds between the buildings. In the orange light of the torches the snowflakes looked like grey flies floating on the growing breeze, swarming around the windows and rooftops. Farden pulled his cloak about him and coughed, watching the hot breath escape from his lips as steam. The cold was doing wonders for his arrow wound.

The city was quiet again. Now that the funeral was over the citizens had gone back to their homes and had locked their doors for the night. Snow quickly covered the streets and blushed orange and yellow in the torchlight and made the alleyways and buildings glow oddly. Farden could barely see ten yards in front of him but he could make out a few people wandering through the cold streets ahead of him. The figures looked odd and misshapen through the thick snow. They passed without a sound, like him their hoods pulled low and hands deep in their pockets. They made a strange sight, with their heads and shoulders covered in a thick layer of white snow, huffing and puffing steam like a chimney as they hurried home. Somewhere to the left a mother shushed a whining child. There was a sudden peal of boyish laughter and two more children wrapped in a dozen scarves bounded through the whiteness. A few seconds later another fatter child raced after them, carrying two sizeable lumps of snow in each chubby hand. Farden shook his head with a hint of a smile, even though the expression felt strangely foreign in his current mood. They were so oblivious to their surroundings, so innocent and carefree. The mage felt a little pang of jealousy and wished he could go running into the snow and forget everything.

Soon he came to a familiar corner and heard the muffled

squeak of a familiar sign. Farden sighed with relief: all he wanted to do was sleep. The mage made his way to the brightly lit doorway and stamped his feet hard on the steps to shake off the snow. The *Bearded Goat* was quiet once again, subdued and half-empty. Thick tobacco smoke filled the air. Farden wandered in and nodded to the innkeeper, who went to pour him another glass of the sweet red wine he was starting to like. It wasn't like him to be so habitual but it was the only thing that seemed to keep him from thinking too much. Melting snow from his leather boots dripped onto the floor and made little puddles. With a sigh he cast a few looks around the place. A few men leant against the end of the bar, swapping words in low murmurs and nods. Farden watched them for a moment, trying to listen, but he soon gave up. Another man, a soldier by the look of him, sipped ale by the hearth. His eyes were glazed in deep thought and he absently swirled his ale in his glass.

The warm wine came in a wooden cup. The smell of spices and nutmeg in the wine smelled good. Farden sipped the hot liquid carefully and savoured the hot steam on his face. Seeing as he had left most of his supplies at the Arkabbey he decided he would order some food later. The only things in his pockets were the Weight, the fjortla, and the daemonstone. He found himself chuckling grimly as he thought how pointless the present was. Farden sighed.

The mage looked to the other figure sat in the corner at the back of the inn and met a pair of beady eyes looking back at him, a pair of very familiar rodent eyes. The old beggar tugged on his hair and nodded slowly. Farden hesitated by the bar, and just looked at the old man. He wore the same patchwork getup as before, his dirty wet cloak was pulled tightly around him like a filthy blanket. Bits of snow clung to his long greasy hair He looked even more haggard than he remembered, like a drowned rat. A yellow smile curled at the corner of his lip. Farden looked away and tasted the hot wine again. He waited patiently by the bar and thought about the sudden strange excitement that stirred in his chest. Farden hadn't even thought of nevermar since that night in the forest with Elessi. But now it was all he could think of. He made his way past the warm fire and the men at the bar and meandered through a copse of stools and tables. He sat down beside the old man without a word.

A moment passed. 'It's a cold night,' said the beggar with a cough.

Farden nodded, keeping his eyes on the fireplace ahead. 'Mm it is, storm's coming.'

'A storm 'e says, hmm.' He clacked the mouthpiece of the pipe against his teeth thoughtfully and then began to chuckle. 'Keep and eye on the weather it'll be comin' sooner than ye think, fine mage, sooner than ye think,' His laugh was a weird hissing sound. The grimy man grinned, flashing blackened gums. Smoke streamed from his nostrils. It made him look like an old dragon, Farden thought.

The mage merely nodded once more and sat in silence, sipping his wine again. The beggar stared at him with a glint in his eye. 'What brings yew t' my table tonight then?'

Farden shrugged. 'Nothing in particular, familiar face and all that.' The excuse sounded stupid. The beggar tapped his nose with a mucky finger. 'Strange that, 'aven't seen yew in a couple o' weeks, mage.'

'I've asked you not to call me that before,' said Farden in a dangerous tone. He sipped his wine again. 'Been busy,' he added.

'Hmm, so I 'ear,' the man chuckled again. The sound made Farden feel uncomfortable. 'What's the matter?' he grinned. 'Nevermar's got yer tongue?' The beggar laughed his little snake laugh and shuffled out of his seat shakily. 'I seen your room already, I'll be in number nine, if ye fancy tryin' some more.' He tottered his way to the stairs and disappeared into the shadows of the upstairs corridor. Farden sighed. His thoughts spoke all at once, clamouring somewhere between his ears. The mage sipped at his wine, feigning calm, and simply stared into the crackling fire.

Half an hour later, when the warmth of the wine had worked its way to his head, Farden found himself striding eagerly up the well-trodden stairs of the *Bearded Goat* and looking at the ascending numbers of the doors. In the dim candlelight he found the room and knocked quietly, looking down the hallway for any onlookers. The corridor was silent and empty.

There was a sound from behind the door and the click of a cheap-sounding lock. An ugly face peered from behind the door and grinned. Farden nodded silently and followed the beggar into the room. Strange that a beggar could afford to stay at the inn, he thought. Maybe he got lucky with a drunk noble. Farden shrugged. He tried not to think of the last night he had spent in a room like this.

The room in question smelled stale, like old shoes mixed with damp, or that earthy smell of dirt. Farden watched the snowflakes outside slip-sliding down the windowpane to join their friends in the street. The city was slowly being covered in a white blanket. Maybe it was a new beginning, he thought, a blank canvas for tomorrow.

The man toyed with a big bag of something on the bed, coughing and murmuring to himself as he rummaged. Gods the man was ugly, thought Farden. In the orange glow from outside he looked like a scrawny rat, bereft of whiskers or tail but just as twitchy. After a short while he cackled softly and produced a long pipe from the folds of his bags. Farden fidgeted.

' 'Ere it is, knew I 'ad it somewhere. Light the fire would yew boy?' said the beggar with a cheeky grin. Farden bit his tongue and went to the fireplace. He crouched low and hunched over so the man couldn't get the gratification of watching the spell. Flame trickled from his fingers and licked at the pile of dry wood. The orange flames hopped from one log to the other like a disease and slowly the fireplace began to smoke and crackle.

The old beggar stooped beside the mage and held the end of the long leaf in the flames until it started to smoke and glow. 'Take a seat,' he said. Farden could smell his rotten breath. He stood up and pulled a threadbare armchair closer to the fire as the old man took a short stool. He grinned his little rodent smile as his seat wobbled unsteadily beneath him. He puffed on the pipe and the sickly-sweet smell began to tickle Farden's nostrils.

'I 'ear yew were in Nelska, with them dragon-riders,' said the beggar. The mage shuffled around uncomfortably in his chair. This old man knew entirely too much about his business. 'You hear a lot, old man,' he said.

'That I do, when my ears still work, heh. Not dead yet then I see?'

The mage gave the man a stony look. 'No apparently not.' This old beggar was starting to worry him a little. Farden didn't trust him one bit, but he couldn't help eying the pipe in the man's claw-like hand. At that moment he shuffled forward on his little stool and pulled his patchwork cloak around his shoulders. Jabbing the air with the bowl of the pipe he pointed to Farden's side, where something strange was happening in his pocket. 'What's that?' he asked.

Farden looked down, confused, and saw a dim glow coming from the inside pocket of his black cloak. 'I don't know,' he replied, and reached to fish out whatever it was. It was the daemonstone and even though it was still wrapped in the thin paper it shone and sparkled with a whitish yellow glow. Farden held it in the palm of his hand and blinked slowly. It felt cold in his hand. 'That's odd.'

The old beggar shook his head and sniffed loudly. 'Don't look safe t' me. Put it away,' he said with narrowed eyes. Farden pretended not to hear him and unwrapped the corner of the paper. The brassy gold rock was definitely glowing. He leant forward and it got brighter still and each of its metallic facets sparkled with pinpricks of white light. Farden wrapped it back up again and held it tightly in his hand. The light shone from between his fingers like one of his light spells.

The beggar sucked his teeth and leant back on his stool. 'Put it away mage. Ain't natural I say. Glowin' rocks.'

'It's fine,' he said, and he couldn't help but think how much Cheska would have liked her present. He sighed and stuffed the daemonstone back in his pocket. He kept his hand on it. Smoke curled up from the pipe as the beggar puffed on it once again. The fire crackled quietly next to them and Farden found himself staring at the smouldering nevermar. The beggar watched the mage's eyes and smiled knowingly. He held out his hand. 'Try some, it's different to the last lot,' he offered.

Farden took the pipe in his hand and watched it burn for a little bit. Grim thoughts shouted loudly in his head. 'You know what happens if you tell anyone about this don't you?' he warned the beggar. He shook his head and waved his hand dismissively. 'I know I know for gods' sake, won't tell a soul.'

The mage watched the thing hovering between his fingers. Trying to justify it was like trying to wrestle a troll. Farden sighed.

'Are yew goin' t' smoke it or kiss it mage?' hissed the beggar, a little impatiently.

Farden glared at him. 'I said don't call me that.'

'Well we ain't got all night boy! Yew goin' to smoke it or not?'

'Fine,' said Farden. He handed him back the pipe and eyed the man with a defiant look. With a grunt he stood up and pulled his hood over his head. 'I think it's time I left.'

The beggar scowled. 'Smoke it,' his eyes flashed with anger.

'Forget it old man,' said Farden, he shoved the armchair out of his way and marched for the door. And then a shout stopped him dead. A shout in a voice he knew very well indeed.

'Farden!'

The mage whirled around to see a different man in the room. The beggar rose slowly from his stool, shaking and groaning as he did so as if he were fighting to keep his limbs still. The man seemed to stretch before Farden's eyes and his black clicked and groaned audibly. His skin shimmered and warped. Years and lines fell from his face like leaves from a tree and his eyes glowed with a sudden dangerous fire. The man threw off his dirty cloak and flexed his arms and fingers. His yellow and black teeth gradually slipped to a whiter shade and they flashed with a snake's grin. The daemonstone glowed brightly in Farden's pocket.

Vice threw the pipe into the fire with a contemptuous snort and watched Farden back up against the door. The mage was aghast, mouth wide open and gaping in disbelief. He stared wide-eyed at his friend of many years, the Vice he had known since his first day at the School, when he had been twelve years old. He wanted to laugh as if it were some sort of sick joke, but the humour was lost somewhere behind that lump in his throat. 'You?' It was all Farden could manage. His world shattered in front of him.

The Undermage picked at something under his nails and chuckled. 'That's what Helyard said. You should think yourself lucky I didn't come while you were sleeping,' he said.

Rage began to boil in the mage's heart and he could feel the white heat along his spine and shoulders. 'After all this time, you were right here under my nose?' Farden clenched his fists until his hands went pale. His stomach churned sickeningly and realisation slowly became a knot in his heart.

Vice clicked his fingers together. 'I'm not here to talk Farden. But as usual you take a while to grasp the obvious.' The smile had disappeared from Vice's face and had been replaced by thin lips and a fiery look in his hazel eyes. 'I suppose your stupidity knows no bounds.'

The mage blinked, unused to the tears that had suddenly

gathered beneath his wide eyes. 'Neither does your treachery!' shouted Farden and he slammed his wrists together with a loud clang. Fire swirled around his fists like a yellow hurricane, burning and hissing with a dragon's roar. Farden cried out, all words forgotten, just pure anger and vengeance came from his throat. He lunged and opened his hands and the fireball leapt across the room. But Vice was ready for it. He threw his hands up in front of him, blade-like, and the fireball slammed into an invisible shield inches before it threatened to consumed him. The flames exploded against the Undermage's spell with a blinding flash and a roar. The yellow fire billowed around him. Still Vice smiled confidently with his sneering grin. Farden shook with anger. He stormed across the room with his hands held high. Lightning flickered and crackled between his fingers.

But Vice was still ready. He spun and dropped to his knees, and jabbed the air. Farden collapsed in abrupt pain and completely doubled over. He had never felt a spell like it. He stumbled against the bed and threw out a hand to steady himself, trying to find breath. The arrow wound between his ribs burnt with agony and he looked up to find the Undermage towering over him. Green light shimmered over his knuckles. Farden saw what was about to happen and dove to the side just as Vice dropped his fist like a hammer. Fortunately he struck empty floor but the shockwave cracked the floorboards and the fireplace split in two.

The brave mage was already on his feet and standing behind the Undermage. He seized his narrow opportunity and brought his knee straight up into Vice ribs, and then he grabbed him roughly by the neck. Sparks coursed along the Undermage's body and he went rigid, crying out suddenly. Lightning shivering over his skin.

'Taste of your own medicine, Vice? Like the scholars at Arfell?!' shouted Farden.

Vice threw an elbow in Farden's face, forcing the mage to break his hold and stumbled backwards. He laughed, and a curved knife appeared in his hands, glinting evilly in the firelight. Farden wiped blood from his lip and backed off. He watched his opponent's hands warily as they moved through the air. The dirty silver blade waved back and forth slowly, calculatedly. That familiar grin curled at the corner of his mouth again, the one Farden had known for over half his life. Vice spat. 'You think you're any different, Farden? Any better than the old men who died at my hand, better than those Siren soldiers or that old fool the Arkmage? I can dispatch you all as easily as insects.' The two of them circled warily, each trying to force the other into a corner. 'I have watched you systematically ruin your life ever since you uncle died. And let me tell you one thing Farden, you are no different from him whatsoever. The temper, the nevermar, the voices in your head, you're both as bad and as useless as each other And what about that pretty girl in the Spire? That Skölgard girl. What was she called again?' laughed Vice.

'Don't you fucking dare speak her name!' bellowed Farden.

'That one you loved so much. Did you think nobody would notice Farden?' The knife flashed briefly and the blade weaved through the air like a cobra. 'She was so easy to get rid of anyway, after all the confusion of the Ritual, and the fire finished her off for me,' said Vice with an evil sneer.

Something inside Farden snapped. With a growl of pure animalistic fury he punched the air above his head with his hands, arms tensed and shaking, fingers bent like claws. The mage shivered and strained, as if he were pulling on the sky, feeling power he had not felt since the *Sarunn*. A rumbling came from below the room, slow at first, but building quickly, until the floor started to shake and rattle violently beneath their boots. Farden's eyes burnt with a vengeful fire, fixed on the Undermage, and he shook as the magick pulsed in his veins as though his blood boiled. Vice began to back away cautiously, a different expression now on his face.

Time stopped once again, just for a second, as though a

moment lasted an hour. The snow froze in midair outside the window. The dust hovered in the room. Still and sparkling.

Then a roar came, a deafening, ear-splitting scream from below them that drowned out the world. Suddenly the floor between them burst into a thousand pieces, as if a volcano had suddenly erupted in the bar. With a blinding flash of searing flame a white-hot pillar of fire tore up through the room and into the ceiling. It blasted the chairs to nothing and turned the door to splinters, ripping through the roof of the inn as if it were no more than a pile of sticks. The bed was catapulted against the wall and the broken fireplace was reduced to a pile of charred bricks in seconds. Both men flew backwards and tried desperately to escape the flames.

The noise was terrifying. The windows exploded under the pressure and sent shards of glass spinning around the room. The mage shielded his face and eyes with his vambraces and scrambled up against the wall behind him to try to get away from the heat. The column of fire now spun like a relentless tornado and tore at the ceiling and walls with teeth made from flames and claws of blinding heat and smoke.

But the spell was slowly waning, Farden could feel it in his hands, and the shivering power slowly began to subside. Between the gaps in his fingers he spied Vice crawling over bits of bed and broken glass towards the cold air outside. The Undermage hopped onto the windowsill and with a quick jump he disappeared into the snow-streaked sky.

Farden gritted his teeth and got to his feet. Tiredness was trying to creep into his arms and legs once again but the rage in his chest stubbornly moved him forward. He skirted the dwindling flames and dashed to the window. The cold air slapped him hard in the face as he leant far over the window ledge and peered into the blizzard. A crowd of people had gathered outside the inn to gape at the fire that billowed from the roof and snapped at the snow-laden sky. The street had been washed of all other colours and turned a bright array of oranges and yellows. Flames dancing on snow. Bits of charred wood and cracked tiles were falling from clouds and littering the street like a strange new type of precipitation. The mage scanned the gawking faces below him and tried to steady his pounding breath. For a brief moment Farden savoured the freezing air in his lungs, but just then he spied a figure hurrying through the crowd, hood up and escaping. Farden grabbed the window frame, ignored the razor-sharp glass tearing at his palms, hoisted himself up, and with a grunt leapt from the room to the dark street below.

The mage landed hard on the icy cobbles and rolled to avoid breaking his ankles. He was on his feet in seconds. Farden barged through the crowd amidst shouts and angry cries. Vice had already broken free of the throng and was making his way further up the street and further into the city. Farden yelled to the bewildered people in his way. 'Get out of the way! Move!'

Up ahead half a dozen soldiers rounded the corner and stood barring the way. Thunderstruck they stared at the fire pouring from the roof of the inn. Farden shouted to them. 'Traitor! Stop him!'

The armoured men broke into a run, heading towards the crowd and towards the hooded Vice. The Undermage scowled: he wasn't about to waste any time dealing with mere soldiers. Vice skidded to a grinding halt and stamped his foot hard in the snow. A wave rippled through the cobbles as if they were marbles floating on a sea and a bubble seemed to expand outwards from him with a dull throbbing sound. The snow scattered in a sudden wind and the soldiers met an invisible brick wall. Their feet flew out from under them as they crashed to the ground with cries of shock. Panic filled the street. The crowd dispersed in all directions. Every one of them screamed and yelled at the top of their lungs.

But a single shout rose above the rest. 'Vice!'

The Undermage turned slowly and carefully, eyes smiling

with a confident air. Vice chuckled mockingly. 'See you at Carn Breagh,' he yelled and he let the words sink in. Then, as fast as lightning, the Undermage moved to grab something from inside his cloak. Farden sprinted forward but before he even got close there was a flash of bright gold and suddenly Vice was gone, leaving the air to shiver and pulse behind him as if he had folded into nothing.

'No no no!' Farden slipped and fell to the cold ground and stared in horror at the empty air. The snowfall became gentle, the wind had died, and a strange quiet fell on the streets. The mage put his forehead to the snow for a moment, fists clenched and frustrated, cheated of his revenge once more. He rolled onto his knees and stayed there and all he could do was stare dazedly at his surroundings. Feet squelched in the wet snow as a few people ran past him, back to their homes and away from the mayhem and the fire. Ahead the soldiers slowly picked themselves up and shook the dizziness from their heads. One still lay unconscious. Farden stared blankly into space and tried to calm himself with deep breaths. Pain slowly crept back into his body and replaced the adrenaline. The deep cuts from the glass in his hands oozed. Farden watched the droplets of blood drip down his fingers and land on the white snow, making little red flowers as they seeped in and froze. He could feel people watching him, he could hear them deciding it was better to leave him be. The fury still burnt in his eyes, he could feel it. His clothes were smoking and charred and his face and arms were a patchwork of old scars and fresh bruises. Farden didn't blame them, he wouldn't have approached him either.

A trumpeting sound broke his reverie but still he couldn't move, finding himself ever more numbed by shock. The sound of wings beating the air grew loud, and Farden lifted his face to the orange-smeared sky, letting the snowflakes land gently on his hot skin.

There were a few loud thuds from behind him that shook the

cobblestones under his knees, and then a scraping of scales and claws on stone. Farden watched the soldiers, eyes wide and nervous, back away and drag their unconscious friend with them. They stared at something behind Farden. A familiar booming voice called to him and echoed through the street, and the mage sighed.

'Farden!'

He rose, feeling his ribs complain to him again, grumbling and arguing that he should stay where he was in the snow. Behind him Farfallen stood with the big red dragon Towerdawn. Only Svarta was there with them. She stood with her arms folded and shaking her head as usual. Farfallen wore a concerned expression on his golden face.

The mage slowly walked to meet them. 'I thought it wouldn't be long until you spotted the fire,' said Farden quietly, regarding the destruction he had caused at the inn. It seemed like everyone had escaped the fire unharmed but sadly the *Bearded Goat* was no more; his favourite inn had been replaced by a smoking shell of a building, roof half gone and fallen in, now no more than a smoking mess of rubble, tiles, doors, and glass lying broken in the street. A handful of patrons, the soldier, the other men, and the innkeeper, stood shivering and confused in the snow. Every eye was fixed on the two huge dragons that had squeezed themselves into the narrow street. Their wings knocked gently against the drainpipes and the gutters.

'It seems that wherever we find destruction and chaos, we find you,' Svarta cast a glance at the smouldering inn behind her.

'It's not like I plan these things,' said Farden. He wiped his bloody hands on his cloak and shunned the pain.

'What happened here?' asked Farfallen. In the light of the flames the dragon's scales shimmered and glittered. The mage took a deep breath and looked him squarely in his big golden eyes. 'It was Vice,' he said. His words rang like cold steel.

The Old Dragon's spines rippled and his back arched like a

cat. 'Vice?' the name was a dark growl in his throat.

'I've been so blind!' Farden cursed and clenched his cold fists. 'It's been him along, this whole time! Helyard, that book from Arfell, your Sirens,' and the most painful of all, 'the Spire, all him!'

'All this time? You never even suspected him?' Svarta's face was the perfect picture of blame.

'You're the one who was so eager to condemn Helyard in the first place! Don't you dare lecture me. Vice has been my friend for years!' Farden eyed her with a dangerous look, daring her to carry on talking. The Siren queen scowled straight back at him and flicked her hair moodily.

The mage's fingers crept to the place where the gold disk hid in his cloak pocket. 'I have the Weight, I can get to him before any of you and stop him,' he said.

'Don't be a fool, you wouldn't even get close,' scoffed Svarta.

'Are you doubting me?' snapped Farden.

'That's enough!' snarled Farfallen impatiently. It was the first time Farden had seen the dragon so angry. 'We have to stop him, now, and put an end to all of this once and for all. Evil such as him does not deserve to live any longer. Where is he now?'

'He escaped using a Weight, probably Åddren's,' Farden kicked at snow and let the frustration froth inside him.

'He's gone?' asked Towerdawn.

Svarta was incredulous. 'You let him go?!' she spat.

Farden took a few steps forward and squared up to her, mere inches from her scaly face. She was unnaturally tall up close. Her yellow eyes glared straight back at him. 'I swear to the gods, Svarta, one more...' he growled.

'I said that's ENOUGH! Both of you back down! How does this help us now?' Farfallen's voice boomed and echoed loudly, and the two slowly separated. 'I'll ask you again, where is this foul worm?'

Farden sighed. 'Carn Breagh in Albion, north of Beinnh. It seems the bastard has deceived us once again.'

'What are you talking about?' Svarta glared.

'Don't you realise? There is no dark elf well near Kiltyrin and Fidlarig, there never was! Vice has been planning to release his monster at Carn Breagh all along, not anywhere near to where we thought he would be. By sending the army south he's left the Arka trapped and powerless to fight back. It would take four or five days hard march before the other Written could reach him.'

'And then it would be too late, by the sounds of it,' offered Towerdawn. His red eyes glinted in the gloom. The dragon sniffed the cold air. 'Something doesn't feel right.'

'We have to stop him,' Farden reminded them stubbornly. 'He has taken everything from us. I will not let him get away!'

Farfallen held up a patient claw. 'But how do you know he has gone to Carn Breagh?'

'He said it just before he escaped,' replied the mage.

The two dragons swapped glances and Svarta nodded quietly, deep in thought but still scowling, staring down at the snow. 'It doesn't feel right,' repeated Towerdawn. Farfallen simply hung his head and closed his eyes and searched for the answer. They all knew what it meant. The word *trap* silently hung unsaid in the air around them, with more than a tinge of dread about it.

'We have no other choice,' muttered Farden.

'It's organised suicide, even with all our dragons,' Svarta asserted quickly.

Towerdawn's crimson face was etched with concern. 'We are not seriously considering this...' his question drifted off.

Farfallen opened his eyes and shook the snow from his spines. 'The mage is right. We have no choice. Vice must be stopped at all costs, and even if it takes our lives we have to end this as quickly as possible.' The Old Dragon let the words sink in before carrying on. 'Towerdawn, assemble all our forces immediately. We have no time to warn the Arka and I doubt they would believe us anyway, not after what happened with Arkmage Helyard. Send two of our fastest, Havenhigh and another, one to Nelska and one to the rest of the dragons in Kiltyrin, we will need all the help we can get. If you want to see this through Farden then you can ride with Brightshow, her rider is in Albion with the others.' The mage simply nodded, but Farfallen could see the zeal burning from behind his eyes and clamping his jaw tight. The mage looked crushed. Blood oozed from his hands and trickled along his knuckles. He looked like he had when they had first met after the shipwreck. Farfallen could see the little dragonscale amulet hiding under the collar of his tunic, and he wondered how much luck the mage had left.

'May the gods fly alongside us tonight,' said the Old Dragon.

Within half an hour the dragons were tearing through the snowy skies. Their wings pounded the turbulent air and their tails swished and whistled across the cloudtops. Once they had cleared the thick snow storm they soared through the crisp air between the clouds and the stars. The bright moon shimmered across their scales and turned everything a different shade of silver, monochrome scales glistening under the stars.

Farfallen was out in front. Both he and Svarta had their eyes fixed on the horizon with resolute determination frozen on their windswept faces. The Old Dragon felt something stirring in him he hadn't felt in a long time. Svarta sensed it, and let her mind entwine with his, each of them mentally preparing themselves for the task ahead. Behind them almost fifty dragons wore the same expression, their riders armed to the teeth and ready to face anything that reared its ugly head. Every single one of them knew the stakes, the costs, and what might await them at Carn Breagh.

Farden pulled himself as close to Brightshow as he could. Using only his spells to keep him warm he desperately tried to breathe through the rushing air. The sick feeling of looking down still hadn't gone since his last flight so he had resigned himself to not looking at all, and just concentrated on conserving his strength. His eyes were sealed tight. Farden felt every single move of the dragon's body underneath him, every sinuous dip and twitch of her wings and tail as she snaked through the skies at their breakneck speed. Farden dug his feet deeper into the saddle to try to remove the ache at the bottom of his spine.

Doubt clouded the mage's mind, coupled with an uneasy uncertainty about facing Vice again. Everything he had ever learnt had come from Vice and that made him twice as dangerous as any other foe. And now it appeared that the Undermage was adept at the dark art of shapeshifting. Farden wondered who or what he really was. There seemed to be something different about Vice now as if he were a different person altogether. It was as if the magick he used was older, more ancient, like Farfallen's. Farden had never known spells like his, and who knew what else he had hidden up his robe. Not to mention that the whole thing, his whole plan, seemed too precise too clockwork. Towerdawn had spoken the truth: nothing seemed right about this. But they were bereft of choices and they had been funnelled into a lack of options with the odds stacked against them. If Jergan had been right about the manual then they were all about to face up to the most terrifying creature Emaneska had ever seen. The mage tried to force confidence into his thoughts and warmth into his fingers. He trusted in his skills, after all he was the best Written there was, and if anyone could take Vice down it was him. After the summoning the Undermage was bound to be weakened. Farden repeated that like a mantra.

A heavy sword rattled and jangled between his shoulders, a loan from one of the other riders. To replace the vial of ice water he had lost the Sirens had given him a tiny bottle of a dark red liquid they had called *syngur*. The strange stuff was constantly warm and tasted of sickly spices with a strange underlying fish taste. Farden could still feel the stuff burning his stomach, but it was helping the spells to keep him warm. He counted the hours until they would arrive above Carn Breagh.

chapter 18

"Let it not be said that Farden is just simply skilled; the man is far and above any mage I have yet to encounter. Despite their downfalls, he is of a powerful family, a pure breed. Whatever the Scribe wrote into his Book awoke a magick beast inside him. I've never seen a mage withstand such draining as he does, nor wield such huge spells with ease. It's a shame he ruins of all it with his anger, his battle-rage if you will, the red mist that has gotten him into trouble and danger many times before. Just look at what happened in Huskar after he killed the chieftain's son in that fist fight, all for some ridiculous wager. If Farden learnt to turn his anger into concentration, he would be greater than the Arkmages, and if that's treason you can hang me for it."
Taken from the diary of Durnus Glassren

Dawn was slowly breaking over Albion, pale shades of red, orange, and yellow smudged the skies in the east as the first hints of the winter sun dared to creep over the horizon. A slight fog hung in the morning air. Thick snow covered everything. It had moulded the landscape into a rolling white sculpture of itself, a simple mess of rolling mounds and bumps hidden under a crisp blanket. The trees were heavy with snow and the weak morning light made them sparkle like clusters of countless little diamonds.

Carn Breagh squatted quietly on its grey-white hill,

unassuming and peaceful. The ruined walls were draped in snow and glistened with the icicles that hung from their ancient ramparts. Its quiet exterior belied the malicious activities deep within the castle.

Far beneath the dripping stone, under the solid rock floors, where not even the rats would go, where the torches struggled to burn through the darkness, Vice pored over a small dragonscale book. He gripped the stone wall tightly and let the magick speak to him and echo in the dark corners of his mind. Figures scurried around behind him, hurrying around and preparing things. Dark soldiers in fire-blackened armour stood in the shadows, only the glint of their spears giving them away. Someone drummed their nails on the stone behind the Undermage and shattered his concentration.

'How long Vice?' they asked.

Vice sighed, and closed his eyes in quiet frustration. 'If I was left to my own devices, instead of being bothered, then I might get it done quicker.'

'You're taking too l…'

'Quiet! Keep yourself hidden like I said,' shouted Vice, and the person behind him huffed in annoyance. The Undermage listened to the sound of their footsteps receding into the shadows. Vice shook his head and watched the buzz of activity around him with narrowed eyes. All was going to plan. He found himself gazing back into the thick darkness of the huge well that took up the entire centre of the room. The shadows lurking in the stone-lined pit were impossibly dark, a matte black darkness that sucked out the light. It was bottomless, unfathomably deep. Vice heard the whispering of the magick from the little black manual calling to him again and gently he ran his fingers across the spidery script without tearing his eyes from the well.

There was an abrupt bang, and then a dull thud somewhere deep beneath them. A shout rang out. 'Lord Vice, we're ready!'

'Good,' he muttered to himself, and then he swept from the

lectern holding the book with his thumb in the page. With his cloak billowing behind him he strode around the pillared walkway that overlooked the great well. His jaw was set proud and confident. He made his way past the others standing in their positions. Vice looked at everyone with an intense, piercing hazel gaze, watching their pale faces melt into a mixture of fear and uncertainty. Weaklings, Vice thought scornfully, quivering like children. All they had to do was stay alive, he snorted.

The Undermage made his way to the small pulpit that perched on the far edge of the dark pit. From there he could lean over and gaze down into the depths and concentrate all the magick into one spot. Vice placed the manual on a stone lectern and let his fingers wander over the pages, peering through the shadows at the script. He took a long breath and tried to empty his mind. With his eyes closed he could hear the magick starting to shiver and pulse, the others shuffling and waiting, the heightened sense of everything around him. This was it, he thought, everything leant on this moment. He had spent too long in hiding, too long pandering to these mere mortals.

There was a sudden creak of a thick oak door and a yell came from the back of the hall and broke the anxious silence. 'Undermage!' All eyes turned to the soldier standing in the torchlight near the doorway. 'They're here!' he called.

The tiniest of smiles might have curled at the corner of Vice's mouth, but it was too dark to see it. He simply nodded and looked around the circular room. 'Let's give them a welcome they'll never forget,' said the Undermage, and they sprang to do his bidding. Vice spread his hands across the summoning manual and put an index finger to the two keys at the corner of the page, the ones that the old Arfell scholars had pointed out to him. A shudder of excitement ran through him. Looking into the impenetrable darkness of the well beneath him he whispered the pivotal words.

'Hear me,' he hissed, and there was a faint rumble from

below.

❦

High in the atmosphere, where the air grew thin, a swarm of dragons wheeled and circled above the snowy countryside that was spread below them like a rather realistic map. The sun was now crouching on the horizon, a pale yellow disk that peered into the morning mists. The snow sparkled even from that height.

Farden rubbed his cold hands together furiously and battled the twists and turns of Brightshow's body with his tired legs. He looked down through the hazy fog and scattered clouds at the tiny ruin below him and cursed to himself, suddenly regretting their decision to come. A dark feeling of dread unfurled inside him. The mage could hear Farfallen yelling to his captains, Towerdawn, Glassthorn, and a huge dragon named Clearhallow who had two riders, one of which looked like Eyrum, armoured up and holding a gigantic hammer-headed axe in one hand.

Farfallen looked at his swarm of dragons, and Farden was sure he could see him smiling. The golden dragon rippled and shone in the dawn light, battling the air with powerful strokes of his wings to hover in one place. He took a breath to speak. 'I will not waste our precious time with heavy-handed words and long speeches! I do no have to remind any of you how dangerous this will be, nor of how high the stakes are. All I can ask is that you remember that we are the first and the last line of defence against this beast. Not since the time of the elves and the gods have we faced such a monstrous foe, such "mouths of darkness." Well I see plenty of mouths here today, hungry mouths filled with teeth, strong claws and wings, brave hearts and strong arms holding sharp weapons! Let us show this ancient beast that things have changed in Emaneska, that we are in charge now!'

A mighty roar followed the Old Dragon's words and there

was a loud metallic screech of metal as scores of weapons were unsheathed and waved in the air. Farden grabbed his own sword and yanked it free. The razor-sharp blade flashed briefly in the sun's rays as he yelled and shouted. Every dragon snarled and unhinged their jaws and spurts of flame darted from their mouths. It felt exhilarating.

With another roar Farfallen folded his wings back and pointed his spiny head to the ground. His body seemed to hover in mid-air for a split second before he suddenly dropped like a stone and plummeted through the air at a frightening speed.

'Hold on Farden!' Brightshow yelled, and in one single dreadfully sickening moment every single dragon tucked their wings to their sides like falcons and plunged into the mists. Farden grabbed on for dear life. The air screamed past his ears like banshees and his heart was pounding frantically in his throat. His insides felt like they were trying to escape from his body and they lurched up and down as though his stomach was fighting his lungs. The mage pressed himself against Brightshow's back and tried desperately to close his eyes, but something inside him couldn't tear itself away from the terrifying ride.

The whole room pulsated and shook with energy. The well was making a deep thrumming sound as if a hammer was striking a drum in its depths, slowly getting faster and louder and gathering momentum for its final terrifying crescendo. Vice shook with the strain of the spell and kept his eyes on the darkness below, feeling the magick swell up from his fingers to his lips as they moved and spoke silent, unfamiliar words. Something was waking up at the roots of the world.

The Undermage was quickly reaching the end of the page, the final hurdle and the most dangerous part of the spell. He could hear the deep booming sounds getting louder. His head throbbed. The whole of Carn Breagh vibrated under the pressure and the walls groaned and bent awkwardly as if they were being squeezed by giant hands. Vice's breath came in laboured gasps. The well pulled at him, thick darkness trying to drag him over the edge of the pulpit and down into the shadows. He braced himself against the stone with a spare hand. He could hear the final few words shouting inside his skull, yelling at him and fighting the deep pounding noise from the well. A sudden wind gusted around the room, blowing out the torches and plunging the hall into darkness. Vice strained and pushed. His heart was beating so fast that it seemed to stand still, like the wings of a hummingbird, like the seconds grinding to a halt around them. The noise was deafening.

There was a yell and a surge in power and a soldier across the room fell to the floor clutching his throat. There was a flash of unearthly light in the well as he tumbled into the well, and for a moment Vice could see the body spinning in the darkness. The Undermage scrabbled to keep the spell intact while his knees buckled underneath him and his lungs burnt. Pain racked his whole body. Suddenly, another flash of light, and Vice reached the last word on the page.

There was a deep rolling crash of thunder from underground and the tremendous noise ground to an abrupt halt. Every single person in the hall lurched and convulsed with the final wave of magick, and there was a dreadful moment of pure silence.

Nothing moved, nobody made a sound, all held their breath, and for an eternity they seemed to wait. Soldiers swapped looks, some concerned, others relieved. Only Vice could feel something stirring beneath their boots. Still holding onto the magick he slowly backed away from the pulpit. Something was awake now. One single last word fell from his burning lips, and then the sky fell in.

Bricks and rock erupted from the ceiling as the roof fell in with an ear-splitting crash, raining stone and mortar on the room. One man was flattened by a huge brick as he dove for cover, another was knocked senseless and tripped over the edge of the well. Stone flew in all directions. The wind turned everything into a swirling storm of stone as deadly chips and shards flew everywhere. Carn Breagh was ripped in two. Daylight suddenly pierced the shadows as room after room and floor after floor was ripped from above them and dragged down to feed the hungry well. Snow fell from the hole above in great clumps and gradually the room was swallowed by a blizzard.

'HOLD!' Vice screamed at the others through the maelstrom, and whoever was left grabbed at anything that would stop them from being torn away. Cries and yells of terror and pain were torn away into the storm. Another boom and a clang came from the well, and a blood-curdling whine from something below. It felt like the entire world was being dragged, piece by piece, into the well.

There was another noise, louder and angrier this time, almost a gurgling scream, and just then three gigantic claws reached over the edge of the pit and grabbed at the wall. They ripped apart stone like rotten wood. Another clawing foot rose up from the well and smashed against the far wall and turned two soldiers to bloody smears on the floor. A stench filled the room that made Vice gag involuntarily, a smell of sulphur and death, of decomposing flesh. The wind had become hot and dry and the blizzard suddenly died.

Out of the darkness below a head rose, a massive, ugly head that was too horrifying to comprehend. Embedded in its dragon-like face were scores of red eyes that glowed like burning coals, and they blinked as one. The beast rattled its horns as a clump of snow fell on its head. It turned to Vice. Hot breath billowed from its nostrils like the steam that had begun to fill the room. The Undermage stood, shakily, to return its gaze, wondering which specific eye to look at. Dark whispers hissed in his head, voices that he hadn't heard for thousands of years. After a moment, Vice looked up, through the hole in the castle to the wintry skies above, to the dark shapes circling above, and then back to the monster. The thing made its whining cry again and lifted itself further out of the steaming well. Another head rose, and another, and another, and yet another, one by one, until almost twenty heads had reared up from the shadows, fighting for space with snarls and screeches. Vice couldn't tear his eyes away, and as he pressed himself flatter against the wall to avoid being crushed by the beast, he watched awestruck as the monstrous thing rose into the air.

Mere seconds before Farden thought they would crash into the ruins Brightshow flared her wings and darted back into the sky. The sudden lurching change in direction made bile jump into the mage's throat, but he forced himself to swallow hard and concentrated on holding on. He opened his mouth to speak but a sudden crash from behind stopped him. They both whirled around just in time to see the castle rip itself in two and erupt in a fountain of broken grey stone. The other dragons roared and dodged the flying chunks with rolls and dives, but one unlucky rider was caught by a shard of rock and was thrown like a rag doll from his saddle. The dragon, a spiny yellowy-orange beast, made a terrible cry and went limp in the air. She crashed to the ground in a shower of snow and brown stone.

'We're too late!' Farfallen yelled, snarling and cursing in some ancient language. They barely had time to think before there was another huge bang. Something was moving around in the gaping hole. Something older than all the dragons combined.

'Look!' Brightshow shouted and everyone turned to watch as the monster ripped its way out of the castle.

'It's a hydra!' shouted Farfallen, and with fearful roars and trumpets every dragon backed away from Carn Breagh. Farden's eyes went wide with shock.

The thing was terrifying, if only by sheer size. With a rumble it pulled the last of its heads from the ruin and stood tall on all four monstrous feet, each one thicker than any tree the mage had ever seen, and rippling with muscle. The hydra dwarfed the swarm of dragons as it stretched to tower high above the castle, easily hundreds of feet tall. A score of heads sprouted from the monster's thick shoulders, and their entangled necks squirmed like a nest of snakes. Each fearsome head was impossibly big, almost as big as a dragon itself. Blinking red eyes and teeth fought for a place amongst bony ridges and bristling crown-like crests of countless dark blue spines. In the weak morning sun the hydra's grey flesh seemed to pulsate and writhe in an unnerving way. Its breath steamed in great clouds like an angry volcano. The mage could smell the thing, a horrible rotting smell of meat that permeated the air and soiled the snow. An ear-splitting cacophony of a roar came from every one of its mouths, an eerie, discordant minor harmony, and the sound chilled everyone to the bone.

Brightshow turned her head to look at Farden, and they swapped fearful glances. Farden felt a cold sweat form on his brow. He had never seen anything like it, not in his dreams, no in his darkest nightmares, not on the wall paintings in Hjaussfen, not even in the wildest parts of his imagination. The thing screeched again, and Farden found himself staring, eyes wide, into the fang-lined mouths of the beast. All thoughts of Vice and revenge had disappeared, replaced only by numbing dread.

There was a huge crash as another part of wall fell in under the weight of the hydra, stones crushed to sand under its four gigantic feet, its thick forked tail swishing back and forth restlessly. A myriad of red eyes blinked as one.

Farfallen swooped close and barrel-rolled overhead. Farden

heard a deep voice in his head as clear as if someone sat behind him. *Go after Vice. We can handle the hydra for now.* The mage looked at the Old Dragon and met his gold-flecked eyes. *Cut the head from the snake and the body dies* said the voice. Farden nodded his head once, grimly, and with that the dragon snarled and flashed a dangerous and toothy grin back at him. He climbed high into the sky, above the hydra, and made a long trumpeting noise like a battle-horn. The others took up the cry and climbed into the air. Below them the hydra snarled and gnashed its countless teeth together, making a sound like snapping trees.

Farden thwacked his dragon's back. 'Brightshow! Take me down to the castle, I have to stop Vice!' he shouted above the roaring and the gnashing.

'Are you sure?' she yelled.

A sudden surge of energy, maybe confidence, maybe fear, he didn't know, but still some sort of mettle coursed through him. 'More than ever, let's go!'

Brightshow lurched and flapped. 'Then hold on!' she cried. Farden was starting to grow tired of hearing those words, but still he tensed his body for the inevitable stomach-churning drop. She dropped like a stone and rolled, making the snow the sky, and then back to the snow again. Farden fought bile again and tried to keep his eyes on the gargantuan hydra that was getting uncomfortably close. There were six dragons behind them, wings tucked and snouts pointed, following him and Brightshow down to the castle. She swerved again and Farden had a blinding moment of fear as one leg slipped from a stirrup. His fingers were frozen to the saddle and he found himself praying, to anyone who would be listening, that he would reach the ground in one piece.

Above them the dark shapes were falling, roaring and screeching and snarling and trumpeting, a riot of colours with claws outstretched and jaws wide. The hydra made its whistling minor chord wail again and its jaws clicked and teeth ground against each other. The swarm and the monster clashed, and chaos filled the cold air. One yellow dragon got too close and was torn in two in a shower of blood and ochre viscera. Another had one wing ripped clean from its side. Farfallen dipped and swooped through the nest of snakes-like heads, blasting searing fire in every direction while Svarta leant far out of her saddle and slashed here and there with her vicious longsword. Towerdawn came up from underneath, flying upside down, and ripped chunks of grey flesh from the hydra's underbelly with his front claws. One head snarled and snapped at him, missing his tail by inches. Fire filled the morning sky.

Go, a voice said again. Farden shouted to Brightshow. 'We don't have much time!'

'I know I know!' she snarled, and rolled left to dodge another snapping head. A blue dragon behind them screeched as the hydra clamped onto its back and yanked it from the air. Sapphire blood splashed the snow as the beast disappeared behind rows of sharp teeth. With a quick flap they were suddenly in the clear, around the back of the monster with only its tail to fear. Brightshow crashed to the snowy ground and gulped air. Farden could feel her huge heart thrumming inside her chest, impossibly fast, pounding with fear. Her yellow eyes were wide and panicky. 'Go, while you still can!' she gasped.

'Just keep clear of that thing!' Farden leapt from her side and drew his sword in midair. The snow crunched and creaked under Farden's boots as he landed and he remembered the first time he had seen Carn Breagh, all those long weeks ago. Beside him the other dragons skidded into the snow while others hovered to let their riders jump to the ground. A big hand grabbed the mage's shoulder and he whirled around to find Eyrum standing behind him. His one good eye stared back at him intently. Even in the excitement of battle, his tone was low and measured. 'Have you still got the scale I gave you?'

asked the big Siren. He held his ridiculously large axe in one hand, hefting it as easily as a toy. The sharp blade glinted in the pale misty light. Farden nodded and patted his chest, and the feeling of the small trinket against his skin suddenly comforted him. A smile hovered on Eyrum's scarred lips. 'Then let us finish this you and I.'

Farden opened his mouth to speak but just as he did so a huge black shadow passed over them. Somebody nearby shouted a warning, which came out more as a blood-curdling scream, and they all ran for cover. Sadly one soldier was too slow, and a tail as big and long as a row of buildings flattened him under a huge explosion of snow.

'Everyone inside, now!' shouted the mage, and the rest of them scampered into the shadows of the castle wall, where a small metal door was sunk into the ice-covered stone. Their work done the dragons leapt into the sky and quickly retreated. The Sirens took cover, crouching behind blocks of stone, weapons shaking and wide eyes fixed on the monster towering above them. Farden didn't blame them, fear chilled his heart like the breath of a tomb.

Doggedly the mage focused his mind and pressed his hand up against the cold door. Closing his eyes he tried to concentrate, blocking out the screams and yells from around him. He could hear the swishes of wings and the rumbling cacophony of the hydra, blasts of fire and the sound of things dying. Farden felt the door creak, and redoubled his efforts. He strained and pulled at the door.

'We don't have time for this,' Eyrum grunted impatiently in his ear.

'Just give me a moment.'

'You and your magick,' muttered the big Siren.

'I said...' there was a clang and a thud, and Farden stepped back to watch the big rusty hinges melt and dissolve. 'Give me a moment.'

Eyrum raised one eyebrow. 'Hmm, stop wasting time. Sirens!

With me!' He shouldered his big axe and strode into the darkness with the others at his back. There were no torches to light their way. Eyrum turned to the mage. 'A little illumination?'

Farden smiled wryly. 'Me and my magick,' he mumbled, and he made a fist. White light shivered around his fingers and suddenly the corridor was bathed in a pale moon-like light. There was a thick burning smell in the air, mixed with rot and ancient damp, a smell that clung stubbornly to the back of the men's throats and made them cough.

'Quiet,' Farden hissed, and they crept on into the ruined castle.

They took every stair they could find, anything that would lead them deeper and deeper into the castle. The sounds of battle raged above them. deafening bangs and tremors that shook the walls whenever the hydra moved. In his head Farden cursed himself over and over, berating his ignorance. He should have realised the first time he came to this dank castle, realised that there was something hiding in the darkness he had felt. Why had he been so blind? He tensed his jaw and consoled his guilt with the fact that Vice was somewhere below them and hopefully weakened by the summoning. Farden would make him pay dearly for what he had taken from him.

After what seemed like an age they came to where the corridors split and the mage looked left, then right and racked his brains to remember the way he had gone before. After a moment, he decided to go left, and quickly found the room he was looking for. The mouldy tapestry was still on the dusty floor, apparently where he had left it, and the narrow spiral staircase still led a path into the darkness below. 'This way,' Farden whispered and the others followed silently. He wiped sweat from his forehead and wiped his palms on his tunic. The castle air was getting hot and clammy and stuffy. The mage could feel something, though what it was he couldn't decide.

They were now in the corridor, and someone had kindly lit all the torches. Farden doused his light spell and momentarily tried to regain his strength. The others strode past him and further down the corridor. He felt a big hand on his shoulder again.

'What is it?' asked Eyrum with barely a whisper. The torches threw strange shadows across his face.

Farden shook his head. He ran his fingertips across the old walls. 'Something is here,' he murmured.

'We know that already.'

'No, something else... something with magick like... I don't know,' the mage looked confused. 'Let's just keep going.'

'Mage!' Someone hissed at them, and they looked up. A Siren with orange scales toting a huge broadsword pointed with his thumb. 'There's a door here,' he said. There was a wide door set deep in the stone, with huge hinges either side of it.

'That's the one,' Farden nodded, and they all spread out and readied their weapons. The mage stood in front of the door and let his hand explore the wood. The massive bolt he had encountered before had been broken open. It was nowhere to be seen. 'It's not locked,' he said, and Eyrum raised his eyebrow again with a questioning look. 'Should it be?'

Farden didn't answer. Instead he stood back and held his sword in one hand, and let a blue spark dance on his other. 'Open it,' he said. The Sirens and Eyrum moved towards the door and seized the thick iron handles that had half-rusted away from age. Farden let his breath slow, felt his heart stop its incessant nervous drumming and start to steady and focus itself. His grey-green eyes closed slowly as the magick pulsed along his shoulders. The spark in his palm fizzed and started to grow. They watched him, waiting for his word.

All it took was a single nod.

There was a squeal of hinges and ancient oak and then the door swung open with a burst of steam and a blinding flash of bright snowy daylight. The sulphurous stench quickly became unbearable. Without even waiting for the others Farden charged inwards. All he wanted was Vice.

But there was no sign of him. Nor anyone for that matter. Nobody alive at least. Farden held his sword high and ready and looked around. Thick mouldy pillars held up a roof that was now split in two and crumbling with snow and dust. Light poured down on a huge pit in the centre of the room that smoked and boiled like a volcano. Dead men littered the floor around him. Some were twisted in grotesque shapes with their eyes staring blankly into the shadows and frozen with their last terrified moments, while others lay smashed and broken under rubble, lying in pools of blood with their limbs crushed, unrecognisable. Crimson smears painted the flagstones. The room shook and vibrated with the fighting above. Farden looked around. Trying to ignore the horrible shapes covering the floor he kept watching the shadows. Nothing. He clenched his fist and the spell extinguished itself. Farden prayed Vice hadn't left.

Behind him the Sirens cautiously spread out and waited. Eyrum leant close to Farden to whisper. 'Where is he?' he asked.

As soon as the words escaped his lips twenty soldiers in fire-blackened armour sprang from their hiding places in the shadows. With shouts and yells they rushed at the little group with their feet stomping through the carnage left by the hydra. For a moment it looked like the odds were stacked high against them, but the attackers hadn't banked on Eyrum being there.

Without a single word or cry the giant Siren calmly stepped forward and twirled his axe in a huge figure-of-eight, cleaving the first man in half without even breaking momentum. The next received a blow to the head and tumbled backwards into his comrades, flailing his arms and screaming through what was left of his face. Blood filled the air. Farden was by his side, trying to stay clear of the windmilling axe and slashing at anything that got in his way. He grabbed one man by the throat and threw him to the floor, digging his sword deep into the soft place beneath his chin. The was a metallic scrape as the blade hit bone. Lightning flickered in his hand and another soldier flew backwards in a flash of blue and white. The other Sirens stabbed and hacked furiously, trying to even the numbers before it was too late.

But the soldiers kept coming, pouring out of hidden doors and shadows like rodents on a sinking ship. Two of the Sirens were already gone, trampled somewhere underneath the chaos. Farden slipped on something wet underneath him. Something whispered to him inside his head.

We're running out of time.

The mage knocked his vambraces together and the ground shook and rippled like a shockwave, pushing everyone nearby to the floor. Farden jumped forwards and swung his longsword in wild arcs to try to clear a path. Then, out of the corner of his eye, he spied a tall figure standing back from the fighting, arms crossed and defiant, a smirk plastered on his smug face, hazel eyes staring implacably at the carnage. Farden snarled, and that all so familiar rage started to burn in his chest once again.

High above the ruins of Carn Breagh Farfallen was watching his dragons fall left and right and by the dozen. The snow was an ugly mess of multicoloured blood, trampled and muddy under the clawing feet of the hydra. Bodies covered the ruins, both dragons and riders, crushed and torn and barely identifiable. Some of the riders still moved, desperately hauling themselves through the rock and snow to get away from the monstrous thing.

As he watched another dragon swooped down and rained bright orange fire on the hydra. The fire engulfed one of the heads and it wailed a cry of pain but another snatched the dragon from the air like a striking cobra and sliced the poor beast in two. The remaining dragons, no more than half their original number, retreated momentarily and hovered around the Old Dragon.

'We can't go on like this Farfallen!' shouted Svarta. 'We aren't even hurting it!'

His tawny eyes narrowed. She was right: most of the heads had been scorched or wounded but they hadn't even slowed it down. The red glowing eyes still watched its attackers with a cold impassive gaze. Its massive claws scratched at the rubble. It hydra whined and swayed in a hypnotising way.

Farfallen knew that Farden was close, he could feel it, they just had to give him some more time. He turned to face his dragons. Every one of them looked exhausted, beaten, and scared. Half of them were wounded, and the other half were covered in grey-blue blood and gasping in the thin air. They all had a certain look in their eyes, of fear and terror, and Farfallen was sure he was no different. The Old Dragon sighed. There was no other choice. 'Everyone will attack one head at a time! We will not rest until they all lie smoking in the ruins, now follow me!' And without another word he dipped a wing and rolled downwards in a sickening spiral.

Farfallen took a deep breath as the air rushed past him. He chose his prey. Jaws snapped at him but he was too fast, ducking between the necks with a speed and grace that belied his size and age. Flame erupted from his jaws, white-hot and searing, and blasted one of the larger heads in a huge stream of fire. Farfallen quickly flapped with all his strength and with two huge wingstrokes he was clear of the monster. The dragons behind him roared together as they followed their leader in a line. Their mouths were full of scorching flame and they enveloped the head in an orange fire storm that made the air crackle and shiver with heat. A few more of them tore at the neck with their teeth and claws and barbed tails. One by one they hacked chunks from the pale skin with swooping attacks, dodging the other snapping jaws by inches. Arrows covered its neck like needles on a porcupine. Fire licked at its glistening skin.

With a bubbling wail the head buckled and started to collapse. The eyes blinked frantically, bluish blood poured from between its fangs. Like a falling tree the thing swayed and then finally toppled with agonising slowness and one last bubbling wail. Skin ripped and tore with a splash of bluish blood, and the head hung at a strange angle, dangling grossly against the hydra's spiny shoulders.

Farfallen grinned victoriously, and joined the others in loud roar. He let the air buoy him up as he circled his dragons. Towerdawn joined him. His rider jabbed the air with a big sword and laughed. 'It worked!' he shouted. The Old Dragon nodded and shook his horns. He smiled a smile of grim satisfaction. Only eighteen more to go, he thought. But the smile died all too quickly, as something was happening below them.

The dangling head shook and quivered and twitched violently. Something moved beneath the skin. The dead eyes began to glow, slowly at first, but then more. They pulsated with a dim red glow as they began to come alive again. The jaws moved slightly. There was a weird crunching sound and then spines started to appear at the base of the broken neck as another head started to peel from the skin and grow upwards. As the wounded head began to heal and stitch itself back together more eyes emerged and blinked, popping up between thick wet spines. Dark liquid dripped from grinning jaws and teeth began to push up through black gums.

The smile faded from Farfallen's golden face and was replaced by a bleak expression of anxiety. The two heads rose up until they stood as tall as the others, good as new and just as dangerous. The hydra whined mockingly.

This is madness. Svarta spoke in his head. The Old Dragon scanned the horizon for any sign of reinforcements. 'I know,' he simply said, thinking of Farden. *We're running out of time.*

☙

Vice smiled contemptuously. Farden took another step forward and emerged into the shaft of sunlight that poured down from above. If he had taken his eyes off the Undermage he would have seen the hydra towering above them, but he kept his glowering eyes fixed on Vice's, trying to burn a hole in his forehead. The mage held his dirty blade out in front of him.

'You never learn do you Farden? You never stop to think,' said Vice. His tone was almost cordial. Farden scowled even more.

'I don't need to think about killing you, it's the obvious choice,' replied the mage.

He laughed. 'Hah! As if you've ever had a choice. You've been wonderfully blind to everything since the start of this, why else do you think I've come so far and achieved so much?' Vice unfolded his arms and began to move sideways, away from the well. Farden moved only his sword, keeping it arms length and aimed at his opponent's neck. The fighting still raged behind them.

'It all ends with you, Vice,' said Farden.

'Does it?' His eyes flashed, and the castle shook as the hydra moved.

Something dark suddenly stirred in Farden's mind, something he had not even dared to conceive up until now. Dread loomed from the shadows.

'We're not about to stop now…' Vice's lip curled with scorn.

'Enough talk!' Farden leapt forward and stabbed at him. But the Undermage was fast. A flash of light from his hand hit the sword and the blade bounced off with a loud ping. Farden slashed again, downwards, and again Vice parried the blow with his spell. The mage kept at it, constantly swinging his blade in all directions like a steel blur. He lunged forward and caught the sleeve of Vice's robe. The swordtip snagged the cloth, and the Undermage seized his chance. He slammed a fist against Farden's wrist and the sword spun out of his grasp, clattering on the stones. He pressed a hand against the mage's forearm and a flash of green light punched the air. Farden flew sideways as if he had been hit by a hammer and he fell against the wall that guarded the edge of the dark well.

'Who are you, Farden?' Vice laughed, with a harsh cackle. The mage breathed hard. The sword was no more than an arms length away but as he went to move Vice shocked him with a swift bolt of lightning and Farden curled up into a ball, squeezing his eyes shut. Ribbons of blue light danced all over his body and shook him with their thunder. He felt like his insides were burning, like his bones were about to snap under the pressure of the spell. He could smell his skin cooking.

'I asked you who you were *mage*. We always thought you would end up like your uncle and run naked through the city gates, but I doubt if we'll ever find out. It seems, Farden, that you've come to the end of your usefulness. And now it's up to me to finish the job the others couldn't.'

Vice's words were a low rumble amidst the noisy hiss that blocked Farden's ears, but he still heard every one of them. The blood thudded noisily and with hasty repetition against the inside of his skull.

'Are you listening to me?' More sparks fluttered around the Undermage's fingers. He reached for the mage and hauled him roughly upright and pressed him against the stone. His eyes burnt with savage anger. 'Who do you think you are, to stand in my way?'

Farden tried to lift a hand to feebly push him away, but his skin felt like it was being stabbed with pins.

Go.

Vice cocked his head to one side, like a vulture, and shook

the mage. He brought his mocking face close and shouted. Spit flew from his lips. 'Hmm? Answer me!'

'I... ' Farden began, and then took a deep breath, but he didn't finish his sentence. With all the speed and strength he could muster he rammed his forehead into the bridge of the Undermage's nose with a loud grunt. At the same time his fingers curled into a fist and he brought it up under his chin. With a pained grimace Vice stumbled backwards and threw a hand out to steady himself. Farden kicked out hard and caught him in the chest. The Undermage sprawled on the flagstones and spat a drop of blood in the dust with a murderous glare.

'Farden, the hydra!' a shout rang out from behind them and Farden spun around to see Eyrum surrounded, with only one Siren still standing by his side, swinging his blood-soaked axe at anything that came within reach. Soldiers hemmed them in on all sides, circling cautiously. At least a dozen of their dead friends lay strewn on the floor, and many of them were missing several large portions of their bodies. The others were not so keen to get in the way of the big Siren's axe.

Something moved in his peripheral vision and Farden turned to meet Vice's fist colliding with his face. Sparks exploded behind the mage's eyes. He pushed the tall man backwards with a flailing arm and swung another punch of his own. It landed hard on his chest and Vice took a step back, briefly winded. Farden wiped crimson blood from his lip and shook his head. His vision was still blurred, so he blinked and tried to move slowly to the left, around to where he had noticed the manual sitting on a pedestal.

Vice began to laugh again with that sadistic cackle and those narrow eyes, mocking his every move. 'You still have no idea. It's dangling right in front of you and you can't even see it. Typical Farden.'

'You don't know me as well as you think you do Vice.'

'Hah! Who taught you? Who arranged for you to go the Schools, to the Ritual? I did. All of it. *I* was the one who sent you to live the life of a Written. It's just a pity you didn't turn out as I'd hoped,' he scowled, his eyes boring a hole into Farden's.

The mage scoffed, and sidled ever so slightly towards the back of the room. 'As one of your loyal servants, like Ridda?'

'Still defending your precious Arka, I see.'

'They're your people as much as they are mine Vice, you traitor!'

Vice shook his head and didn't break his gaze for a second. 'I watched the Arka crawl from their filthy beginnings! I was there when the first stone of Krauslung was carved from the mountains and I will be there when it falls. I have watched you people grow for a thousand years and I've seen what you've become, bureaucratic fools pissing their gold away with the whores and the drunks in the street, meddling in magick they'll never understand. Fools, Farden, fools that need removing from these lands. And I shall be the one to do it.

Farden shook his head. 'And the Sirens?' he muttered.

'Two dragons with one stone.'

Farden glared, trying to convey as much hate as possible in one look. He thought of all the evenings he had spent sat with the Undermage and his dark wine, swapping stories with him, discussing the world and its matters. He thought of every lesson Vice had ever taught him, how many things they had both confided in the other. All this time, he said to himself. The anger and sorrow felt like lead in his chest. 'It must have been painful to play dumb all these years, faking all those smiles and kind words,' said the mage. 'I think you've enjoyed every moment of this. Relished every bit of your despicable plan.'

Vice flashed white teeth and rubbed his hands together, making a little yellow spark float upwards towards the broken ceiling. 'Immensely.'

Farden kept inching sideways and made sure he held Vice's gaze for as long as possible. He didn't trust his eyes to look at the manual and betray him. Orange fire started to curl up between the Undermage's fingers. Farden raised his hands, slowly, to be ready to fend off the spell, and took a long inward breath and held it. He could feel magick pulsating along his arms but he pushed it to his legs and feet and tried to remember everything he had seen in Hjaussfen, everything he had learnt that night, sitting beside the fireplace in the Old Dragon's room, listening long into the morning to the quiet one-eyed Siren called Eyrum.

Go!

Vice flicked his hands outwards and the blistering fireball flew straight at the mage in an orange blur. Farden breathed out. With one tiny step he slipped to the side and made the room slow and smudge like a ruined oil painting, pastel shades of grey and white like nebulous fog wiping the world to one side. He watched the crackling orb of flame roll through the air and lazily make its way towards him. The crystalline flames blossomed and whirled and strangely in that moment he felt like reaching out to touch them, to see if they would snap in his hands. But he was still moving and Farden slid to the left as though the earth had suddenly tripped beneath his boots.

The fireball burst against the wall with an angry flash and Farden was already several yards away. Without wasting a second he sprinted to the pedestal and the manual.

'No!' Vice yelled, and leapt to catch him. Farden skidded to a halt and grabbed the little book, letting the magick flow back into his hands and erupt in white hot flame from his fingers. There was a dull thud deep from somewhere in the well and the room started to shake around them. The yellow pages curled and crumbled as the fire ate into the book and the room shook even more. Farden lifted the manual up in his fist and let the flames consume his entire forearm until the book was a smouldering mess, just the time it took for Vice to reach him and land a blow to his ribs right where the arrow had hit him. Blinding pain knocked him to the floor. Something or someone was standing behind him, but as he turned a heavy object collided with his skull, and the world went black.

Farfallen took another deep breath and blinked the smoke from his amber-flecked eyes. A pitiful amount of dragons were left and the sound of their roars and screams below made his heart feel heavy in his chest. He felt Svarta putting her cold hand on his scales and felt her voice in his head.

'We have to fall back, the mage has failed,' she said aloud.

But the Old Dragon shook his head stubbornly. 'I can still feel him, somewhere in there.'

'Farfallen…' she said, and he couldn't ignore that she was right. He looked down at the hydra below them, still snarling and biting at his dragons. They fought on bravely. Riders still swung their swords as their mounts ducked and wheeled under and over the squirming heads to breathe fire on the monster's back and legs. Farfallen could feel their exhaustion. He watched with sad eyes as yet another of his dragons was ripped to pieces by two ravenous heads. One held the screaming beast by its tail while the other tore at its back and head. Sulphurous breath steamed in clouds through its spear-like teeth. Emerald blood ran in rivers down the hydra's shoulder. Farfallen let a wave of pain pass over him, and nodded slowly.

'Then let us get away from this thing. We have done our best. Emaneska will have to fend for itself,' said Farfallen, and let out a mighty, if not slightly tired and disappointed, roar. With screeches the dragons quickly flapped away from the snapping jaws. Every single eye, of rider and beast, was wide with terror, or relief, or both. The hydra kept coming at them, hissing and whining, drenched in blood and gore and obviously still not satiated.

'Keep clear of it!' Towerdawn yelled to the others, and the diminished ranks flapped higher into the clear blue sky. One unlucky dragon lost the tip of its tail as one head snapped its grey fangs but it managed to escape with the rest and joined the others. They could barely summon the strength to flap their wings. They watched Farfallen and waited. As the Old Dragon opened his mouth to speak a low moaning groan from below interrupted him. They all looked down. Dust was starting to rise up into the air around the hydra's claws and its eyes were starting to blink and flicker, pulsating like its skin which was now writhing and sweating.

'Something's happening!' shouted a nearby rider. Farfallen quietly prayed that it was not another one of its tricks and that it wasn't about to sprout wings. The dragons backed away even further as smoke began to pour from one of its mouths. The dust turned to ash and cinders and began to billow in great clouds around its legs. A huge boom resonated from somewhere inside Carn Breagh. Farfallen squinted at the monster. Its skin was starting to darken and great black blotches erupted under his skin like bruises. The marks seethed and smoked until all of the hydra's flesh smouldered like burning paper. The smell was horrible. The remaining dragons soared on the rising air to get clear of the beast and save their strength, and from high above they watched the hydra burn and smoke and wondered what would happen next.

With a lurch and a stumble there came another deep boom from within castle. One of the hydra's legs dissolved into ash and then the tail started to deliquesce in thick bursts of smoke. Just before its heads started to fall and topple like fire-gutted towers to crash and burn against each other it cried out with its minor chord wail for one last time. Then there was a loud sucking noise as the air rushed inwards and the hydra seemed to fold in on itself with a low rumble. It was like watching a mountain burn up and die. As the noise reached its crescendo the hydra gurgled and exploded in a huge cloud of ash. The shockwave turned the snow black and filled the air with dust. Trees were flattened. The dragons rode the blast, and in a moment it was over. They flew in its wake and glided towards the ruined castle, swapping exhausted smiles and toothy grins.

Farfallen had only one thing on his mind: Farden, the little spark that had disappeared in his mind shortly before the hydra had collapsed.

chapter 19

*"A long time ago, when elves and daemons still haunted the lands,
the oldest of the gods held a secret meeting deep in the deepest
woods, and fearful of being heard they whispered no louder than the
softest leaf. 'The daemons are growing bolder by the day,' said one, a
tall glowing goddess. 'They have called on Orion, the oldest of the
daemons,' replied a second, one of the earth-gods. 'He roams the
shores as we speak, hunting for us.'*

*"In return the ageless one nodded, and listened to the cawing of the
ravens in the firs. He sighed with a rustling of ropes. 'He will spell
our downfall if the elves have their way. We grow weaker,' he said.
'Above and below us the lands of fire cool and the lands of ice melt
with every year. We must take action now or be lost forever.' The
others hummed and murmured in agreement, but the god of the earth,
a great beast of stone and moss wagged his mistletoe finger. 'We have
forgotten the others.' And with that he pointed, through copse and
bramble, to a scrawny group of figures huddling around a campfire in
the distance. Another god, a scaled man with wings that fell like
hammers, shook his head. 'They are the slaves of the elves, they will
never amount to anything.'*

*"The tall pale goddess held up a hand. 'They have my gifts, and none
will stand in their way when we are finished,' she said. The ageless
one knocked his stick against an oak tree. 'It is decided. We will go
forth.'*

"And so the gods decided. They burst forth from their hiding place

and fell upon the elves. Orion himself was almost overwhelmed as he lay with his slave mistress, but they fought and they fought for a thousand years, until finally the gods pulled the elves and the daemons into the sky to remain there for ever more. Only three escaped that fate, the dark spawn of the daemon Orion, and taking their shapes they hid amongst the campfires with the slaves, pale kings in drab clothes.

"And as the stars began to sparkle and the wolves howled at the ghostly moon they decided to split the barren land in three, to go their separate ways as each saw fit. The red sun rose above the cold and empty land and they left, to the three corners of the world, to carve their own destinies and rule over the new people."

Old fairytale

Something smelled like burning. Like the smell of scorched flesh that clung to the rags that were the mage's clothes.

Something tugged at his wrists and rasped at the skin underneath and turned it rough and bloody.

Something in his head ached like a firework had gone off inside his skull, as if his brain was trying to smash its way out.

Something made his skin tingle and burn, itchy like ants biting, or cats scratching. It made him think of a cat from a ship he had been on once, perhaps.

Something was deeply wrong.

Fragments of a fight, or maybe a great battle, floated in his memories. Flashes of a great beast towering above a snowy land, orange blood splashing on rocks. Screams. It was like waking from a dream he could have sworn was real, a strange familiarity with the scattered images. Farden attempted to open his eyes, but the pain was too much. He consented himself to just resting. After all he had hours to sit there.

Suddenly it was all too real and Farden could picture himself there being punched and kicked, watching the world blur all over again and wanting to reach out and grab the tendrils of a crystalline flame that floated mere inches in front of his face. His skin burnt under the yellow light. A smile sneered from the shadows, something collided with his skull.

He had been there, in that place, with a daemon towering over him and reptile shapes in the pale blue sky high above. He had fought a man, a tall man with piercing eyes. He had done something, or was in the process of doing something. Farden remembered fire and a book.

Then it came to him, and the realisation of being tied to a chair in a cold and empty room struck him like a wet rag around the face. Farden jumped and forced his eyelids to open and his eyes to focus. Blurry shapes and dark objects slowly started to take shape around him. There was blood on the floor as if something had been dragged along it. He rubbed his fingers and felt something sticky between them. Farden's head ached.

The mage started to look around, slowly, and began to recognise the walls and pillars that lined the walls of the hall. Light was coming from somewhere behind him but it was too painful to turn his head. It seemed that his arms were tied fast it with rough ropes, and so were his legs, and they felt dead and heavy as if no blood could get to them. Farden strained and listened to the creaking of the rope and chair but the agony of pulling against the bonds was too much, and he slumped into his seat feeling very exhausted and quite alone. A subtle but annoying noise whined in his ear. At least it let him know he was alive. Farden waited, for exactly what he didn't know, but it was all he could do, so he closed his eyes and let the rhythm of his breathing take over.

❦

Outside the room, behind the locked door, down the long hallway and up several flights of curling stairs, in the highest part of the fortress, Vice strode back and forth between the pillars and tall windows. His boot scuffed softly across the smooth marble. Anticipation bubbled up inside him as he felt the final pieces of his plan sliding and clicking into place. His victory felt very close at hand now. There was only one final problem to deal with, and he was tied to a chair downstairs in one of the empty dining halls. He would take care of him in a moment.

There was a clattering or armour and the sound of boots on marble, and the Undermage turned around. A soldier ran up to him and saluted quickly. The man seemed very agitated. Vice gestured for him to speak. 'Your Mage, they're here, in the city,' he blurted.

Vice allowed himself a brief shiver of excitement. 'King Bane?'

The soldier nodded eagerly. 'Yes my lord. His soldiers are rounding up our men and going about the streets telling everyone to stay inside.'

'Good. Tell them not to resist and to follow their orders. Bane comes in peace, do you understand me? None of the Skölgard are to be harmed in any way. You can escort the King to the great hall at his leisure, and tell him I will await him there,' ordered the Undermage. The soldier clicked his heels together with a metallic twang and hurried back down the hallway.

Vice smiled with pride. He could almost hear the pieces clicking into place now. It was time to pay someone a brief visit.

❦

Farden was concentrating on staying conscious. He hadn't felt like so close to slipping away since the shipwreck, when he lay on the cold table with the healer standing over him humming to himself as he worked. He focused all his energy on simply breathing and tried to get some of the magick to creep back into his body. The warm glow started to warm his cold aching bones. There must have been something wrong with his eyes because the floor and the walls in front of him were painted with harlequin patterns of different coloured light. Everything had been turned shades of red, green, yellow, and blue. Farden blinked, hard, but the colours didn't go away. There looked to be a wide door at the end of the room, and a small flight of steps. A long hardwood table lay against the wall on the left, surrounded by wooden chairs, some lying awkwardly on the floor, others stacked in twos and threes between the pillars. He squinted at the crest hanging on the wall to his right, a golden pair of scales, equally balanced, emblazoned on a white shield topped with tiny mountain flowers shaped from polished steel.

Farden was in the Arkathedral. He was somehow back in Krauslung, not Albion. He pondered how long he could have been there, tied to the chair in that empty room. His tongue was dry enough and his stomach ached enough for it to have been days. Farden had no way of knowing.

There was an abrupt bang and the metallic sound of dangling keys twisting in locks. There was another bang, and a slow creak. Two blurry figures walked in to the hall, a tall one and another, Farden couldn't make them out. The tall one walked straight towards him while rubbing his hands. He appeared to be smiling. The other disappeared into the shadows. Farden blinked slowly like an owl, and lifted his head to look at the stranger walking slowly across the floor. The multicoloured light swirled over him and turned his robe into its canvas. It painted his face strange hues of red and yellow. Vice leant close to Farden and chuckled. He was in a good mood. 'I'll take these,' he said, and reached into Farden's pockets to retrieve the Weight and the daemonstone. It glowed in his hand and Vice narrowed his eyes at it. 'Aptly named,' he muttered, and slipped it and the Weight into a pocket of his own.

Farden tried to spit at him, but there was nothing in his mouth, so he just panted instead, feeling his furry tongue rasp against his dry teeth.

'Manners Farden, we have company,' said the Undermage.

'Wh…' the mage croaked.

'Why? When? What? You still have no idea what's going on do you? Poor Farden, so blind.' Vice stepped back to admire his prey, helpless and weak, bound tightly to a chair. He looked up at the huge stained glass window that took up the whole of the back wall. It depicted a huge arching portrait of the sun shining over the port of Rós with a man standing in the centre of it, a proud looking old mage accepting a ball of light from the white goddess above him. Vice scowled, and began to pace back and forth.

Farden coughed and spluttered. He managed some hoarse words. 'I killed your hydra, it's over.'

'Hah, I find that very unlikely. I might as well tell you that at this very moment the good King Bane is perusing the newest addition to his realms. After all of this trouble with his lovely daughter, he is most anxious to see order restored to the Arka, especially after all the mess they have made.' Vice sneered and his teeth glowed red in the odd light. 'And Farden, the so-called saviour of the proud Arka, will be charged with treason and sent to the gallows to hang for all to see. It seems that you have gone mad, my good mage, just like your uncle did. It was you who committed the murders at Arfell, it was you who stole the tearbook from the Sirens, and it was you who tried to summon the hydra for yourself. Thank the gods that I was there to stop you in time. You see Farden, Bane is here to announce the new and only Arkmage, his very loyal subject, the Lord Vice. I wouldn't be too surprised if Åddren did not survive the night.' Vice grinned, his masterpiece divulged. There was a moment of silence as the pieces finally slid into position, and Farden was left to stare into space. It was all just for power. Utter, ruthless, and absolute power.

'You're nothing but a common thief,' mumbled Farden.

'Oh I am much more than that dear boy, I am a merchant of chaos. There will be all out war again, if the King of Skölgard and I have anything to do with it. The fall of the Siren kingdoms will take a year or two at most, but we will break them in the end.'

'With another of your plots?' Farden narrowed his eyes, thinking of all the things Vice had taken from him. 'You disgust me Vice. It should be you in the gallows, not me,' he said.

'Then tell me why it's you that's tied to a chair, bound and beaten, and confused as usual? It has taken us years to get this far. And if you hadn't been such a disappointment then you wouldn't be in this current situation,' replied Vice. He jabbed a finger at the mage.

Farden grinned a weary but insolent smile. 'Then why is it so hard to kill me?'

The Undermage shot him a dark look. 'Because you're a stubborn bastard, and I needed your stupidity. Of course it's not that things went without any complications. The sorcerer I placed on the *Sarunn* with you was one of my oldest but he was a complete moronic fool. He was supposed to wait until you got back from Nelska, once you had delivered the precious tearbook to that Siren Queen, Svarta. He obviously got a little too greedy. And after all this time to think that Farfallen, that ugly beast, had survived his wounds? That I did not expect. But despite these things it all fell into my lap, and my plan went ahead accordingly.'

'What about Helyard?'

'That dreary old fool was doomed from the start. His hatred for the Sirens made him an easy target, and with the power he had it made sense that he was behind it all. You saw for yourself how quick the dragon-riders were to condemn him, and the amount of dignity he displayed on leaving the hall. The old bastard deserved everything he got.'

'You love hearing the sound of your own voice don't you Vice?' interrupted Farden. The Undermage backhanded him hard and he spat blood on the floor. The slap made his head throb even more. He rolled his eyes and tried to focus again. Vice was still talking.

'What did I say about manners in front of guests? You're about to miss the best part Farden, patience please. Do you want to know what you are, why you were so perfect to manipulate?'

The mage shook his head, suddenly very wary that a pair of eyes were watching him from the shadows. Vice laughed with a dark tone and crossed his arms triumphantly.

'You were an experiment Farden,' he lectured, 'a test to see if a Written could withstand the deeper magicks and attain a new state of perfection. I was the one who originally brought the Scribe to the Arka all those years ago, and with you I had him write a few special things into your Book, a few extra things an ordinary Written couldn't survive, things that in the end, turned your own uncle mad.' Vice paused to sneer once again as Farden glared. 'That's right, you heard me, you were to be a weapon just like your uncle Tyrfing.

'But you weren't perfect either, oh no, by all definitions you were yet another disaster: a reclusive self-involved individual with a perverse sense of right and wrong, hanging on every word that dreary vampyre of yours had to say and too stupid to see past your own anger. So you became a tool Farden, a pawn for me to manoeuvre and exploit as I wished while I waited for another exceptional individual such as yourself to come along. Someone of better upbringing, with ideals and power, somebody who would follow and serve the true power in Emaneska.'

'I guess that true power would be you then?' Farden spat, straining uncomfortably against the ropes.

Vice's eyes momentarily flashed with a deep murderous fire

that Farden had never seen before. 'You Arka are like lambs for slaughter to me, meat to be sold and bartered with. I have watched you since the first sun rose above the mountains, when you were over-confident and weak, and I have watched you grow into a spineless nation of magicians and prostitutes. I've spent too long simply watching, and now what is there left to do with the Arka except destroy them? I just happened to save two of the better ones for myself,' he snarled. Vice slowly lowered his head until his eyes were level with the mage's, only a few inches from his face. Farden stared straight back at him. 'What are you?' he asked, and the Undermage tapped him on the cheek.

'That's a story for another day, my dear mage, one that you won't be hearing.' He tapped him again, harder. 'You're not curious Farden? Not at all? Who else could I have under my wing besides Ridda and that idiot, Karga? Could it be Åddren? No of course not, he's catatonic after the loss of his precious Helyard, too busy soiling his robe with fear and weak indecision.' *Slap*. Farden's cheek stung. He didn't care any more. Vice had taken everything away from him that there was to take. The Undermage continued.

'Not any of the Sirens, no, who could get closer to you than anyone. Let me see, maybe the man you buy nevermar from, that good friend of mine? No closer still, even more than your precious Durnus...' Vice chuckled, and stepped back to swing an arm wide. He pointed to the shadows. 'Say hello to Farden,' he said.

Footsteps echoed on the stone, and then a very familiar figure walked from the darkness, a figure he had let his hands explore every inch of, a smile he had kissed countless times, eyes he had stared into for hours on end, that he had emptied himself into, that he had told his darkest secrets to except one, that he loved this person more than anything or anyone he had ever encountered, that she was the only thing that made him feel normal.

Cheska performed a little wave and smiled at him coyly. Farden was breathless. There was one more thing to take. His heart felt like it was slowly grinding to a halt. The love of his life stood in front of him with her hands on her hips, smiling with those mountain-lake eyes, reflecting purple and green in the strange light.

'You died... in that fire...' managed Farden.

Cheska wandered closer. 'The fire was Vice's idea, but it was necessary to make you believe I was gone.' She shook her head. 'You always were a strange one, Farden, so emotionally complex for a Written. You're so concerned with not becoming your uncle you didn't give any thought to who you were.' She leant in to whisper in his ear. 'You're like fire, you only come alive in the dark.'

Farden could smell her, that scent that she had left on his pillow. He choked back something, and didn't dare himself to speak. She smiled. 'It was fun, for a while,' she said. 'And we got what we needed.'

'If you're curious Farden, the only thing I needed from you was you,' said Vice, in a low tone.

The mage looked up suddenly, feeling the same darkness he had felt in the bowels of Carn Breagh. Something felt deeply wrong. He stared straight into Cheska's complacent eyes and saw only sick truth hidden there. She stepped slowly back, now with a very serious expression. There was no fondness there. Vice walked up behind her and let a pale hand rest on one of her shoulders. He watched Farden with glowing eyes, victorious and supercilious. His other hand curled around her waist and pressed her against her stomach.

'A little spark of life grows inside Cheska's womb, a child of pure power born from two Written. There is a reason the offspring of such a union is outlawed, Farden, and that reason is very simple. Your child will be the finest mage Emaneska has ever seen, and my finest weapon.'

Farden strained against his ropes, seething with anger and grinding his teeth at the two of them. His face went red with exertion, and his breath came in ragged gasps. The ropes held fast.

'At least you were useful in the end, hmm?' Vice chuckled, and then he whispered in Cheska's ear. 'We have to go upstairs, your father will be eager to see you,' he said, and she nodded.

Vice took a step forward and examined Farden with a faint mocking smile as he rocked and pulled at the chair feebly. The Undermage put his foot on Farden's leg and pressed his foot against his ribs. The mage squinted and gasped, still unable to speak through his rage. Vice pressed once more and then relented, stamping his foot back on the floor with hubris. 'I will be back for you momentarily. I have a princess to return,' he said, and then turned to leave.

Without another word they left and the door slammed behind them. Farden started to convulse, yanking and straining the ropes in all directions. The chair and the knots protested with squeaks and groans but still they didn't budge. He was too weak to try magick. All he could do was tug and pull and hope something would give way at any moment.

Minutes passed and still he fought, and with each twist and pull he growled and coughed, fighting against the grief and anger and sorrow and rage growing in his chest. He sucked in air, exhausted, and sagged in the chair with his head down and spit hanging from his mouth. A tear crawled from his eye and started to fall down his dirty cheek. Farden watched it drip onto his shredded tunic and soak into the fabric.

He gave in then, and cried, with long uncontrollable sobs and deep breaths, letting the hot tears of frustration burn channels through the dust on his skin. Farden closed his eyes and wept.

❦

'I don't understand why you had to tell him about the child, he's already going to hang why rub it in?'

'Are you turning soft on me Cheska? The man has caused us endless trouble, he deserves to suffer. And if I recall, you were the one who wanted to come and show your face, not me, so don't you dare lecture me on rubbing it in.' Vice glowered at her, and she looked away.

Cheska remained quiet. She watched her feet tread on the marble steps and took several long deep breaths. They walked up another flight of stairs and emerged in to the long hallway leading to the great hall. The council and the king would be there waiting. Vice rubbed Farden's blood from the back of his hand and straightened his black and green robe. There was no need for haste, he reminded himself, he had all the time in the world. He turned to Cheska as they reached the huge gilded doors of the hall. 'Just remember what I told you,' hissed the Undermage. The two soldiers standing guard raised their spears and pushed hard on the big heavy handles, and the doors swung inwards with a low moan. Vice pasted an affable smile on his face and walked into the bright sunlight inside the hall. He looked around at the council and noted the mass of Skölgard soldiers that surrounded them all, holding tall halberds and wearing thick pale armour that was a rusty copper colour. Arkmage Åddren sat on his throne looking very small and agitated. There was a hollow look in his dark sapphire eyes. His hair looked thin and unwashed. There was an awkward hush in the hall. Vice inwardly laughed.

The King of Skölgard turned around to face the newcomers. He stood in front of the statue of Evernia with his hands on his hips. Bane was a huge man, maybe seven feet tall and just as wide. He looked half-man half-bear, with a hungry smile and dark green eyes that seemed to shine even in the daylight. His hair was short and slicked down with wax and his beard was braided into two forks. A scar carved its way down one side of his jaw. A silver necklace of miniature skulls hung around his thick bristly neck and dangled over an enormous silver and pale green breastplate depicting two wolves fighting. Wrapped around his shoulders was a long fur cloak and the tails of it had dragged muddy streaks across the pure white marble. When he saw Cheska King Bane opened his massive arms wide, and his numerous bracelets rattled noisily. With two big steps he closed the gap between them and swept her up into her arms, looking at Vice as he did so. Vice nodded almost imperceptibly.

'Cheska my daughter, it is good to have you back in my arms once again,' said Bane in a booming voice. 'Where is the bastard who dared to endanger the first princess of Skölgard?' he glared, looking around at the council.

'You have caught the traitor Vice?' called Åddren, looking suddenly confused. The Arkmage's voice cracked shrilly as he raised his voice to shout. 'Who is it?'

Vice sighed and looked to Åddren with a gracious and somewhat patient smile. 'Your Mage, esteemed council members. I was just about to explain. The traitor behind all of this has been none other than one of our own Written, a mage this council put a lot of faith in, a man we have honoured more than once. He has been in league with the dragons this entire time and together they sought to destroy this council from within.'

'What of the beast?' came a shout from the council. Vice held up a hand and nodded. 'That, at least, is good news. I have just returned from Albion where this traitor attempted to summon the hydra. The beast was stopped, luckily by myself.' Vice paused for affect. He heard more than a few sighs of relief. He continued. 'I caught the traitor and brought him back here.'

Åddren sat up, feebly, in his throne. 'Well tell us Vice, who is it?'

The Undermage pointed a long finger at the Arkmage. 'You should know Åddren, he's the mage you put so much trust in, the mage that you gave Helyard's Weight to, allowing him escape to Albion before I had a chance to stop him. He is none other than Farden.' Vice glared at his superior. A wave of dissent and shocked murmurs rustled through the crowd.

Bane took a few giant steps forward and put his giant hands on his waist. 'You allowed him to escape Arkmage, after what he did in Manesmark, after he almost killed my daughter?' The king was incredulous, and played his part well, Vice thought to himself. Bane signalled to his men. 'Drag him from the throne!' he shouted, and his soldiers sprang to his bidding. Åddren started to panic. The council and the Arka guards seemed torn, but any that moved forward quickly found blades in their faces. The Skölgard soldiers had the great hall surrounded. Åddren leapt up from his throne and tried to call for order but before he could get any further a soldier grabbed him and escorted him roughly across the hall to stand in front of Bane. Shouts echoed around the hall.

'Leave him alone!'

'Arrest the traitor!' they cried.

'Quiet!' yelled the king. He looked the frail-looking old man up and down and curled his lip in scorn. 'You are not fit to rule these people.' Bane waved a hand dismissively. 'Take him to the cells,' he ordered, and his soldiers dragged Åddren away towards the doors. Unlike Helyard the Arkmage didn't even protest. He allowed himself to be silently removed from the hall, simply gazing back at Vice with sorrow in his eyes.

But the Undermage smiled, and looked to the King of Skölgard. Bane nodded back, and turned to the council members and the Arka soldiers standing in small groups behind his men. His voice boomed and echoed around the marble hall. 'You are all witnesses to this! From henceforth the lands belonging to the Arka will be held as a vassal of the Skölgard empire! My soldiers will remain here to keep order as your new Arkmage sees fit. Since he has saved this council from betrayal and chaos more than once I am appointing Lord Vice as the head of this council, to rule alone. My word is final! Do we all understand?'

There was a resounding chorus of agreement from everyone there including the Skölgard soldiers. Vice flashed a victorious smile and started to walk towards his new throne. As he passed the statue of Evernia he reached inside his robe and dropped his two Weights into each of the scale pans with two loud clangs. Fire trickled from his fingertips and he lit each candle in turn, as tradition stated. He flashed the goddess a mocking glance and carried on walking. The council began to clap as he put his foot on the marble steps. One by one he marched up them, and then turned to take his place on the throne. He looked over the gathered members of the council and then to Bane, who stared confidently back at him with what could have been a smile. The crowd was on the verge of cheering when suddenly there came a huge rending crash from somewhere below the hall. The room vibrated with the impact and the goddess's statue trembled ever so slightly. Dust fell from the marble beams. Vice pointed to a group of soldiers and barked orders at them. 'Go find out what that was, immediately!'

'Yes Your Mage!' they shouted, and bowing quickly they ran off. They slammed the doors with a bang and then an eerie silence fell in the great hall, broken only by the tolling of the twin bells below. Vice drummed his fingers on the marble throne, and stared at Bane.

Farden's chest heaved with the breathless sobs that racked him. He choked and spluttered again, and then tried to squeeze the tears from his blurry eyes. His wrists, head, ribs, and legs ached with mind-numbing pain. And his brain was going crazy. He relentlessly repeated every word, every tortuous poignant moment of the last half hour in his head, every heart-wrenching wave and whisper drenched him with sorrow. He stared into the coloured patterns on the floor and tried to clear his thoughts. But nothing happened. Farden squeezed his eyes together and let the painful darkness envelop him.

Sunlight burnt his skin, making it prickle and sweat. It was a dry heat, and the hot wind on his face did nothing to cool him. There was sand between his toes. Farden sighed; this was not what he needed now. He tried to keep his eyes shut but they itched as the fine grains of sand wormed their way beneath his eyelids and scratched his eyes. Something pawed at his leg. Farden opened his eyes to find the sun and a black cat staring at him. He blinked, momentarily blinded, and looked around. Only sand greeted him. There were no mountains, no cliffs, no birds, just endless sand from horizon to horizon, east to west. The sky was as big and blue as it had ever been, and Farden wished he could just melt into it and never wake up.

The cat yowled at him and he looked down. Farden could feel the tears drying on his cheek. The wind whipped his naked body. His red and gold vambraces glinted and flashed in the sun. He stared into the cat's impassive obsidian eyes and tried to match its gaze. He knew it was waiting for him to speak. Farden shook his head.

'I told you to leave me alone.'

You're not finished yet said the familiar voice in his head.

'I'm done. I give up. All I have to look forward to is the rope around my neck. I don't care who you are but I would appreciate it if you left me to enjoy my last few hours.'

So this is it? All the help I've given you and you just give up?

Farden hung his head and the cat hissed at him through its needle-like teeth. 'I don't even know who you are.'

For the third time, I'm just like you. We never ask for this, nor do we ever complain, we just do what we're told. It's what people like you and I do; we fight, and we never ask for anything in return.

'I want to be left alone,' replied Farden.

No you don't. You want to fight. You want to march upstairs and take a sword to his head and watch the blood drip on the floor, for both of us. The voice was becoming impatient.

The mage shook his head. The cat crept a little closer. 'It's useless. He's won. I'm a failure just like my uncle.' Farden slumped to the sand and felt the hot yellow stuff buoy him up. The sky seemed so blue and empty.

The voice hesitated for a moment. The cat crept closer and raked a claw down Farden's leg. The mage didn't even flinch. The sand shifted and moved around his shoulders and he closed his eyes, letting the warmth surround him. *They found me naked and screaming. They found me painted in someone else's blood. They found me biting the tips from my fingers. They found me scraping words into my legs with shards of window glass. They found me swearing and cursing and yelling his name until they filled my mouth with rags. They found me clawing at the city walls and wanting to run. Then they gave me a blanket and a gold coin to do with as I saw fit. They sent me out into the wilderness. They didn't kill me, they let me go, I didn't fight, I left. I was lucky. I was not becoming someone different, I was getting to know the person I was already. He had changed me, he had tried to use me, but I failed. He had failed.*

The sand crept over Farden's neck and swallowed one of his arms. The cat bit his thigh and drew blood. Why him? Why had all this happened to him? Was it his destiny to be tortured and chased, just because he was some failed idea Vice once had? The hot sand moved up to his ears and blocked out the noise of the wind. But the voice still spoke deep in his head.

All the help I've given you, and you're just going to give up.

Farden nodded and felt the sand tugging and pulling at his

legs. It wanted to eat him and he wanted to let it. He didn't care any more. Vice had taken everything from him.

Who are you, Farden, what have you done with yourself?

His foot was enveloped by the warm gritty earth.

Are you his tool Farden? His weapon? I asked you a question mage!

The sand sucked him further into the ground. The cat scratched furiously at the sand and dug for his limbs. He was now up to his chest.

What have you done with your life?

The sand moved over his skin like a yellow river, like time falling through the waist of an hourglass. It swallowed his chest and arms and crept up his neck. The dragonscale pulled at his skin and he opened his eyes to find the cat staring at him, her two black eyes like scrying mirrors reflecting his bruised and battered face. What had he done? Farden felt the sand on his chin. There was a reason he had been so useless to Vice, and it was that reason that suddenly burnt like a little candle in the mage's dark and stormy mind.

You are not becoming someone different... shouted the voice in his head.

Instead of doing what Vice wanted, instead of falling into treachery, he had gone out and sought his own life, to try to make a difference in the wild world. Farden thought of all creatures he had slain, all the towns he had saved, even the bandits back in Beinnh he had slaughtered, and decided, yes, he had made a difference, at least somewhere in Emaneska. Farden sat up a little, and felt the claws of the cat on his chest. The sand fell back slightly. Whatever was woven into his book made him angry, and vengeful, but it also made him powerful, and if he could learn to tame it he could make everything right. With Vice's cards now spread clearly on the table, it was his turn to make a decision. Farden began to tug and pull against the hot sand. He heaved and strained and yanked his limbs from the ground.

'I am simply getting to know the person I already am,' whispered Farden, feeling the hot wind in his throat. The cat danced on its hindlegs as he pulled his body from the sand and stood up. He raised his hands to the blue sky and felt something he had never known before.

Keep an eye on the weather, Farden said the voice, as a single wispy cloud appeared above him in the endless blue and the desert began to fade.

❦

Farden snapped back to consciousness. With a wave of dizziness the colours on the floor swirled and shifted, and he took a deep breath to steady his pounding heart and the sickening nausea. A large dark shadow scudded across the patchwork of colours and a deep repetitive whooshing sound grew loud in the dark room. Farden blinked owlishly and wondered why the blood was pounding so loudly in his ears. Before he realised what was happening there came an almighty crash from behind the mage and his chair tipped forward onto the floor in a huge gust of air. Gold wings towered over him, glittering and shimmering in the sunlight. Shattered pieces of stained glass cracked and crunched under heavy claws. The dragon raked a razor-sharp talon over the back of the chair and Farden's bonds sprang open with a twang. Completely ignoring the shredding glass underneath him the mage wriggled and shimmied his way out and bent to tackle the rope binding his ankles. Once the ropes were a tangled frayed mess on the floor Farden stood and drowsily started picking bits of glass from his clothes. The whistling noise in his ears was back. He wiggled a finger in his ear to no avail. Shielding his eyes with a hand he stared out of the smashed window. It was a clear crisp day over Krauslung for a change, and the bright sun made the mountains sparkle. Farden looked up at the Old Dragon and Farfallen grinned at him, flashing his teeth, and then he made a hurried movement with his wings.

'The King of Skölgard has taken over the city, you don't have much time to stop Vice!' said Farfallen.

'I have to try! Just keep them off my back!' replied the mage, and with that he hobbled towards the door. With a nod Farfallen crouched to move further into the hall. Behind him other dragons swooped and circled the fortress. The twin bells were singing over their roars and screeches. Archers were filling the ramparts.

Farden reached the door just as it flew open under the boots of a dozen men. They stormed into the room waving their swords but Farden quickly limped to one side, still holding his ribs. 'Farfallen!' he shouted. The Old Dragon closed one golden eye and blew a jet of orange fire from his jaws that ripped the door from its hinges and sent the men diving for cover. Farden was already up and running. Ignoring the flames at his heels he darted down the corridor and then sprinted up several flights of stairs, towards the highest part of the Arkathedral, to the great hall. Farden heard shouts and the banging of weapons behind him but he kept running and skidded on bloody feet down the marble hallway. The Arka soldiers at the door saw him coming and lowered their spears. Farden didn't break his pace. 'Out of my way!' he yelled.

'Halt!' they shouted, and they marched forward with their spears far in front of them. Farden didn't stop. One of them held up his hand in an authoritative gesture. 'Stop I say!' he bellowed.

Farden simply moved the bedraggled hair out of his face and pushed against the air with both hands as he ran forward. There was a dull thudding sound and the soldiers flew backwards against the wall with a loud crash of armour against stone. The mage didn't waste a second. He made a run for the gilded doors and kicked them open. Gritting his teeth, Farden strode into the hall and slammed the doors behind him. He was breathing heavily.

The great hall was deathly quiet. Every eye was on Farden as he stood there, dishevelled and dusty, with blood pooling around his feet. There were no whispers, no shouts, no clamouring of any kind from the gathered men and women, only silence. Farden looked around as he tried to calm himself. A huge man, who Farden correctly assumed was Bane the King of Skölgard, was standing in front of him, holding Cheska with one hand and his other at his belt, resting gently on the hilt of a big sword. Vice was standing in front of the throne, glaring daggers at him. Farden looked at the statue Evernia, at her calm expression, and then at the unbalanced scales swinging gently from side to side, two gold disks sitting in each pan. The sunlight was just touching the edges of the skylight above her marble head. The sky was as blue as it was in his dreams. A voice whispered in his head, and suddenly Farden understood.

A booming shout broke his reverie. 'Seize him!' yelled Vice and a group of nearby soldiers ran to the mage and grabbed him roughly by the arms. Weak though he was Farden struggled and pushed against them. Vice stormed across the hall towards him. Shadows fluttered across the floor and the new Arkmage peered up into the clear sky to see a swarm of dragons circling above like vultures. They would be dealt with soon enough, he thought.

'Have you told them what you told me Vice? Have you told them about the fire? About Helyard?' A soldier elbowed him in the ribs and the breath flew out of him.

Vice marched straight up to Farden and struck him hard in the face. Indescribably hard. It was a fast punch without grace nor mercy and the mage sprawled in the hands of the soldiers. Vice hauled him to his feet and shook him. His eyes blazed with murderous fire. The council were talking now. Bane moved Cheska behind him and his soldiers inched forward.

'I've had enough of you,' snarled Vice.

'Tell the council what you really are, old friend' Farden

gasped.

Vice shook with rage. His hazel eyes bored into Farden's, but the mage kept staring straight back at him. 'You're a stubborn bastard Farden, just like your uncle. I will have you hanged immediately!'

'You'll have to catch me first,' whispered the mage, and he grinned through bloody teeth, breaking his gaze for just a second to see a small white cloud drift across the crystal blue sky above Evernia's head. With every ounce of magick he had left in his exhausted body Farden pushed against the floor. And pushed he did.

Amidst shouts and yells Farden flew out of the grasp of the soldiers and soared into the air. He swung his fist as he flew, focusing all his energy into that one crucial swing, and like a sudden lightning strike he hit Vice squarely on the jaw. Sparks exploded from the mage's fist and in a blinding flash of light Vice fell to his knees dazed and stunned. Chaos erupted in the great hall as screams and yells filled the air.

Farden landed awkwardly, stumbling on his injured feet, but then ran for the centre of the room. With a metallic scrape Bane unsheathed his huge broadsword and swung it with a loud grunt at Farden's neck. The mage quickly dove into a roll and heard the blade whine over his head, missing all but a strand of his dark hair. The king roared and darted after him with speed unnatural for a man of his size. Farden could hear the huge man bearing down on him, but he kept running, eyeing the others closing in on him. All he had to do was get to the statue and it could all be over, Vice, Cheska, the Arka, they could all disappear. His chest was about to burst with exhaustion but still his legs pounded the floor and propelled him forwards.

Just as Bane reached out to snatch at Farden's clothes the mage leapt forward in a mad jump for the scales. The King grabbed at empty air and the mage crashed into the scales with a pained cry. Farden rolled to the floor in a shower of hot wax and spitting candles. He grabbed at the gold disk as it almost tumbled out of his hands and quickly bent his whole concentration on it. He felt the magick bite and suddenly it started to pull him in.

He watched as the world ground to a halt for the last time, ignoring the men poised over him with swords and halberds, ignoring Vice staggering to his feet, ignoring Bane frozen only mere inches away, hands outstretched and his face a boiling mass of anger, the very picture of rage. Farden looked only at Cheska, staring into her pale blue expression. He wondered what his child would look like, whether it would have his hair, her eyes, and whether she would miss him in any way whatsoever. He looked into her eyes and found she wasn't the same person any more, just a hollow shell of what she had pretended to be for all those years. There was a sudden rush of air as the world folded in on itself, and he was dragged into the blinding light.

Epilogue

for all the things to come

As the orange sun peered over the craggy ice-locked mountains in the east, a pair of grey-green eyes watched the light spill over the rocks and ignite the drifts of snow in a warm yellow glow. The man stood atop the highest mountain for miles and miles, braving the icy winds that tugged at his skin. He closed his eyes and let the cold bite his cheeks. The air was so clear. Below him, in the places the sun hadn't touched yet, the shadows fell amongst the black rocks and turned the snow a deep blue colour. The man squinted as he peered at the jagged skyline in the distance, where the wispy clouds huddled together. He could see smoke rising from the city in the south. Beyond that the sea sparkled like a blanket full of jewels.

The mage crouched and pulled his cloak around him, careful not to drop the gold disk he clutched in his hand. His clothes were ripped and torn and his pale face was a mess of bruises and scratches, but he didn't seem to care. For the first time in his life he felt true peace.

Farden stayed for a while, letting the sun warm him, letting his calm thoughts wander, and then he stood. With a flash of light and a flurry of powdery snow he was gone.

Later that morning the mages found that the old vampyre and his chubby servant had disappeared some time in the night. Their tent was empty but for their possessions and some of their clothes. At midday hawks arrived carrying messages saying that they should return home. The dragons flapped away northwards, silent and brooding. Modren watched them as they left, as he stood on the shore on the outskirts of Dunyra harbour. The waves licked his boots. He watched the dark shapes disappear into the sky one by one. With a sigh he crumpled the parchment in his fist and threw it into the sea. He left without a sound, heading for the bubbling quickdoor and Krauslung.

A few months later, a small boat approached the snowy shores of Nelska with three passengers sitting on its wet benches. The man in the middle of them was plying the oars. The gentle grey waves lapped at the soggy boat and made gentle splashing noises against its sides. The thing creaked and moaned with every move. The wind was cold, but calm, and it gently ruffled their hair and played with their clothes. It looked as though it was about to rain.

Farden paused his rowing and looked behind him. He noticed a welcome party standing on the shingles. The people looked cold and wet, but the dragons glistened as usual.

Durnus looked uncomfortable, and shuffled around in his seat. He was a touch paler than usual.

'What's wrong?' asked Elessi. 'You've been fidgeting around the whole time.'

'Nothing is wrong, maid, I am merely tired and not fond of the sea,' he said.

'You told me you loved the sea,' Farden said.

'Not in small boats, now leave me alone,' replied the vampyre. Farden nodded.

Elessi wrung her hands, and tapped Farden on the back. 'Are the dragons dangerous? I've never seen a dragon.'

'Well, you're about to meet one, but they're as docile as big cats. It's their queen you have to look out for,' he said. The mage pulled hard on the oars and the little boat skipped across the waves. His ribs twitched momentarily and he felt a little stab of pain, but then it was gone again.

After a few minutes of rowing they reached the shore and a pair of Siren soldiers dragged the boat up above tideline where the others were waiting for them. Farden hopped out of the boat and offered his hand to Elessi. She smiled and jumped to the sand with ease. Durnus scrabbled out of the other side and got as far away from the water as he could.

Farden walked to the dragons and smiled at Farfallen. Svarta and Eyrum were on his left, Towerdawn, Havenhigh, and Brightshow stood on his right with their riders. The Old Dragon smiled his toothy smile. Farden felt Elessi jump a little behind him. 'Well met and good wishes, friend.'

'And to you Farfallen. Thank you for your offer of hospitality, but I'm afraid we won't be staying long. As soon as the weather improves I'm heading to the east.'

'You may stay as long as you want Farden,' replied the gold dragon. He wore a sombre expression for a moment and he lowered his voice. 'Any news from Krauslung?'

Farden shook his head. 'None. That last we heard she was out of the city and in the north, with her father. Vice remains in the Arkathedral for now.'

Towerdawn crunched pebbles as he shifted his wait from foot to foot. 'Dark times are ahead; he has no love for us dragons.'

'You should have killed him when you had the chance,' said Svarta quietly, more like a regret rather than an accusation. Farden nodded.

'Who have you brought with you?' asked Brightshow, with a hint of excitement in her yellow-flecked eyes. Farden smiled and moved Elessi out from behind him. 'This is my friend Elessi, from Albion. She's never met a dragon before,' he said.

Farfallen bowed his head in a formal gesture. The others followed suit. 'And it is a pleasure to meet you Elessi of Albion.' She smiled and looked as if she would start giggling. Farden rolled his eyes. 'And this is my superior, Durnus,' said the mage. Durnus stared at Farfallen with his pale blue eyes and bowed low to the ground. 'I've heard a lot about you, and let me tell you what an honour it is to meet you,' said the vampyre with a smile. Svarta looked slightly taken aback at the sight of his fangs but Farfallen lowered his head once again 'Well met Durnus. It is a pleasure to have you all in Nelska,' replied the Old Dragon.

Brightshow piped up again. 'In case you forgot, Farden, you left something behind the last time you were here,' she said, looking behind her at her rider, Lakkin. The tall Siren moved forward holding a box, and Farden looked slightly confused. Slowly he crouched down and tipped the box gently on one side, and out came a small black cat. Farden's weathered face creased into a smile. It was Lazy, the ship's cat. The little creature stretched and looked around, but when it saw Durnus standing there it made a curious sound and wandered forward ponderously, daintily stepping over the wet pebbles. She came to a stop a few feet from him and curled her tail around her body. To everyone's utter surprise the cat opened its mouth, and spoke aloud. 'I have a message for the vampyre,' it said calmly. Every eye turned to Durnus, and his mouth hung agape. Elessi leant close to Farden and whispered in his ear. 'Is this normal in Nelska?' she asked.

Farden couldn't tear his eyes away from the cat. 'Not in the slightest,' he replied.

acknowledgements

This was my first book, and mark my words it shall not be the last. It's also been a long time in the writing, and thanks to the following people I actually finished it! So without any further or much ado at all here we go:

First I would like to thank my parents Paul and Carol, and this is for two quite basic reasons. The first is that they quite obviously and simply produced me, and the second is that as a child they insisted, nay demanded, that I read everything in sight, and without those two reasons I would not be where I am right now, scribbling this on the back of an envelope. (I'd like to thank Royal Mail for the envelope).

I'd like to thank the incredibly tolerant people who, for the last sixteen months, have had to put up with my constant badgering. Nancy Clark read and edited the first ever manuscript, as did Roger Clark, and their feedback and suggestions were invaluable to me. Nancy made sure it was suitable for all you Americans out there. Charlie Elwess was there to keep the Yorkshire tea brewing and point out any irregularities. (He has a band called Arcady Bliss, you should listen to them. No excuses). Sarah West, my eternal thanks, for the final edits, and for a room in her house, for which I am utterly grateful. Spotify, for your musical archivery, and my thanks to the music of the innumerable artists that have provided the emotions. Thomas Bulfinch, for the stories and myths, Mikael Westman for the cover, and Oliver Latham, for giving me a book that changed my whole perception of writing. I don't think he even realises what he's done. I'm expecting a phone call any day now...

And to Claudia, for putting up with the constant summons to my office, for reading all the little snippets and excerpts and experiments and dialogue, for nodding and smiling all the while, and for the encouragement and love and faith (and she drew the cover!) thank you. One day she might read the whole thing.

And thank you, for reading my debut book, I promise I won't take this long to write the next one.

Coming soon in 2012:

Emaneska is crying out to be saved.
The only one who can save it
is covering his ears...

www.bengalley.com

Did you like this Book?

Then help Ben out by showing your support.

For today's Authors, every bit of exposure helps. Authors like Ben survive because of your recommendations and your encouragement. If you liked **The Written**, then please tell your friends.

You can now follow and support Ben Galley on Facebook and Twitter!

Facebook.com/BenGalleyAuthor

@BenGalley

Thank you for your support!

Lightning Source UK Ltd.
Milton Keynes UK
UKOW051331200112

185756UK00001B/5/P